Also by
Helene Sinclair

Stranger in My Heart

Published by
WARNER BOOKS

ATTENTION: SCHOOLS AND CORPORATIONS

WARNER books are available at quantity discounts with bulk
purchase for educational, business, or sales promotional use. For
information, please write to: SPECIAL SALES DEPARTMENT,
WARNER BOOKS, 666 FIFTH AVENUE, NEW YORK, N.Y. 10103

ARE THERE WARNER BOOKS
YOU WANT BUT CANNOT FIND IN YOUR LOCAL STORES?

You can get any WARNER BOOKS title in print. Simply send title
and retail price, plus 50¢ per order and 50¢ per copy to cover
mailing and handling costs for each book desired. New York State
and California residents add applicable sales tax. Enclose check
or money order only, no cash please, to: WARNER BOOKS, P.O.
BOX 690, NEW YORK, N.Y. 10019

His eyes held a longing she could not help but see...

When his arms went around her, Bethany couldn't prevent herself from entering his embrace. His mouth claimed hers, and she gave herself willingly to the remembered sweetness of his kiss.

Drawing back, Edward looked down at her. With his finger he traced the lovely curve of her cheek.

"You're a beautiful woman, Bethany Kincaid," he said huskily.

Bethany shivered and suddenly felt cold. The desire she saw kindled in the blue flame of his eyes was not for her, Bethany Forrester; it was for a woman gambler named Kincaid. That was not who she was. Edward didn't even know her name or why she was here.

And if he knew, would he still be looking at her like he was now doing? Once more he drew her toward him, and when her body came in contact with his, she gasped. If he kissed her again, she was certain she would be lost. "Please," she whispered breathlessly. "I..." She was saying one thing, but her traitorous body was conveying an entirely different message...

The Bayou Fox

The Bayou Fox

Helene Sinclair

WARNER BOOKS

A Warner Communications Company

For my good friends,
Jean and Tom Tucker

WARNER BOOKS EDITION

Copyright © 1987 by Helene Lehr
All rights reserved.

Cover illustration by Sharon Spiak

Warner Books, Inc.
666 Fifth Avenue
New York, N.Y. 10103

 A Warner Communications Company

Printed in the United States of America

First Printing: July, 1987

10 9 8 7 6 5 4 3 2 1

Chapter 1

"I'll see him in hell!" exclaimed Bethany Forrester through clenched teeth. Amber eyes reflected the intense anger she was feeling. She was holding herself so rigidly that her nerves screamed in protest.

Although the words were spoken heatedly, no one heard them. She was alone in what used to be her bedroom, postponing if only for a few minutes the trip to the cemetery, to attend her father's funeral.

A gray and dismal light poured in through the curtainless window, creating dark shadows that flowed across the oak floor and crept up the rose-patterned wallpaper.

Taking a deep breath, Bethany sought to gain control of herself. She had been trembling with repressed fury ever since she had walked into the house ten minutes ago, hearing her footsteps echo throughout its emptiness as she went from room to room.

Removing a small mirror from her reticule, she put a dab of powder on her eyelids, noting how swollen they were from weeping. Shadows created by thick, dark lashes accented the faint smudges of lilac beneath her eyes, attesting to a lack of sleep the night before. But even these deficiencies couldn't detract from her fine-featured beauty. Taller than average, Bethany Forrester possessed a well-rounded slimness that caused most men to eye her in an appreciative manner.

Still viewing her reflection, Bethany raised a hand to smooth her jet-black hair, hesitated, then let it fall to her side. On this of all days, it hardly mattered what she looked like.

Returning the mirror to her purse, her fingertips touched the white envelope given to her by her father's attorney the previous day. It contained just over five hundred dollars. With the exception of her jewelry, it was the sum total of her assets.

Pensive now, Bethany turned and surveyed the room that only two days ago had been furnished with a canopy bed trimmed with yellow ruffles and an embroidered quilt that had taken her many hours of painstaking work to complete. There had been a teakwood armoire, a truly exquisite piece of craftsmanship that her father had had shipped all the way from New Orleans. The Turkish rug was gone now, as were her dressing table and chairs. With the exception of her clothing and jewelry, everything had been auctioned off to satisfy her father's gambling debt. Even the house had been sold.

And for what? She thought bitterly. *To pay a man who had won it all by cheating.* Had she been a man, Bethany would have called him out and demanded satisfaction. That avenue was closed to her; but there

2

were others that were open, and she meant to travel them until she reached her destination: the total ruin of Edward Hammond. Bethany knew next to nothing about him, but she planned to learn everything there was to know. Then she would destroy him, just the way he had destroyed her father.

Noting the time revealed on the small gold watch pinned to the lapel of her black wool jacket, Bethany realized she could delay her departure no longer.

With a last look about her, she left the empty room that held so many memories of happier times. Her personal belongings were at the Hotel Louisville, where she had spent the previous two nights. This afternoon, before attending the funeral, she hadn't been able to resist coming back here for a last, poignant look at the house in which she had lived all her life.

Stepping out into the cold February day, Bethany glanced up at the leaden skies. A few flakes of snow had begun to fall but were not, as yet, sticking to the ground.

"Hurry, Bethany!" Hattie McDowell, who had raised Bethany ever since her mother died, leaned out the window of the hired cab waiting at the curb. "We don't want to be late." As she motioned Bethany forward with a gloved hand, her angular face fell into concern. Pencil thin and energetic, Hattie was nearing sixty, but her face was unlined except for a few tiny crinkles around her hazel eyes. Her hair, too, belied her age, it being the same dark chestnut brown of her girlhood years.

As Bethany settled herself, Hattie reached over and

patted the slim hand, then sighed deeply as she leaned back against the cushioned seat.

The cab moved forward over the cobblestoned street, the horse's hoofs pounding a rhythmic cadence that was almost musical. Although they were several blocks from the river, the whistles of the steamers moored at the busy wharf could easily be heard.

The sounds never reached Bethany's surface awareness. She was thinking of her father. Had it been only two days since he had died? It seemed so much longer to her.

"Hammond cheated. I know he did, but I don't know how," her father had said, for perhaps the hundredth time since he had come home six weeks ago. By then the house had been sold, and they were watching as the furniture was being auctioned off to the highest bidder. One minute her father had been standing at her side, and the next he had fallen to the ground. There had been no warning, no cry of pain, which was the only solace in which Bethany found a degree of comfort.

"I can't believe he's gone," Hattie murmured with a catch in her voice.

Bethany forced her words through a tight throat. "I'll get even with that man if it takes me the rest of my life."

"Oh, my dear, I wish you would reconsider and come with me to Harrodsburg," Hattie implored. She had spent the better part of the morning trying to convince Bethany to do this, and although she had declined, Hattie wasn't ready to give up. "I know my sister would welcome us both."

"No." Bethany gave a sharp shake of her head.

4

"When I've accomplished what I've set out to do, I'll come to visit you. But for now, I have other plans." She turned her head to stare out the window, her chin set in a stubborn tilt that was all too recognizable to her companion.

Hattie's eyes clouded as she viewed the headstrong young woman seated beside her. Almost twenty-two, Bethany was more than beautiful. With those amber eyes and black hair—a true black, having no reddish or gold tints in it—Bethany could have her pick of any number of eligible young men, and she had indeed turned down several marriage proposals. Instead she was going off on what Hattie considered to be a wild-goose chase.

"Bethany, you cannot do this thing," she cried out, unable to contain her agitation. Reaching beneath her shawl, she plucked a handkerchief from the sleeve of her black bombazine dress and mopped her eyes. "You know your father wouldn't approve; he always wanted the best for you. . . ."

"If I were my father's son, it would be expected of me, even by you," Bethany pointed out. "He told me everything that happened in that last game. He didn't lose . . . he was cheated."

"But, Bethany, you can't prove that," Hattie said, wiping her nose. "And neither could your father or he would have done something about it at the time." She felt heartsick as she looked into the lovely eyes of the young woman who was as much her daughter as if she had come from her own womb.

"He couldn't prove it because Edward Hammond is too good at what he does. I intend to see that that man gets what's coming to him," she concluded grimly, clasping her gloved hands tightly in her lap.

"Bethany, please listen to me." Hattie's voice took on a note of urgency. "You know what type of women play in those games. Your father would be appalled if he knew what you were going to do." Her hand fluttered in a helpless gesture. "Besides, you know nothing about playing poker."

"I know enough," Bethany replied tersely. She gave the older woman a quick glance. "And what I don't know, I plan to learn." Her features softened as she saw that Hattie was truly upset. Quickly, she put an arm around her and pressed her lips against the cool cheek. "Please don't worry about me," she said quietly. "This is something I must do. . . ."

"But what will people think? You're not even allowing a proper time for mourning!"

Bethany turned away. *I will mourn him for the rest of my life*, she thought to herself, but she made no verbal comment. Nor did she care what people thought. That was one legacy her father had left to her. "Always be your own woman, Bethany," her father used to tell her. "Never let anyone tell you what you can or cannot do. Answer only to your conscience."

Hattie sighed, her shoulders moving in a shrug of futility. She knew that when Bethany was set on something, it was next to impossible to change her mind. Under normal circumstances, Bethany was tolerant, generous, good-humored; but she could not abide underhandedness in any form. Putting the handkerchief to her eyes again, Hattie fell silent as the carriage turned onto the dirt road that led to the small cemetery on the outskirts of Louisville.

There were about twenty-five people who had come to pay their last respects, almost all of them men. Two of Bethany's friends, Joan Princeton and Emily Simmons, stood to the side of the freshly mounded earth that was now dusted with a light covering of snow. Their expressions were grave as they viewed her. Joan, who had already tried to talk Bethany into coming to live with her and her husband, had tears streaming down her pale cheeks, prompting the young man at her side to pat her arm in an awkward gesture of comfort.

Not having the ready funds with which to purchase an elaborate headstone, Bethany had commissioned a plain white marble marker that read, simply:

GEORGE FORRESTER

1828–1880

BELOVED FATHER

The minister, a tall thin man with a mop of unruly hair that curled about his clerical collar, nodded in a sympathetic way as Bethany and Hattie approached. Then he cleared his throat and proceeded with the simple ceremony.

Bethany hardly heard his words. Her father, George Forrester, had been a professional gambler, riding the riverboats up and down the Mississippi for several months a year. In spite of his sometimes lengthy absences, she and her father had been close. While he had not been wealthy, there had been enough money to furnish the house on Bristol Street in a more than comfortable manner and to supply Bethany with an education and even a trip to Europe the year before.

Now it was all gone. Even her father was gone. And all because of one man.

While heads were bowed all around her, Bethany held her chin high, willing away the tears that stung her eyelids. She had shed her tears and wept her sorrow. Now it was time to act.

"Ashes to ashes..."

With a start, Bethany brought her attention back to the proceedings, seeing the minister drop a handful of dirt mixed with snow onto the casket.

A smothered sob came from Hattie, who had her handkerchief pressed to her lips. Her fingers went to the silver crucifix around her neck, and she clutched at it, as if for support.

Bethany turned away. The funeral was over; her quest for vengeance had begun. Never in her life had Bethany hated another human being, but she found herself doing so now. It was not a pleasant feeling, but she welcomed it nonetheless because, in some strange way, it overshadowed the pain of her loss.

Joan, her husband at her side, walked back with Bethany and Hattie to the waiting carriage where she paused and gave Bethany an earnest look from beneath her plain black bonnet.

"Richard and I... we'd hoped you'd stay with us for a while," she said softly, blue eyes imploring. "At least until you decide what you want to do. We know what a shock all this has been for you. First the house and all your lovely things, and now this..." Her voice broke. "It really is too much for you to bear."

"We are never given more than we can bear."
Bethany hugged her friend and mentally chided herself
for her words; the loss of everything she held dear *was*
more than she could bear. "Thank you for your invitation, but I'm...for now, I'm going with Hattie."
Bethany flushed with the lie and refused to meet Hattie's
disapproving stare. Giving her friend a final hug, she
entered the carriage.

They made the trip to the station in silence, although
Bethany was very much aware of Hattie's thoughts.
Bethany had only vague memories of her own mother,
who had died more than eighteen years ago. For a while
the house seemed empty and hollow, as did her father.
Then one day Hattie appeared. A widow and childless,
Hattie was infused with an efficient energy that soon
made the house comfortable again. It grieved Bethany
to cause even a measure of unhappiness for the woman
who had shown her nothing but kindness and love for
all these years, yet she knew she could not rest easy
until she did this one last thing for her father.

After they arrived at their destination and got down
from the carriage, Bethany dismissed the cab and watched
as the porter put the trunks aboard the train. One of
them contained her father's clothes, which Hattie had
agreed to keep until Bethany sent for them.

Hattie turned, her expression hinting that she might
be about to make one more attempt to dissuade Bethany
from her course of action. Instead, she said simply, "I
offered to give your father my savings, but he wouldn't
take it."

"I know," Bethany murmured, pressing Hattie's hand.
"And he was right not to accept your money. But I

know your offer touched him; he appreciated it very much.''

The whistle blew a strident command for passengers to board, startling them both. With a sob, Hattie reached for Bethany. ''You will write and let me know how you are?''

''I will. I promise.'' Bethany kissed the older woman with sincere affection.

Hattie clung to Bethany until the conductor bellowed a final call, then she hurried away without a backward glance.

White steam enveloped Bethany with a fleeting warmth as the train strained forward, the screech of iron against iron assaulting the ears of passengers and well-wishers alike.

Bethany remained on the platform until the train was out of sight, certain that the image of Hattie's tear-stained face framed in the dirty window would be with her for a long time.

The wind now had a cutting edge to it, and the snow began to fall in ever-thickening flakes. Paying no mind to the worsening weather, Bethany began to walk the four blocks that would take her to the home of Wilbur Kane, one of her father's closest friends. Kane hadn't attended the funeral, for he was now so crippled with gout that he could barely walk. He was in his early sixties, some ten years older than her father had been, yet the two men had formed a friendship that had spanned a decade.

The streets were almost deserted, hosting only a few hardy pedestrians willing to brave the elements. Behind the closed doors of the neat brick and clapboard houses, dinner was doubtless in progress; now and again an enticing aroma reached Bethany, who suddenly realized that she had not eaten anything since breakfast. Shivering with cold, she quickened her steps, almost running up the snow-covered walk that led to Kane's two-story house.

She found him in the back parlor, settled comfortably in a cushioned chair by the fireplace. Kane's wife had died childless after five years of marriage, and although more than thirty years had passed since then, he had never married again.

His florid face lightened when he caught sight of her. He was slight of build, appearing even more shrunken within the confines of the large wing chair in which he was seated. Although his brown hair was thinning noticeably, his sideburns were long and thick.

"Bethany, my dear girl." He extended a gnarled hand to her.

As Bethany crossed the room, she felt the chill in her bones ease. The parlor was warm and cozy. On a table near the bookcase, a lamp burned brightly. The pale-blue velvet draperies had been tightly drawn against the gloom of the day, hiding the delicate tracings of ice patterns that were forming on the glass, allowing only amber and gold light to reflect on the furniture and flocked wallpaper.

"I don't have to tell you how sorry I was to hear about your father," Kane said, clasping her hand. "Forgive me for being unable to attend the ceremony."

Bending forward, Bethany placed a gentle kiss on the weathered cheek. "I understand. I wanted to stop by and thank you for your note of condolence."

He nodded gravely. Noticing how pale and chilled she looked, he gestured toward the table beside his chair. "Can I offer you a sherry?"

"No, thank you." Bethany seated herself in the chair opposite him. Feeling the warmth of the burning fire, she unbuttoned her jacket, then spoke quietly. "Mr. Kane, what can you tell me about a man named Edward Hammond?"

He raised a brow in surprise. "Your father spoke of him?"

"Yes," she answered carefully, not wanting to reveal her purpose. She knew that Kane, like Hattie, would strongly disapprove of what she planned to do and would make every effort to change her mind.

Absently, he rubbed his nose with a knuckle. "Well, I don't know Hammond very well. He's a young man, at least by my standards, not yet thirty. I've only played cards with him once or twice. That was about three years ago, but he's made quite a reputation for himself." His mouth twisted in sardonic amusement. "They call him the Bayou Fox."

Fox, indeed! thought Bethany. *Snake would be more like it.* Renewed anger kindled in her eyes. With effort, she kept her face bland as Kane continued.

"Hammond owns a farm a couple of miles east of Lexington, in the Bluegrass region," Kane went on. "Glencoe, Glenhaven, something like that. He raises horses."

Bethany's eyes widened. "He isn't a gambler?"

"Oh, yes, that he is. But he spends a great deal of time on his farm. Good player. Only one I know who's as good as Colin Thatcher."

Bethany inclined her head, trying not to show too much interest. "Colin Thatcher?"

He nodded. "One of the best players along the Mississippi."

"I've never heard the name before." Bethany kept her voice casual. "Is he from around here?"

Kane chuckled and rearranged the blanket that was draped over his legs. "Colin doesn't have a house that I know of. When he's on land he hangs his hat in the Peabody Hotel in Memphis." Another chuckle erupted as Kane warmed to the subject. "Saw Thatcher and Hammond play once. The game went on for three days! Neither one of them won." He shook his head from side to side. "There's bad blood between those two," he confided. "Something to do with a woman. I never did learn the details."

Kane fell silent as his housekeeper, Nellie Ingersoll, came into the room. Nellie was small, thin, and utterly devoted to Kane, having been in his employ for more than twenty years. With a friendly nod at Bethany, she announced that dinner was ready.

"Good!" Kane said enthusiastically, rapping the arm of his chair. Then he looked at Bethany. "You will join me?" he asked, smiling broadly at her ready acceptance. Rising, he leaned stiffly on his cane, favoring his right foot, which was bandaged to the ankle, and on which he wore no shoe.

Aware of her friend's pride, Bethany made no move to assist him, walking slowly beside him as they headed for the dining room.

A while later, having assuaged her immediate hunger with several spoonfuls of Nellie's hearty beef ragout, Bethany regarded her host. "Mr. Kane, did my father tell you what happened on this last trip?''

Kane paused a moment, as if giving her question serious thought. Then his watery blue eyes found hers again. "Yes. Yes, he told me," he answered in a low voice, not trying to hide his distress.

Bethany put down her spoon, her appetite suddenly gone. "How could my father not have seen what was happening?" she cried out. "If he knew the game was dishonest, why didn't he leave?" It troubled her that she had raised her voice, but the question had been tormenting her.

Reaching for his glass, Kane took a sip of wine before he replied. "It's not as easy as it sounds, Bethany. Some card mechanics are obvious. Those can be handled with no problem. But the others..." He sighed, buttering a generous slice of bread. He took a bite, then continued. "Some of them can be smooth as silk."

Bethany's forehead creased. "You think my father was uncertain, that he was only guessing?"

Inclining his head, Kane stared into his plate a moment. "No," he said with a sigh. "George was very certain; and he was not one to accuse a man falsely."

"I know," Bethany said in a small voice. "I've never heard him accuse anyone before..." She caught her breath against the tightness in her throat.

Kane reached out and patted her hand. "You must put it from your mind. I believe your father, but he had no proof," he added, echoing Hattie's sentiment. "The Bayou Fox took him for all he was worth—and there's nothing to be done about it now."

Bethany lowered dark lashes over amber eyes. *Oh, yes,* she thought to herself, *something can be done,...and I will do it!*

Settling himself comfortably, Kane lit a cigar and viewed the tip reflectively. "You know, I remember once, some years ago, I was in a game with a couple of cotton brokers from Georgia." He made a sound of disgust. "At least that's how they represented themselves. One of them was signaling the other with his cigar smoke." Noticing Bethany's startled expression, he gave a rueful shake of his head. "I swear an Indian couldn't have done it better. The game was almost over and my money about gone before I caught on to what they were doing." He inhaled deeply, blew a ring of smoke, then looked at her in an almost apologetic manner. "How're you going to accuse a man of smoking his cigar in a suspicious manner? Certainly you'd better be prepared to prove it, else you'll find yourself staring at the business end of his derringer."

Bethany leaned back in her chair, trying to analyze what she had been told. She hadn't for one moment envisioned something as bizarre as cigar smoke. Could she do it? she wondered, feeling a moment's uncertainty. But there was no choice, she realized; not for her. Her father's memory cried out for vengeance. She owed it to him to at least make the attempt.

Bethany stayed a while longer, listening to Kane reminisce in the way a man will when he can no longer be a part of the life he knew, and who now has only memories with which to sustain himself.

Later, on her way back to the hotel, Bethany's amber eyes were lit with determination. If she had to learn to play cards in a professional manner, she might as well learn from the best, she decided.

Chapter 2

A cold wind howled through Memphis, driving sheets of rain along its path.

From her hotel window, Bethany gazed down at the wet street, watching people struggle with umbrellas that were almost useless against the wind, trying to avoid the continuous spray of water kicked up by fast-moving drays and carriages.

For the past ten days she had been waiting impatiently for Colin Thatcher to check into the Peabody Hotel. During that time she had sold most of her jewelry. Since her father had always purchased the best stones he could find, they had brought her a tidy sum, one which had taken her completely by surprise.

How she wished her father would have taken the gems, but he had refused to touch them, insisting that they were her inheritance. He could not, of course, have known that he would not be given the opportunity to recoup his losses. Even so, Bethany had had no idea of their worth. She shuddered to think what would have become of her if she'd not had this resource.

Nor would Bethany allow her thoughts to dwell on circumstances too far in the future. It would come as it always did, one day at a time. For now it was enough that she had a goal and the means with which to attain it.

This morning the desk clerk had sent word that Colin Thatcher had finally checked in the night before. Bethany had spent several hours in restless anticipation, feeling the morning an inappropriate time to call on the man she hoped would help her.

Turning from the window, she glanced at her watch. It was now one thirty in the afternoon, and her nerves would tolerate no further delay.

Crossing the room, she paused before the pier mirror, staring at her reflection with a critical eye, turning once or twice to see the overall effect. She had dressed with care, not wanting to appear frivolous. With that in mind, she had chosen to wear a plain black bombazine skirt with a high, pointed waist, gathered around her hips to form a soft bustle in back. Her blouse was of white silk, high-necked and long-sleeved, with no frills or furbelows to mar its clean lines. She had arranged her hair simply. Parted in the center, it was drawn back from her face, falling into soft curls at the nape of her neck.

Satisfied that all was well, she went out into the hall, walking slowly along the carpeted floor until she reached room 23. Lifting her hand, she knocked on the door. When it opened a moment later she smiled at the man who stood on the threshold.

Bethany didn't know what she had expected, but it certainly wasn't the type of man she saw before her now. There was a certain Continental air about his dark attractiveness, and she guessed him to be in his early thirties. His hair was a deep, rich brown, almost black. And his eyes, too, were dark. Beneath a trim mustache his upper lip was narrow, the lower full. He was dressed casually, his white ruffled shirt open at the neck.

Bethany averted her gaze from the sight of the thick curly hair on his chest. "Mr. Thatcher?"

He smiled, his eyes frankly appraising her trim figure. "Yes?"

"I . . . I would like to talk to you. My name is Bethany Forrester."

His brows lifted. "Forrester? Would you be related to George Forrester?"

She nodded slowly. "He was my father."

Colin considered her for a moment. "Was?" he asked in a low voice.

"Yes." She lowered her eyes, then looked up at him again, bracing herself against the words she knew would cause her fresh pain. "He . . . he died two weeks ago. A heart attack."

A frown creased his forehead. "I'm sorry to hear that." Moving quickly, he stepped aside, swinging the door wider. "Come in." As Bethany walked past him he picked up a gray broadcloth jacket that matched his trousers and hastily donned it. "Sorry," he murmured with a grin. "I wasn't expecting company."

"Please don't apologize," she said quickly, turning to face him. "If I'm intruding I can come back at another time."

"Oh, no," he said quickly, buttoning his shirt. "Please sit down."

Glancing around, Bethany realized that Colin apparently occupied a suite, for she found herself in a sitting room. A comfortable-looking horsehair sofa dominated one side of the room, flanked by mahogany tables supporting brass lamps, both of which were now lit. A rolltop desk was in a corner, but appeared to be unused. A table and two straight-backed chairs were placed by the curtained window. Bethany headed for one of them.

After she had seated herself, Colin settled himself on the sofa.

"What can I do for you, Miss Forrester?" he asked politely.

Bethany hesitated, toying with the strings of her reticule, suddenly nervous. Then she inhaled deeply, knowing she would have to be straightforward and honest if she were to convince this man to help her.

"Mr. Thatcher, . . . I would like you to teach me to play cards in a professional manner."

He stared blankly, obviously taken aback by her request. "I beg your pardon?" He began to laugh.

Bethany moved restlessly in her chair, upset with the sound of his mirth, then decided it was preferable to shocked disapproval.

"Please, it's no joke." She viewed Colin Thatcher with all the seriousness she could muster. "My father lost everything he had; it destroyed him." She looked away, her breath coming in a soft sigh. "It isn't the losing that bothers me," she went on quietly. "My father was a gambler all his life. He knew the risks."

Colin cleared his throat. "I really am sorry to hear

about your father's untimely death, Miss Forrester," he murmured, still nonplussed by her unorthodox request. "George was a fine man, but I don't understand why you have come to me...."

"My father was cheated; he told me so." Bethany's amber eyes were level and direct. "I want to beat that man at his own game." She raised her chin. "And I will, if it's the last thing I do."

Leaning forward, Colin placed his elbows on his knees, hands clasped between them. His demeanor turned somber as he viewed her. "I take it that you hold this man . . . accountable for your father's death?"

"I do," she stated flatly.

"Would you care to give me his name?"

"Edward Hammond."

Colin's laughter erupted with a force that brought tears to his eyes. Settling back, he wiped them with the back of his hand. "I have trouble beating him. What makes you think you can do it?"

"I will do it," Bethany insisted in a firm voice that cut through his laughter, "with your help." She stared at him, more than a little annoyed by his continued display of amusement. "Mr. Thatcher, I already know how to play poker!" she went on in a forceful voice, refusing to be intimidated. "I know the rudiments of the game very well, but I'm not good enough to sit with professionals," she added in a disarming display of candor.

The rain was coming down harder, and the wind had gained enough momentum to seep through the windowpane. Bethany shivered, feeling the icy breeze against her back.

"You're cold!" Colin exclaimed. He sounded contrite. "I'll light the fire—"

"Please don't trouble yourself . . ." she said quickly.

But he had already gotten to his feet. "No trouble at all."

Bethany watched as he busied himself at the small hearth in a corner of the room, and when the flames took hold, she welcomed the added warmth.

Turning from the fireplace, Colin regarded her curiously. "Do you really believe your father was cheated?" he asked.

"He believed so." Bethany's response was immediate. "And my father was too experienced to be wrong in his assumption."

Colin studied her for a long moment before he spoke, impressed by her beauty and spirit. Quite the loveliest woman he'd ever seen, he thought to himself, noticing how the white silk blouse lovingly molded her firm breasts. Although her skirt was long he'd caught a tantalizing glimpse of a well-turned ankle when she had seated herself. It took little effort on his part to envision the shapely limb above that slender ankle.

"I was in that game with Hammond and your father," he murmured finally, returning to the sofa. "In all honesty, I saw nothing amiss—although I wouldn't put it beyond Hammond to do something of that nature. The man's an odd mixture of hot temper and cold blood. Still, what you're suggesting . . ." He spread his hands. "I'm afraid it's out of the question."

Bethany chewed her lower lip, disappointed, but she wasn't about to give up so easily. She recalled Kane mentioning that there was bad blood between Hammond and Thatcher, and she wondered if perhaps their differences had been resolved.

"Are you a friend of his—is that it?" Her voice was low, but clear.

"Hardly," he answered with a wry chuckle. "Oh, I've stayed at Glencoe several times as Edward's guest. But Hammond and I had . . . well, you might say we had a disagreement some months back." He rubbed his jaw, remembering the blow that had almost unhinged it. "At any rate, since that time we've met only during the course of . . . our business."

She had to smile. "Playing cards is a business?"

"It's the way I make my living," he admitted.

As he spoke, Colin removed a silver dollar from his pocket and absently began to toy with it. Bethany watched as the coin slipped through his slender fingers, one by one, then made the return trip with an effortlessness she found fascinating.

"Let's say for the sake of argument," he went on, staring across the room at the now brightly burning fire, "that you could beat Hammond in a game of poker. I sincerely doubt that you can take it a step further and force him into betting more than he can lose. Hammond is shrewd." He said this with a nod of his head. "And he has one purpose in mind: the restoration of Glencoe. He'll go to any lengths to accomplish that."

"I suspect that man would go to any lengths to get *anything* he wanted," Bethany replied dryly. She made no attempt to hide the bitterness in her voice. Glancing out the window, she regarded the silvery ribbons threading down the glass, determined to remain calm. "Why not let me cross that bridge when I come to it?'' she suggested at last, turning to look at him.

He hesitated, making no comment, and Bethany pressed on. "You must understand that I am very serious about this. I will do it with or without your assistance. It is, after all, a question of honor. My father's debts have been paid. All that remains is for me to collect one that is due him, or at least his memory. I cannot rest easy until it is done," she concluded with a fierceness that took him by surprise.

Inclining his head, Colin studied the tips of his polished boots. "It might work," he mused after a long moment. He was thoughtful, then went on. "You do have one advantage." His dark eyes held a twinkle as he viewed her again. "You're a woman. Very few men will credit a woman with having enough expertise to play poker."

Amusement dimpled Bethany's cheeks. "Do you?"

"I never underestimate a woman," Colin stated with a laugh, raising a hand. "To me, women are fascinating creatures," he admitted candidly. "I don't always agree with how their minds work; but I never underestimate them."

Bethany leaned forward, her manner intense. "Please, Mr. Thatcher, I need your help. I really do know how to play poker. . . ."

Beneath the trim mustache, his lips twitched with a repressed smile as his eyes swept the length of her. Idly, he wondered if this woman knew how sensuous and alluring she looked.

"In other words, you are your father's daughter?" Colin got to his feet, returning the silver coin to his pocket. "Very well, let's see what you can do." Walking across the carpeted floor, he opened the door that led to the bedroom, returning only moments later. "Here, use these." He put a pile of chips in front of her and an equal amount in front of himself as he sat down opposite her.

For more than thirty minutes they played, only the required responses breaking the silence.

Finally, Colin leaned back in his chair, again toying with the silver dollar. He had a thoughtful, somewhat enigmatic expression on his attractive face. Bethany was more knowledgeable than he had supposed her to be—and she was beautiful. Looking into those amber eyes, Colin couldn't think of a better way to spend some time than in her company. He rubbed his chin again, imagining he could still feel the pain of the blow dealt by Hammond. Certainly he had a score to settle with that man, Colin thought to himself.

"All right," he said at last, making up his mind with a suddenness that startled her. "I'll teach you as much as I can."

Bethany issued a small sigh of relief and relaxed for the first time since she had entered the room. "I'll be glad to pay you for your time," she offered.

Shaking his head, Colin smiled at her. "No need. Believe me, it would be payment enough to see Hammond bested by a woman." He gave a quick laugh at the idea. "He'd never be able to live it down." Putting aside the silver dollar, he picked up the cards again.

For the next few days, much to Bethany's dismay, for she was anxious to get on with it, Colin taught her nothing about the game of poker. Instead, for hour after endless hour, she shuffled cards, dealt them out, picked them up, and started all over again.

She was clumsy at first. At least half the time the slick cards popped out of her hands and onto the floor. Patiently, Colin would retrieve them and once again demonstrate how they should be held. His fingers were long and slender, the type one might expect to see on an accomplished pianist, displaying a dexterity that astonished her.

Bethany found herself viewing her tutor with increasing respect, convinced that Wilbur Kane had been accurate in his assessment of Colin Thatcher as the best cardplayer along the Mississippi.

Gradually, Bethany's own dexterity increased until she was able to perform the relatively simple operation with little effort or thought.

"Now," Colin said to her on the fourth day, "we begin to learn the game."

Removing his jacket, he draped it over his chair. Picking up the cards, he dealt out three hands, two of which he intended to play. Hers were dealt face up so that he could see what she was doing. For a while they played in silence.

"Raise it," Colin advised her at one point.

Bethany gave him a puzzled look, then viewed her cards. "But why? I have only a pair of fours. . . ."

"Yes, but your opponent doesn't know that," he pointed out with a lopsided smile. "Bluffing is a very important, very subtle part of the game. And if you want to bluff, you must raise before the cards are drawn. Don't show your hand if you drop out or lose, however; it reveals too much to the other players."

Somewhat hesitantly, she pushed a few chips to the center of the table.

He made a sound of disapproval. "No, no. Be assertive! The object is to win, and that takes money. Don't be afraid to bet if you have a good hand or if you want your opponent to *think* you have one."

Bethany sighed. Some of Colin's advice seemed contradictory to her. The following day, holding an eight of clubs and a nine of spades, she drew three cards.

"Why did you draw with that hand?" he questioned sharply.

"I might have gotten something," she said, feeling defensive at his tone.

His attractive features settled into a stern look. "Always remember this: When you are dealt a hand with no possibilities, get out immediately. Don't wait for the draw." He tapped his cards with a fingertip. "I have already opened. Obviously, I have you beat right now."

By the end of the week, which Bethany thought consisted of marathon days, they were playing on a one-to-one basis, Colin no longer looking at her cards.

They fell into the habit of dining together in the evening. Whether they ate in the hotel or at a restaurant, Bethany noticed that Colin was always shown to the finest table in the room and was catered to with a degree of attention that bordered on fawning.

Occasionally, when they did eat in the hotel dining room, Bethany was aware of more than one curious glance in her direction. She supposed, with some amusement, that her reputation was more than compromised by now. She could just imagine what people were whispering about her in speculation, for she was certain it was common knowledge that she was spending day after day in Colin's room.

One evening, after a particularly satisfying meal of oyster bisque, soft-shell crabs, and rich *crème brûlée,* Bethany sipped her wine and regarded Colin from beneath her dark lashes. He was dressed stylishly in a double-breasted dark green frock coat, the cuffs and lapels of which were velvet. He favored white shirts with ruffled fronts and was wearing one tonight.

"How did you become a gambler?" she asked him, realizing how little she knew about the man with whom she was spending so much of her time.

He laughed easily, admiring the play of candlelight in her hair. She had it fashioned into thick braids that coiled softly about her small ears. Her peach silk dress was high waisted, in the Empire style, and had flowing, lace-trimmed sleeves that flared at the elbows.

Had she been any other woman, Colin suspected he would have made love to her by now. But he knew instinctively that Bethany was unlike any other woman he'd known. For openers, in addition to being beautiful, she was intelligent, quick, resourceful—traits he knew to be all too rare in a woman. He had an idea that Bethany Forrester was going to mean a great deal to him.

"Quite by accident, actually," he answered at last. "My family lives in San Francisco. When I was sixteen I was determined to become the most successful prospector in California. It wasn't long, however, before I discovered that it was plain hard work for little reward. In a mining camp, there are only a few diversions:

drinking, gambling, and . . ." Colin was about to add whoring, then thought better of it. He toyed with the stem of his wineglass, his lips in a half-smile. "I am a man who drinks only lightly."

Bethany tried but couldn't hide her smile, having guessed the unmentioned diversion. "So you learned to . . . gamble in the mining camps."

"Yes." His mood shifted, and he regarded her seriously. "I realized there was more money on a poker table than at the bottom of a tin pan." Noticing that she had finished her wine, he picked up the bottle.

"And have you never married?" she asked, watching as he refilled her glass.

"Lord, no!" Colin exclaimed with another laugh. He put the bottle back on the table. Then, as he looked at her, he added quietly, "I suspect you might be able to make me change my mind, however . . . if you play your cards right."

A faint blush tinted her creamy cheeks. "I have no intention of changing your mind," she said firmly, then grinned at him. "Besides, it's best not to tamper with success. We're doing fine just the way we are."

The following afternoon, again at the card table in Colin's sitting room, Bethany viewed her hand attentively. Despite the fact that she was holding only a pair of sevens, she decided to raise the pot. Waiting for Colin's response, she absently patted her hair.

Observing her movements, Colin frowned. "Bethany, you must break yourself of the habit of playing with your hair," he admonished quietly.

Her eyes widened, and her hand paused in midair. "What?"

"You've done it twice now, both times when you're bluffing. It's a dead giveaway."

She blinked in astonishment. And of course Colin was right; she had been trying to bluff him. "I hadn't realized that I was doing that," she murmured with a laugh, feeling a bit foolish.

"Well, now that you are aware of it, always look for the same type of weakness in your opponents," he advised. "Most people aren't aware of what they're doing. Watch for involuntary gestures: a yank on the earlobe, a shifting of the eyes, a bead of perspiration."

Finally, there came a day when Colin settled back in his chair and smiled at her. Although he had repeatedly cautioned her not to reveal her hand, Bethany, feeling mischievous, hadn't been able to resist doing so on this particular occasion.

This time she had bluffed him and won.

"I think you're ready," Colin said softly, obviously impressed. "There's no more that I can teach you." He regarded her with new interest and a bit of respect. He detested coy, simpering women who fluttered their eyelashes as fast as their fans and who giggled inanely every time a man opened his mouth. Bethany Forrester was like a cool, fresh breeze after a spring rain.

Bethany was elated with her small victory. If she could outwit a man like Colin Thatcher, certainly she could do the same with a scoundrel like Edward Hammond.

"Tomorrow," Colin was saying, "I'll book passage for us both on the *Nola Star*."

"Is that where Edward Hammond will be?" she asked, watching as he returned the chips to the enameled box in which they were kept.

"He'll be there. He boards at Louisville."

Chapter 3

Edward Hammond stuffed the last of his clean shirts into his portmanteau, secured the straps, then nodded at his manservant.

Coming forward, Henry picked up the leather suitcase and placed it by the door. A huge strapping Negro in his late thirties, Henry Mason and his wife Clarissa were the only house servants at Glencoe, since the only residents were Edward and his father, Cyrus Hammond, who was confined to his bed. The Masons' two young sons, Paul and Robert, worked in the stables.

Compared to the farms that surrounded it, Glencoe was not especially large. It covered a mere seventy-eight acres, but it was prime land, encompassing fenced-in meadows of bluegrass, a small lake, and an oval training track.

There was even a smithy adjoining the stables, but the forge and tools were long since gone. Nowadays the horses were taken to a farrier in nearby Lexington when it was time for them to be reshod.

In addition to the main house, there was also a stone cottage by the edge of the lake. Having only two rooms, it was badly in need of repair, an eyesore that irritated Edward each time he looked at it. But there had been so much else to do that he had never gotten around to refurbishing it. Not that anyone lived there now. At one time it had housed the overseer, but Glencoe no longer had an overseer. That post had been unoccupied since the war, during which time most of their horses had been confiscated.

Being a border state, Kentucky had at first tried to maintain a position of neutrality, but finally opted for the Union. Fully a third of Kentucky's sons, however, had fought for the Confederacy. Edward's father had been one. In the hands of the Federals, Glencoe had fared badly during those years.

Edward slipped his arms into the sharply tailored frock coat held by Henry. "Has my father eaten his breakfast yet?" he asked.

"Brought it to him over an hour ago, Mistah Edward," replied Henry, a deep sigh following his words. "But all he did was drink his coffee." Crossing the room, he fetched a brush from a dresser drawer. "Rissa's gonna be unhappy when she finds out that he didn't even touch his food," he went on, deftly brushing the broad shoulders of his employer. "She got up early this morning just to make him some of those honey biscuits he likes."

Adjusting his silk cravat, Edward gave a rueful shake

of his head. "I suspect he's in a mood because he knows I'm leaving this morning."

Henry's face broke into a wide grin that revealed startlingly white teeth. "Bet that's what it is," he said, nodding his woolly head in agreement. "Mistah Cyrus always sulks when he knows you're going away. Like as not he'll be hungry before you reach Lexington."

Edward answered with a smile, then said, "I'll stop in to see him before I go."

"You do that, Mistah Edward," Henry responded, returning the brush to its accustomed place. "Cheers him up every time he sees you."

With long strides, Edward left his room and went downstairs, bracing himself for the confrontation he knew was coming.

Sunlight streamed through the stained-glass fanlight over the front door, creating a rainbow of color on the white tiled floor of the foyer. At the foot of the stairs, Edward turned and headed for the back of the house.

What had originally been the rear parlor was now his father's bedroom. An addition to the house, the room was angled out from the main structure and contained two large windows.

Entering, Edward smiled at the man who was in bed, propped up by pillows. The four-poster was placed in such a way that Cyrus could see out of either window, one of which offered a view of the stables, and the other, the carriage drive.

Facing south, the room was sunny, the cheerful ambience enhanced by a crackling fire in the hearth. Edward had personally selected the furniture and carpeting with an eye toward his father's comfort. He had also purchased the wheelchair that sat forlornly in a corner, never having been used since the day he brought it home.

Cyrus Hammond was fifty-one, but he looked like a man who was fifteen years older than that. His hair was snow white and sparse, his face lined, his eyes dulled by years of pain and helplessness. He had spent the last two years of the war in the prison camp at Elmira. Both of his feet had suffered severe frostbite in that first harsh winter. The ball of his right foot and the toes of his left had been amputated due to the resulting gangrene.

But more than his body had suffered. Cyrus's spirit had received a blow from which he had never recovered.

When he returned from the war it was to find his wife dead, his home ramshackled, his horses gone. He had taken to his bed and had never left it since. Only one thing truly occupied his mind: the large, leather-bound volume that held his meticulous notations regarding the lineage of the horses raised at Glencoe. Cyrus studied the log for endless hours in an effort to determine which combination of dam and sire might be expected to produce a champion.

Edward had been thirteen when the war ended, and for the following two years he had worked at any odd job he could find in order to feed them both. But in his fifteenth year, with renewed purpose and determination, Edward began to bring Glencoe back to life. Now, at twenty-eight, it pleased him to know that his goal was in sight.

"How are you feeling, Pa?" Edward's smile broadened as he came into the room, though his heart twisted at the sight of the ravaged figure on the bed.

The elder Hammond ignored the greeting. He never felt well, so he saw no need of replying to the obvious. "You're going off again, are you?"

The words sounded querulous, but Edward was used to that. "Yes. I'll be back in two weeks, as always."

"Damned foolishness," the old man muttered, his fingers plucking restlessly at the quilt. "Didn't raise my son to be a gambler."

"I'm not really. You know that." Walking across the room, Edward stoked the fire and added another log.

Cyrus's grunt was explicit. "Traipsing up and down the Ohio and Mississippi, playing for high stakes." He glared. "Don't know what else to call it. A spade's a spade; no quibbling about it."

Brushing his hands together, Edward repressed a sigh. "It'll only be for another year—two at the outside." He gave his father a level look as he came to stand at the foot of the bed, one hand wrapped around the post. "I made a great deal of money this last trip. Without those winnings, I could never have purchased Dawn's Light."

"And that's another thing," Cyrus said, his lined face falling into a scowl. "You just got back from London two days ago. You spent a small fortune on that horse! I know, I know—" He raised a hand to forestall his son's comments. "She's the best-looking mare I've ever seen. But now, here you are, off again. Who's to see to things when you're not around?"

Edward took a deep breath. "Now, Pa, you know very well that Matthew has things under control—"

"That whippersnapper!" Cyrus scoffed and looked away. "He's just a boy."

"Matt's twenty-two. Hardly a boy, I'd say," Edward retorted mildly, refusing to be drawn into an argument. "And he handles horses with the best of them. He'll be a great trainer one day."

Shifting his weight in the bed, Cyrus stared at his son. "The bay mare is coming to foal, you know," he tried again, his expression intent. Although he always made the effort to fight the loneliness he felt when his son was gone, he was never successful. Without Edward, the days stretched long and empty.

"I'll be back in plenty of time," Edward assured, starting for the door.

"Edward, . . ." Cyrus called to him, "that Madison girl—Lydia. I haven't seen her around lately. . . ."

Pausing, Edward turned toward his father. "The engagement's off, Pa. Don't you remember? I told you some months ago."

"Good! Never did like her. Sam Madison and his son—traitors! Both of them." The statement was issued through pinched lips that conveyed bitter condemnation.

Edward released the sigh that he'd been holding in check. "That was a long time ago, Pa. . . ."

"What's time got to do with it?" came the swift retort.

"Some things are better forgotten," Edward murmured in a low voice.

Cyrus made a noise that sounded suspiciously like a snort. "Forget? You ask me to forget that Glencoe was ravished by the bluecoats while The Willows suffered no damage at all?" His voice wavered with his emotion. "Not a stone out of place!"

"Glencoe will soon be on a par with The Willows," Edward said quietly, returning to the bed. Placing a hand on his father's thin shoulder, he gave it a gentle squeeze. "I'll do anything I have to do; I promise you that."

"Well . . . ," Cyrus said, sounding comforted, but issuing a great sigh, "I guess you'd better get going then."

About to turn away, Edward looked down at the tray with its uneaten food, and frowned. "Henry says Rissa got up early to make your favorite biscuits."

Cyrus waved an impatient hand. "I'm not hungry. . . ."

"Seems like you could have eaten one of them," Edward speculated, his tone giving no indication of the concern he was feeling. Lately, it seemed his father was eating less and less.

"I could have, if I was hungry; but I'm not," Cyrus replied with irrefutable logic.

Giving his father a somewhat exasperated look, Edward picked up the tray and left the room, heading for the kitchen.

Rissa was seated at the table, peeling potatoes. She was short and plump, her skin the color of cinnamon. Her dark eyes more often than not sparkled with a merry twinkle that was usually accompanied by a wide smile. She was garbed in the attire she wore almost every day: a short-sleeved black cotton dress, over which she wore a starched white apron. A bright red bandanna covered her kinky hair and was fashioned into an elaborate tignon of the sort worn by black women in New Orleans, which was, in fact, where she had been born.

As Edward placed the tray on the table, Rissa regarded the untouched food with a deep, despairing sigh. "Don't know what keeps that man alive," she muttered, shaking her head, then looked up at Edward. "You had your breakfast?"

He smiled. "Just a cup of coffee, Rissa. And," he added, picking up one of the biscuits from the tray, "one of these."

Going to the stove, Rissa poured coffee into a cup and handed it to him. "You going off on that boat again?" she asked, sounding every bit as disapproving as Cyrus.

He nodded. Swallowing the last of the biscuit, he drank the coffee, then noted the time. "And I'd better be on my way. The *Nola Star* doesn't wait for anyone." He put an arm around her plump shoulders and gave her a quick hug. "You'll take care of Pa while I'm gone?"

Her lips stretched into a wide smile that clearly conveyed her adoration. "You just leave everything to Rissa," she assured him.

Edward came out onto the porch a while later, breathing deeply of the clean-scented air. He lingered a moment, running his hand over one of the smooth white columns that soared to the second-story veranda. All the columns in the front of the house had been replaced with new ones, the originals having been badly gouged and scratched during the time the Federals had occupied Glencoe.

Coming down the steps, Edward's handsome face fell into a scowl as he saw the horse and rider coming up the drive. The woman was tall, with flaming red hair and a body that was, he knew from experience, voluptuous.

Alighting from the chestnut gelding with the easy grace of someone who's been around horses all her life, the woman came sauntering toward him, full hips swaying provocatively beneath her Spanish-style riding habit, the skirt of which was tightly laced at her waist. With each step she took, the skirt parted to reveal the soft leather chaps underneath. Over a long-sleeved wool blouse, she wore a smart little bolero jacket that curved temptingly over the swell of her generous breasts, outlining them in a tantalizing manner. Few people looked at Lydia Madison, in the full bloom of womanhood at twenty-six, and termed her less than stunning.

"What are you doing here?" Edward growled as she paused before him.

A finely molded brow arched upward. "Darling, we were engaged not too long ago. Surely you can manage a warmer greeting than that." Despite her flip words, there was an undercurrent of intensity in her voice as she spoke.

"We are no longer engaged," Edward said flatly. "You know that as well as I do." He was irritated with her unexpected visit and made no attempt to conceal it from her.

Her green eyes darkened a shade. "Just because we had a slight misunderstanding is no reason why we can't still be friends." A small white hand reached out to caress the lapel of his jacket.

"I do not call finding my fiancée in bed with another man a misunderstanding!" he shot back. Grabbing her wrist firmly, he moved her hand away from him.

"Oh, Edward." She forced a gay laugh. "Don't be provincial. Honestly, I didn't come here to argue with you. I knew you'd be leaving for Louisville today, and I merely wanted to wish you luck."

Henry had brought the carriage to the front, and Edward now flung his portmanteau in the back seat. He gave her a brief glance that held no trace of warmth. "I have to go now, Lydia."

Before he could step into the carriage, she caught his arm. Standing on tiptoe, she planted a light kiss on his cheek, ignoring his withdrawal.

"When you return, we must talk," she whispered softly. Her voice held the slightly breathless quality that always afflicted her when she was close to him. A sudden breeze ruffled his golden hair. Lydia clenched her hands to prevent herself from reaching out and smoothing the wayward curl that tumbled across his forehead. His face was all planes and angles, his body lean and muscular, and every inch of him was seared into her memory.

"There's nothing to talk about." Annoyance altered his voice as he moved away from her.

Lydia pouted in the way that once moved his heart. "Edward, we've known each other practically all our lives, since we were children. Surely you don't intend to let a moment's foolishness on my part destroy all we've meant to each other."

Settling himself in the carriage, Edward spoke tersely, blue eyes narrowed. "Lydia . . . listen to me! It's all over. I want nothing more to do with you. Go back to The Willows and play your little games with someone else." He motioned to Henry. "Go on! I don't want to miss the boat."

Lydia watched as the carriage proceeded down the drive. Then, a deep frown marring her otherwise pretty face, she mounted the chestnut gelding.

Damn, she thought, noticing that Edward did not turn to look at her. *If only they hadn't had that silly spat; if only she hadn't had that extra glass of wine; if only Colin Thatcher wasn't so handsome....*

Lydia urged her horse forward, her mouth set firmly. Colin meant nothing to her; Edward meant everything. She vowed to get him back in any way she could.

Just then, looking toward the west field, Lydia saw the horse. After a moment she nudged her own mount in that direction. A young man, Edward's groom, was leaning on the fence, oblivious to everything except the prancing animal.

"Matthew!" Lydia called out.

Straightening, Matthew Fletcher looked at her and immediately removed his cap. "Good morning, Miss Lydia." His broad, boyish grin revealed white, even teeth. Although his manner was cordial, Matthew didn't especially like Lydia Madison. There was a harsh, grating tone to her voice that made him want to cover his ears. But she was knowledgeable about horses, and for that alone he gave her a measure of respect.

She nodded curtly, then pointed toward the horse. "I've not seen her before."

The young man nodded enthusiastically as he leaned on the fence again, one foot on the bottom railing. "Her name is Dawn's Light. Isn't she beautiful? Edward bought her in Europe a few weeks back."

"What breed is it?" she inquired, noting that the horse appeared just under fifteen hands high.

"An Akhal-Teke. Edward's hoping to breed her, but he needs to find a stallion of good quality first. He's so proud of her. He just loves that horse, and I can't say I blame him."

Lydia pursed her lips, thinking that she had never seen an animal move with such a clear, flowing stride as this one was displaying. The head was delicately formed, the large eyes expressive and intelligent. "What's her speed?" she asked.

Running a hand through his light brown hair, Matthew put his cap back on his head. "I've just breezed her around the track a few times. I've not let her out yet." He gave a small laugh, shaking his head. "But I swear she runs like she's got wings."

Lydia watched the magnificent animal a moment longer, impressed by the long lean body. Its coat had a metallic sheen, catching the sunlight and reflecting it in rippling waves of gold that flowed across sinewy muscles, withers, and flanks.

Finally, without offering a good-bye, Lydia nudged her own horse forward. Halfway down the drive, she reined in and turned in the saddle for another look at Dawn's Light. Her eye then lit on the house, and she saw Cyrus Hammond peering at her through the window.

The man didn't like her; she knew that. She wondered whether Edward had given his father any reason for his broken engagement, then decided it didn't matter one way or the other.

Turning, Lydia prodded the chestnut gelding to a canter, heading for her home, which adjoined Glencoe.

Chapter 4

The _Nola Star_ was one of seven steamers that had put in at Memphis on this day, her twin chimneys rising like towering rubies against the cerulean sky. Linking the two red stacks was a fanciful bit of intricately worked gilt with a star in the center.

On the bow of the boat, a bright red flag hung limply from the jack staff, waiting for an accommodating breeze to quicken it to life.

Fully four hundred feet in length, the _Nola Star_ was a side-wheeler, her white and shallow hull resting easily in the water. Eight boilers supplied high-pressure steam to two engines, one on each paddle wheel, the gaily painted boxes of which depicted the name _Nola Star_ in gold leaf.

A sense of excitement pervaded the levee. It was crowded with bales of cotton, hogsheads of sugar, various sized crates, boxes, and burlap bags.

Passengers and onlookers alike milled about in haphazard fashion, giving the impression that no one had a destination in mind. Roustabouts worked steadily, if noisely, loading and unloading cargoes, their shouts and curses coloring the air with a steady din.

Mary Dennison, owner of the *Nola Star,* stood on the texas deck, her brown eyes carefully observing those passengers who were now boarding. There were only a few; most had embarked at Louisville.

Two levels below where she was standing, deck passengers congregated on the main deck, but Mary gave them scant notice. Most were emigrants, the rest down on their luck. Neither accommodations nor food were offered to deck passengers. Their trip was made with whatever provisions they brought with them.

Glancing down at the levee, Mary saw Owen Tully, his wife and daughter close on his heels, coming up the gangway. She turned to the eighteen-year-old girl who was standing at her side. ''Amy, did you assign the Tullys their usual stateroom?''

Her daughter checked the passenger list she was holding, then nodded, her silver-blond hair catching the sunlight and reflecting little sequins of light with her movement. Amy didn't speak, for she couldn't. She hadn't said a word since she was four years old. Methodically, she made a check mark next to the name of Tully, then looked down at the new arrivals.

At that moment, Harriet Tully raised her head to look at Amy, her plain face set in a smirk.

Amy turned away. The girl, who was a year younger than Amy, had a sharp tongue, with a cutting edge to her remarks. Amy knew malice when she saw it. The few times she had been in Harriet's company the girl had turned her nose up at her. Her mother, Martha, wasn't much better, always talking down to her as people sometimes did, for they thought that her mind was as faulty as her tongue.

Still, the Tullys were repeat guests—her mother always referred to the passengers as guests—and Mary went out of her way to make them feel welcome.

Bethany and Colin boarded the *Nola Star* at half past four in the afternoon, using the gangway that led to the hurricane deck. The late February day, although cool, was bright and sunny, causing dancing rays of sunlight to play across the water, shifting and coyly changing shape, as if flirting with the eye.

Colin had secured staterooms for them both on the texas deck. The only thing higher was the pilothouse, an extravagantly glassed aerie that offered a commanding view of the river.

When she entered her cabin, Bethany gave a little gasp of pleasure. It was more lavish than she had expected. While not overly large, it was beautifully furnished. The Brussels carpet was a dark crimson, patterned in a warm gold that was repeated in the velvet draperies that covered the single window. The walnut writing table was flanked by two chairs covered in pale green damask.

Overall, the effect was one of restrained elegance.

Seeing her trunk in a corner, Bethany removed some of her clothing and hung it in the wardrobe. After she washed, she brushed her hair, twisting it into a soft chignon at the nape of her neck.

Deciding to change her dress for the evening, Bethany

45

selected a pastel-blue silk gown with a fine lace over-skirt. It was an off-the-shoulder creation with the merest hint of a bustle, the skirt falling snugly about her slim hips.

Promptly at five o'clock the chimneys poured forth pitch-pine smoke, the mooring lines were cast off, and the ship's whistle invaded the stillness of the afternoon. The *Nola Star* moved confidently in the muddy waters of the Mississippi.

Picking up her shawl, Bethany opened the door, smiling as she saw Colin patiently waiting for her. He, too, had changed his clothes and was wearing a black broadcloth jacket over gray-striped trousers. A diamond breast pin winked darts of light from the folds of his silk cravat. His eyes widened when he caught sight of her.

"You look beautiful!" he exclaimed, quite overwhelmed at the sight of her. "I hadn't realized..." He grinned. "You're not going to tell me that you bought that dress in Memphis."

She laughed lightly, pleased with his admiring look. "No. I bought this dress in Paris."

With an exaggerated display of gallantry, Colin extended his arm and escorted her downstairs to the dining room. Located on the hurricane deck, it was more than one hundred feet long with staterooms on either side, each one of which had a magnificent oil painting on its door. From above, light poured in through stained-glass clerestory windows, as well as from two gigantic crystal chandeliers.

As they crossed the room, Bethany studied the people around her, relieved to see that there was no one aboard that she knew. She'd had a moment's apprehension before she came downstairs, praying she would not run into any of her father's friends, knowing she would be hard-pressed to explain her reasons for being on the *Nola Star.*

The men in particular came under her close scrutiny. Which of them, Bethany wondered, was Edward Hammond?

Colin held her chair while she seated herself at one of the dining tables, all of which supported starched white linen cloths and a narrow crystal vase filled with fresh flowers.

"I think you'll enjoy the food," he said as he sat down. "The owner, Mary Dennison, sets a fine table. It's one of the reasons I favor the *Nola Star.* That, and the fact that the cargo is at a minimum." He gave a short laugh. "I've been on a few where the bales were piled so high it was impossible to walk the deck."

"The *Nola Star* is more of a passenger boat then?" Bethany inquired, studying the extensive bill of fare that had been handed to her by a hovering steward.

Colin nodded. "One of the best. It wasn't always so, though. When Mary's husband was alive, it was just like all the others. At that time the *Nola Star* made the trip from Memphis to New Orleans and back again. Now, of course, it terminates in Louisville." Colin glanced briefly at the bill of fare, then at Bethany.

Bemused, Bethany saw there were fully fifteen entrées to choose from, consisting of five types of fish, seven of meat, and three of roast game. That did not include soups, salads, and desserts, of which there were more than twenty listed. With a laugh, she put down the menu and requested that Colin order for her.

While he did so, Bethany viewed her surroundings with interest.

The room hummed with muted voices, occasional laughter, and soft music played by a string quartet situated at the far side of the dining room. For the most part, the passengers were elegantly dressed, the ladies gowned in silks and satins, the men sporting elaborate shirtfronts and jeweled breast pins.

The stewards, all of whom were Negroes, moved quietly and efficiently, their snowy white gloves in sharp contrast with their black suits.

Bethany had just dipped her spoon into a steaming bowl of gumbo when Colin directed her attention to a table not far from where they were sitting.

"The Bayou Fox has just made an appearance," he murmured, lifting his napkin to his lips to hide a half smile.

Turning her head slightly, Bethany blinked in surprise. Again she found herself looking at a man who was vastly different from what she had expected. He was tall, lean, tanned, and golden-haired. His clean-shaven face was all angular planes.

Bethany's mouth tightened as she stared at him. Handsome? Yes, he was that. But his looks had little to do with his attraction, she realized. An aura of maleness emanated from him. She had a suspicion that every female in the room was aware of Edward Hammond. Indeed, she noticed that more than one woman was throwing coy glances in his direction. His eyes were like blue flames; vivid, intelligent, direct.

Too direct. She became aware that he was staring at her in a compelling way.

Bethany turned away and concentrated on her food. Absently, Colin retrieved the silver dollar from the pocket of his vest and began to manipulate it through his fingers. Bethany hardly noticed. She was by now growing used to this peculiar nervous habit of his.

They had just finished their dessert, a frothy chocolate mousse, when Bethany looked up to see Edward Hammond coming toward them.

"Good evening, Colin," he said, pausing by their table. "I didn't expect to see you on this trip. If I remember correctly, your last voyage wasn't too successful."

Raising her head, Bethany regarded Edward Hammond with understandable curiosity. His stance was relaxed, perfectly at ease. One hand rested lightly on top of the empty chair on the other side of the table. Bethany stared at the suntanned skin. His was not the smooth hand of a gentleman. It was large and powerful, the hand of a man used to physical labor.

Colin had leaned back in his chair, the smile on his face less than sincere. A flash of enmity crackled between the two men, but as quickly as it appeared, it subsided. Both of them had come to terms with the fact that the nature of their livelihoods threw them into contact with each other. Consequently, both had adopted a thin veneer of civility toward one another.

"Last time I had a bit of bad luck, Hammond. This time I've brought a good-luck charm with me." As Colin glanced at Bethany his smile turned genuine.

"I've never believed in luck," Edward murmured, his gaze coming to rest on Bethany with a directness that was almost insulting in its implications.

I'll bet you don't, Bethany silently fumed. *A man who cheats has no need of luck.*

"Might I be presented to your . . . good-luck charm?" Although he had addressed Colin, Edward's eyes never left Bethany's face. A vast improvement, he was thinking, over the tarts that Colin usually brought with him.

"Of course. Forgive the oversight. This is Miss Bethany . . . Kincaid," Colin quickly improvised, knowing that Edward would recognize the name Forrester.

"Miss Kincaid," Edward acknowledged with a small bow. "I'm certain you'll provide an admirable distraction . . . for most of the players." His expression plainly told her that he would not be one of them.

Bethany took a sip of her wine, put down her glass, and gave him a level look. "I do not intend to be a distraction, Mr. Hammond," she retorted in her coldest voice. "I intend to play cards."

Surprise momentarily erased the mocking expression, but when it returned, it was even more pronounced.

"I should like to be on the receiving end of anything you'd care to deal out," he said, emitting a vibrant chuckle Bethany felt certain sent a tingle down the spine of every female within earshot.

With a brief nod at Colin, he strolled away without a backward glance.

"My God," Bethany gasped in anger. "He's just as rude as he is unscrupulous!"

"Don't let his attitude throw you," Colin advised,

patting her hand. "If you do, you won't be able to think clearly." He got up. "The games won't begin for a good hour yet. Let's walk the deck." He picked up her shawl and draped it around her shoulders.

As Bethany got to her feet, she realized she was trembling and made a conscious effort to control herself. Colin was right, she thought. Anger would only cloud her judgment and slow her reflexes—neither of which she could afford.

It was growing dark now, the air chilly and a trifle damp. Nevertheless, couples strolled the promenade, relaxed on deck chairs, or stood in small groups, conversing and laughing.

The surface of the river changed dramatically as twilight cast deepening shadows along the banks. Last year, in 1879, the Mississippi River Commission had been formed. Snag boats had set to clearing the river, and the navigable channel was now defined by beacon lamps that threw golden ribbons of light across the water.

Bethany leaned on the white wooden railing that was decorated with lavish filigrees, appreciating the loveliness of it all. How beautiful, how benign it looked. But having lived in its proximity all her life, Bethany was well aware of its capricious nature. Periodically, the water would rise to flood stage and higher, devouring the land and the flimsy structures built by man in defiance of the river's supremacy.

Glancing toward the prow, Bethany saw a woman and a girl heading in their direction. The woman, who appeared to be in her early forties, was tall and of impressive proportions, though certainly not fat. The strong features of her face were offset by eyes that were dark and luminous. She was dressed fashionably in a mauve pannier skirt and a short spencer jacket. Her Windsor hat was perched atop dark hair worn in a sweeping pompadour that revealed a becoming streak of silver at her temples.

Colin touched Bethany's arm. "That's Mary Dennison. She owns the *Nola Star*. The girl with her is her daughter. Amy doesn't speak." Bethany flashed him a questioning look, but Colin only shrugged. "I don't know why. Something to do with the war, I think. Mary doesn't talk much about it."

"Colin!" the woman called out as they neared. "Glad to see you could join us again."

Colin laughed. "Don't I always?" Turning, he introduced Bethany, again using the name Kincaid.

Amy offered a sweet smile to which Bethany promptly responded in kind. The girl could be no more than eighteen, Bethany thought, but she was a true beauty. She was fine-boned to the point of appearing fragile. Silvery blond hair was drawn back from her face, falling into soft, long curls about her slim shoulders. An odd mixture of innocence and wisdom shone from her gray eyes; *it was as if she were at once both older and younger than her years*, Bethany mused, startled by her observation.

"If I can do anything to make your trip more comfortable, you just let me know," Mary said to Bethany with a nod of her head.

"Oh, this isn't a pleasure trip for Bethany," Colin put in. "She's here to play poker."

Mary raised a brow, giving Bethany a closer look.

"Well, you'll certainly add some class to the table," she remarked with a broad grin.

Removing his watch from a vest pocket, Colin noted the time. "Let's get back inside," he said to Bethany, nodding at Mary and Amy as they moved away.

Chapter 5

In spite of the more than fifty men and a spattering of women in the room, the Grand Saloon seemed almost hushed. A few people were playing roulette or faro, but most were at the felt-topped poker tables.

A large, rectangular sign hanging over the bar in plain view informed everyone that firearms were not permitted in the Grand Saloon. Anyone who chose to overlook this rule, the sign read, would be required to disembark at the next landing.

Pushing the door inward, Colin saw that Edward was seated at his usual corner table. Bethany began to head in that direction, but Colin's arm detained her.

"Not yet," he said in a low voice. "The table next to his." He nodded at the three men sitting there. "The man with the muttonchop whiskers is Owen Tully. He's in railroads. The other two are planters. They'll all be in their cups before the night's gone."

Approaching the table, Colin smiled at the three

men. "Mind if we join you?" he asked, his tone indicating that he would very much mind if any exception were taken.

Tully immediately got to his feet, straightening his brown cravat, eyes fastened on Bethany with open admiration. He was a thin man in his early fifties, not overly tall, with stooped shoulders and an anxious expression that appeared carved into his face from years of use.

"Pleased to have you both join us," he said. His rather close-set blue eyes were friendly as he nodded.

The other two men didn't bother to stand. They offered only a sullen nod, apparently having serious reservations about playing cards with a woman.

As the game progressed, Bethany realized that Colin's decision had been a wise one. Owen Tully was a nervous player who gave himself away time and again. He invariably tugged at his cravat when he had a bad hand and beamed when he had a good one. The two planters, Josh Middleton and Robert Endicott, were not so obvious, but they both were drinking heavily, their responses delayed and, at times, reckless.

At the next table, Edward lit a cigar and, as had happened several times during the last half hour, his eyes strayed to his adversary's beautiful companion.

Edward was annoyed with himself for letting his attention wander. But the woman couldn't be as innocent, as honest as that face led him to believe . . . not doing what she was doing, not traveling around with a rogue like Colin Thatcher. Edward felt certain Colin wasn't just indulging himself in a protégée. Kincaid. . . .

Edward gave a slight shake of his head. He'd never heard the name before.

Almost as if she felt his gaze, Bethany turned toward him. For a long moment his eyes held hers as if they were alone in the room. Bethany's ears tingled with the flush that crept up her neck. She quickly attributed her reaction to anger, for what other emotion could she possibly feel for that man?

Turning away, she played out the hand—which she won—then stole another glance at Edward Hammond, but he was talking to Mary, who had stopped by his table. With a strange feeling of relief, Bethany shuffled the cards and began to deal.

Having concluded her conversation with Edward, Mary inspected the long table that had been set up as a buffet, nodding in satisfaction at the array of cold meats and cheeses.

While she sipped from a steaming cup of coffee, Mary's eyes scanned the room, resting with a practiced casualness on those men she had never seen before. Although the *Nola Star* had a reputation for honest games, on more than one occasion a card mechanic had slipped aboard. The stewards were under strict instructions to report to her immediately if they noticed anyone acting suspiciously.

She also made certain that the cards being used at each table were the ones she supplied. The backs were engraved in an intricate geometric pattern, with the name of the *Nola Star* in the center. Mary had them made to order by a firm in Chicago. At the end of each evening's play, stewards gathered all the used cards and destroyed them.

Satisfied that all was well, Mary took a seat at an

empty table. She watched Bethany for awhile, admiring the cool assurance the young woman was displaying. She'd known several women gamblers in her time, but Bethany didn't seem to fit any mold. She was obviously well-educated, a lady. That alone set her apart.

And what the devil was she doing with the likes of Colin Thatcher? Mary wondered, finishing the last of her coffee. She'd known Colin for some years now. His taste ran toward well-dressed harlots, most of whom applied their makeup with a more than liberal hand.

Mary put down her cup, then headed for the Ladies' Cabin, which adjoined the Grand Saloon. Although smaller, it was furnished more elaborately, the ceiling rich in Gothic ornamentation. The carpeting was plush, the chairs comfortably cushioned, the glasses and silverware of the same high quality as was used in the dining room.

Due to the lateness of the hour, the Ladies' Cabin was almost empty. Seated at a small upright piano in a corner of the room, a bored-looking young man was offering an insipid rendition of Schubert's Symphony in C Minor.

Seeing Martha Tully wave to her, Mary repressed a sigh as she headed in her direction. Like Amy, she didn't especially like the woman or her daughter. But the Tullys made the trip downriver and back at least twice a year, spending a great deal of money each time they did so.

"We will be in New Orleans in time for Mardi Gras, won't we?" Martha asked as Mary approached. She was, as always, sitting stiffly in her chair, her back as straight as an arrow. This was not the result of good posture; rather it was due to the fact that she insisted on wearing a corset at least a size smaller than her large frame required.

"Captain Baxter assures me that we're right on schedule," Mary replied with a smile that included the other ladies at the table.

"Would you care to join us?" Martha gestured. "Madame Jordaine is reading the cards for us. . . ."

"No, thank you." Mary's gaze swung to the thin, dark woman who had the Tarot cards spread on the table before her. "Another time perhaps."

"And where is Amy this evening?" Martha continued in a voice that could be heard all over the room. "Harriet was so disappointed that she didn't join us after supper."

Mary glanced at Harriet but saw no sign of disappointment. The girl was placidly devouring a large piece of chocolate cake, never taking her eyes from her plate.

Mary turned to Martha again, the fixed smile still in place. "I believe Amy has retired," she replied quietly, noting the diamond necklace Martha Tully was wearing. It fit so snugly it was almost hidden in the folds of her neck.

"Ahh, the poor child. . . ," Martha said with an exaggerated sigh of sympathy and a knowing nod at her companions.

Mary's brows dipped. "Amy is neither poor nor a child," she retorted tartly.

"Oh, yes, of course." The woman waved a ringed hand and had the grace to flush. "I just meant . . ." She lowered her voice to a conspiratorial level. "Well, you know what I mean...."

Yes, you old cow, Mary thought to herself, refusing to let her anger show on her face. *I know very well what you mean.*

"If you ladies will excuse me..."

Without waiting to see whether they would or not, Mary walked away, heading for the two-room suite she shared with Amy on the texas deck.

When she was out of sight of the women, Mary allowed herself an irritated sigh. She supposed that, over the years, she should have gotten used to the ridiculous notion held by so many people who knew her daughter that Amy was someone to be pitied. But she never did. Her heart ached for Amy—for the lost years of her childhood, for the terror and the nightmares that had been the lot of her daughter.

Days went by when Mary never even thought of it. Then someone like Martha Tully would bring it all back again.

It was after one o'clock in the morning when Robert Endicott finally got to his feet and stretched.

"That's it for me," he announced, his words slurred from whiskey. Having removed his jacket earlier in the evening, he plucked it from the back of his chair and pushed his arms into it. Collecting the few coins that remained in front of him, he stumbled away.

Josh Middleton had long since retired, but Owen Tully played another hand. He seemed to Bethany to be a bit desperate, his forehead glistening with a fine sheen of perspiration as he raised the pot several times in a row. Bethany dropped out, but Colin stayed, his face revealing no indication of whether he was holding a good hand or not.

Finally, Tully called.

"Full house," Colin murmured, putting his cards on the table. "Aces over fours."

Tully threw his cards down and exhaled a breath that caused them to flutter. "Have to give you a marker, Mr. Thatcher," he mumbled.

Colin nodded affably, smiling broadly. "My pleasure, Mr. Tully."

After the man had left, Colin turned to Bethany and winked. "You did well tonight." Getting to his feet, he held her chair as she got up. "But keep in mind that not all players are as accommodating as our Mr. Tully," he went on. "He's a goose waiting to be plucked."

"I'll remember." Bethany nodded more solemnly than she felt. She was in the grip of a feeling of excitement. She had won! Not much, to be sure; only sixty-two dollars. Still, it was proof of her capabilities. She gave a small start as she realized that Edward Hammond was suddenly at her side.

"Calling it a night, Colin?" he said, speaking over her head and not acknowledging her presence.

"Looks that way," Colin muttered, sounding annoyed as they all headed for their staterooms.

Walking between the two men, Bethany kept her eyes lowered, not wanting to look at Edward Hammond for reasons she couldn't explain to herself.

When they reached the texas deck, Colin paused with Bethany before her cabin. Edward continued a short distance down the corridor, where he halted before his own door. Unlocking it, he paused a moment, glancing back in their direction, a half smile on his face as he looked at Bethany. She flushed, knowing very well what his thoughts were; it was quite evident that he assumed that she and Colin were sharing the same room.

She moistened her lips, inserted the key into the lock, and told herself it didn't matter what that man thought.

Before she could enter, Colin clasped her hand. "Again I want to say how lovely you look." He brought his face closer to hers, hesitating when she drew away from him. "I want you, Bethany," he whispered softly. His fingers traced a finely tapered wrist, then slid up her arm to her shoulder in a caressing manner. A pulse throbbed at his temple, and his eyes blazed with a desire that was not lost on her.

Unaccountably, Bethany glanced towards Edward's door, then took a step back. "Please . . . don't." The sudden act of familiarity surprised her.

Colin ignored her. Pulling her toward him, he kissed her, his mouth working against her lips in an almost feverish way, as if he wanted to consume her.

Even through the impediment of her clothing, Bethany could feel his urgent need, but there was no answering response within her. She drew away from him, her expression leaving no doubt that she was unwilling for matters to progress any further.

Colin's hands fell away, and he gave her a crooked smile. It had been a long time since any woman had rejected him. It made Bethany that much more desirable. She had no idea of the fire she ignited in him.

"Very well," he murmured. "I'll wait until you feel more comfortable with me." His hand cupped her chin, tilted her face upward. "But don't make me wait too long," he added quietly, giving her a level look. "I'm not a man who likes to be kept dangling."

Bethany frowned. Until now, Colin had acted the perfect gentleman, never by word or action indicating that he had carnal thoughts. Never once while they were together in the privacy of his room had he sought to take advantage.

"I offered to pay you, Colin. You declined." She injected a note of sharpness into her voice, annoyed that he had placed her in this position in the first place. "Have you now changed your mind—and the method of payment?"

His jaw tightened, and she saw the flush on his neck. "Of course not! I meant nothing of the sort." His voice softened, grew husky. "You must know how your beauty taunts a man. I know it would be good between us, if you'll only give it a chance." His dark eyes pleaded with her.

Bethany put a hand behind her, fumbling for the doorknob. "Goodnight, Colin," she said firmly.

Inside her room, Bethany issued a long sigh. Colin's actions left her vaguely uncomfortable. He was an attractive man; in fact Bethany had no doubt that many women would consider him to be very handsome. But she couldn't bring herself to feel that way about him. Something was missing—the spark wasn't there. She knew the feeling, having had a brief affair while in Paris the year before. Louis had been married, and nothing could have come of it. Bethany wasn't even certain now whether she'd been in love with him, but the physical attraction had been like a spray of fireworks, and having experienced it once, Bethany knew she would never settle for less.

After she undressed, Bethany slipped into bed, mulling over the evening's events.

Having won, even nominally, gave her a confidence that till now she had been lacking. No longer did she doubt that she could beat Edward Hammond.

She moved restlessly at the thought of that man, still stung by his condescending attitude toward her. Before today she had only a sense of determination prodding her on.

Now, she decided, finding a more comfortable position, not only would it be satisfying to bring that man to his knees—it would be a pleasure!

Chapter 6

Despite having stayed up late the night before, Bethany awakened early the next morning. It was not yet eight o'clock.

Glancing out the window, she saw the day was cloudy and heavy with the threat of rain, giving a grayish cast to the water. The *Nola Star* was at this moment angling toward shore, heading for one of the many refueling stations that dotted the banks of the river.

Getting out of bed, she washed herself in the porcelain basin, missing the warm tub she was used to having at the start of each day. When she was finished, she went to the small dressing table and brushed her hair, piling it high on her head, securing it with pins and an onyx comb. Then she donned a gray knitted wool skirt with a matching jacket and a soft-rose silk blouse. A smart little velvet hat with a saucy yellow feather completed her ensemble.

Picking up her parasol, she went down to the dining room.

Not seeing Colin in evidence, Bethany hesitated in the doorway. It was not considered proper for a lady to dine alone.

The absurdity of the situation caused her amber eyes to sparkle in amusement. After last night, no one would consider her a proper lady anyway, so what difference did it make?

Bethany walked calmly toward an empty table, ignoring the condemning expressions she was receiving from some of the ladies in the room. Hands were raised to cover rosy lips as they whispered to one another with pointed looks in her direction.

Opening the bill of fare, Bethany had to smile. It was only slightly less elaborate than the evening presentation. Pursing her lips, she wondered if anyone actually ate roast lamb for breakfast.

After a moment's reflection, Bethany decided this was not a day to be adventurous, and she ordered scrambled eggs, biscuits, and café au lait.

While she waited for her food, Bethany absently traced an aimless pattern on the white tablecloth with her fingernail. Almost as clearly as if he were standing in front of her, she could see those blue eyes of Edward Hammond fixed upon her.

It was a most disturbing sensation, and she did her best to shake it off, sternly reminding herself that she must remain detached, must not allow her anger to get the better of her.

The steward put her breakfast on the table, but she made no immediate move to eat it.

Funny how things change, she thought. Just a few short weeks ago she had been an average young woman going about her rather normal life, nothing more pressing on her mind than what dress to wear to her next social function. Now she was notorious, a woman with vengeance on her mind.

But with good reason, she thought grimly, picking up her fork. Someone had to make that man pay for what he did.

Raising her head just then, Bethany saw Mary and Amy coming toward her.

"May we join you?" Mary asked, pausing by the table.

Bethany smiled warmly. "Please do. I dislike eating alone."

"Where's Colin?" Mary seated herself and arranged the skirt of her russet silk morning dress, the sleeves of which ended in myriad ruffles at her elbows. Amy sat down next to her. Unlike her mother, she was garbed simply, her floral-print muslin dress unadorned by either lace or ribbons.

Bethany shrugged. "Still sleeping, I guess."

Mary tilted her head and raised a brow. The few words and the disinterested expression told her that Bethany and Colin had each spent the night in their own cabin. *An unusual state of affairs for Colin,* she thought with malicious glee. Being a woman who made her own way in this man's world, and who had done so for many years, Mary saw nothing wrong with a woman playing poker. But it increased her curiosity about Bethany. She was drawn to the young woman who was such a contradiction in terms.

"Have you and Colin known each other long?" Mary inquired. She leaned back in her chair as the steward placed her usual breakfast before her: a fruit compote, dry toast, and coffee. Amy was served more substantial fare in the form of griddle cakes that shimmered beneath a coating of melted butter and honey.

Bethany shook her head. "Not very. Colin's been . . . helpful."

Mary gave a slow nod but refrained from pursuing the enigmatic statement. She frowned slightly, noticing that Bethany appeared distracted, as if her thoughts were elsewhere. "I do hope you slept well," she ventured, taking a spoonful of fruit.

"Oh, yes," Bethany answered quickly, in order to dispel the concern she was noting. "Very well." She gave a small laugh. "It's the day: the grayness depresses me," she added, thinking of the day her father had been buried.

At that moment, Martha Tully walked by, Harriet at her side, her husband traveling a few steps behind. She offered a greeting to Mary. Bethany could have been invisible for all the outward notice the woman bestowed on her.

"Oh, dear," Bethany said with a light laugh when the woman moved on. "I fear I've been branded a pariah."

"Don't let the old biddy upset you," Mary said, waving a disparaging hand. "Mrs. Tully likes to think of herself as a social trendsetter; in fact, her father was the town drunk, and her mother took in laundry."

This time Bethany's laughter was genuine. "Is that really true?"

Mary tilted her head to one side and raised her brows. "Unless people who know her are spreading vicious rumors, it is." Her eyes twinkled. "To be perfectly honest, I have heard it said, but I can't vouch for its authenticity."

For the next thirty minutes, Mary and Bethany continued to chat amicably, gradually growing more at ease with each other; by the time Amy rose from the table, both women had relaxed, enjoying each other's company.

"Amy works in the office," Mary explained, as the girl walked away. "I used to have a clerk, but he was so addle-brained that I fired him. Amy handles all clerical matters now, and she's damn good at it."

"She's a beautiful girl," Bethany remarked, biting into the last of her biscuit.

"That she is. And bright, too." Mary gave an emphatic nod. "Make no mistake about that. Just because she doesn't talk, doesn't mean she can't think. And she can read and write with the best of them," she added with no little pride. "When she was younger, I used to give free passage to any teacher who'd give her lessons during the time they were on board."

"You've spent a lot of time on the river," Bethany murmured. She had supposed that Mary and Amy lived in a house somewhere and only occasionally traveled on the *Nola Star*. It came as a surprise to learn that they actually lived on the boat.

Mary inclined her head. "It's a way of life. Not as good as some, but better than most." She paused, watching as the steward refilled her coffee cup. "We had another boat before the *Nola Star*," she went on. "But the *Wayfarer* carried cargo. Oh, we took on a few passengers now and then, but mostly it was cotton. Since the war that trade's dwindled. Everybody's using the railroad now." She added sugar to her coffee and stirred it vigorously.

"You no longer own that boat?" Bethany inquired.

"No. When the war came we sold the *Wayfarer*. Couldn't stay on the river in those years; too dangerous. The Federals had their gunboats going up and down, shooting everything in sight." Mary put down her spoon. "Have you ever been on a steamboat before?"

Bethany nodded. "Yes, several times. But none as grand as the *Nola Star*," she confessed, with a smile. "It's like a floating hotel."

A hearty laugh greeted that. "More like a floating gambling house, I'd say." Mary wiped her mouth with the linen napkin. "But I keep it as honest as I can," she continued, not noticing that Bethany had tensed and was now sitting stiffly in her chair. "I won't even sell a ticket to any man who has a reputation for being a river sharper."

"Have you had much trouble with people like that?" Bethany asked, as casually as she could.

Mary gave an offhand shrug. "Now and again. Shills are harder to spot, but I never forget a face. And believe me, in my time I've seen all the tricks."

Bethany looked away. She did not for a moment doubt Mary's sincerity. Obviously, though, there was at least one card mechanic who was so good that his actions had gone unnoticed by Mary's astute eye.

Mary stood up. "We'll be in Vicksburg tomorrow. Amy's birthday is coming up, and I promised her a new outfit. Would you care to go shopping with us?"

"Thank you. I'd enjoy that." Bethany felt a moment's unease as she looked up at Mary's trusting face. Of necessity, she'd had to tell several lies while they had talked in order to conceal her identity, inventing, as it were, a fictitious and nonexistent background for herself. Now, as she watched the older woman walk away, she couldn't help but wonder whether her budding friendship with Mary Dennison would fade when the truth came out.

When Mary left, Bethany finished her coffee, then went for a walk on deck.

Smoke trailed from the tall red stacks and mingled with the damp, gray air. The day was still overcast and growing more humid. A low patch of mist clung to the riverbank and drifted lazily along the surface of the water.

She had not gone very far when she saw Edward Hammond leaning on the railing. Even on a dismal day like this his golden hair seemed colored by the sun. He was impeccably dressed in a fawn-colored frock coat and matching breeches that molded well-muscled thighs. His boots were highly polished, and his vest appeared to be hand-embroidered.

Reluctantly, Bethany admitted to herself that he was damnably attractive. She suspected he had only to walk into a room to dominate it. But for all that, the man was not to be trusted. Gambler though he was, her father had been a man of honor and had instilled that precept firmly in the mind of his daughter.

"Well, Miss Kincaid," Edward said to her, straightening. "Out for a morning stroll?"

Without asking for permission, he fell in step beside

her. She was taller than he had first supposed and moved with a lissomeness that caught his admiration. He had a strong suspicion that if he were to place his hands on that slim waist of hers, he would find only softness and not the bony interference of a corset or stay.

Bethany had made no response to his greeting or his presence, so he said, "I understand you enjoyed moderate success last night."

"As a matter of fact, I did, Mr. Hammond," she replied, wondering how he knew that. "And you?"

He offered a rueful grin. "Not too well, I'm afraid. Perhaps I, too, should have a lucky charm."

"Oh, I don't think you need any," she murmured, with a lift of her brow. "I feel certain you have quite a few tricks up your sleeve."

She gazed out over the water, seeing a stern-wheeler heading upriver. It was a fine-looking vessel, but Bethany thought it couldn't compete with the grandeur of the *Nola Star* as she sailed proudly down the river, gleaming like a jewel. As the two boats came abreast of each other, both pilots tapped their ship's bell in greeting.

Edward turned his head in her direction. "I'm surprised to see you walking alone," he commented.

"I don't see anything surprising about it," she responded, without looking at him.

"Well, you are . . . traveling with Colin, aren't you?" A note of caution shaded the question.

She gave him a brief glance, hoping her cheeks weren't flushed. Then she was angry with herself. Why should she care what he thought?

"I am," she replied at last, unreasonably annoyed by

the easy grace of his long strides as he walked beside her. His body moved like a well-oiled machine.

The corners of Edward's mouth gave a slight twitch as he considered her admission. It was just as he thought it to be. Well, she was fair game for anyone then. Including himself.

He cleared his throat. "Have you been doing this sort of thing long?"

"What sort of thing?" There was a sharp edge to her voice.

"Umm . . . playing poker, of course."

"Not very."

"I've never known a woman gambler before," he remarked conversationally, nodding to an acquaintance who was walking in the opposite direction.

"Well, now you do," she tossed back at him tartly.

Bemused by her brusque manner, Edward fell silent. He glanced sideways at her but couldn't read anything in her face. He took the time to appreciate her small straight nose, high cheekbones that flowed into a delicately molded chin, and graceful white neck. And those eyes! God, they were beautiful. Amber jewels set in a frame of dark silky lashes.

"I suppose you think it's not proper for a woman to play cards," Bethany said to him. Although she wasn't looking at him, she knew he was looking at her. *Why does he keep staring at me?* she wondered, irritated.

"Good heavens," he laughed, "you're not one of those militant females, are you? One of those suffragettes? I do hope I'm not in for a lecture on women's rights."

Bethany gave him an annoyed look. "I take it you're

against that sort of frivolity." Her tone was distinctly sarcastic. "You believe a woman's place is in the home, is that correct?"

"I confess never to have given it much thought," he replied easily.

Her shining black hair was so neatly coiffed beneath the pert little hat she was wearing that Edward found himself wondering what it would be like to remove the pins that confined it and let it come tumbling free. Would it fall to her shoulders? Halfway down her back?

"Where do you live, Miss Kincaid?" he asked after a moment.

She paused, looking up at him, wondering how to answer. Nowhere? "Ah . . . in Louisville," she said at last.

"That makes us neighbors, then! My home is a farm just outside of Lexington."

Although he spoke enthusiastically, Bethany made no response. She began to walk again, seething with hot resentment, wondering what he would say if she told him she had no home, and that it was his fault she was in that predicament.

Edward motioned to the stairs that led up to the pilothouse. "Would you care to go up and take a look?" he asked.

She hesitated. "Is it permissible?"

"For me, it is." He put his hand on her elbow. "Come on. Mr. Forbes is a good friend of mine. He won't mind if we visit."

The room was larger than Bethany had expected it to

be. Wood paneling rose to a height of about four feet. From that point on all was glass, right up to the ceiling. The huge steering wheel was a work of art, intricately carved and highly polished. A high-backed bench with leather cushions was positioned along the rear wall. There was also a deep-cushioned sofa and, in a corner, a big black stove, now unlit. Polished brass was everywhere.

"Edward! Good to see you again."

John T. Forbes, senior pilot of the _Nola Star_, came forward to shake Edward's hand as they entered. He was an imposing-looking man of fifty-four, with thick, black hair and bright blue eyes that widened in appreciation when they landed on Bethany.

The only other person in the room was Will Bishop, a thin, gangly lad of fifteen, who was learning to be a pilot under the tutelage of Forbes.

Forbes now gestured to the boy. "Will, take the wheel. And make sure you keep her in the water!" He turned to Edward. "I was just about to have some coffee. Will you both join me?" At Edward's murmured acceptance, Forbes reached for the coffee pot.

"Have you been a pilot for long, Mr. Forbes?" Bethany asked as she seated herself on the sofa.

"Better than twenty-five years," he answered proudly, handing her a cup of hot, chicory-flavored coffee. He poured one for Edward and one for himself, then sat down on the bench. "And before that I was an apprentice, much as Will here." He nodded to the lad, whose bearing and manner gave every indication of the sense of importance he was feeling in being allowed to guide the boat single-handedly.

"It must be an exciting occupation," Bethany said, sipping from her cup, looking toward Edward. He had remained standing and was staring pensively out over the river. She wondered why she had thought he would sit beside her. At this moment, he seemed totally unaware of her presence.

Forbes nodded in agreement. "Wouldn't want to do anything else."

"Why would you?" Edward remarked dryly, turning to look at Forbes. "Pilots are the next best thing to presidents."

For that observation Edward received a hearty laugh from Forbes. "Even better! If Mr. Hayes was on board, I'd still have the final say." He picked up his pipe from the table beside him, lit it, then regarded Bethany. "The river's full of history, you know. It has many interesting stories to tell, if you know where to look." He bent forward slightly, pointing outside. "This bend we're going around right now, for instance. This was where the *Sultana* first experienced the trouble that would later sink her."

Bethany tilted her head to look outside, then regarded Forbes again. "The *Sultana*? Isn't that the steamer that sank with almost two thousand people on board?"

He took a puff on his pipe, then removed it from his mouth. "Right you are, young lady. It was in April of '65. When the *Sultana* left New Orleans, she was carrying a regular crew and less than a hundred passengers. But when she reached Vicksburg, more than eighteen hundred Union soldiers clambered aboard, anxious to get home. There wasn't a spare foot of room left, I can tell you that. They even crowded into the pilothouse.''

Bethany frowned. "How big a boat was it?"

"Smaller than this one," Forbes answered. "She was a side-wheeler designed to carry about three hundred and seventy passengers." He shook his head and sighed. "She might have made it, too. Captain Mason was a good man. But the river was at flood stage, and the *Sultana* was breasting a strong current. She was right about here when one of her boilers started acting up. They patched the leak and kept going. Made it as far as Memphis, which is where they refueled. When they headed upriver again, they got as far as a group of islands called The Hen and Chickens. That's when the boilers exploded."

Bethany shivered. "Did anyone survive?"

"Not many," Forbes replied somberly, putting his pipe back on the table. "Better than fifteen hundred died."

"I hope there's nothing wrong with our boilers," Bethany said with a shaky laugh.

"Don't you worry about that." Forbes smiled broadly. "I've never lost a boat yet."

When they had finished their coffee, Bethany and Edward descended to the hurricane deck.

A few drops of rain began to fall, and Edward regarded the lowering weather with a quick frown. "Looks like we're in for a shower...."

Before Bethany could react, Edward had taken hold of her arm. Opening the door that led to the dining room, he moved his hand to the small of her back and propelled her inside. Stepping over the threshold, Bethany hastily moved away from the disturbing warmth of his palm.

Edward grinned down at her. "You know, I rather suspected that slim waist of yours had no need of support. I see I was right."

She was so shocked by his words that for a moment Bethany couldn't speak. In defiance of convention, she seldom wore a corset. Her reasons were simple: in an age when full and rounded hips were considered to be the epitome of womanly appeal, hers were, so she thought, unfashionably slim. The effect of a corset only magnified that slimness.

Still staring at him, she saw his blue eyes boldly sweep the length of her from head to toe. And, she noticed, he took his own damn sweet time about doing it! Bethany's eyes widened, then she flushed, finding his lazy smile infuriating.

"You are the rudest man I've ever met!" she flared indignantly. The force of her anger deepened the crimson in her cheeks.

Still grinning, Edward put his hands in his pockets. "My apologies, Miss Kincaid. I meant that as a compliment. . . ."

Bethany was trembling with outrage. The insolence of the man! The fact that he had the churlishness to insult her by referring to something she considered to be a physical deficiency was bad enough, but that he sought to make it sound like flattery was the mark of unmitigated gall! "I am not complimented by your boorish words, Mr. Hammond. And I'll thank you to keep your hands to yourself!'' Glaring at him a moment longer, she turned quickly on her heel and stormed away.

A puzzled look replaced Edward's smile. *Now why,* he wondered, *would a woman like that take offense at such an innocuous remark?*

Chapter 7

Bethany spent the rest of that morning assiduously avoiding Edward Hammond. Just the thought of him raised her hackles and caused her to tremble with anger. She had always thought of herself as being cool and level-headed. Why then was she finding it so difficult to maintain her composure when in the company of that man?

Soon after the midday meal, the *Nola Star* put in at Greenville. Colin was sprawled in a deck chair, deep in conversation with one of his cronies. Not wishing to join them and feeling the need to be alone for a while, Bethany went ashore.

The day was still humid and overcast, but the rain had ceased. Bethany strolled along the one main street, absently looking into shop windows, pausing now and again when something caught her eye.

She was uncertain as to when she became aware that someone was following her, but when she did, only a glance told her that it was Edward Hammond. There was no mistaking that easy stance and those broad shoulders. Whenever she crossed the street, he did. Whenever she paused in front of a store, so did he, maintaining a distance of about a half a block.

For the better part of twenty minutes, Bethany refused to acknowledge him, hoping he would return to the boat, for she had no desire to be in his company. But his presence was so distracting, so persistent, that she was left with no alternative but to confront him.

He was dressed in the same fawn-colored breeches and matching jacket he had been wearing earlier in the day. He was also wearing the same smile, and as she stormed in his direction, it broadened.

"Miss Kincaid. . ." He tipped his hat and offered a brief nod of his head.

"Why are you following me?" she demanded, halting before him.

"There is only one street," he pointed out with a wave of his hand, giving no indication of having noticed her agitated state. "It would be difficult to walk elsewhere, even if one had a reason to do so."

Her eyes widened. "Are you denying the fact that you were deliberately following me?" Exasperated, she resisted the urge to stamp her foot.

"I would imagine that any man who caught sight of you would be tempted to do just that," Edward Hammond answered easily. "But, if you can believe it, my intentions were a bit more altruistic."

"Somehow I doubt that," Bethany retorted with a toss of her head.

She began to walk away, and he positioned himself at

her side, matching her pace. Annoyance pinked her cheeks. Obviously the man couldn't take a hint.

"Mr. Hammond!" She paused and glared at him. "Just what does it take to inform you that I prefer to be alone?" Her hand tightened on her parasol as if she were holding a weapon.

Without realizing it, Bethany had halted in front of a saloon. The doors now swung out, and a man emerged, his inebriated state all too evident from his stumbling gait. Bethany was so close to the doors that he plowed right into her, causing her to almost lose her footing. In an effort to maintain his own balance, the man clutched at her shoulders.

"Oh, my," he said, grinning inanely. "What have we here?" He hung onto her, swaying from side to side, visibly trying to focus his eyes as he peered at her.

"Get away from me!" Bethany put her hands on the man's chest and pushed, but he only tightened his grip. Her hat went askew and her parasol fell to the ground.

"Come inside, little lady," the man mumbled in her ear, his words slurred to the point of incoherency. "I'll be glad to buy you a drink . . ." Bethany slapped at the hand that reached out to touch her hair.

Edward, his hands clasped behind him, bent forward to look at Bethany. "Do you still wish to be alone, Miss Kincaid?" he asked in an infuriatingly mild voice. He raised his brows while he waited for an answer, his relaxed demeanor suggesting he saw nothing out of the ordinary in the situation.

"Will you do something!" she snapped, beginning to struggle as the man's arms went around her waist. She averted her face, trying to avoid the alcohol-infused breath that was almost overpowering in its intensity.

With an ease that thoroughly astonished Bethany, Edward disengaged the man's hold on her and firmly turned him around. A slight shove sent him back through the swinging doors of the saloon. Bending over, he retrieved her parasol, the smile returning to his face.

Muttering to herself, Bethany reached up and straightened her hat as best she could, then grabbed her parasol from his hand in a most ungracious manner.

Edward tried to keep a straight face, and if he hadn't found her so adorable in her piqued state, he might have succeeded. He didn't dare tell her that the feather on her hat was broken in half, the hat itself sitting at a strange angle, nor did he have the courage to mention that her bustle was slightly off center. Some things, he reasoned somberly, were better left unsaid.

"I think it would be wise if you would allow me to escort you back to the boat," he murmured after a moment, then nodded toward the swinging doors. "No telling when your friend might return."

"He's no friend of mine!" she declared indignantly.

Edward pulled on an earlobe, still trying to maintain a serious mien. "Well, he did seem to be quite taken with you. . . ."

A boisterous sound erupted from within the saloon, but it was difficult to tell whether it was based on merriment or argument. A sudden shattering of glass indicated that it might be the latter.

Edward was regarding her with a quizzical look. Shaken, Bethany made no further protest.

"Are you always so impetuous?" Edward inquired as they headed toward the wharf. He shortened his stride so that she would not be forced to hurry.

"I hardly consider going for a walk impetuous," she countered, a bit more heatedly than she had intended. She didn't know which upset her more: the fact that she had needed him to come to her assistance, or the fact that he delayed so long in doing so.

"It could be, if you walk into the unknown," he observed quietly. "You're very independent, aren't you?"

Bethany stared at him, but his expression was unreadable, indicating neither approval nor disapproval. "I like to think so," she replied airily, raising her chin.

His mouth twitched. "Independence goeth before a fall," he murmured with a slight smile.

She bristled, annoyed by his teasing tone. "That's pride!"

"So it is," he agreed pleasantly, not in the least bit daunted by the sharp correction.

A wagon came rumbling up behind them on its way to the dock. Turning his head, Edward noted its progress, then placed a hand on Bethany's elbow to guide her to the side of the dirt road. With the contact, she became uncomfortably aware of his nearness, of the warmth his body emanated. Although the pressure he was exerting was no more than firm, she could sense the underlying strength and power that was held in check. When the wagon passed, his hand released its hold but left in its place a tingling sensation that unnerved her.

Striving to regain her equilibrium, Bethany turned her face to the cool breeze that swept up from the river and tried to ignore the man who walked beside her. It was not so easily done.

She stole a glance at his handsome profile, noting the straight, perfectly formed nose, the strong line of his jaw, the sensual mouth. The thought crossed her mind that he certainly didn't look like what he was; in fact, he didn't even look like a gambler, much less a dishonest one. Bethany considered herself wise enough, however, to know how deceiving appearances could be. Probably not many people saw through his façade, she thought smugly. And wouldn't he be surprised to know that she did!

It was an edge in her favor, one that Bethany promised herself to take advantage of when the proper time presented itself.

Just before they reached the gangway, she stopped and looked up at him. "I . . . suppose I owe you an apology." She hoped her tone didn't express the aversion she felt at having to say the words.

"On the contrary, I'm the one who should apologize. Apparently I offended you this morning by offering an unwanted compliment."

Bethany blinked. She had forgotten about that. "Oh, yes . . . well . . . I'm sure you didn't mean to be deliberately insulting." Even having said that, she didn't believe it for a minute.

"You have my word on it," Edward said in a voice too solemn to be truthful. His mouth quirked, and he refrained from looking at her hat, staring instead into those lovely amber eyes.

Clearing her throat, Bethany straightened her shoulders. "At any rate, I do thank you for your assistance a while ago . . ." Her mouth tightened primly, and she fixed him with a pointed look. "But you had no business following me."

Edward cocked his head, his blue eyes glinting with amusement. "But I wasn't following you, Miss Kincaid. I told you that. I had no idea you were ashore when I left the boat. When I did see you, it was quite obvious that you didn't know what kind of town this is. Only Natchez-under-the-Hill can be more troublesome for an unescorted woman. I assure you I would have done the same for any woman of my acquaintance." He touched the brim of his hat. "If you'll excuse me. I feel certain you can find your way on board without further incident."

Saying no more, Edward made his way leisurely up the gangway without a backward glance.

Bethany glowered, then made a face at his receding figure. She had never met such an exasperating man in her life!

At that moment, the ship's whistle sounded shrilly, startling her into the realization that the *Nola Star* was preparing to leave.

Hoisting her skirts, Bethany hastily ascended the wooden walkway that led to the hurricane deck. Several people turned to stare at her in such a blatant manner that Bethany wondered irritably whether she had suddenly grown a wart on her nose. Disconcerted, she decided she was just imagining the amused looks she was seeing.

Inside her stateroom, Bethany put her parasol on a chair. Catching sight of her reflection in the mirror, she gave a strangled cry of outrage, not believing what she was seeing.

In a quick movement, she spun on her heel, flung open the door and flounced up the corridor to Edward's room, where she knocked loudly.

"Why didn't you tell me?" she shrieked when he opened the door. "How could you have let me walk around in public looking like this!"

The look he gave her bore an innocence that enraged her. She felt like screaming. Plucking her hat from her head, Bethany thrust it under his nose. "You knew!" she accused.

Viewing the bobbing feather, Edward chuckled. "I once had a dog with an ear like that. He was devoted to me."

"Well, I'm not! And as if this were not enough" —she waved the hat—"you could have at least told me about . . ." She swallowed, certain he knew she was referring to the awkward position of her bustle. She felt her lower lip tremble and caught it between her teeth. "People were staring at me!" she blurted out.

"I don't doubt that for an instant," he murmured, more to himself than to her. Extending a hand, he touched her cheek. It was as satin-smooth as he expected it would be. "You have no cause for worry," he said gently. "Regardless of what you wear, you could look nothing less than beautiful. As you do even now," he added, his voice growing husky.

Blushing, Bethany drew in a sharp breath, clenching her hands at her sides and, in the process, what remained of her hat. "You're impossible," she muttered. With as much dignity as she could muster under the circumstances, she marched back to her stateroom, never seeing his smile soften as he watched her go.

Closing her door with a slam, Bethany heaved a great sigh and tossed the ruined hat onto the chair next to her parasol. Peering over her shoulder, she viewed the offending bustle. During her struggles, the padding that formed its foundation had shifted to one side.

In spite of herself, Bethany's lips twitched in the beginnings of a reluctant smile. No wonder people had been staring at her, she thought, now unable to repress a giggle. It was difficult to deny that her appearance warranted more than casual attention.

Shaking her head, Bethany moved about the room, taking off her outer clothes and hanging them neatly in the wardrobe.

Although her anger had dissipated, she felt unsettled and restless, which seemed to be her usual reaction each time she met Edward Hammond. Well, she wasn't about to let it continue, she decided firmly. A bit of determination on her part was all that was necessary. She would ignore him. It was no more than he deserved.

Glancing at the bed, she hesitated a moment, then turned down the covers. A nap was just what she needed, Bethany mused, reasoning that she had been up late the night before and probably would be again tonight.

But when she did fall asleep it was to dream of smoldering blue eyes staring at her and a sensual mouth curved into a mocking smile. When she awoke an hour later, Bethany didn't feel at all refreshed.

That evening, Bethany made certain that Colin was at her side when she went downstairs. Crossing the dining room, she smiled at Mary and Amy, both of whom were eating with the Tullys.

Martha Tully, garbed in a bright pink dress decorated with enough ruffles, flounces, flowers, and ribbons for two gowns, gave Bethany a sharp look that displayed both disapproval and intense curiosity. When she and Colin had moved out of earshot, Martha turned her gaze on Mary, leaning forward as she spoke.

"Mr. Tully tells me that that woman was in the Grand Saloon last night, playing poker with the men!" Her fleshy face reflected scandalous shock, but her black eyes glittered with greedy interest.

"I believe Miss Kincaid was playing," Mary murmured quietly. In some fascination, she watched as Martha's ample bosom hovered dangerously close to her plate of beef Stroganoff, and she was a bit disappointed when Martha sat up straight again.

"I've never heard of such a thing!" the woman gasped in outrage. "Unless of course she's a . . ." She paused, glancing sideways at her daughter. "Unless she's not a lady," she amended carefully.

"Oh, I'd say Bethany is very much a lady." Mary cut into her veal and brought a forkful of it to her mouth, trying hard to conceal her amusement. It didn't take much to shock the Martha Tullys of this world, she thought to herself.

"Humph!" Beneath the pink bodice, Martha's bosom heaved with indignation. "I really don't think you should allow such goings-on," she declared in a strong and righteous voice.

Seated beside Martha, Harriet's mouth was set primly. Her brown hair was swept up in back, and at the sides was a profusion of ringlets that now bobbed as she nodded her head in sharp agreement with her mother.

"After all," Martha continued in the same voice, "there are decent ladies on board, not to mention young, impressionable girls." She patted Harriet's hand as if offering comfort. "And I for one am not happy to have to be in the company of that type of woman. She should stay with her own kind!"

"And what kind might that be?" Mary asked innocently, widening her dark eyes as she viewed the other woman.

Frowning, Martha stared at Mary, uncertain as to whether she was being facetious or not. Still mindful of the presence of her daughter, however, Martha chose to ignore the question. Even the discussion of such a subject was unfitting for a woman of refinement and breeding.

"At any rate," Martha continued, giving her husband a venomous look that caused his face to redden, "I've told Mr. Tully that if he must gamble, then he should do so with the gentlemen!"

Exchanging a glance with her mother, Amy raised her napkin to cover her smile. Unfortunately, she wasn't quick enough to escape the eagle eye of Martha Tully, who glared at her.

Amy tried not to fidget through the rest of the meal, having wished it was over before it had begun. Mr. Tully was pleasant enough, trying to include her in his conversation whenever he spoke. That, unhappily, was rarely. His wife did most of the talking, and most of it was an endless litany of her daughter's virtues, punctuated by pointed looks in Amy's direction.

With a degree of uncharitableness that was unusual for her, Amy decided that Martha Tully could take lessons from Bethany Kincaid on how to conduct herself as a lady. Not that it would do much good—the woman's caustic personality was beyond the reach of mere instruction. Although she thought that, Amy bore no real resentment toward Martha Tully, or anyone else for that matter. She expected very little from people, and she was rarely disappointed. Some people were nice, some were not. To Amy, it was as simple as that.

Chapter 8

In her office the next morning, Amy removed the ledger from the top drawer of her desk, picked up a pen, and discovered the ink pot was empty.

Hell's bells, she thought, using the favorite imprecation of one of her teachers. Getting up, she smoothed the skirt of her yellow lawn dress, then walked gracefully across the carpetless floor to a cabinet in the corner.

Locating a new ink pot, she turned, startled to see a young man standing uncertainly in the doorway. He was in his early twenties and pleasant-looking, with dark brown hair that fell into neat sideburns. Mentally, her mind swiftly scanned the passenger list. Charles Reddington. Traveling alone, and on his way to New Orleans where he was scheduled to disembark for parts unknown.

He took a step forward, removing his hat as he did so. "Excuse me, miss. I seem to have misplaced the key to my stateroom. The name's Reddington. I'm on the hurricane deck.'' He tilted his head to one side as he became aware of her classic beauty, for he was an artist of sorts. As his gaze traveled the length of her, he thought to himself that he had seldom seen such perfection of face and form. What a challenge it would be to try to capture that ethereal quality on canvas.

Amy smiled and nodded. Going behind her desk again, she opened the door of a shallow metal cabinet positioned on the wall. Inside, in neat rows, were hung duplicate keys to all the cabins, arranged by deck. She quickly located the right key. Removing it from its designated slot, she handed it to the young man.

''Thank you,'' he murmured, still bemused by the sight of her. A smile turned into a bashful grin. Amy had no trouble seeing the admiration in his eyes. ''I can't imagine where I lost it,'' he went on with a small laugh. ''I'm usually not so careless.'' He paused, obviously waiting for a response. When none was forthcoming, he looked confused. ''I mean, I had it with me when I went to breakfast. But when I returned to my room, I couldn't seem to find it.''

He fell silent and again stared at her. With a sigh, Amy picked up a pencil. ''Don't concern yourself, Mr. Reddington,'' she wrote in her neat script. ''People lose keys all the time.''

She handed him the paper and watched as he read it. His expression, as he put the paper back on the desk, was all too familiar to her: dawning comprehension, followed by acute embarrassment.

''Thank you,'' he stammered, smiling and backing away. ''I'm sorry to have troubled you. . . .''

As the door closed, Amy gave a rueful shake of her head. The predictability with which most people reacted to her was a constant source of amazement.

A moment later, the door opened again, and she looked up to see Jeb Fitzsimmons. Tall and thin, with carroty-red hair that darkened to brown when it reached his sideburns, Jeb was, in a sense, Amy's assistant. While she did the paperwork, tallied the bills, and assigned passengers to their quarters, he did the over-seeing of the roustabouts and supervised the loading and unloading of any cargo the *Nola Star* might be carrying.

"What was that all about?" Jeb asked, with a nod in the direction taken by Charles Reddington.

Raising a hand, Amy pointed to the cabinet behind her.

"Oh. Another lost key." Jeb placed the papers he had brought with him in front of Amy. "Some people would lose their head if it wasn't screwed on tight." He gave her a broad smile. Unlike most people, Jeb never underestimated Amy Dennison. Having worked with her for the better part of a year, he knew she was capable, astute, and intelligent.

Pursing her lips, Amy nodded in agreement. Initialing the lading bills, she handed them back to Jeb.

Alone again, Amy stared into space, her gaze reflective. She knew she was different from other girls her age, and the fact that she did not speak was only one of the reasons. She was very observant, very perceptive, and listened a great deal. What she learned about people more often than not depressed her. Few young men gave her a second glance—the first ones were given when her beauty caught their eye, the second never being offered once they learned she could not speak to them.

The situation, however, didn't trouble her in the least; Amy had yet to meet the man from whom she wanted that second glance.

The ship's bell sounded three times, breaking into her musings. Amy got to her feet, aware that the boat was making for shore. A shopping excursion was just what she needed. Her spirits rose at the prospect.

In times past, reaching Vicksburg had depended in large part on the river being at a high stage, for the city was situated atop a high bluff. In 1876, however, the capricious Mississippi took one of the turns for which it was notorious, cut across a curve, and left Vicksburg stranded a full three miles from the channel. Army engineers worked diligently to rectify the situation, diverting the lower part of the Yazoo into the Mississippi, thereby allowing steamers to again land at Vicksburg.

Bethany, Mary, and Amy went ashore as soon as the *Nola Star* was secured.

The air was clean and fresh-scented after yesterday's rain. Large mansions and manor houses graced the hillsides, and below the city the restless river moved inexorably on its way to the gulf.

Despite the passage of more than a decade, Bethany saw remnants of the ravages of war that still remained, most notably in the scarred and pitted land. More than half the inhabitants of Vicksburg had dug caves to house and shelter themselves during the devastating forty-eight day siege that had resulted in the capture of the city.

The streets of the business district were crowded, a goodly portion of the people being passengers from the steamers moored at the wharf. Bethany watched Amy in some amusement. The girl's eyes shone with anticipation as they went from shop to shop inspecting materials, laces, and ribbons, while an indulgent Mary tried to keep up with her daughter's enthusiasm.

Their selections and purchases finally made, Mary led them to a café, claiming her feet needed a well-deserved rest.

The café was no more than a large room with a counter on one side. There were only five tables, their tops bare of any amenities. The diamond-paned window in front was uncurtained.

"Not much to look at," Mary said in a low voice as they entered. "But they serve the best damn coffee this side of New Orleans."

The proprietor, an aging Irishman named Liam O'Donnell, was a small, thin man with overlarge teeth, which he displayed in a grin when he saw Mary and Amy.

Coming from behind the counter he greeted them effusively, then touched Amy's arm. "Chantilly has become a mama since you were last here. Look!" He pointed to a box in a corner where a large gray cat rested with lazy assurance among her litter.

Amy's face lit up. She immediately headed for the box while Bethany and Mary sat down at one of the tables.

Observing her daughter, Mary's lips curved into a half smile. "She loves animals, does my Amy," she said to Bethany. "She'd have a zoo if I didn't put my foot down."

Bethany glanced over at Amy, who was cuddling one of the kittens in her arms. Then she looked at Mary curiously. "What happened to her?" Bethany asked the question a bit hesitantly, not wanting to upset Mary.

But the older woman only shrugged. "It happened during the war. When it came, we sold the *Wayfarer* and took a house outside New Orleans. My sister lived nearby. My husband, Lucian, wouldn't take the oath, so we couldn't live in the city. The Federals were everywhere then, and Amy was born during that first year of the war. Lucian had joined the Confederacy and was somewhere in Tennessee. For the next four years we stayed put, Amy, Jason, and me."

"Jason?"

"My son. He was only twelve when he died," Mary said quietly. "The Federals had come by once or twice, pillaging food, trampling crops. But for the most part we were left alone. Of course, the soldiers were always looking for gold and silver, but Lucian had hidden our savings well. It was buried more than three miles from the house, at the edge of the swamp."

Mary fell silent as O'Donnell, still displaying his toothy grin, placed cups of coffee and a plate of small cakes on the table.

"During that last summer," Mary continued when the man left, "my sister came down with yellow fever. Her daughter was the one who came to fetch me. Two of her sons and her husband were here in Vicksburg at the time. The other son was in a prison camp. He didn't survive."

The sigh she emitted seemed to come from deep inside her. "Well, I couldn't take Amy with me under the circumstances, so I left her and Jason at the house while I went to care for my sister. The war was winding down. We all knew by then that it was a lost cause. The Federals came the next day, or maybe it was the day after," she waved a hand, "I never was sure. They were like madmen: looting, rampaging after anything that was of any value."

Mary closed her eyes, squeezing them tightly, to blot out the memory or to regain her equilibrium, Bethany was uncertain.

"When they came to our house," Mary went on, "I guess . . . I guess Jason tried to protect it. They put a bayonet through his chest and set fire to the house."

Dismay was thick in Bethany's throat as Mary continued.

"It was almost ten days before I got back." Her voice fell to a ragged whisper. "By then the heat and sun had done its work. My boy was all but unrecognizable. He was in the front yard. Amy was sitting next to him. She was half starved." Mary's face twisted in bitter anger. "What the bastards didn't burn, they took with them."

Bethany reached out and put a hand on Mary's arm. "My God, that's terrible! What that child must have gone through!"

Blinking against the sting of tears, Mary said, "She hasn't spoken a word since that day I found her. She wasn't quite five then. I don't think she remembers it, though. I guess she just sort of blocked it out of her mind."

"Has she been to a doctor?"

Mary gave a short, humorless laugh. "Every one of any note in every city up and down the Mississippi." She moved her shoulders. "They all said the same thing. Shock caused it, and only shock will undo it." She paused, taking a deep swallow of her coffee.

"Your sister . . ." Bethany said after a moment. "Did she survive?"

Slowly, Mary shook her head. "No." Her mouth went grim as she added, "I keep thinking that if I hadn't left, if I'd taken Amy with me . . ."

"Oh, Mary. You mustn't torment yourself with such thoughts," Bethany said quickly. "Taking Amy with you could have resulted in her death from the fever. You know that. And if you hadn't gone, you would never have forgiven yourself if your sister had died alone and uncared for."

Mary lowered her head. "I know," she sighed. "I know. I guess we all have our own personal little parade of *if*s that march through our lives."

Bethany opened her mouth to speak, but a deep, rich voice preempted her words.

"Good afternoon, ladies. Mind if I join you?"

Mary looked up and immediately brightened as she saw Edward. "Of course not. Sit down, Edward. Bethany and I would be pleased to have your company."

Edward's mocking eyes rested on Bethany as if challenging her to say otherwise. Bethany said nothing. Only a slight tensing at the corners of her mouth indicated she might be something other than pleased.

Amy returned to the table, smiling shyly at Edward as he held her chair while she seated herself.

"I have to be the most fortunate of men," Edward commented as he sat down, "to be in the company of three of the loveliest ladies in the Mississippi Valley."

Bethany gave him a stony look but noticed that both Mary and Amy were beaming with delight. Leaning forward, Edward playfully tweaked Amy's chin, and the girl blushed furiously with the attention.

"Been shopping?" he asked, nodding at the packages on the table. His brows lifted as he regarded Bethany, who was staring intently at her coffee cup.

"Yes."

Hearing the curt answer, Mary's brow wrinkled in perplexity. Her gaze swung from Bethany to Edward and back again. Bethany was scowling into her cup as if she'd discovered a fly swimming in her coffee. Mary sensed the suddenly charged atmosphere, an undercurrent of . . . animosity? But she couldn't understand the cause of it. As far as she knew, Bethany and Edward had met for the first time only a few days ago.

"Bethany bought a lovely costume for Mardi Gras," Mary said finally, in an effort to break the strained silence.

"Perhaps you'll allow me to show you the sights when we get there," Edward suggested to Bethany. He stretched out in his chair, positioning his long legs at an angle and then crossing his ankles, which put his muscular thighs very much in evidence. Bethany was annoyed with herself for being unable to resist letting her gaze sweep over them.

She moistened her lips. "Thank you. But that won't be possible. Colin is escorting me."

"Well, if I cannot join you on your tour of the

Crescent City, perhaps you will join me at the tables tonight.'' He glanced at her sideways. ''That is, if you can handle competition a little stronger than Owen Tully,'' he added, the slant of his mouth hinting at sarcasm.

Irritation stiffened Bethany's shoulders. She was convinced now that that infuriating smile of his was glued in place each morning before he went out to face the world. She straightened in the chair and arched a brow.

''I just might do that,'' she said with a brief nod of her head, keeping her tone casual so he wouldn't think her too eager. Bethany didn't fool herself into thinking she could beat him the first time they played, but it would give her the opportunity to see just what kind of a player he was. And certainly she'd keep an eye out for any suspicious moves on his part.

Edward held her gaze a moment longer, then stood up. ''I look forward to it,'' he said softly.

Taking his leave of the café, Edward walked slowly back to the wharf, his brow furrowed with thoughts of Bethany. He couldn't figure her out. Something about her was not right. She was like a puzzle with half the pieces missing. He had an idea that there was great strength and purpose behind that porcelain façade. It intrigued him. He had watched her for a few minutes through the front window of the café before entering. Her expressions and mannerisms were altogether different from when he was in her company. Was it himself? Edward wondered. Did he cause the icy reserve that suddenly came over her when he approached?

He paused at an intersection, waiting for a carriage to go by, then crossed the street, his step unhurried.

And why did he care? Why did he keep looking at her whenever she was in proximity? She was beautiful, yes, but he knew a score of beautiful women.

Having reached the levee, Edward's eye took in the usual frantic turmoil that accompanied the comings and goings of the steamers. The noise was ear-shattering. Two young boys were standing close to the edge of the water, mouths agape in wonder as they stared at the *Nola Star*. One of them nudged his companion and pointed to the pilothouse. Edward smiled at their wistful expressions, remembering his own burning ambition as a boy to ride on one of the splendid steamers.

He was about to ascend the gangway when he paused dead in his tracks.

Standing demurely to the side of the wooden walkway, her green eyes wide and expectant, was Lydia.

A rush of annoyance flushed Edward's cheeks and tightened his jaw.

She came toward him, looking fetching in a bottle-green pelisse and a pert little hat trimmed with yellow silk ribbons. In the afternoon sun her hair was a red flame, her skin the delicate shade of apricots.

"Hello, Edward," she said in a small voice, her green eyes anxious as she viewed his frowning face. "You're not angry with me, are you?" She put a hand on his arm, feeling the solid strength of him beneath her fingertips. The racing beat of her heart caused her breast to rise and fall in a quickening fashion.

Edward stared at her but said nothing.

She pouted in what she hoped was a charming way. "Oh, Edward, tell me you're not angry. I only wanted to be with you. It's all I've ever wanted." A tear glistened in the emerald eyes.

Edward sighed and ran a hand through his hair. "I'm not angry with you, Lydia." He kept his voice under tight control. "It's just that I see no point in your being here. I've told you before: it's all over between us."

"It may be over for you, Edward," she said softly, "but it will never be over for me. Besides, I...I decided to go to New Orleans for Mardi Gras." She moved closer, slipping her arm through his. "I persuaded Captain Baxter to give me the stateroom next to yours. That was naughty of me, wasn't it?" She watched him intently, unaware that she was holding her breath.

In spite of himself, Edward was reminded of how passionate her full lips could be. A smile began to work its way through the frown, erasing lines in his forehead, replacing them with crinkles at the corners of his eyes. "Well," he said at last, "far be it from me to deprive you of the pleasures of Mardi Gras."

Lydia's laughter was infused with delight as they walked up the gangway. A feeling of relief combined with anticipation made her step light. She felt positively giddy. She knew Edward very well. His physical needs were as great as her own. Given time, she'd make him forget all that had happened, make him realize that they were meant for each other. The first round belonged to her. Edward might not have been too pleased to see her—but neither had he ordered her away.

Edward went directly to his stateroom to wash, shave, and dress for the evening, still a bit annoyed at Lydia's arrival. While he admitted to feeling a small degree of physical attraction for her, he also knew that any emotional ties between them were severed and wondered now whether those ties had been love or habit.

Wearing only his trousers, Edward had just finished shaving when the door opened to reveal Lydia.

Turning, he gave her an irritated look. "Don't you ever knock?"

Closing the door behind her, Lydia's green eyes darkened with desire in the way he knew so well. The sight of his broad, muscled shoulders and his bare chest with its mat of golden hair made her legs so weak she had to lean against the door. Her heart thudded wildly and a trickle of perspiration dampened the valley between her full breasts.

"Oh, Edward. . . ." The longing in her voice reached out to him with suffocating persistence.

Before he could speak or respond to her unexpected appearance, Lydia had flung herself at him, moist lips covering his own, her arms about his waist as she pulled him tight against her. The answering hardness of his body made her own go limp. Removing her lips from his, she fastened them at the hollow of his throat.

"Do you remember how it was between us, Edward?" she whispered. Her touch was as light as a feather. Her fingertips trailed down his chest and paused on his abdomen. Slowly, she undid the buttons of his trousers, then slipped her hand inside, where it rested warmly against the throbbing flesh of his manhood. She began to stroke him in the way he had taught her, knowing exactly the rhythm and pressure that would please him the most.

His jaw worked with a visible effort, but he could not

control his body's fiery response to her questing mouth and wanton caresses. Lydia had been an avid pupil of love, and she had learned her lessons well.

"You have the morals of an alley cat," he growled. His fingers dug into the softness of her upper arms. He wanted to push her away but couldn't quite bring himself to do it.

Her eyes grew hooded and her lips parted with her quickening breath. "You never seemed to mind before," she said, her voice tremulous. Her hands continued to move with familiarity over his lean and muscular body, and Lydia was more than gratified at the sound of the long shuddering breath he took.

Pressing her advantage, Lydia leaned her body full against his. Brushing her lips along the column of his neck, she bit on his ear, then ran her tongue along the outside of it.

Edward muttered a curse. Things had gone too far for him to stop now. In a quick motion, he picked her up and deposited her none too gently on the bed, then he removed his trousers. Pushing up her skirt, he was more than a bit startled to discover that she was wearing nothing beneath her dress.

As he glanced at her, Lydia flashed her most bewitching smile and was rewarded by a grin that was only half-exasperated.

Reaching out, Lydia pulled him closer, guiding him into her, impatient for the total fulfillment only Edward could give her. He displayed no tenderness as he took her roughly, slamming into her with something that resembled anger rather than passion. Nevertheless, Lydia clung to his rocking body, murmuring his name until her voice became garbled with her own heightened excitement. Beneath him, her body moved like a tormented thing with a will of its own.

Raising her hips, Lydia tightened her vaginal muscles, and the sound of his groan sent a hot, sweet fire singing through her veins. It was not a trick that had been taught to her; this one she had learned on her own. For this precious moment Edward belonged to her and to no other. She would have gladly given everything she owned to prolong it for all eternity.

Lydia felt herself elevated to the pinnacle of sensation and could not check the moan that was torn from her throat when her body shuddered in a flooding release.

Even then, Lydia kept her arms around Edward, reluctant to release him. Despite being sated, her body still yearned for his touch. She couldn't seem to get enough of him.

But as soon as his breath calmed, Edward moved away from her. Sitting on the edge of the bed, he reached for his trousers.

Raising herself up, Lydia again put her arms around him, resting her cheek on his back, running her hands through the soft golden hair on his chest, her fingers tracing the hard muscles beneath his warm skin.

"I love you," she whispered.

Firmly, Edward disengaged her hands and stood up.

"This doesn't change anything," he said quietly, not looking at her, sorry now that he hadn't been able to control himself.

Lydia bit her lip. "I don't understand why we can't still see each other." She paused and gave him a sharp look, her eyes diamond bright. "There isn't anyone else, is there?"

The answer was slow in coming. "No . . ."

Getting to his feet, Edward frowned, wondering why he had hesitated, wondering why Bethany's face came to mind. Damn, he was attracted to her. He didn't want to be. There were enough complications in his life right now without adding one more.

Lydia had straightened her clothing and smoothed her hair. Now she came toward him.

"I've wanted you so badly," she told him. "Nights without you have no meaning for me. There's been no one else." She raised her head to look at him. "And you?" Her emerald eyes pleaded with him to give her the only answer she wanted to hear.

"Lydia . . ." He drew a deep breath.

"You don't need anyone else," she said quickly, fearing he was going to tell her something she didn't want to know. "I'm all the woman you'll never need." Putting her arms around his waist, she rested her head on his chest. His clean scent acted like an aphrodisiac on her. "Will you have supper with me, Edward?" she pleaded softly.

Looking down at her shining hair, Edward sighed in resignation. "Of course."

Lydia's smile of satisfaction was hidden from him. *Round two,* she thought, hugging him tightly.

Chapter 9

The *Nola Star* had departed from Vicksburg and was once again heading downriver when Edward and Lydia entered the dining room some forty minutes later.

Having changed her dress, Lydia was now garbed in a magnificent dark green velvet gown, the color and cut of which set off her charms to perfection, a fact of which she was well aware. Her red hair was worn high, swept to one side, where it fell into a single lush curl that rested on her collarbone.

Catching sight of them, Colin put down his fork and frowned. "Now, what the devil is she doing here?" he muttered.

Bethany followed his glance, her eyes widening at the sight of the beautiful woman with Edward. She looked cool and elegant, not a hair out of place, and was moving across the room with a glacial superiority that suggested she possessed a great measure of self-confidence.

"Who is she?" Bethany turned to look at Colin.

"Lydia Madison. Edward was engaged to her not too long ago. And from the look on her face," he mused thoughtfully, "the wedding would appear to be on again." Colin hadn't seen Lydia since that night at Glencoe when she had so unexpectedly entered his room. He had forgotten how stunning she was. He gave a short sigh, wishing again that Edward hadn't interrupted them at such a crucial moment. His loins still tightened when he thought of what had almost taken place.

"She must have just gotten on the boat," Bethany murmured, uncomfortably aware that Edward and his beautiful companion were heading in their direction. "I've not seen her before."

"I think you're right," Colin responded. "Although I can't imagine why she didn't get on at Louisville if she planned to be on board." Picking up his fork again, he resumed eating.

As the couple approached, Edward paused. His burning gaze swept over Bethany, lingering for a significant moment on the creamy swell of breast revealed above her blue satin gown.

Disconcerted, Bethany could feel herself blush to the tip of her toes. With great effort she met his gaze, keeping her eyes level and unwavering.

"Good evening, Miss Kincaid," he murmured. "I hope you still plan to join me at the tables tonight." At her slow nod, he smiled. "Shall we say ten o'clock?"

With an almost imperceptible nod, Lydia's eyes flicked over Colin and came to rest on Bethany, whom she studied with the cool appraisal one beautiful woman affords another. She heard Edward's murmured words, detecting a certain tone in his voice, an inflection that told her that his greeting was not a casual one. Lydia decided it wasn't Colin that had prompted Edward to stop at this particular table. Her eyes narrowed slightly and fixed upon Bethany with all the hauteur she could summon forth.

Bethany's flush deepened until her cheeks were tinted a becoming deep rose. Lowering her head, she made a determined effort to concentrate on her food as Edward and Lydia moved away.

And just why was she so startled? she demanded of herself, slicing into her roast beef with a vicious thrust of her knife. Whatever else he was, there was no denying the fact that Edward Hammond was a handsome man. Even that didn't say it all. He possessed an easy grace and charm that she had no doubt appealed to many females of all ages. Hadn't she seen with her own eyes how even Mary and Amy responded to him?

An unreasonable anger jolted her, surprising her with its force. But she could find no explanation as to why she should be feeling that emotion. Just because Edward Hammond had appeared with a beautiful woman draped on his arm was no reason at all for her to be upset.

Just after ten o'clock, trying to hide her nervousness beneath an assumed air of nonchalance, Bethany sat down at the table with Colin and Edward. Owen Tully, ignoring his wife's instructions, had joined the game and gave Bethany a friendly smile. Bethany acknowledged his greeting as she gracefully slipped into her seat.

As she played, Bethany studied Edward very carefully, looking for any outward indications or mannerisms as Colin had taught her to do. Except for that damned mocking smile, which he bestowed upon her each time they made direct eye contact, there was nothing at all. He gave his cards a brief, almost cursory glance when they were dealt to him, then he laid them down on the table, where they remained until he won or lost.

Bethany had never seen anyone play that way before. Even Colin held his cards in his hands, occasionally studying them.

Just then, Bethany raised her eyes and found herself looking into those of Lydia Madison, who was standing behind Edward's chair, one perfectly manicured hand resting possessively on his broad shoulder. The woman was not smiling, and her green eyes were decidedly unfriendly.

Lydia stared intensely. She couldn't remember the last time she had considered any woman a threat. She was well aware of, and secure in, her own beauty. She'd seen very few women who could even come close to her in physical appearance. Never had she met one who could surpass it.

Until now.

And just who the hell was she? She had asked Edward about the identity of Colin's companion, but his answer offered no enlightenment. The name meant nothing to her.

Lydia leveled another hard look at Bethany. Why was a woman like this sitting at a table playing poker with men? She did not at first glance appear to be a whore; but she could be no better than one. Lydia relaxed a bit with this assumption. Men like Edward didn't waste their time with whores, no matter how beautiful they were.

Bethany grew uncomfortable under the relentless, icy stare. Flustered, she picked up the cards and began to shuffle them. To her horror, some of them slipped out of her hands and skidded across the felt-topped table, landing in Edward's lap.

Oh, Lord, she thought, chagrined. She saw them all looking at her: Colin, sharply; Tully, puzzled; Lydia, icily. And Edward—damn him—was grinning from ear to ear, making no effort to hide his amusement.

"An unusual way of dealing," he commented, pushing the cards back across the table. "I'll bet you didn't learn that from Colin," he added with a wicked glint in his eye.

She knew her face was crimson, but she did her best to ignore him, forcing her attention on the task of dealing the cards.

Beside her, Colin pursed his lips. Dark amusement shone on his face as he studied Edward. The man seemed unable to take his eyes off Bethany. Most likely, Edward expected her to fall at his feet, like most women did. This time, however, the Bayou Fox was in for a surprise.

A thought struck, and Colin had to smile. Wouldn't it be too funny for words if Edward were to fall in love with Bethany, while he, Colin, claimed her for his own? The idea so pleased him that Colin could hardly contain the laugh that bubbled in his throat.

As the evening progressed, Bethany, to her dismay, found herself making one foolish mistake after another.

Lydia's frosty expression had dissolved into cold disdain, which didn't help matters any.

When the game finally ended some three and a half hours after it had begun, Bethany gave into a great feeling of relief. She had lost close to two hundred dollars and counted herself lucky that it hadn't been more.

"What on earth was the matter with you tonight?" Colin demanded testily as they both sat down for a late night snack. "You played better the day you came to my hotel room."

Bethany's hands worked restlessly against each other. "I don't know. It was just—I guess I was too anxious," she concluded lamely.

With a sigh, she placed her hands around the coffee cup, feeling the warmth on her palms. She was miserable in the aftermath of the evening's debacle. Twice she had tried to bluff Edward, without success. Worse, she suspected that he had been aware of what she had been trying to do. Even though she had been careful not to display her cards, on both occasions Edward had regarded her with open amusement. She had made certain that she didn't touch her hair, didn't even hardly move, if the truth be told; despite her precautions, however, he had known.

Colin, Bethany thought now, had every right to be annoyed with her.

Leaning toward her, Colin placed a hand on her arm, his features relaxing. "Don't worry about it," he said softly, seeing how upset she was. "You were nervous, that's all. Next time you'll be more in control of yourself."

Reaching for his glass, Colin took a swallow of the amber liquid, enjoying the sting of the whiskey as it flowed down his throat. Except for a glass of wine with his supper, he never drank before a game and permitted himself this indulgence only when he was through for the evening.

"I've never seen anyone play like that," Bethany lamented. "He barely looked at his cards."

"Edward has a peculiar style," Colin admitted. "Perhaps I should have alerted you about it. Usually, it's a death-knell for anyone to adhere rigidly to a recognizable style; but for Edward it seems to work. People are a bit thrown by this, and he knows it."

"Well, it had the desired effect on me," Bethany said wryly.

"Actually, it could work to your advantage," Colin speculated after a moment, putting down the glass.

She made a face. "How can making a fool of myself work to my advantage?"

Colin's smile was slow. "It'll put Hammond off his guard, for one thing." His expression turned pensive. "Yes. The more I think of it, the more I'm convinced that what happened tonight will eventually work to your benefit."

Bethany stared at him doubtfully. "Do you think I can really beat him?"

Colin pursed his lips and looked away for a moment before answering. "Just how much does it mean to you?"

Her brow furrowed. "It means a lot to me. I've already told you I cannot rest easy until that man gets what's coming to him. When I think of what he did to my father . . ." The breath caught in her throat, and she bit her lip, unable to complete the thought.

Colin glanced sideways at her. "Then perhaps it's unwise of you to leave such things to chance," he suggested, watching her closely.

"What do you mean?"

He hesitated, then said, "I'm sure I don't have to tell you how fickle Lady Luck can be. One can only play the cards one is dealt . . ."

Bethany shook her head, and a shadow of annoyance crept into her voice. "I don't understand what you're saying, Colin! Of course one can only play the cards one is dealt. What other way is there?"

He shrugged, in what appeared to be a careless gesture. "There are ways to ensure that a player receives only the cards he, or she, needs for a winning hand."

For a moment, Bethany's stare was blank, uncomprehending. When his meaning finally became clear to her, she gave a startled gasp. "Are you suggesting that I should cheat?" Shock rippled through her, leaving her cheeks pinked with color.

Shifting in his chair, Colin glanced uneasily around their immediate vicinity, for Bethany's voice had unintentionally risen. "That's a strong word, Bethany," he admonished quietly. "And one that I urge you to refrain from using around here."

Bethany's jaw tightened. "Whatever word I use, the meaning will be the same!" She gave him a sharp glance. "Do you actually know how to do something like that?"

"Every professional player knows how, Bethany,"

Colin said dryly. "Even your father knew the mechanics of manipulating cards."

"If he did, he never used that knowledge," Bethany said quickly.

"I'm not saying he did. No one ever questioned your father's reputation for honesty. All I am saying is that he knew how to do it. The knowledge is not only useful, but also necessary," Colin went on to explain. "If a man doesn't know how to cheat, how is he going to recognize it when another player tries to rook him?"

Bethany caught her lower lip between her teeth, then sighed deeply. "I suppose you're right, but I'll have no part of it!"

Colin settled back in his chair again. "As you wish," he murmured. "But in this case it wouldn't be the same thing," he added reflectively. "It would be...ummn...a retribution."

She turned away in disgust, surprised that Colin could have brought up such a subject. "Two wrongs have never made a right. If I even considered such a thing, I would be no better than he is. At any rate, I don't know how. And," she held up a hand to forestall any comment, "I don't want you to give me any lessons. That is one talent I can do without. I will win on my own, or not at all!" she added firmly.

"Of course," Colin said quickly. "Please don't be upset—it was only a suggestion. In fact, there is no doubt in my mind that you can beat him on your own."

His words calmed her, and Bethany was silent a moment, assailed by fresh doubt. "Well, I hope your confidence isn't misplaced," she murmured at last.

Colin leaned forward, suddenly serious. "Bethany,"

he said, "you must know that I'm beginning to care a great deal for you...."

A look of dismay came into her eyes.

Taking hold of her hand, Colin squeezed it. "I hope you're coming to feel the same way about me," he whispered.

Feeling a nudge of distaste with the physical contact, Bethany staunchly resisted the urge to remove her hand, but a slight frown creased her forehead.

"Colin..." She stared into her cup, wishing he had not steered the conversation to a personal level. Best if she were blunt and to the point, she decided. "I like you; really, I do. But... please believe me when I say there can be nothing more between us than friendship."

Raising her hand to his lips, Colin kissed her fingertips. "One of the best foundations on which to build," he noted quietly.

Bethany averted her gaze from Colin and happened to glance across the room, seeing Edward in conversation with Winston Baxter, captain of the *Nola Star*.

Edward cocked his head, apparently listening to the man, but his eyes were fastened on Bethany and Colin, who still had her hand to his lips.

Bethany returned Edward's look hesitantly, choosing not to analyze the emotion she was seeing on his face. Quickly, she withdrew her hand and stood up.

"Please... stay and finish your drink, Colin," she said, annoyed that her voice sounded breathless. "If you'll excuse me, I'm going to retire."

He got to his feet, looking surprised at her sudden move. "Of course. Good night." He watched her leave the Grand Saloon, then sat down again.

At the top of the stairs, Bethany began to fumble within her reticule, searching for her key. Not looking where she was going, she never saw the broom on the floor, apparently having been left there by a careless cabin boy.

When she stepped on the rounded handle, Bethany felt her ankle turn in a painful way that caused her to lose her balance, sending her sprawling to the floor amid a tangle of skirt.

"Oooh. . . ." She grimaced, bending forward to touch her throbbing flesh. Experimentally, she wiggled her toes, flexed her foot. Although it hurt, she was relieved to discover she hadn't broken any bones.

"Well, . . . Miss Kincaid . . . ," said Edward Hammond. He squatted down on his haunches and grinned at her. "I think you'd be more comfortable if you sat in a chair. . . ."

She glared at him, all too aware of her undignified state. "I tripped over that damn broom and almost broke my ankle!" God, the man had made an art form out of being annoying!

His eyes traveled the length of her. "Let's have a look."

Before she could protest, he took her foot in his hands. Calmly, he removed her black kid shoe, then began to manipulate her foot. "Doesn't seem to be broken," he murmured.

"I know that!"

"You have lovely eyes," he said, turning to look at her. Gazing into those amber depths, his hand moved slowly from her ankle to the calf of her leg.

Angrily, Bethany jerked away from him, refusing to

acknowledge the sudden flare of heat that swept over her. Still grinning in a way that Bethany found maddening, Edward got up, assisting her to her feet.

"If you'll lean on me, I'll help you to your cabin." He put an arm around her waist after retrieving her shoe.

She was about to move away, but as soon as she put her weight on the injured ankle, she realized it would not support her.

"I have a better idea," Edward said softly. Without warning, he picked her up in his arms. "Now, which one of these cabins is yours?"

Bethany felt his warm breath on her cheek and a tremor shot through her, causing her to shiver.

His mouth quirked and his brows rose. "Chilly, are we?" He tightened his arms around her. "That's more easily taken care of than a sprained ankle."

Bethany knew her face was red. She had never felt so mortified in her whole life. She pointed. "That one," she said weakly.

Carefully, he stood her on her feet, took the key from her trembling hand and unlocked the door. Then he picked her up again. Entering, his eyes toured the cabin quickly, pleased but a bit surprised to see no sign of male occupancy. Crossing the room, he set her down on the bed.

"I suggest you bandage that ankle as soon as possible." He inclined his head, staring at her. "Now, can I be of any further assistance, Miss Kincaid?"

"No, thank you," she said stiffly. The pulse at the base of her throat was throbbing noticeably. "You've done quite enough."

"Not half as much as I'd like to," he murmured, making no immediate move to leave.

For a long moment his eyes held hers, and Bethany found herself unable to look away, unable to slow the increasing tempo of her heartbeat. She wanted to tell him to get out of her room, formed the words in her mind, but couldn't speak them. She was caught, as if hypnotized.

Her focus narrowed sharply to a pair of blue eyes that seemed to draw the breath from her lungs. There was something so utterly sensual in those eyes that she felt they pierced to the deepest, most secret part of her.

Finally, after what seemed to her an eternity, he turned and left, closing the door quietly behind him.

Still sitting on the bed, Bethany stared at the closed door, her hands clenched in her lap, her mouth a white line of incensed fury. Her body felt so weak that she was afraid to stand up.

She hadn't known it was possible for a man to make love to a woman with his eyes; yet Bethany had the strange feeling that that's exactly what had happened to her tonight.

Bethany shook her head sharply, as if to rid her mind of all thoughts of Edward Hammond. With a hand that still trembled, she leaned forward and removed her other shoe and her stockings.

Then, her movements unsteady as she tried to stand on one foot, Bethany took off her clothes, throwing them carelessly onto the nearest chair. Just as awkwardly, she wriggled into a nightdress, then crawled into bed. She didn't bother to extinguish the lamp, certain she would be unable to sleep. Her ankle was beginning to throb in a really painful way. She tried shifting her weight several times, but it didn't help any.

At the sound of a knock on the door and someone calling her name, she sat up. "Come in," she called out, recognizing Mary's voice.

"Edward told me you'd taken a fall and hurt your ankle," Mary said as she approached the bed. Bending over, she reached for Bethany's foot and studied it with anxious eyes. "Thank goodness there's no swelling. I've brought some bandages and a jar of liniment." She put the bandages on the table and unscrewed the lid of the jar, smiling as Bethany wrinkled her nose. "Smells awful, doesn't it? Works like a charm, though."

Her movements precise and efficient, Mary rubbed Bethany's ankle with the liniment, bandaged it, then put a pillow beneath her foot.

"Oh, that feels a lot more comfortable," Bethany said gratefully. The effects of the liniment were immediate, causing heat that seemed to seep right into the pores of her skin.

Mary frowned, obviously still upset. "I've a mind to fire that boy for leaving the broom in the hall like that," she declared. "It was just plain carelessness."

"Please don't do that," Bethany said hastily. "It was my own fault. I should have been paying attention to where I was walking. I was the one who was careless."

Mary pursed her lips as she considered that. "Well, at the very least I'll have a few words to say to him." She rearranged the covers, gave them a pat, then said, "You'd better stay off that foot for a day or so. I'll have your meals sent up."

"Thank you, Mary. I appreciate that."

When Mary left, Bethany extinguished the lamp, now feeling pleasantly drowsy, and was soon lulled to sleep by the gentle rocking of the boat as it wended its way downriver.

The following morning, Bethany awoke to a soft tapping on the door. At first she thought she had imagined it, for when she opened her eyes, the sound had momentarily stilled. She was about to snuggle down again when the tapping resumed, a bit more insistent than before. Quickly, she sat up, pulling the blanket higher as she did so, thinking it was the cabin boy with her breakfast. But when the door opened, she gave a start of surprise at the sight of Edward carrying a tray.

"Good morning," he said cheerfully, as if it were a most ordinary occurrence for him to be entering her bedroom. Crossing the room in a few long strides, he placed the tray on her lap. "How are you feeling?"

Momentarily at a loss for words, Bethany's hand automatically went to her throat to assure herself that all the buttons on her nightdress were closed. He saw the gesture and grinned at her.

"Don't be alarmed," he said, chuckling at her expression. "I'm not in the habit of ravishing helpless females. At least not this early in the morning." His eyes dwelled for a moment on the delightful contrast of ebony curls framing luminous ivory skin.

"What are you doing here?" Bethany stared at the tray in her lap and hoped she didn't look as flustered as she felt. In dismay, she then regarded the chair where she had thrown her clothes. Even her undergarments were in plain sight!

There was a twinkle in his blue eyes as Edward said, "I confess to having waylaid the cabin boy in the hall." He picked up the napkin and snapped it open with a flourish. Before she could protest he had tucked one end of it into the neck of her nightdress.

"This isn't necessary," she said weakly, growing more upset by the minute and wishing he'd keep his distance. The touch of his fingers on her throat had produced the oddest sensation in the pit of her stomach.

"No trouble," he assured her. "I've always had a secret desire to be a waiter," he mused, taking a step back to view the effect. "Now I know why." He lifted the small silver pot from the tray and deftly poured her coffee. "I'd join you," he remarked in the same cheerful voice, "but there's only one cup."

Feeling at a definite disadvantage, Bethany tried to smooth her hair with her hands. She must look terrible, she thought in some annoyance. She hadn't bothered to brush her hair the night before, as she normally did before retiring. Nor had she fashioned it into its usual braid. She had no doubt that it was a tangled mess, but why should she worry about what she looked like in front of him?

"How is your ankle?" Edward inquired, viewing her elevated foot.

"Much better," she replied, not entirely truthful. It still hurt like a sore tooth. She moistened her lips, hesitated, then said, "Thank you for sending Mary to me last night." Her tone was curt because the necessity of having to thank him was galling.

He laughed. "I didn't think you had any spare bandages around."

Coming closer, Edward plumped the pillow behind her back, and for a moment his hand rested warmly on her shoulder. It was a casual gesture. She could detect nothing suggestive or sensual in the brief touch and was at a loss to explain the sudden stab of current that flashed through her whole body.

Bethany sat very still, not looking at him as he moved to the foot of the bed again. She was uncomfortably aware that the heat she felt in her cheeks was most likely reflected by crimson color. Suddenly remembering her almost mesmerized state the night before, she gave Edward a wary glance, trying to gauge his expression. It was open, guileless, good-humored. Bethany relaxed, chiding herself for her foolishness. Surely she had imagine the intensity of that moment. It had been no more than a trick of light and shadow.

Edward pointed to the tray. "You'd better eat that before it gets cold," he instructed jovially.

Bethany frowned up at him. Did he plan to stay all day? she wondered, finding herself irritated not only with his presence but with her reaction to it as well. "I don't think you should be here," she sputtered at last.

He raised a brow. "Why not?"

"Someone might have seen you come into my room." She waved a hand in a vague gesture. "I mean, they might . . . get the wrong idea," she concluded lamely.

Lowering his head, Edward looked thoughtful. "You know, they just might," he agreed in mock seriousness. "My reputation could be ruined like that!" He snapped his fingers.

Anger brightened her eyes. "I wasn't thinking of *your* reputation!" His answering laugh set her teeth on edge, but Bethany felt a rush of relief when he finally went to the door.

"By the way," he said, hesitating a moment on the threshold and speaking as though the thought had just come to him. "You look lovely in the morning. Not many women do." The door closed before she could respond.

Taking a deep breath, Bethany picked up a roll and bit into it, wondering whether he had spoken the words sarcastically.

Bethany spent the rest of that day half expecting Edward to make another surprise appearance, but he did not. Colin visited her briefly, and Mary and Amy insisted on taking their evening meal in her room so that she would not have to eat alone. But Edward did not return, and when the cabin boy brought her breakfast the following morning, Bethany had a moment's uncertainty as to whether she felt relief or disappointment.

Chapter _10_

The water was still high, almost to the top of the levee by the time the _Nola Star_ approached New Orleans.

Even on this day the waterfront bustled with frantic activity. Side-wheelers and stern-wheelers were tied up next to each other, some so close it appeared that a person could walk from deck to deck without touching the water. Closer to the gulf one could see a profusion of foreign brigs and frigates, creating a forest of masts and riggings that towered toward a twilight sky dotted with swooping and wheeling sea gulls.

The _Nola Star_ eased her way alongside the _Robert E. Lee,_ on which conveyance Rex—the King of Carnival—had arrived. The boat was so festooned with ribbons and flowers that it gave the appearance of being gift-wrapped.

Garbed as a gypsy, her dark hair falling loosely about her shoulders, Bethany stood on the texas deck beside Colin, who looked dashing in his buccaneer's outfit.

The pain in her ankle had completely subsided, and Bethany had removed the bandage she'd worn for the past two days. Mary had seen to it that her meals were brought to her and had severely reprimanded the cabin boy responsible for leaving the broom in the hallway.

Last night she had returned to the tables, sitting with a group that had included Edward. This time she had played with confidence, refusing to be distracted by anyone or anything, and in the process had managed to recoup some of her losses. She still hadn't been able to beat Edward Hammond, however, nor had she made any further attempt to bluff him.

But the time would come, she promised herself. When it did, she'd be ready.

Feeling a slight chill in the evening air, Bethany pulled her cashmere shawl closer about her. With absolute amazement, she looked up Canal Street. It was so crowded with costumed revelers that at first glance there didn't seem to be a square foot of unoccupied space.

"Have you ever been to Mardi Gras?" Colin asked her, amused by her expression.

"No," Bethany replied, still astonished by what she was seeing. Music, laughter, and drunken shouts of glee created a not unpleasant din that was enhanced by the sing-song cries of vendors hawking everything from oysters to pralines to steaming cups of chicory-laced coffee.

"I think you'll enjoy it. I understand the theme this year is The Aztecs. Momus will be in rare form, I'm sure."

"There are so many people," Bethany murmured.

126

Colin laughed at her observation. "People come from all over the world to witness Carnival in New Orleans. I've been told that last year there were more than seventy thousand visitors."

"Is there always a special theme?" Bethany asked, turning to look at him.

He nodded. "Several, actually. Each krewe has its own. Momus is supposed to present 'A Dream of Fair Women.'" He grinned down at her, noticing how white her skin appeared against the vivid red dress she was wearing, and how her full breasts strained temptingly beneath her bodice. "You would be an excellent choice to lead off that parade."

Bethany smiled, then asked: "What is a krewe?"

Colin shrugged. "Nothing more than a group of men who meet to discuss next year's Mardi Gras. They host fancy balls during carnival, but their invitations go to only a select few." He glanced at his watch. "The parades have already begun." He put on his mask and took her arm. "Let's see if we can battle our way through the crowd to the French Quarter."

The music, combined with the noise of the crowd, was almost deafening, but Bethany found herself caught up in the gregarious display of frivolity that surrounded her. It was as if, once masked, people shed their inhibitions. They cavorted and danced in the streets, on the banquettes, even on the roofs of buildings. Some formed living chains, linking hands and rushing through the crowd, occasionally taking a hapless bystander with them.

By the time Colin managed to weave a path through

the boisterous revelers to the French Quarter, Bethany was breathless.

The doors to all restaurants and cabarets were opened wide: an invitation to any and all to come inside. There was no place to sit, but Colin managed to find an advantageous spot for them to stand on Royal Street.

A delightful scent of roasting coffee and pralines filled the air. Buildings painted in soft pastels were now draped in carnival colors of purple, green, and gold, none of which hid the exquisite grillwork for which the Vieux Carré was so famous.

The first of the bands came into view, followed by four young lads dressed as pages who were scattering flowers in preparation for the arrival of his majesty. Flambeaux-bearers dressed in bright red satin marched to the side of the towering papier-mâché float, their torches casting wavering shadows of deep rose and soft gold over everything in their path.

When Rex finally appeared, Bethany caught her breath at the sight of his attire. His robe literally sparkled with brilliants, as did his crown. Behind him, his entourage were no less impressive.

Bethany dissolved into helpless laughter as the Momus parade finally came into view. All the "fair women" were in fact brawny men dressed in beautiful gowns, masked in the visage of women.

Colin bent close to her. "Certainly you're lovelier than any of those fair damsels," he remarked with a short laugh. He touched her arm. "Are you thirsty? Shall I get us both a bit of refreshment?"

"Oh, yes," Bethany said enthusiastically. "I'd like that."

"All right. Wait for me right here. I'll be back in a few minutes."

Bethany watched as he elbowed his way through the crowd, heading for a cabaret not too far distant, then returned her attention to the seemingly endless parades. Men dressed as Egyptian soldiers were now tramping through the streets, breastplates glinting like gold in the torchlight.

Hearing raucous laughter and raised voices, Bethany turned and stared at the chain of revelers pushing their way through the crowded banquette. She gave a gasp of startled surprise when one of the men grabbed her hand, dragging her along with them.

"No! Let go of me," she shouted, half laughing. But her words were lost in the unending pandemonium that surrounded her.

She tried to break free, but the man behind the garish mask paid her no mind. Looking behind her, she tried to catch a glimpse of Colin, but he was nowhere in sight. She stumbled, almost fell, and was jerked upright again by the relentless hand that clutched her wrist.

"Let go of me!" she said again, a bit frightened now. The pressure of the crowd was so great she feared being trampled to death.

The chain rounded a corner, whipping her along. Her shawl slipped from her shoulders and in only seconds was lost from view.

Suddenly a man stepped out from a doorway. A fist shot out, landing on the jaw of the person who had been pulling her along, and the pressure on her hand finally gave way.

Bethany found herself lifted off her feet as the man

drew her into the relative seclusion of the shadowed doorway. Firm hands went around her waist, gripping her tightly. For a moment Bethany allowed herself to rest against a broad chest, breathing her relief in long shuddering gasps.

Then the hands around her waist moved to her back as he pulled her against him. Bethany looked up into the masked face that was now so dangerously close to her own. In that split second, she recognized the blue eyes and golden hair of Edward Hammond.

He gave a low, throaty chuckle. "On this night of nights, a man is usually granted a favor for rescuing a lady in distress."

Before she could protest, his warm mouth had claimed her own.

Bethany began to struggle, but she was no match for the strong arms that held her fast. His mouth worked against hers, forcing her lips to part, his tongue seeking the sweetness of her own. His body was fitted so close to hers that Bethany was acutely aware of every hard muscle he possessed.

She felt seared by the burning heat he emanated, and her struggles dissolved into ineffectual movements. Never in her life had a kiss produced such heated emotions as she was feeling now. Blood pounded in her ears, and her heart thudded wildly in her breast.

For a timeless moment, Bethany found herself unable to resist. Her mind whirled in a vortex of emotion so complete that she was oblivious to the crowd of revelers, nor did she hear the strains of music that rode on the soft air.

At last he drew back, his handsome face as flushed as her own.

Wrenching free, Bethany bolted into the crowded street, arms flailing at the sea of bodies that swirled around her. Above the noisy din she could easily hear Edward's mocking laughter. Even after she had fought her way a distance of several blocks, the sound of it echoed in her mind, creating waves of fresh fury that washed over her.

From the doorway, Edward watched her until she was lost in the crowd. He was sorely tempted to follow her. But then, after a moment's consideration, he purchased a bottle of wine and made his way back to the grandstand that had been erected on the banquette, where Lydia was waiting for him.

"A regular Sir Galahad, aren't you?" Lydia's voice was tight, her bearing stiff as he sat down beside her.

Turning his head, Edward regarded her in surprise. "You know, Lydia, people who eavesdrop hear things about themselves they wish they hadn't," he said mildly. "And people who spy usually see things they wish they hadn't."

Lydia's mouth was a thin line. "Who was that woman?"

Edward reached for one of the glasses Mary had supplied and poured some of the wine into it. "I've no idea," he said easily, handing her the glass. "During Mardi Gras it's impolite for anyone to ask for names."

Lydia was so furious that she could barely contain herself. "Am I to believe that you've turned into such a rake that you've taken to grabbing strange women off the street and kissing them?"

"You can believe anything you like." Pouring himself some wine, Edward sipped it thoughtfully, watching the parade of devils now passing by the grandstand. Despite his easy tone, he was at a loss to explain his feelings. The tide of emotion that had swept him away a short while ago left him baffled. In retrospect, Edward realized that he had forced himself to release that soft and tantalizing body. Even now he could feel the imprint of it against his own.

God, I must be bewitched, he thought to himself, draining his glass.

Behind her silk domino, Lydia's green eyes had narrowed to slits. She was certain she knew the identity of the woman—and she was convinced that Edward knew, too. Unless she was way off the mark, that lush black hair belonged to Bethany Kincaid.

Lydia pursed her lips, paying no mind to the panorama of color and papier-mâché in front of her. Perhaps, she thought to herself, she should have a talk with Colin; one that would benefit them both.

Chapter 11

Tears of anger blinded her as Bethany ran up the gangway and fled to her stateroom. She was shaking to such a degree that she collapsed on the bed. Balling her hands into fists she pounded her frustration on her pillow. _Cheat! Cheat!_ her mind cried out, and Bethany was unaware of the tears that slipped silently down her cheeks.

Feeling a hand on her shoulder, she quickly raised herself up on an elbow and, through the shimmering curtain of tears, viewed Mary's concerned face.

"Bethany, are you all right? You ran right past me in the hallway. What happened? Where's Colin?"

The barrage of questions drew a rueful laugh from Bethany. She hadn't even thought of Colin in these past harrowing minutes.

"Colin is getting refreshments." The sight of Mary's puzzled face provoked another short, humorless laugh.

"I don't know where he is," she confessed. "We became separated in the crowd."

"Ahh . . ." Mary relaxed, sitting on the edge of the bed. "It can get pretty frightening when you get caught in that crowd of rabble-rousers. Amy and I usually watch from the pilothouse. Not as exciting, but safer."

Bethany sat up, pushing her tumbling curls from her face and brushing the droplets from her lashes. "It wasn't that . . ." She bit her lip, then grasped the older woman's hand. "Mary—there's something I have to tell you—but I would ask that you say nothing of it to anyone else. . . ."

"Of course, Bethany." Mary's concern heightened at the sight of the young woman's pale face.

"I . . . my name isn't Kincaid," Bethany began in a hesitant voice. She sat up straighter, putting her feet on the floor. "It's Forrester. My father was George Forrester."

"Well, I'll be damned," Mary breathed, her eyes widening. "You're George's daughter! But, I don't understand. . . ."

Taking a deep breath, Bethany explained, watching the play of incredulity that colored Mary's face.

"And you think it was Edward who cheated?" Mary asked at the conclusion of the recitation, now understanding Bethany's peculiar attitude toward him.

"I know he did."

Slowly, Mary shook her head. "I've never known him to do that. Quite frankly, he has no need to." She gave Bethany an earnest look. "There are some players I wouldn't trust, but Edward Hammond isn't one of them."

Bethany remained unconvinced. "My father wasn't a

134

novice," she said, more stiffly than she had intended. "If he said it happened that way, then it did." The analysis was delivered in a flat voice of unshakable conviction.

"Why don't you just confront Edward?" Mary suggested. "I'm sure he could tell you what happened."

With a sigh, Bethany got to her feet. Crossing the room, she glanced outside, seeing the glimmering lights of lanterns and torches play across the night sky. The whole city seemed to glow.

"I'm certain Edward would have a fine explanation for what happened," she said at last, still looking out the window. "Trouble is, I'm sure I won't believe it."

Mary took a deep breath. "But what do you hope to accomplish with this . . ." she gestured, momentarily at a loss for words, "this impersonation of yours?"

Bethany turned to face her. "I'm going to beat him at his own game," she answered in a low voice. "Ruin him, if I can."

Mary blinked in utter astonishment. "You? You plan to beat Edward in a game of poker?" She laughed and shook her head. "You can't be serious."

Bethany raised her chin slightly, looking down at Mary through half-closed eyes. "Oh, I'm serious, all right. My father is dead because of that man. . . ."

"Oh, Bethany . . ." Mary's face crumpled with her distress. "Such harsh words. . . ."

"Indeed they are. The truth often is; but I'm convinced that my father's attack was caused by his despair over losing everything he owned," Bethany went on in a stronger voice. "The man who cheated him could just as easily have held a gun to his head and gotten the same result!''

There was an awkward silence. Bethany turned away a moment to compose herself. When she faced Mary again, her voice was calm.

"How well did you know my father?" she asked.

"Well enough to know that he was an honest and decent man," Mary replied quietly.

Bethany tilted her head to one side. "Do you think he would have accused a man falsely? Without just cause?"

Mary sighed and shook her head sadly. "No," she admitted slowly. "I don't." She gave Bethany a level look. "But I just can't believe Edward is capable of playing dishonestly."

"Can't? Or don't want to?"

Mary flinched, but she answered truthfully. "A bit of both, I guess," she admitted ruefully. Seeing Bethany's implacable expression, she sighed again. "I suppose there's nothing I can say that would change your mind."

"No," Bethany agreed, coming back to sit on the bed. "But there is something you can do to help me." Reaching over, Bethany clutched Mary's hand again. "Were you there during that game?"

Mary nodded. "I was there."

"Tell me what happened."

Mary's brow creased with her effort to assimilate her thoughts. "Except for the fact that your father lost so heavily, there was nothing out of the ordinary."

"There must have been!" Bethany cried out. "Please, Mary, think. . . ."

Mary sighed and shook her head. "I'm sorry, Bethany. I don't remember anything unusual."

"How many were at the table at the beginning?" Bethany prompted, shifting her weight so that she was facing Mary directly.

"Five. But two of the men left early. By eleven o'clock only Edward, Colin, and your father were playing." She pursed her lips. "If I remember correctly, it was pretty much put and take for a few hours. But by one thirty or so, it got intense."

Tilting her head, Bethany said, "There was no impartial dealer?"

"No. As you've already discovered, we have no house dealers aboard. The expense of hiring professional dealers is one I've never felt to be justified, although it's standard policy on some other boats."

Bethany frowned in some perplexity. "But wouldn't you be getting a cut of each pot?"

"Yes," Mary admitted with a nod of her head. "But the profit isn't all that much. Most of it would go to pay wages. What I do is a lot simpler. In effect, I rent the chairs." At Bethany's quizzical look, Mary smiled, then went on to explain. "Anyone who wants to gamble in the Grand Saloon pays me five dollars for the night . . . in advance."

Bethany's face was a study in confusion. "But I've not paid you any money. . . ."

Mary laughed. "I know. Colin has picked up your tab."

Chewing her lip, Bethany made a mental note to repay Colin. Then she asked, "Who else was there that night? Was anyone watching?"

"Oh, yes. Some of the other tables were in play, and as always, there were a few spectators." Mary gave a short laugh. "One of them was a woman who came with Colin. She drank wine like it was water. Never a night passed that she wasn't tipsy. Colin was furious with her. I've never seen him lose his temper like that."

Bethany repressed an impatient sigh, wanting Mary to tell her about the game, not about Colin's girlfriend. But she calmed herself and let Mary tell the story in her own way.

"Silly woman bumped into the table on her way to the bar," Mary went on, laughing at the recollection. "Edward's drink was knocked over. That's when Colin got so angry. He told her in no uncertain terms to go back to her room."

"Then what happened?"

Mary made a vague gesture. "Well, after one of the stewards mopped the table, they continued with the hand."

"Who won that hand?" Bethany asked, watching Mary closely.

"Edward."

Bethany's mouth compressed into a thin line. "I should have guessed."

"Your father was betting heavily all night, Bethany," Mary said gently. "He must have had great confidence in that last hand. He had no money left and had to offer Edward a marker. Your father, of course, had a good reputation and so Edward readily accepted."

"I'll bet he did," Bethany muttered maliciously.

Both women were silent for a time. Then Mary

glanced sideways at Bethany, who had a thoughtful expression on her face.

"Getting separated from Colin and lost in the crowd isn't what upset you tonight. What did happen, Bethany?" she asked quietly.

Bethany bit her lip. "A man grabbed my hand and dragged me through the crowd. I . . ." She shifted uneasily. "It was Edward who pulled me to safety. He . . ."

Mary lowered her head so Bethany wouldn't see her smile. "Strange things happen during Mardi Gras," she murmured, then got to her feet. "I remember once some years ago when a man grabbed me around the waist and danced me through the streets. Then he kissed me. . . ." She shook her head, her eyes soft with remembrance. "I never did know who he was, or even if he was handsome. But I've never forgotten that kiss. . . ."

Bethany looked at her friend, then turned away to hide her flaming cheeks. She had the disconcerting feeling that she, too, would never forget the kiss she had received during Mardi Gras.

Mary had been gone only a few minutes when Bethany heard a knock on her door. She froze. What would she do if she found Edward standing there?

"Bethany?"

She relaxed when she heard Colin's anxious voice. Opening the door, she smiled at him.

"My God, I looked all over for you," he exclaimed, appearing unsettled. "What happened?"

In as few words as possible, Bethany told him, leaving out her encounter with Edward.

"I really am tired, Colin," she concluded. "It's late, and I would like to get some rest."

When she had closed the door again, Bethany lay down. She felt exhausted. But no matter how fiercely she sought oblivion, sleep eluded her. Each time she closed her eyes she found herself remembering that hard body pressed against her own. How was it possible for one man's kiss to be so different from all others? She clenched her teeth at the thought. He had acted despicably, taking advantage of her like that. The man had no scruples, she realized; none whatsoever.

Bethany moved restlessly on cool sheets, her flesh throbbing with a sweet torment until finally she got out of bed and paced her stateroom, cursing the day she had first heard the name Edward Hammond.

Having removed his costume, Colin went downstairs to the Grand Saloon and seated himself at an unoccupied table. It was after eleven, but the room was almost empty; most passengers were still ashore.

Toying with the silver dollar, he stared moodily at the untouched drink before him, wondering when he had fallen in love with Bethany Forrester. Had it been that first day when he had opened his door to find her unexpectedly standing there, looking lovelier than any woman had a right to look? Or had it happened now, tonight, when he'd experienced panic upon discovering her absence? He had searched for her for the better part of an hour before returning to the boat, feeling a weakening sense of relief when he found her safe in her room.

How had he gotten himself into this predicament?

Colin demanded of himself. In the beginning, she was just another lovely woman, and all women were alike. A man took his pleasure and was done with it. What the devil was so special about this one that she could churn his insides without the slightest effort?

Colin was forced to admit to himself that he wanted Bethany more than he'd ever wanted any other woman. He had always shied away from marriage, refusing to be tied down. Now, suddenly, the idea seemed inviting. Colin dismissed the fact that Bethany would not allow him to get too close. Women like that didn't jump in and out of a man's bed.

He was so deep in thought that Lydia's voice caused him to start in surprise. She hadn't changed and still wore her costume, a blue and gold silk gown cut in a Grecian style, leaving one rounded shoulder bare. A white wig covered her flaming red tresses and caused her eyes to appear even greener than they were.

As she sat down, she said, "You can buy me a drink, Colin."

"Still the same?" he asked, beckoning to the steward. At her nod, he turned to the waiter. "A mint julip for the lady." He studied Lydia's glacial expression with an arched brow. "You look like a cat that has its tail caught beneath a rocker," he observed, trying not to smile.

Emerald eyes flashed at him. "Stop playing with that damned coin and listen to me!" She was still rankled over the evening's events and the fact that Edward had barely spoken to her on the way back.

"You have my full attention," Colin said, placing the dollar back in his vest pocket.

Lydia leaned forward, inadvertently displaying her lush bosom. "Who is Bethany Kincaid?"

Dragging his eyes from the tempting sight, Colin gave a short laugh. "So that's it." He grinned at her. "Imagine you being jealous of my . . . companion."

She made a face. "Don't be obtuse, Colin. It doesn't become you. Who you spend your time with doesn't concern me in the least."

Colin assumed a hurt look and tried to sound wounded. "And I thought you cared."

They fell silent a moment as the steward placed Lydia's drink on the table.

"Who is she?" Lydia repeated in a stronger voice.

He shrugged and took a sip of his drink before he answered. "She's just a friend. I met her in Memphis."

"Are you having an affair with her?" Lydia asked bluntly.

Dark brows shot up. "My, we are inquisitive, aren't we?" At the sight of her angry face, Colin stopped smiling. "Why are you so interested in Bethany?"

Removing the mint from her glass, Lydia took a deep swallow. Then she quickly explained to Colin what had taken place between Edward and Bethany earlier in the evening. The amused expression on his face only fueled her irritation.

"I thought she was with you!" She made it sound as if the whole thing was his fault.

"She was. We became separated." For just a moment Colin was tempted to tell her the truth. But if he did, he was certain she would tell Edward, if for no other reason than to make him stay away from Bethany. *Best to say nothing,* he decided.

"Damn it! You don't look all that concerned. I assumed you were interested in her." Lydia moved restlessly in her chair, her tone irate.

Colin held up a placating hand. "I am. But you yourself said that Bethany seemed upset by what happened. Edward is not foolish enough to pursue a woman who wants nothing to do with him."

Secretly, Colin was pleased, though he took great pains to hide that fact from Lydia. Under the circumstances, he was certain Bethany would continue to rebuff Edward. How delicious, he thought, to have Edward fall in love with a woman who despised him; a woman who, by her own words, vowed to ruin him.

Reaching over, Colin took Lydia's hand in his own, his thumb rubbing the smooth, tapered fingers. "I don't think you have any cause for concern, my pet." He regarded her curiously and with a certain degree of fondness. "I thought it was all over between you and Edward."

"For me it will never be over," she answered quietly, lowering her head.

"I cannot see how he can resist," Colin said, giving in to his desire to ogle those generous breasts, remembering how they had filled his hands to overflowing. She was a luscious piece, all right. Edward would do well to count his blessings. "God knows you're a fetching temptress," he murmured.

Lydia raised her head to look at him. The compliment had not raised her spirits.

"Why do you think I'm here?" she said after a long moment. "I want him back," she continued before he could speak. "And I'm going to get him. Nothing will stand in my way.'' She gritted her teeth. "Not even your precious Miss Kincaid. Keep her out of my way!''

Colin was careful to display no amusement. He thought Lydia a most attractive woman, but a bit too strong-willed for his taste. She would lead Edward a merry chase when they finally married, he thought to himself. Colin had no doubt that Lydia would get Edward back. She always got what she wanted, even if she had to use devious means to accomplish it.

"We are not at cross purposes, my dear Lydia.'' Colin squeezed her hand. "Bethany is very special to me.'' He leaned back in his chair, hooking his thumbs in his vest pocket. "In fact, I'm seriously considering asking her to marry me.''

Hearing that, Lydia relaxed visibly. Picking up her glass, she toasted him. "I wish you every success, Colin. I hope the two of you will be very happy.''

Colin leaned toward her, lowering his voice. "In the meantime, if I can offer you any . . . consolation, you have only to say the word. If I remember correctly, we never did finish what we started.''

Lydia smiled for the first time since she sat down. While she had to admit, even now, that she was attracted to Colin's dark, devilishly good looks, she certainly wasn't in love with him. Edward was the only man she'd ever loved, despite her brief encounter with Colin. Six months ago, when the *Nola Star* had anchored in Louisville, Edward had invited Colin Thatcher to spend a few weeks at Glencoe.

That night she and Edward had had heated words over their wedding date. Edward had insisted on waiting two years, saying he wasn't ready to settle down until he had Glencoe back on firm footing and in the black. Lydia saw no need to wait that long and told him so in no uncertain terms. He refused to listen. Angry, and more than a little tipsy, she had gone storming upstairs, heading for the room that was hers when she stayed at Glencoe.

Noticing that Colin's door was ajar, she had entered his room, for what purpose she could not remember now. The next thing she knew they were in bed together. She hadn't bothered to close the door because she hadn't intended for anything to happen.

When Edward passed by a few minutes later and saw what was taking place, he'd become furious. He and Colin had gotten into a fight, but the extent of Edward's anger had fallen upon herself. The events of that night had culminated in their broken engagement.

"One of these days I just might accept your offer, Colin," Lydia said at last. Then she turned somber again. "But not now. If Edward even suspected anything was taking place between us, it surely would be the end." She shook her head and spoke firmly. "I can't take that chance."

Colin's shoulders moved, and he gave a deep sigh. "I suppose you're right," he said, sounding regretful and allowing himself one more look at those tempting globes.

Chapter 12

The following day, just after five in the afternoon, the _Nola Star_ moved away from the levee and began the return trip upriver.

Beneath a setting sun the Mississippi flowed like liquid bronze. Trees appeared to have been painted with raw umber against the luminous sky. Along the banks, herons and egrets swooped among moss-covered trees.

It was Amy's favorite time of day. She was convinced that nowhere else in the world did the sun set so splendidly as it did right here on the Mississippi. Having tallied the lading bills necessary to any departure, she strolled along the texas deck, enjoying the cool breeze that pinked her cheeks and caused silvery tendrils of her hair to flutter beneath the wide-brimmed straw hat she was wearing.

Pausing, she watched the paddle wheel churn, seeing the resulting spray of water catch the sunlight and fashion itself into a rainbow.

"Amy!"

Startled, she turned to see Harriet Tully seated in a chair, an open book and a box of candy on her lap. The girl called to her again, but Amy hesitated, feeling much as a cornered animal would. From long experience she was always able to tell whether someone did or did not like her. Harriet did not.

"Come and sit with me for a while," Harriet insisted, sounding annoyed that Amy hadn't come forward immediately. "Surely the boat will run without your attention for a few minutes." She waved an imperious hand, as if beckoning a servant. Even at sixteen, Harriet was showing a tendency toward her mother's corpulence. Her hips and upper thighs were heavy, her cheeks plump to the point of making her face appear as round as a melon.

Hearing the shrill titter, Amy walked resignedly toward Harriet. Well, she thought ruefully, it was implausible to have supposed that she could avoid the girl for the whole trip.

In a graceful movement, Amy seated herself on the edge of the chair next to Harriet, folding her hands in her lap.

"You're looking a bit peaked," Harriet noted, effectively concealing her envy as she looked at the flawless, creamy complexion of Amy's face. Having a sweet tooth of monumental proportions usually resulted in her own skin looking blotched and red. Today was no exception.

Viewing Amy's dress, Harriet's nose wrinkled in distaste. Muslin! She would rather have been caught dead than wearing such a cheap fabric. And it was so plain! High-necked, long-sleeved, and simple, simple, simple!

With some satisfaction, Harriet's hand went to the ruffle at her neck. It flowed to her waist and was repeated in the flounces of her red taffeta skirt, which was gathered at intervals with yellow velvet roses.

"I daresay you're working too hard," she speculated with a lift of her brow.

Why, Amy wondered irritably, *does the girl find it necessary to shout each time she talks to me?* Harriet seemed to be of the opinion that she was hard of hearing.

"I would hate it dreadfully if I had to do work of any kind," Harriet went on, her voice at the same raised level. "Naturally, Papa will see to it that the man I marry is rich enough so that I will have servants to do all those nasty chores that make life so uncomfortable for a lady."

Reaching into the box of sweets, Harriet fingered several pieces of chocolate before selecting the one of her choice. She popped it into her mouth, but saw no need to offer one to Amy. Her mouth worked around the candy, bulging her cheeks as if she were a squirrel intent upon storing a winter's supply of food in one trip.

The sight sparked a twinge of nausea, and Amy viewed her hands, still folded in her lap.

"A gentleman has already approached my father and requested permission to court me," Harriet confided, not mentioning that the man in question was all of twenty-one years her senior. She studied a tapered fingernail. "I've not made up my mind as to whether I will accept him or not." Her narrow lips curved into a smirk as she reached for another candy. Swallowing noisily, she glanced sideways at Amy, taking the clear brow and level eyes to be galvanized interest. "I don't suppose any gentlemen have shown an interest in you, have they?" she goaded, watching for Amy's reaction with wide-eyed interest. But if Harriet was expecting anger or embarrassment, she was sadly disappointed.

Harriet frowned, annoyed by the slight smile on those lovely lips. Suddenly she could no longer bear the sight of the beautiful, serene face that stared back at her. She was only wasting her time trying to talk with a dim-witted fool, she decided.

With a snort of derision, Harriet picked up her book, her attitude leaving no doubt that she was through with her one-sided conversation.

The smile still hovering about her lips, Amy beat a hasty retreat. Going down to the hurricane deck, she saw Edward. She flashed him a bright smile and nodded as he waved to her.

Turning, Edward leaned on the railing. He threw a half-smoked cigar into the swirling, muddy water, noting that the sky to the west was streaked with orange and gold, the setting sun piercing trees and foliage with bright swords of light.

Edward rubbed the back of his neck, feeling tired and restless at the same time. He'd slept fitfully the night before, unable to erase Bethany's image from his mind, remembering the feel of her satiny lips beneath his own mouth.

Finally, he straightened. Mary had invited Bethany and Colin, as well as Lydia and himself to dine at the captain's table tonight to celebrate Amy's nineteenth birthday.

Edward wasn't at all certain he was looking forward to the evening. He had seen Bethany in the dining room earlier in the day, but she had given him a stare that would have frozen the devil's backyard. And Lydia, too, was still miffed over last night's events.

All in all, he thought morosely, *it should prove to be an interesting evening*.

Despite his misgivings, however, the meal progressed in a congenial manner, due mainly to the efforts of Captain Baxter, a jovial man in his late forties with Dundreary whiskers and prematurely white hair. He regaled them all with tales of his years on the river, and the way it had been in the early days of steamboating when a man had to have a sixth sense to navigate the Mississippi's perilous course.

"In those days," Captain Baxter said as the first course was being cleared away, "a pilot had to have his wits about him. He had to know the river like the back of his hand, and even that wasn't enough. Old Miss is as capricious as a woman when it comes to changing the way she looks."

As he spoke, his gaze swung from Bethany to Lydia, enjoying the sight of them both, trying to make up his mind which was more beautiful. Fire and ice, he thought to himself.

But while he couldn't say which was the loveliest, he decided that Bethany was definitely the more interesting. She was like deep water; a man would do well to plumb her depths and discover what delights lay beneath that cool reserve. Lydia, on the other hand, was like a shallow, fast moving stream. Her thoughts were written on her face; and not all of them were pleasant, he mused, looking into her emerald eyes.

He leaned back in his chair as the steward placed their dessert on the table and viewed the rich, rum-laced pecan pie with an appreciative eye. The concoction had been prepared in lieu of a birthday cake, for it was Amy's favorite dessert.

To Captain's Baxter's right, Amy saw her mother lift a forkful of pie to her mouth and wince as she bit into a piece of nut shell.

Oh dear, Amy thought uneasily. *The kitchen staff would certainly hear about this*. Nothing irritated her mother so much as finding the food ill-prepared. Some weeks back Mary had found a clam shell in her chowder and came close to actually dismissing Theresa Ruiz. It was a foregone conclusion that her mother would be heading for the kitchen as soon as the meal ended.

Not finding anything amiss with his own pie, Captain Baxter cleaned his plate and gave a great sigh of satisfaction. He motioned to the steward, and the man came forward to fill their wineglasses with champagne. Picking his up, Captain Baxter turned to Amy with a fond smile.

"It is always a milestone to reach the age of nineteen," he said. "And few have done it as gracefully as our guest of honor." He raised his glass to her. "Many happy returns, my dear. I wish you health, happiness, and love."

Amy's cheeks were tinted with color as she received congratulations from them all.

Knowing the girl always became embarrassed when

she was the center of attention, Captain Baxter kindly diverted that attention as he addressed the group at large. "Well, I hope you all are enjoying your trip," he said congenially, swallowing the last of his champagne.

"I'm sure we are," Lydia murmured, giving him a dazzling smile. The green eyes then sought Bethany, who was seated across from her. She was wearing a satin dress the color of honey. It very nearly matched her eyes, but of course Bethany knew that. "And you, Miss Kincaid?" Lydia said in a voice that fairly dripped snow. "Did you enjoy Mardi Gras?"

Beside her, Edward shifted uneasily and murmured a sound of warning, which Lydia chose to ignore.

"Yes, it was very nice," Bethany replied, a bit surprised by the question.

"One meets such interesting people during carnival, don't you agree?" Her full red lips curved into a tight, restrained smile. "And it's so easy to relinquish the proprieties." Her tone remained ice cold. "One can, in a sense, do anything one wishes."

Bethany felt heat fan her cheeks. Instinctively, she knew with certainty that Lydia was aware of what had taken place between Edward and her the night before; though for the life of her she couldn't figure out *how* Lydia knew. Had Edward told her? That thought was even more upsetting.

A look flashed between Bethany and Edward, fleeting, but, to Lydia, holding a world of meaning. Seeing it, she felt as though an icy hand had gripped her heart. She wanted to leap out of her chair and rake her nails across those flawless cheeks. She, better than anyone, knew what it was like to be held in the arms of Edward

Hammond, to be kissed by him. Few women could resist him, and Lydia didn't think Bethany was one of them. Well, if this woman had any designs on Edward, she would have to be put in her place, quickly, in no uncertain terms.

"Edward!" Lydia spoke with a brittle brightness that effectively cut through the silence that had fallen. "I would like to go out on the promenade; a walk would be welcome after such a splendid and satisfying meal."

Before Edward could respond, Lydia, with catlike grace, had gotten to her feet. Having no alternative, Edward stood up, as did Captain Baxter, whose white brows had risen in amused perplexity. Lydia handed Edward her cape, and, his mouth tight, he draped it around her shoulders.

Outside, Edward led Lydia once around the deck, then firmly directed her to her cabin.

"Edward, . . . you haven't spoken a word to me in the last ten minutes," she complained; *nor*, she thought, *had he even looked at her.*

"Perhaps I didn't want to risk another one of your tantrums," he said calmly, making a mental note to bar his door when he retired for the evening. He knew Lydia was his for the taking, but no stirring of desire moved within him. Absently, he wondered how he had put up with her all these years.

Her hand clutched his arm. "Please come inside with me," she whispered, her yearning all too clear for him to see. Her fingers took on the appearance of talons as she tightened her grip on his arm. "Stay with me tonight—" She broke off, seeing the answer on his face. Her cheeks flamed with humiliation at his unspoken rejection. Rage boiled inside her, for she thought she knew the reason. Edward went to move her hand from his arm, but she snatched it away before he could touch her.

The venomous fury displayed on Lydia's face was so overt that Edward turned away from the sight of it. No longer did he see beauty, only a twisted mask of jealousy that repelled him.

Lydia bit her lip but couldn't prevent her words from rushing out. "What is that woman to you?" she demanded.

He raised a tolerant brow. "What woman?"

Her face colored to an even deeper crimson. "You know perfectly well who I mean! That little trollop with the black hair and cat eyes!" Her chin thrust out. "I suppose now you're going downstairs to play cards with her!"

"If she's at the tables, there's an excellent chance of that happening," Edward replied.

His unruffled appearance enraged her. She could, she thought desperately, handle anything except the boredom she was seeing on his handsome face.

Lydia's hands balled into fists. "You're a fool!" she said through clenched teeth. Unmindful of her temper, she let her voice rise to shrillness. "You seem to think she's a lady. Well, she's not! Why do you suppose that tramp is traveling with Colin?"

Dark color suffused Edward's face. He didn't want to think about that. "Go to sleep, Lydia," he said wearily, turning on his heel. "You'll feel better in the morning."

As he descended the stairs, Edward couldn't help but wonder if he would feel better in the morning, for there was no doubt in his mind that Bethany Kincaid, lady or trollop, had him thoroughly intrigued.

Chapter 13

The kitchen had been in the throes of frantic activity all day. In addition to the three meals of the day, countless dozens of hors d'oeuvres had to be prepared for the party that would begin at ten o'clock. The final touches were accomplished after dinner was served at six. Mary personally supervised the making of the delicacies before she went to her cabin to dress for the evening.

This last Saturday night of the trip was always tumultuous for everyone involved, but the guests enjoyed it, and those who had been on the _Nola Star_ before not only looked forward to the occasion, but they also expected it as their due.

Even on this night, however, there were a few diehards who insisted on playing cards in the Grand Saloon. Colin was among them, promising Bethany he would join her before the party ended.

Bethany gave great thought to what she would wear for the festive occasion, finally selecting a velvet gown that was a soft rose color with an overskirt of Mechlin lace dyed the hue of deep red wine. The sleeves were set low on her shoulders, emphasizing their ivory roundness. Her hair was worn high, cleverly entwined with pink pearls.

It was half past ten by the time Bethany went downstairs, and the party was already in full swing.

The dining room was ablaze with light. Stewards scurried back and forth, holding trays laden with canapés, small pastries, and endless glasses of chilled champagne. Tables had been moved aside for dancing. The string quartet, now accompanied by the bored-looking pianist at his upright, which had been moved from the Ladies' Cabin for the evening, was currently offering a mellifluous waltz.

The many fabrics and colors of the womens' dresses as they glided and whirled gave one the impression of a huge multicolored bouquet.

Lydia, too, had dressed with care. On her white throat, an emerald and diamond necklace threw tiny, sparkling darts of light with each movement she made. She had again chosen to wear green; this time a lavish creation of iridescent silk with a décolletage so startling that her breasts appeared to be in imminent danger of being presented in their entirety to any interested onlooker. As she moved about the room, more than one man was watching her with unabashed lechery in anticipation of that delicious happenstance.

Bethany was standing with Mary and Amy, who looked especially lovely in a pearl-gray silk dress with puffed sleeves that narrowed at her elbow before continuing to her delicate wrists. It was, Mary was explaining to Bethany, her first "grown-up" gown.

The evening was well under way when Bethany saw Edward heading in their direction. She tensed as he approached. She refused to admit to herself that she had been aware of him from the first moment she had entered the room, aware of where he was standing, aware of with whom he was speaking, and with whom he was dancing.

Coming closer, Edward gave a small bow that included all three women, his blue eyes touching Bethany like a casual caress. Like the other men, he was dressed in formal attire, the black broadcloth of his suit and snowy white shirtfront enhancing his golden hair and tanned skin.

Then he turned to Amy and extended his hand. "May I have the honor of dancing with the loveliest young lady in the room?" he asked with a gentle smile.

Amy blushed prettily as she took his arm, allowing him to lead her onto the dance floor. Mary's face held a soft smile as she watched her daughter's graceful movements.

"She's growing up so fast," she murmured to Bethany with a slight catch in her voice. "It seems only yesterday that she was a child . . ."

Bethany put her hand on Mary's arm and gave a gentle squeeze. "Edward was right," she said quietly. "Amy's quite the loveliest woman here. You must be very proud."

"I am," Mary said simply, then viewed Bethany with worried eyes. "If only—"

"I know," Bethany said quickly. "But you mustn't

lose hope." she fell silent, seeing Edward return with Amy. After thanking the girl, he turned to Bethany.

"Miss Kincaid?"

Not wishing to cause a scene, Bethany placed her hand on his extended arm. As the quartet played "Tales from the Vienna Woods," Edward led her into the waltz, and she was mildly astonished at how well he danced. His movements were effortless, his rhythm precise.

"Somehow I knew you'd be a good dancer," he murmured, smiling down at her. A faint scent of jasmine rose from her hair to intoxicate his senses.

She looked up, and the blue flame of his eyes seemed to scorch her whole body. "Thank you," she managed to say, praying that he didn't notice how her hands were trembling.

Glancing over Edward's shoulder, Bethany saw Lydia dancing with Captain Baxter. Amber eyes met green ones. If there was any truth to the saying "if looks could kill," Bethany suspected she would have fallen over by now.

Sensing that the song was coming to an end, Edward danced Bethany to the door. Before she knew what was happening, she found herself outside.

"It was a bit warm in there," Edward said in a casual way. "I thought you might welcome a breath of fresh air," Taking her arm, he began to walk.

Bethany raised her head to stare up into the star-filled night. A yellow moon had risen in the velvety-black sky, looking for all the world as if it had been deliberately hung there. Beneath its glow the river flowed like a white satin ribbon.

Edward glanced down at her. "You look very beautiful tonight," he said in a low voice.

A whistle sounded from a distant steamer, but the *Nola Star* was currently making her way through a serpentine maze of bends in the river, and neither boat nor lights were visible. They seemed to be alone in a pocket of wilderness.

Bethany clasped her hands at her waist, suddenly feeling nervous and unsettled. "Why did you bring me out here?"

He cocked an eyebrow, feigning astonishment at the question. "Because I thought you'd like to be alone with me."

She halted abruptly, hearing the mocking inflection that was becoming all too familiar to her.

Having paused when she did, Edward put his hands on her smooth shoulders and pulled her toward him.

"No . . ." Even having said that, her legs refused to move.

"You don't mean that," he said softly.

Did his voice sound as breathless as hers?

Bethany felt his hot mouth on hers, shivered when his arms went around her. Against her will, her lips parted. She fell into an abyss of emotion, infuriated with her own heated response. She didn't want to feel anything and fought against the wave of liquid fire that inflamed her whole body. Feeling his hand cup her breast, Bethany whimpered.

Struggling for composure that was almost beyond her reach, Bethany managed to break away. On legs that felt like quivering aspic, she ran back into the dining room. Standing just inside the doorway, she tried to catch her breath, but her heart was beating so rapidly that she felt the need to gasp for air. She took several deep breaths in an effort to control herself. Then, spying Mary, she gratefully headed in her direction.

Mary regarded Bethany's flushed face curiously as the young woman sat down beside her, but said nothing.

"Where's Amy?" Bethany asked in an overly bright voice, more for something to say than really wanting to know. Her lips parted as she took another deep breath.

"She's gone to bed." Mary sighed. "And, frankly, I wish I could do the same. I sometimes wonder why I let these affairs go on for such a length of time. . . ."

Mary continued to talk, and Bethany listened with half an ear, her thoughts a confused jumble within her mind. Looking up, she saw Edward standing by the door, a small smile tugging the corners of his mouth. A sparkle of blue flame glowed warmly as he viewed her through half-closed eyes. Their gazes locked, hers a reluctant prisoner of his.

Bethany balled her hands in her lap, and anger provided the strength for her to look away.

Damned conceited oaf! she fumed silently, still hearing Mary's voice but not her words. How dare that man assume she wanted to be in the same room with him, much less alone with him.

Ooh! She gripped her hands even tighter, perversely wishing they were around his neck. Of all the egotistical, aggravating, mendacious males in the world, Edward Hammond was surely the prize one of them all, the prince of that elite group.

She turned to give him her frostiest glare, only to see him dancing with Lydia. The woman flashed a cold smile at Bethany. She said something to Edward. Bending his head, he listened, then laughed.

Bethany stiffened noticeably at the rich sound, wondering whether she was the cause of the merriment, then started when Mary touched her arm.

"Excuse me, Bethany," she said, getting to her feet. "Much as I would rather not, I feel I must circulate among my guests."

"Of course," Bethany said quickly. She was about to get up and go to her stateroom when she saw Colin coming toward her, a big smile on his face.

"There you are!" he said jovially, in a tone that told Bethany he had won. "I told you I'd be here before the party ended."

Bethany viewed the outstretched hand and, resignedly, rose to dance with him.

Chapter 14_____

Memories of the past evening came rushing forward to awaken Bethany with a start the following morning. A pale gray light crept in the window, and she realized it was quite early yet. A glance at her watch showed that it was a few minutes past six o'clock.

Getting out of bed, Bethany looked outside, surprised to see the _Nola Star_ angling toward the wharf at Louisville. They had apparently traveled at great speed during the night.

Bethany dressed quickly, then began to pack her clothes. She was almost finished with this task when she heard a knock on the door. Moving forward, she opened it to see Edward Hammond standing there. He was dressed for traveling in a knee-length, dark gray broadcloth coat, white ruffled shirt and a dark crimson silk vest over which was looped a gold watch chain. His leather boots were, as usual, highly polished.

"I want to talk to you," he said, before she could

speak. He put a hand on the door to prevent her from closing it.

Her chin lifted. "I don't think my stateroom is an appropriate place for any discussion between us," she said stiffly.

"It's private," he pointed out. He lowered his hand but leaned on the door frame. When she still hesitated, he grinned at her. "I can be persistent when I put my mind to it," he murmured. "On the other hand, I suppose we could have a conversation right here." He deliberately raised his voice, seeing two elderly ladies coming down the hallway. He gave them a mock bow, and they stared curiously at Bethany, their eyes telling her of their disapproval.

Bethany's delicate nostrils flared, but she made no comment until the women descended the stairs. With the exception of Mary and Amy, most of the women on board had been treating her as though she had a contagious disease. Her amber eyes flashed when she again looked at Edward.

"I cannot imagine any basis for conversation between us," she snapped.

"Can't you?"

He took a step closer. Bethany took a step back. Edward closed the door behind him.

"What would your fiancée say if she knew you were in my room?" Bethany clasped her hands at her waist, annoyed to hear the quaver in her voice.

"I have no fiancée," he replied. "Unless, of course, you would like to apply for that position," he added.

Bethany heard the light, bantering tone of his voice, but failed to notice the intense look in his eyes. Her knuckles went white as she squeezed her hands tighter. Her palms itched with the urge to wipe that smug smile from his face.

He was standing so close that Bethany could feel his warm breath on her face. Raising her head to look at him, she swayed, then caught her balance.

With a jolt of surprise, Bethany realized she had been expecting him to kiss her. Looking into those blue eyes, she saw that he knew it, too!

Quickly, she turned away and swallowed, furious with herself. "You said you wanted to talk. Please get on with it." Oh, Lord, why couldn't she keep her voice steady?

Standing behind her, Edward put a hand on her shoulder. She felt the pressure, the warmth, and was suddenly alert to him. Emotion warred with logic. What, she wondered frantically, would she do if he turned her around and took her in his arms?

"Do you really dislike me as much as you pretend?" His voice came softly at her.

Her back stiffened. "You flatter yourself! I have no feelings about you, one way or the other." There, she thought, satisfied. Her voice was again level and in control, even if her legs were trembling.

His hand fell away, and she could feel him staring at her. Those eyes seemed to burn right through her. "Somehow I don't quite believe that."

She took a step away from him and picked up a dress from the back of the chair. "I'm not in the habit of saying things I don't mean."

"I think this time might be an exception," he said so softly that Bethany had to strain to hear his words.

She gave him a sharp glance. The man truly was impossible. "You have an outrageous conceit!" Folding the dress neatly, she placed it in the valise that rested on the bed.

"Really?" He sounded surprised. "You're the first one to tell me so." Before she could respond, he spoke quietly. "Mary tells me that she plans to stay in Louisville for a few weeks." Bethany turned to look at him, wondering what he was leading up to. "I've told Mary that she and Amy are welcome to stay at Glencoe when their business in Louisville is completed. I thought perhaps that you, too, would like to spend some time at Glencoe . . . unless, of course, you have other plans." He watched her expectantly.

She opened her mouth to say no, then closed it again. The idea of spending several weeks in a hotel didn't appeal to her; neither did living with Joan and her husband. Besides, she had promised herself that she would learn everything there was to know about Edward Hammond; and, so far, she knew little more than when she started.

Finally, she nodded slowly. "Very well. In view of the fact that Mary and Amy will be there, I'll accept your invitation."

A while later, having eaten a hurried breakfast, Bethany went to find Mary while Edward saw to their luggage.

Concern quickened her steps. She had seen neither Mary nor Amy in the dining room. But when she knocked on the door, there was no answer.

Cornering one of the cabin boys, Bethany asked him if he knew where Mary was.

"Mrs. Dennison and her daughter got off as soon as the boat docked," the lad reported. "Didn't even take the time to eat breakfast."

With a sigh, Bethany made her way down to the hurricane deck, where Edward was waiting for her.

Bethany was of a mind to wait for Mary's return, but Edward assured her that both Mary and Amy would head for Glencoe as soon as they concluded their errands and to wait for them here would be to chance missing them.

Seeing Lydia, who was standing with Colin and Captain Baxter, Edward called to her.

"I'll be glad to drive you home, Lydia," he offered politely. "Miss Kincaid is coming with me, but there's plenty of room."

Lydia, whose expression had brightened with his approach, now stared coldly from beneath her wide-brimmed hat, her eyes glinting with anger.

"There's no need to trouble yourself," she said haughtily. "I've made other arrangements. As a matter of fact, I've invited Colin to stay at The Willows." Beside her Colin gave her a look of surprise; this was the first he'd heard of an invitation.

"Fine," Edward said, and meant it. His hand cupping Bethany's elbow, he led her to the gangway.

With a sour expression on her face, Lydia moved to the railing, watching as Edward and Bethany stepped into the waiting carriage, which Matthew had driven to the wharf. This was Edward's way of getting even with her; Lydia was certain of it. *Well, let him have his little fling*, she thought. *He'd tire of that trollop soon enough.*

Then she turned to Colin, whose shoulders were slumped in dejection.

She gave him a baleful glance. "I take it you haven't gotten around to proposing yet," she said acidly. "Ever the procrastinator, aren't you?"

He looked sheepish, unable to meet her eye. "There hasn't been time," he said, not wanting to tell her Bethany continued to rebuff his admittedly tentative advances. But he didn't want to press her, fearing she would refuse him in no uncertain terms. "I was waiting for the right opportunity . . ."

"Moonlight and roses?" Lydia suggested sarcastically with a lift of her brow. "Come on . . ." Walking quickly, she headed for the gangway. "At least you'll be close enough to visit her . . . if you've a mind," she added in a tone that suggested he'd be a fool to even contemplate such a step.

Colin followed her, trying not to look as confused as he felt. This development had caught him totally unaware; he was, if anything, more surprised than Lydia. When had this all come about? he wondered.

Then he relaxed. The reason was so obvious that he wished he could tell Lydia and set her mind at ease. Bethany had said she wanted to learn everything there was to know about Edward. And what better way to keep him off his guard than to agree to be his houseguest?

Oh, it was perfect, he thought, feeling much better, resisting the urge to rub his hands together in satisfaction. When Bethany returned to the *Nola Star,* she would most certainly be ready to put her plan into action.

And he, Colin, would have his own little revenge on the Bayou Fox.

*   *   *   *   *

When Mary and Amy returned to the boat later on in the day, Captain Baxter had some bad news. The strain of having to move at full speed for such a length of time the night before had damaged one of the boilers.

"I don't think we should even consider leaving until it's repaired," Baxter said to Mary.

"How bad is it?" she asked.

He shook his head. "I don't know. Jeb's checking it out now."

Mary frowned. "It could take weeks before we can get another boiler shipped down from Cincinnati."

"That might not be necessary," he said. "Although I do think we should go ahead and order one right now. If this one can be patched, we can keep the *Nola Star* in service until such time as we can get the new one."

Mary nodded. "All right. I'll take the next packet to Cincinnati. You stay here, Winston. I know you'd like to spend some time with your family." She turned to Amy, noted the girl's crestfallen face, then made a quick decision. "Just because I have to stay," she said, "is no reason why you have to. I'll send word to Edward and ask him to come and get you."

Her mother's words caused Amy's face to brighten. In a much happier frame of mind, she went to pack her clothes.

Chapter 15

Lamplight shone from the downstairs windows and spilled onto the front porch. Beneath a full moon that glowed with shimmering whiteness, Glencoe appeared to Bethany to have been constructed from alabaster.

Before the carriage drew to a halt, Henry opened the door. Smiling a welcome, he hurried forward to fetch their valises.

"Nice to have you home again, Mistah Edward," he said, nodding his head.

"Thank you, Henry. This is Miss Kincaid. She'll be staying with us for a while. Please ask Rissa to prepare one of the guest bedrooms for her use."

"I'll do that right now," Henry responded quickly as they entered the foyer. He put down the suitcases and gave Edward a questioning look. "Rissa has supper about ready," he said. "Would you be wantin' to eat in the dining room?" Often Edward took his evening meal with his father. Henry didn't think that would be the case tonight.

"Yes, that'll be fine. I'll stop in to see my father first." Edward put a hand on Bethany's elbow. "Please come with me. I'm sure he'd like to meet you."

He led her down the hallway, giving her a brief explanation of why his father was bedridden.

As they entered, Cyrus looked up, his lined face brightening with his first glimpse of his son.

"How're you doing, Pa?" Edward said by way of a greeting and then introduced Bethany.

Cyrus regarded Bethany curiously, well aware that this was the first woman Edward had brought to Glencoe since Lydia. In fact, discounting that harlot, this was the first woman Edward had ever brought home. Although Edward had never said anything, Cyrus was well aware of the reason for his son's broken engagement. Though his feet were impaired, there was nothing wrong with his ears, and the shouting and scuffling that had taken place on that night had informed him of everything that had happened.

"Are you from Kentucky?" he asked Bethany. This one, he thought approvingly, was a lady—no question about it. That she was beautiful was of no importance to Cyrus. There was more to a woman than beauty; any man worth his salt knew that.

Bethany nodded, gaining a quick impression of a man with whom life had dealt harshly. The resemblance between Edward and his father was miniscule, the older man being far shorter and thinner than his son. A man without purpose, Bethany suspected, feeling saddened by her deduction. Only the eyes held hope, sharp and penetrating as they viewed her. "I was born in Louisville."

Narrowing his eyes, Cyrus gave her a sharp look. "Were you on the side of the Confederacy?" he demanded, a quick frown wrinkling his brow.

"Now, Pa...," Edward murmured with a low laugh. "The war's been over for many years...."

"It'll never be over for those of us who were in it," the old man snapped. His glance at Edward was filled with annoyance, then his gaze swung to Bethany again as he waited for her answer.

"Yes, Mr. Hammond," Bethany responded gently. "I was on the side of the Confederacy."

The old man looked mollified and gave Edward a curt nod. "Better than that Madison girl. Damned Unionists, the whole bunch of them."

Hearing Henry's announcement that supper was ready, Edward hastily ushered Bethany from the room.

They followed the Negro along the hall.

Pausing, Henry opened the gleaming black doors that led into the dining room. The long table, chairs, and sideboard were Chippendale, dark, and highly polished. The Persian rug was patterned in muted gray and soft yellow, the same colors to be found in the wallpaper. Although a crystal chandelier hung from the ceiling, it was unlit; the room was bathed in the soft glow created by two brass candelabras on the table, now covered with a lace cloth and set with fine silver.

They sat down to a sumptuous meal of roast quail, sweet potatoes, and buttered carrots, accompanied by Rissa's homemade biscuits.

"I must apologize for my father . . . ," Edward said to Bethany when they were settled.

"Please don't," Bethany interrupted sincerely. "There's no need. I've known many people his age, men and women, who can't seem to let go of their memories of that terrible time." She thought of Mary and Amy. Surely their memories would remain with them for a lifetime.

Edward nodded thoughtfully as he speared a carrot with his fork. "Still and all, fourteen years is a long time to hold a grudge."

Bethany cut into the quail, appreciating its savory aroma. "Is his grudge against the Unionists or the Madisons?" she asked.

"Both, I guess," Edward replied somberly. "Pa's especially bitter because no other farm in this area suffered as much damage as ours did. And more than anything else was the fact that The Willows, only five miles away, was untouched. You see, in their earlier years, Sam Madison and my father had a sort of friendly rivalry, an ongoing competition to see which of them could raise the finest breed of horse." His smile was wry and a bit sad as he continued. "They were, in a sense, neck to neck when the war broke out. My father elected to fight for the Confederacy—with dire results. Madison, on the other hand, sided with the Federals. To this day, my father has never forgiven him."

"And you?" she asked softly, putting down her fork. "You don't resent the Madisons?"

As soon as the words were out, Bethany could have

bitten her tongue. Obviously he didn't resent them; he had been engaged to their daughter.

Slowly, Edward shook his head. "I owe them too much to resent them. After my mother died of pneumonia, I stayed here alone, seeing to things as best I could. But then the Yankees came, confiscated our horses, and in general took over." There was an edge of anger in his voice as he related this, but it disappeared as he continued. "Sam Madison gave me food and shelter. I lived at The Willows for the better part of three years until the war ended."

Bethany leaned back in her chair, her eyes wide with surprise. "Does your father know that?" She found it hard to believe that anyone could hate a man who had helped his son.

Edward nodded, finishing the last of his coffee. "Yes, he knows." He sighed as he put down his cup. "But he was a very bitter man when he returned. Hatred kept him alive while he was in Elmira, and it only increased when he came home and saw Glencoe in ruins."

She looked about the graciously furnished room. "It's certainly not in ruins now," she murmured.

"Nor will it ever be again if I have anything to say about it!" Edward spoke with a forcefulness that tensed his jaw.

Giving him a quick glance, Bethany saw how the blue flame of Edward's eyes glowed with decisiveness. His home and his land meant a great deal to him, she realized. *Enough to reach his goals by any means?* she wondered. *Even if the means were dishonest?* The thought was a weight that depressed her, for reasons she didn't fully understand.

"More coffee for you and the lady?" Henry asked softly.

As they nodded in response, he refilled their cups, then removed the dishes from the table. When they were alone again, Edward looked at Bethany, noticing how the candlelight accented the fine bone structure of her face and deepened the amber of her eyes.

"Where did you learn how to play cards?" he asked, adding cream to his coffee.

"Where did you?" she countered, amused. "I suspect you've never yet asked a man that question."

"I've never cared before," he responded quickly, aware that she was parrying with him. "What are you going to do with your life?" he went on, changing his strategy. "Ride the riverboats up and down the Mississippi?"

"Isn't that what you do?" she challenged.

"Yes," Edward admitted seriously. "But it certainly isn't the way I plan to spend the rest of my life. I'm doing it for a reason. . . ."

Bethany gave him a level look. "Perhaps I, too, have a reason," she said in a low voice.

Suddenly Bethany felt weary; she wanted only to lie down and go to sleep, to halt the churning indecision that filled her mind with questions she couldn't answer.

Murmuring what she hoped was a gracious leave-taking, Bethany hurried upstairs, on the verge of tears and not knowing why.

On the landing, she halted abruptly, realizing she didn't know which of the bedrooms to enter.

"This one is yours. . . ."

Through the soft shadows Edward's quiet voice came to her. Bethany turned, seeing him standing in front of an open door she had already passed.

Feeling a bit foolish, she retraced her steps.

"It was inconsiderate of me not to realize that you'd be tired from the long drive," he said as she paused in front of him. His hands were warm on her shoulders. "Tomorrow, when you're rested, I'll take you on a tour of Glencoe," he informed her softly, but his eyes spoke another language, held a longing she could not help but see.

When his arms went around her, Bethany couldn't prevent herself from entering his embrace. His mouth claimed hers, and she gave herself willingly to the remembered sweetness of his kiss.

Drawing back, Edward looked down at her. With his finger he traced the lovely curve of her cheek.

"You're a beautiful woman, Bethany Kincaid," he said huskily.

Bethany shivered and suddenly felt cold. The desire she saw kindled in the blue flame of his eyes was not for her, Bethany Forrester; it was for a woman gambler named Kincaid. That was not who she was. Edward didn't even know her name, or why she was here.

And if he knew, would he still be looking at her as he was doing now? His eyes held a question she could not permit herself to acknowledge even, much less answer. Once more he drew her toward him; and when her body came in contact with his, she could feel his arousal and gasped. Putting her hands on his chest, Bethany held him at a distance. If he kissed her again, she was certain she would be lost.

"Please," she whispered breathlessly. "I . . ."

His hands fell away. Bethany saw the confusion that played across his face as he gave her one of those intense looks that made her knees weak. And of course he had every reason to be mystified, she thought ruefully. She was saying one thing, and her traitorous body was conveying an entirely different message to him.

In a quick movement, Bethany turned away and entered the room, closing the door firmly behind her.

The room was lovely. The wallpaper was of a cream-colored background against pale green vines. The carpet was blue. A sofa was positioned at one end of the room, in front of a marble fireplace. A lamp burned on a low table. In a corner was a rosewood writing table. At the other end was a four-poster bed, a cherrywood armoire, and a dressing table. The single window was draped with dark blue velvet.

As she stepped to the dressing table, Bethany began to remove the pins from her hair, suddenly aware of how she was trembling.

She pressed her hands to her temples, her thoughts offering nothing but confusion.

Oh, God, how could she think? When she had started out, everything had been crystal clear in her mind. Now. . . . What upset her the most was that she was uncertain as to the nature of her vacillating thoughts. Was it because she was honestly beginning to think her father had made a mistake? Or was her confusion due to the fact that she found Edward Hammond so compelling?

She bit her lip, not wanting to think about it anymore.

But when she undressed and crawled into bed, Bethany's thoughts would give her no peace. She tossed and turned for hours until she finally fell into a restless sleep.

The following morning dawned clear and sunny. After breakfast, Edward took Bethany on a tour of Glencoe. Most of the horses Bethany saw in the stables were Thoroughbreds or Standardbreds.

Bethany watched with interest as Matthew worked with a large chestnut mare. The horse was circling Matthew, who was leading her with a longe line. The rein was long, fully sixty feet in length, designed, Bethany knew, to prevent strain on the hindquarters. For the better part of five minutes, Bethany watched as the horse moved at a quick canter, Matthew correcting it when it occasionally broke into a trot.

Race horses, Bethany knew, were never allowed to trot unless they were being trained in that pace. A race horse galloped, cantered, or walked; but he never trotted. Standardbreds, on the other hand, were trotters, registered if they could cover one mile in or under two and a half minutes.

"He's very good," she said at last, admiring the firm, yet gentle way in which Matthew was handling the spirited animal.

Edward nodded his agreement. "Matthew has a way with horses." He turned to look at her. "I've always thought a man had to be born with that quality; I sincerely doubt that it can be learned."

"She moves impressively," Bethany noted, wishing he wouldn't look at her like that. It quite unnerved her.

He nodded again. "That she does. I'm going to race

her in Lexington this Saturday. I think she's ready to show us what she can do. Would you care to come along and watch?''

"I would indeed."

Edward touched her arm. "Come on. I've saved the best for last."

When they reached the west field, Bethany stared in amazement at Dawn's Light. "That's not a Standard-bred, is it?''

"She's an Akhal-Teke," Edward said. "An offshoot of the Turkoman, older than the Arabian; in fact, some say it's the ancestor of that breed. Originally, they came from the Turkoman Steppes. In addition to being beautiful, they have remarkable endurance."

Having lived most of her life in Kentucky, Bethany was no stranger to horseflesh. But never in her life had she seen an animal like this one. Beautiful suddenly seemed an inadequate and trifling word.

"You found her here, in Kentucky?" she asked, still looking at the horse.

"No," he answered. "I was attending a horse show in London when someone told me of an auction to be held in Brussels. The quality was to be such that even the czar planned to attend." He laughed. "Happily for me, the czar wasn't interested in Dawn's Light. I sincerely doubt that I could have outbid him."

"An animal like that must have cost a small fortune," Bethany said, her voice low. And where did he get the money to buy it? she wondered.

"She did," Edward agreed cheerfully. "And I would have willingly paid twice the price. Fortunately, I made a great deal of money during my last trip on the *Nola*

Star. I used most of those winnings to buy Dawn's Light." A sigh of satisfaction followed his words.

Bethany stiffened and felt ice cold beneath the warm sun. "Do you always win?" she asked quietly, keeping her face averted.

He laughed and shook his head. "No. Not always."

Oh, God, Bethany thought, turning to look at his handsome face. How could she so betray her father as to let herself be taken in by the soft smiles of the man who was responsible for his downfall? She stared at Edward, seeing the golden hair. Now wind-tossed, it seemed to beckon to her fingertips to smooth it. She clenched her hands, feeling a tightening in the pit of her stomach; for the moment, she felt almost physically ill.

Edward didn't notice Bethany's expression, for he caught sight of Henry hurrying toward him.

"It's a letter for you, Mistah Edward. Was just delivered."

"Thank you, Henry." He opened the envelope, read it, and smiled. "It's from Mary," he said to Bethany. "Apparently there's trouble with one of the boilers. She's decided to go to Cincinnati to order a new one, then return to Louisville until the *Nola Star's* ready to go." He put the letter in his pocket. "But she wants Amy to stay here. Henry, bring the carriage to the front. I'll ride into town to fetch her." He put his hands on Bethany's shoulders. "I probably won't get back until tomorrow afternoon. If you need anything, just let Henry know."

Bethany nodded, still feeling unsettled.

That night, after she had eaten supper, Bethany selected a book at random from the well-stocked library and retired to her room, but after reading the same paragraph three times in a row, she laid the book aside.

Getting up, she went to the window and stared out into the moon-washed night, her thoughts a confused jumble. She put her cheek against the cool pane of the window, blinking back tears of frustration.

No, she thought in rising anguish, fate wouldn't be so cruel as to allow her to fall in love with the man who had been responsible for her father's death. She straightened. Was Edward the man she thought him to be? Or was he the man her father had declared him to be?

Bethany knew she had to find out, but the method of accomplishing this escaped her. Crossing the room, she sat down in a cushioned chair, thinking of Mary's advice: confront him! But that was implausible. No one would admit to doing something like that.

Leaning her head back, Bethany closed her eyes, taking stock of the situation as she knew it, making a mental list of facts:

One, her father had been emphatic in his denunciation.

Two, Edward gambled for one purpose only: to make money in order to restore Glencoe to its former glory. Unlike most men, he didn't gamble for the thrill or excitement of it; unlike Colin, he didn't gamble for a living. Nor was he compulsive. He gambled for a reason; and by virtue of either contrivance or skill, he was good at it.

And finally, Colin thought Edward capable of cheating. Mary did not.

The fact that Edward had purchased that magnificent horse with what was most assuredly her father's money was one thing Bethany could not in all fairness hold against him. The question still remained: did he come by that money honestly, or had he cheated to get it?

Reviewing all this, Bethany chewed her inner lip. It was the sum total of facts at her disposal.

It told her nothing.

But one way or the other, Bethany knew she would have to uncover the truth. She would have no peace of mind until she did so.

Chapter 16

Sitting beside Edward, Amy viewed her surroundings with a keen eye. As the carriage rolled up the drive, a shiver of delight coursed through her as she viewed the horses. Tails swished lazily, and sinewy muscles caught sunlight and rippled it across silky coats. Large, velvety eyes gazed at her with what she was certain was an invitation to become better acquainted—an invitation she sincerely wanted to accept.

Beautiful. The word echoed reverently in her mind. If paradise existed, surely this must be its earthly counterpart.

Watching her, Edward smiled at her enthralled expression. Seldom had he seen her so animated. She could hardly sit still and was trying to look everywhere at once.

"You like the horses?" he asked. He didn't need to see her quick nod to know the answer. "Would you like to learn how to ride them?"

Amy's eyes widened and her lips parted. Edward laughed and patted her arm. "All right," he said. "If that's what you want, that's what you shall have."

When Edward first met Mary, six years ago, Amy had been only a wisp of a child. He still had a tendency to think of her as such, though at nineteen, Edward knew she was to be considered a young woman. He was fond of her then, and he was fond of her now.

The carriage drew up to the front entrance, and Edward waved at Bethany, who was standing on the front porch. As Amy got out, Bethany came forward and put her arm around the girl.

"It's good to see you again," she said warmly.

"Do you have a riding habit that Amy can borrow?" Edward asked as they entered the house.

"Yes, indeed," Bethany responded, then smiled at Amy. "But we'll have to do a few alterations. I'm afraid mine will be much too large for you."

Leading Amy up to her room, Bethany located the outfit in her trunk. She and Amy spent the rest of the afternoon pulling out seams and sewing them back together again, but the result was satisfying to them both. The bottle-green velvet was especially flattering to Amy's fair coloring.

After dinner, Amy retired. Bethany and Edward went into the library where Henry served them a glass of burgundy, then discreetly withdrew.

"Amy's a lovely child," Edward noted as he sat down in one of the wing chairs.

Bethany gave a small laugh. Moving toward the fireplace she gazed down at the glowing embers. "I don't think she'd like to hear herself described in that way.''

"No, I suppose not," Edward said, taking a sip of his wine. "But when I first met her, she was only thirteen years old."

She turned to look at him. "You've been traveling on the *Nola Star* that long?" She sounded surprised.

He nodded. "And you?" His blue eyes fixed her with a penetrating look. "Why were you on the *Nola Star*?"

She put her glass on the mantel. "For the same reason you were," she said quietly. "To play cards."

"Why would a woman like you feel the need to do something like that?" he asked, puzzlement drawing his brows together.

A small smile pulled at the corners of her mouth. "And what kind of woman am I?"

Putting his glass on the table next to him, Edward got up to stand beside her. "Beautiful," he answered simply. "Certainly you must have had at least one offer of marriage. . . ."

"I have," she said lightly. "But I will not marry a man just for the sake of being married." He was staring at her in that intense manner that always caused a quiver deep inside her. Bethany drew a deep breath, wet her lips, and moved away from him.

His forehead creasing, Edward watched as she walked toward the window. He had the distinct impression that she was trying to put distance between them. His eyes took in the lovely curve of her back, and he moved toward her.

"And what of your family," he asked quietly. "Do they approve of what you're doing?"

Bethany shuddered, feeling his breath on the back of her neck. In a swift movement, she turned to face him. "Is it my family's disapproval or your own that concerns you?"

He had raised his hand to touch her cheek but let it fall to his side upon hearing the suddenly altered tone of her voice. *There it was again*, he thought to himself. *The sudden reserve, the barricade she managed to erect with a lightning-like change of pace.* Each time it happened, it took him by surprise.

"I . . . never said I disapproved," he murmured, turning away from her. He walked back to the table, finished his drink, and looked at her again. "I usually stop in to say good night to my father before I retire. If you'll excuse me, I'll see you in the morning." He crossed the room, his easy stride betraying no indication of his inner tension. Her nearness was torturing him.

Watching him leave, Bethany bit her lip. She put her fingertips to her forehead, expelling a long, drawn-out breath.

What is the matter with me! she thought irritably. A few minutes ago, they had been having a congenial conversation. Why did she react so strongly each time he got too close to her? She couldn't even think straight! No man had ever had such an effect on her before.

Walking to the mantel, Bethany picked up her glass and downed the wine in one long swallow. Edward had been going to kiss her, she knew that. She had wanted him to; she admitted that. And she also knew that the next time he took her in his arms, she would be lost.

Pressing her hands together, Bethany walked from the room and went upstairs, praying for the strength she knew that sooner or later she was going to need.

The next morning was calm, with a pale sun that drifted gauzily through the trees. Unusually mild for March, the weather hinted at an early spring. With Amy in tow, Edward headed for the stables, having already informed Matthew of her inability to speak and that he was to teach the girl to ride.

Matthew, curry brush in one hand, paused at the sight of Amy, struck by her delicate beauty, noting how her hair shimmered with silvery light in the sun.

To his utter chagrin, Matthew heard himself stammer in acknowledgment of the introduction offered by his employer. Edward seemed not to notice, and for that Matthew was thankful. But the girl—what did he say her name was? Amy?—had a slight smile on her rose-tinted lips, a smile that lit her gray eyes, and Matthew found himself basking in the warm glow.

"I think Sea Foam would be a good choice to start her off," Edward was saying.

"I'll saddle him right away," Matthew said, still unable to look away from Amy. He almost tripped over a bale of hay, offering a weak grin as he righted himself.

Turning, he went to get the horse and returned in record time. Holding the reins firmly, he led the stallion to Amy, who immediately reached up and stroked the silky mane.

"First lesson," Matthew said to her. "Always mount a horse on the near side, which is the left."

Amy studied him as he spoke and she liked what she

saw. His crisp brown hair was wavy and somewhat unruly. In deference to the cool morning air, he wore a light jacket and tan breeches that were tucked into well-worn boots.

Matthew held out his hand. Amy hesitated only a moment, then shyly placed her hand in his. It felt warm to her and very solid.

Watching Amy as she settled herself, Edward nodded in satisfaction as he returned to the house.

Amy spent the remainder of the morning learning to ride under Matthew's expert tutelage. Finally, they went back to the stables, and Matthew helped Amy dismount.

Handing the reins to Robert, Henry's eldest son, Matthew instructed the thirteen-year-old boy to care for Sea Foam. Then, turning back to Amy, he felt his face blanch at the sight of the large German shepherd. The dog, who belonged to Robert, was unaccustomed to strangers and could, on occasion, act in a threatening manner. Right now, he was standing a few feet from Amy, who had taken a step in his direction. The dog was very still, eyes alert, his ears flattened in unmistakable warning.

A cold stab of fear prickled Matthew's spine. "Adam!" he called, keeping his voice calm and firm.

Amy was about two feet from the dog now. Getting down on her haunches, she held out a hand, palm up, making eye contact with the animal.

Hearing a low, menacing growl, Matthew opened his mouth to order the dog away when to his amazement Adam came forward, ears suddenly perked up. He sniffed the smooth palm held out for his inspection; then, tail wagging, he came close enough to be petted.

Walking toward Amy, Matthew hunched down at her side. "I've never seen him do that before," he said in wonder. "Usually he avoids strangers," Reaching out, he ruffled the dog's fur, and then he stood up, assisting Amy as she stood upright again. "I guess he likes you," he murmured. *But then, who wouldn't,* he added silently, studying her. The thought occurred to him that he would dearly love to spend the rest of his life looking at that sunny smile.

Taking hold of her small hand, Matthew led Amy down to the lake. Removing his jacket he spread it on the ground for her to sit on.

For a while, Matthew sat in silence, watching the ducks gliding smoothly through the blue water.

From beneath thick silvery lashes that were darkly tipped, Amy studied him, noting his lean, well-muscled body. His eyes were a deep brown, crinkled at the corners, and when he smiled, the little lines deepened as if in agreement. Since he wasn't all that much older than herself, Amy decided it was the wind and sun rather than time that had left its mark. Amy knew very few young men, and those that she had known were transitory, coming into her life one week and leaving it the next. None of them had ever appealed to her.

Looking now at Matthew's strong hands, clasped between his knees, Amy felt a small tremor in the pit of her stomach, a sensation she had never experienced before.

She liked his voice, too, even when he hesitated, as if he were giving careful thought to his words. She sat up straighter, suddenly aware that she had met the young man from whom she wanted that second look.

Reaching into her pocket, Amy brought forth pencil and paper. She touched Matthew's arm, and he turned to her.

"How long have you been here?" she wrote.

"Five years," he said. "I was born in New York. My folks have a business there—a shoe-repair shop. But," he explained, "I was never happy in the city. I've loved horses all my life." He paused as she again put pencil to paper.

"Was your family sad to see you go?"

He smiled and gave a careless shrug. "Well, my mother, I guess. I have two brothers and a sister. I don't expect my leaving was too much of a burden. We lived in a four-room flat above the store. My eldest brother, Alexander, had already moved out when I left." He shrugged and plucked at a blade of grass. "I had no destination in mind, you understand. I just knew I had to get out where I could breathe."

Amy raised her knees to support her elbows and cupped her chin in her hands, her gray eyes never leaving his face.

Matthew was more than a bit disturbed by those eyes that were suddenly looking so intensely into his own. He couldn't recall ever having seen such a beautiful face. He noticed the same thing that Bethany had when she first met Amy: youth and innocence curiously offset by age and wisdom. He wondered what her voice would sound like. Beautiful, he decided, just like the rest of her. And why didn't she speak? All Edward had told him was that something happened to her as a child, something so dreadful that it robbed her of speech.

"At any rate," he went on, visibly trying to collect

his thoughts, "I had a few dollars put away, and when I set out I had no idea where I was going. I thought at first I would head west, maybe settle there. But I wanted to see a bit of the country before I made my decision. When I got here . . . well," he laughed, twirling the piece of grass between his thumb and forefinger. "I knew I had come home." He looked at her. "Does that sound odd?"

Slowly, she shook her head.

"Well, it was like that, odd or not. Here was where I belonged."

Pensively, Amy stared across the water, wishing that she, too, belonged here.

Chapter 17

The following day Amy gobbled her breakfast and headed for the stables. Above the pungent smell of horses and manure she caught the clean scent of hay and saddle soap.

Shading her eyes with her hand, Amy peered about her, spying Matthew in a fenced-in meadow not too far from where she was standing. She ran toward him, seeing his face light up as she approached.

Ashamed of her exuberance, Amy shyly tore her gaze away from him, then caught her breath at the sight of the horse. She stepped up onto the bottom rail of the fence and tentatively touched the mane of Dawn's Light. Her eyes widened, and her hand flew to her own hair.

Matthew grinned at her. "Yes," he said softly. "It's as silky as your own." Reaching out, he placed her fingertips on the horse's neck. "Feel her coat. It's as smooth as satin."

Amy was delighted. She put her arms around the horse's neck and pressed her cheek against the soft muzzle. Dawn's Light nickered, swishing her tail in approval of the attention.

Jumping to the ground, Amy balled her small hands into loose fists. Watching Matthew closely, she held them before her, then drew them back to her chest.

Matthew's brow creased. "You want to ride her?" At her quick nod, he scratched his head. "I don't know, Amy. She's a bit spirited. Maybe you better wait awhile. Besides, I don't know if Edward would approve . . ." At her imploring look, his heart melted.

Matthew saddled Dawn's Light, giving Amy a little tip as he did so. "Always make sure that the cinches are secure and that the saddle fits snugly," he told her. "You might find it hard to believe, but some horses are actually smart enough to take a deep breath while they're being saddled. Then, when they exhale, the saddle doesn't fit as tightly as it should and can slip to the side while you're on it."

Giving a final check to see that everything was secure, Matthew helped Amy mount. At her expression of pure delight, he had to smile.

Settling herself, Amy looked down at him, seeing the suntanned skin against the white of her own flesh. He had nice hands. They were strong, but their strength was contained by gentleness that she could see when he handled the horses and could feel when he touched her.

Matthew handed her the reins, resisting the urge to tell her to be careful.

Her booted feet nudged the golden flanks of Dawn's

Light. The animal responded quickly, galloping along the track with long, flowing strides that seemed effortless.

As the horse and rider came into the back turn, Matthew cupped his hands over his mouth.

"Shorten up on the reins!" he shouted, fearing she was going too fast. But Amy paid him no mind, allowing the horse to run at its own speed. Plunging his hands into his pockets, Matthew watched intently. He was so engrossed, he didn't immediately notice Edward as he came to stand beside him.

Edward shook his head in wonder. "Truly, she's poetry in motion," he murmured, eyes fastened on Dawn's Light.

His own eyes never leaving the slim figure of Amy, Matthew nodded his agreement. Her hair had come undone and streamed behind her like a silvery veil. "She rides like a champion. . . ."

Caught by the tone of Matthew's voice, Edward glanced at him, eyes glinting in amusement. "Do I detect a spark of interest, Matthew? Offhand, I'd say it wasn't Dawn's Light that put that expression on your face."

Matthew's ears burned with the furious blush that swept up from his neck. "I meant no disrespect. . . ."

Edward laughed and clapped the young man on the shoulder. "I'm sure you didn't," he said kindly. "Come on—we'd better stop this particular horse race before they're both worn out."

That night, Matthew inspected all the stables, making certain that Paul and Robert had mucked them out and laid clean straw. He checked the water and feed levels, patted a few rumps, then headed back to the house.

Halfway there, he paused, looking up at the lighted window of Amy's bedroom.

Was it possible, he wondered, for a man simply to look at a woman . . . and know? Until now, he'd not believed such a thing possible. He'd made fun of his own brother Alexander, when he had declared himself to be in love with a woman whose name he didn't even know, a woman he'd caught a glimpse of one Sunday afternoon in Central Park. A woman he'd married four months later.

And Matthew remembered his mother's words to her eldest son, for she, too, had not believed. "You don't love that woman," she had scoffed to Alexander. "You're *in* love with her. There's a big difference: one lasts and the other doesn't. Being in love is like sitting on a picket fence. Sooner or later you're gonna fall off. And when you do, there's only two places to go: you fall into love, or out of it."

But apparently Alexander had fallen in the right direction, Matthew mused. After almost seven years, he and Roberta still had a happy marriage.

An owl hooted from the security of a leafy perch, breaking into his thoughts.

Matthew looked up at the window again. It was dark. No doubt she was fast asleep.

And that's where you should be, Matthew told himself, instead of dreaming up foolish notions to puzzle your brain.

The following days passed swiftly, too swiftly for Amy, who fervently wished for time to stand still. She rode every morning, spending the rest of the day trailing after Matthew, helping him with his chores when she could. She learned how to put vinegar in the water when washing tails or manes, the addition of which helped to untangle the hair. Matthew taught her how to bridle a horse—the saddles were too heavy for her to lift—and stressed the importance of fitting the bit properly so there would be no discomfort to the horse's mouth.

And what she liked best, what put her so much at ease in Matthew's company, was the fact that he talked *to* her, not up, down, or around. Mostly, he spoke of the one thing that interested him above all others: horses.

Amy listened in rapt attention as he told her how the Thoroughbreds came into being, explaining that their ancestry could be traced to one of three oriental sires: the Byerly Turk, the Darley Arabian, and the Godolphin Arabian.

Sea Foam, Matthew reported proudly, could trace his ancestry in an unbroken line back to Godolphin. Although Sea Foam was too old to race now, he was kept for breeding purposes.

"But he was great in his day," Matthew said. "He'd spend his heart to win." Matthew drew her attention to the only white marking, just above the heel, on Sea Foam's otherwise bay coat. "That," he informed her, "is a sure sign of speed. If an animal has heart and stamina as well, it has the makings of a champion. And right here, in Kentucky, is where more champions are born than in any other part of the world," he boasted unabashedly.

On the following Saturday afternoon, Amy met Matthew

by the lake. Having dragged a small boat out of the shed next to the cottage, he put it in the water. Edward and Bethany had gone to the races in Lexington. Matthew was happy that they hadn't taken Amy with them, unaware that Edward had indeed invited her, and that she had declined.

He helped her into the small boat, then rowed to the center of the lake. Watching Amy's expressive face as she eagerly took in her surroundings, Matthew thought to himself that he had never truly seen beauty before. All else was a blurred imitation of the perfection he was viewing now. He ached, although he wasn't quite sure why he did so. When he spoke, his words caught in his throat.

"You'll be leaving in a couple of days," he said. "I . . . I wish you didn't have to go."

Hearing the slightly altered tone in his voice, Amy turned to look at him.

They stared into each other's eyes for a moment suspended in eternity. The breeze sighed through the trees and rippled across the water, the gentle sounds washing over them both like a caress.

Impulsively, Matthew leaned forward, brushing his lips across her petal-smooth cheek. Drawing back, he stared at her with awe. He had never in his life felt this way; he felt shaken to the core of his being. The very place where his soul dwelled had been invaded by this slip of a girl.

Hearing his name called with sharp urgency, Matthew tore his gaze away from Amy and turned to see Paul, Henry's youngest son, beckoning frantically from the shore.

"The foal's comin'," the boy shouted, dancing with excitement.

Matthew broke into a wide grin as he picked up the oars. "Looks like we'll be in for a busy night," he speculated, rowing as fast as he could. Reaching land, he helped Amy out of the boat. "Would you like to come along?" he asked. At her enthusiastic nod, he squeezed her hand.

Edward held the reins loosely, allowing the horse to amble at its own pace. He glanced at Bethany, seated beside him in the buggy. Although her face was composed, looking pale and lovely in the moonlight, he easily remembered how she looked only a few hours ago: eyes sparkling with anticipation, cheeks flushed with excitement as Red Cloud strained toward the finish line.

"Did you enjoy yourself?" he asked softly.

"Oh, yes," she answered quickly, turning to look at him. "I've been to the races before, but this is the first time I . . . well, it's the first time I got so caught up in it." She gave a little laugh that tugged at his heart. "Then again, I've never been personally introduced to a horse that was competing." She paused, then asked, "Are you upset that Red Cloud didn't win?"

"Of course not. She came in third, and that's a very good showing for a maiden race. Besides, horses are like people. They have their good days and their bad ones. You can't expect them to perform at their peak all the time."

The breeze quickened, and Bethany removed her wide-brimmed hat, enjoying the refreshing coolness.

As if it were the most natural thing in the world, Edward put his arm around her. Bethany leaned against him, a small sigh of contentment escaping her lips with the motion. She felt relaxed and comfortable. The rhythmic clip-clop of the horse's hoofs seemed to be in harmony with the night sounds, an accompaniment rather than a discordant note.

The buggy rumbled up a hill, and Edward halted the vehicle at the top. Below them, the meadow of blue-grass rippled beneath a full moon like a silver lake, flowing into the ebony shadows of the trees that formed its bank.

"It's beautiful," Bethany whispered, drinking in the lovely sight. She tilted her head, hearing the sweet melody the breeze evoked from each blade of grass as it wended its way through the night air. "Do you hear it?" she said in the same hushed tone of voice.

Edward lowered his head. "Yes," he answered quietly. "Nature's own symphony, performed for an audience of two."

For a long moment they gazed into each other's eyes, caught in the magic of the moment. His lips were soft as they found her own, and Bethany did not draw away from him. Her reasons for being here suddenly seemed to have no substance. She did not know when her arms went around his neck, or when his kiss became infused with urgency, but Bethany was well aware of the hot flame of desire that sprang to life deep inside her.

When he finally drew away, Bethany could feel her body trembling, aching with a need she tried to repress but couldn't. Edward's arms were still around her, holding her tight, and Bethany rested her hand on his chest. Her body's response to this man was something she recognized, something she could deal with. But there was more, a deeper feeling that was beginning to alarm her.

Bethany closed her eyes, not wanting to examine this feeling too closely, not even willing to admit its existence. But it was there, teasing her mind, prodding her awareness for an acceptance she refused to give.

"What are you thinking about?"

Edward's quiet voice broke into her musings, and Bethany raised her head to look at him. What *had* she been thinking? she thought with a start. Quickly, she drew away from him, and her hand shook as she raised it to smooth her hair. Edward was staring at her, a perplexed frown creasing his brow, and her mind searched frantically for a reply.

"Bethany? Is anything wrong?" Concern deepened the lines in his forehead as he looked at her.

Wrong? Bethany felt the beginnings of an hysterical laugh gather in her throat, and she swallowed. Everything was wrong. Even her being here with this man was wrong. She stared at the handsome face before her, noting how the hard planes and angles were softened in the night shadows. An almost irresistible urge came over her, and Bethany wanted to fling her arms around him, to hold him close, to never let go.

Anxiety tightened her stomach. Was she beginning to care for him? Even in the privacy of her mind, Bethany wouldn't allow herself to use the word love.

"Bethany," he murmured softly, "if there is anything troubling you, I wish you would confide in me, trust me. . . ."

"There is nothing," she said too quickly, amber eyes clouding with the untruth. Trust him? Could she ever do that? she wondered miserably.

Clasping her hands in her lap, Bethany took a deep breath. "There's nothing wrong," she repeated, as calmly as she could. "Perhaps. . . ." She wet her lips. "Perhaps we should be getting back." Averting her face, she stared outside, refusing to meet his eye.

Edward continued to look at her for a moment longer, then sighed, realizing the futility of pressing her further. And even if he did, and she responded, that was not the way in which he wanted to receive her confidence. It must be open, freely given, or it was worthless.

They didn't speak for the rest of the journey, but to Bethany it seemed as though the silence resounded with questions for which she had no answer. By every accounting she should hate this man. Then why was she so attracted to him? Why did his slightest touch set her heart to racing?

It's only a physical attraction, she told herself firmly. But the words, even unspoken, rang hollow.

Edward's silence was just as charged with emotion as was Bethany's. They had shared a moment of togetherness, of oneness; but then she had withdrawn from him in a most deliberate way. It was as if she was fighting any feeling she might have for him. But why? What reason could she possibly have for doing something like that? It made no sense.

When they finally turned into the drive, Edward gave a sharp glance in the direction of the stables, seeing the lighted interior. Instead of driving up to the front door, he headed directly for the stables.

"What is it?" Bethany asked in quick concern, sensing a sudden tension in him. "Do you think that one of the horses is ill?"

"I don't know," Edward replied, helping her down from the buggy. "I hope not." He turned at the sound of Paul's voice.

"It's the foal, Mistah Edward," the boy said, still feeling a tingling excitement, and pleased to be the first one to impart the news.

Edward relaxed and gave a sigh of relief. "Has it been born yet?" he asked, dropping a hand on the thin shoulder of the lad.

"No, sir. But it's comin' any minute now." Paul confided this information with a seriousness that caused Edward to smile.

The boy trotted happily inside, Bethany and Edward following closely behind.

The mare was well along in her labor. Amy was sitting in the straw, her hand gentle and soothing as she petted the horse's neck. Edward removed his jacket and knelt beside Matthew, who was regarding the animal intensely. Finally, Matthew gave a delighted yelp. "It's time!"

Edward and Matthew both lent steady hands to guide the little foal into the world. Edward gave a sigh of relief, seeing the forefeet emerge first, knowing that the delivery would be a normal one. In only seconds the head appeared, and a short while later the newborn foal rested in the straw.

Matthew sponged the animal with care, then watched

as it tried to struggle to its feet. Spindly forefeet searched for firm ground and after a few false starts found it. The back end came up then, and at last the colt was upright, standing stiffly and somewhat unsure of himself.

Bethany brushed her cheeks, unaware of the tears that had fallen as she witnessed this miracle of life.

Having gotten to her feet, the mare now started to lick her baby, making certain he was clean enough to suit her own standards. With her nose, she nudged the colt toward her teats, where it began to suckle contentedly.

"Only minutes old and hungry as a bear!" Matthew exclaimed in delight.

With a display of excitement she couldn't contain, Amy crept toward the colt and pointed to its heels, looking at Matthew with shining eyes.

"Yes," he breathed with a wide grin. "He has the emblem, the mark of the champion."

Later, as she and Edward and Amy walked back to the house, Bethany said, "I'm glad I was here to see that."

Edward put his jacket around her shoulders. "I know what you mean," he murmured with a chuckle. "A newborn foal is one of the most enchanting things nature has to offer."

Inside, Bethany handed him his jacket and bid him goodnight as they parted. He stood at the foot of the stairs, watching her as she and Amy went upstairs. After a few thoughtful moments, he went to tell his father about the new foal.

Closing the door to her bedroom, Amy leaned against it and sighed deeply. She put a hand to her cheek, remembering the feel of Matthew's mouth on her flesh.

How she wished he'd been bolder and given her a real kiss. For the first time since she could remember, she wished she could talk . . . to Matthew.

Contrary to her mother's assumptions, Amy remembered that horrible day of her childhood very well. When she was younger, all her dreams had been nightmares. Even now, when she closed her eyes and thought about it, she could still see her brother Jason's slim body being lifted off the ground, skewered at the end of the bayonet. Her screams had been lost in the ribald laughter of the men in blue.

Terrified, she had run and run till her heart threatened to pop out of her mouth, plowing into brambles and thickets that tore at her clothes and ripped her skin. From a distance she had seen the flames as their house was set ablaze and saw, finally, the soldiers riding up the lane and disappearing from view. She had then raced back to her brother's side. There seemed to be so much blood that her eyes couldn't take it all in.

Her legs had weakened and she sank to the ground. The heat from the sun and the fire pressed down on her with a relentless ferocity, plunging her into a hot pool of light from which there was no escape.

That was as far as her memory took her. The next thing she remembered was being in bed, her mother leaning over her, a cool hand on her brow.

Although her mother had questioned her, Amy found the words frozen in her throat. From that time forward she had been unable to utter a sound.

But if she could talk, Amy wondered now, what would she say to Matthew? She had never in her adult life conversed with a man.

Crossing the room, she sat down at the dressing table and removed the ribbon from her hair. Picking up a brush, she applied it vigorously to the silvery cascade.

Then she paused, studying her face in the mirror. She put the brush down and leaned closer to her reflection, her eyes staring at her rose-tinted lips.

Matthew. . . .

Her mouth formed the name, but no sound emerged. With another sigh, Amy got up and undressed. After donning her nightgown, she extinguished the lamp and crawled between cool sheets, watching the pale shafts of moonlight that crept in through the window.

Desolation came over her, and she made no attempt to brush away the tears that coursed silently down her cheeks.

Chapter 18__

In her own room, Bethany removed her clothes, hanging them neatly in the armoire. In the yellow-tiled bathroom, she washed herself and then donned a pale-blue silk nightgown. When she returned to the bedroom, she sat down at the dressing table and brushed her hair until the dark and silky tresses gleamed with highlights. It was well after eleven o'clock, but she wasn't at all tired. Sleep was out of the question, at least for a while.

Still feeling the excitement of the evening, she put on a satin peignoir. Then, crossing the room, she went to sit before the fire, which Henry had thoughtfully prepared against the evening's chill.

Settling herself comfortably, Bethany tucked her legs under her, propped the cushions to support her back, and gave a sigh of contentment. She couldn't remember a day she had so thoroughly enjoyed as this one.

As soon as they had finished breakfast she and

Edward had left Glencoe. Although not as impressive as Churchill Downs in Louisville, the track at Lexington was more than adequate.

With a soft smile, Bethany now turned her head and stared into the flames, thinking of the little foal, seeing again in her mind's eye the hesitant first steps toward a new life.

Bethany was still sitting there when she heard a soft knock on her door some ten minutes later.

"Come in," she called, thinking it might be Amy.

The door opened and Edward entered, filling the room with his presence. He held up a decanter and two brandy glasses.

"Will you help me celebrate the new addition to our family?"

She laughed. "Yes, of course."

Edward threw the sofa pillows on the floor before the fire, patting one of them as an invitation for her to join him. Filling the glasses with brandy, he handed one to her as she came to sit beside him.

"To Celtic Warrior," he toasted. "May he be as fleet-footed as Mercury."

He touched his glass to hers, and the fine crystal rang with a sweet-toned clarity. Leaning on an elbow, he studied her face, now awash with a golden glow in the soft, flickering light of the fire. Unbound, her ebony hair fell in shining curls that seemed to beg his hands to explore its softness.

"Tell me about yourself," he said quietly. "I know next to nothing about you."

"There's not much to tell," Bethany said evasively as she sipped the brandy.

"You have no past?" he teased. "A husband that you might have forgotten to mention?"

Her laughter was pleasant to his ear. "No, nothing like that. No husbands . . . and no family," she added quietly, her manner turning subdued. She swirled the liquid in her glass, watching the play of color that changed from gold to deep red in the firelight. She took another sip.

Edward stared at her for a long moment in silence. There was a mystery about this woman that he found both intriguing and disquieting. At times he was certain she was being less than honest with him. Every time he brought up the subject of her past, she managed to avoid giving him a direct answer.

Placing a hand on her arm, he bent toward her. "You know, I suddenly find myself not caring about your past. Only your present—and your future." Giving in to temptation, he ran his fingers through her thick, soft hair. "It's just past your shoulders," he murmured.

Bethany inclined her head. "What did you say?"

"Your hair," he whispered. "I wondered how long it would be."

She giggled, feeling warm and relaxed. "You could have asked. I would have told you."

"There are some things a man likes to find out for himself. . . ."

Turning to look at him, Bethany saw the tenderness in the blue flame of his eyes and could not help but respond to it. When he took the glass from her hand she made no protest. Lifting her head slightly, Bethany's lips met his as she moved further into the embrace of his arms. His tongue sought the satin softness of her mouth, and Bethany found herself consumed by the same fire that had possessed her when last they kissed.

Drawing away, Edward gently pushed her back on the cushions, his hands undoing buttons and ribbons. Bethany slipped out of her peignoir, then raised her arms as he lifted her nightgown over her head. Quickly, he removed his own clothing.

Seeing him unclothed simply verified what Bethany already knew. His muscular frame was superbly made: hips narrow, abdomen flat and hard. Resting back on the pillows she saw his eyes take in the perfection of her body.

"God, you're beautiful," he murmured with a catch in his voice. His hands traced the length of her as if he wanted to memorize every inch of her. Bending forward, he nuzzled the softness of her breast, inhaling the clean scent she exuded.

Capturing a nipple between his lips, he coaxed it to tautness. Bethany gave a soft moan as his touch became more insistent, creating a need she could no longer deny. Her breath quickened to a pant, and her heart began to beat wildly as his mouth moved down her quivering abdomen and found her most secret place. She let out a whimpering cry, her fingers weaving through his golden hair.

Unhurriedly, Edward's tongue teased her body until she felt mad with desire.

Feeling her flesh trembling beneath his touch, Edward eased himself on top of her. Entering her moist warmth, he fought for control, moving slowly inside her: long, fluid strokes that evoked a moan of pleasure from her. She began to move her hips with increasing urgency, and Edward quickened his thrusts. Her nails raked his back as she arched her body to meet his demanding pace.

Bethany's world spun inward until she was conscious of nothing but the sweet hardness that filled her so completely. She heard a low cry and knew it had come from her throat. Then, when she thought she could bear no more, she shuddered with a rapturous release that seemed to reach every nerve she possessed. Edward groaned and gripped her tighter as his body convulsed, and he collapsed against her, breathing deeply.

When his heart had ceased its pounding and slowed to its normal rate, Edward again gathered her in his arms. With her head pillowed on the golden hair of his chest, the blazing fire warming them both, Bethany felt a great and satisfying lassitude envelop her as she closed her eyes.

Some minutes later, hearing her deep and even breathing, Edward pressed his lips to the silky black tresses. Carefully then, so as not to awaken her, he picked her up and put her in bed, tucking the covers snugly about her.

He dressed, then stood there, looking down at her sleeping form, seeing the ebony curls splayed against snowy white sheets. She was beautiful beyond comparison. Bending forward, he brushed the delicate curve of her cheek with his lips, then quietly left the room.

The fire burned low, the moon rose and waned in its journey across the night sky, and Bethany stirred, in the grip of a dream.

She murmured and gave a small gasp, seeing the figure of her father standing some distance away. With a cry of joy, she began to run toward him, arms outstretched.

But her father stood very still, arms folded across his chest, visage stern and forbidding. Black eyes viewed her in a condemning manner from beneath flattened brows.

Still running, Bethany came to an abrupt halt as her father's voice came to her through the mists of time.

"Hammond cheated," he intoned, staring at her. "I know he did, but I don't know how...."

Bethany sat bolt upright in bed, wide awake now, heart slamming against her ribcage, breath caught in her throat. Her skin felt clammy and cold, and she ran a trembling hand through perspiration-dampened hair.

The words echoed with frightening finality through the corridors of her mind. She shivered and rubbed her bare arms. In the darkness of her room, the dream seemed very real.

Tears welled in her eyes and hung in droplets on her lashes. Burying her head in her pillow, Bethany's sobs seemed wrenched from the deepest part of her.

It was a long time before she could fall asleep again.

Chapter 19

Warm sunlight poured in through parted draperies, touched Bethany's face and gently prodded her to wakefulness. Opening her eyes, she made no immediate move to get up, feeling emotionally and physically drained.

Although she didn't want to, Bethany remembered the dream vividly; it depressed her with its implications.

With a deep sigh, she finally swung her long legs over the side of the bed, only then becoming aware that she was still naked. In a hasty movement, cheeks aflame as she recalled last night's activity, Bethany got to her feet, busying herself with washing and dressing, refusing to think of anything else for the time being.

Wearing a morning gown of turquoise chiffon, her hair swept back into a soft chignon, Bethany descended the stairs and entered the dining room a while later, relieved to learn that Edward had already eaten and that he and Amy had gone to the stables to check on the new foal.

Alone at the table, Bethany ate the substantial breakfast put before her by Henry, chewing and swallowing without making note of what she was eating. She had prayed for strength, but her prayers had gone unanswered. Declining a second cup of coffee, she went outside, feeling the need to be alone, knowing that sooner or later she would have to confront her troublesome thoughts.

The day was mild, and no clouds marred the morning sky. Bethany walked aimlessly, finally halting by the lake. She was too restless to sit down, so she just stood there looking at the expanse of blue water. The late morning air was filled with the sound of chirping birds, punctuated by the occasional quacking of the ducks.

Bright sunlight seemed to probe relentlessly at Bethany's conscience. Memory cut sharp and clear, defying her to ignore its existence

She was appalled at what she had allowed to happen the night before. Her face flamed when she thought of her eager responses to the man she had sworn vengeance against. Never had she thought herself capable of such passion as he had aroused within her. Bethany thought there must be a core of wantonness inside her that Edward had discovered, one she never knew existed.

It must have been the brandy, she decided, promising herself to avoid that fiery liquid in the future.

But was it the brandy?

Oh, God! She gave a soft moan, pressing a hand to her forehead. She could not be in love with this man, could she? The idea was intolerable; . . . she wouldn't let it happen!

Moving toward a broad oak, Bethany leaned against it as if she were too weak to stand up.

And what would her father have thought if he had known what had taken place last night? She winced, her mind trying to skirt the issue without success. She had made a promise to his memory, one she had not only failed to keep, but one which she had betrayed.

Hearing the sound of horse's hoofs just then, Bethany turned, almost relieved to see Colin Thatcher riding in her direction, welcoming the interruption of her dismaying thoughts. She watched as he swung out of the saddle, a broad smile on his face.

Colin had enjoyed his stay at The Willows in spite of himself. He and Lydia had gone bicycling, riding, and to the races. They had also played tennis, a sport of which Colin was not too fond. He'd had no idea that Lydia was so deadly with a racquet. The six grandchildren of Samuel Madison had gotten on his nerves, but he and Lydia had been gone for most of the day, and the children, thankfully, were barred from the dinner table, having their meals served to them at an earlier hour than the adults.

The evenings, however, had been a crashing bore. When Lydia had invited him to her home, he had hoped they might share a few nights of intimacy; such had not been the case. He and Lydia had played endless games of backgammon, while her sister-in-law Margaret had offered endless songs on the piano. Colin had been unable to decide which was worse: Margaret's playing or her singing. Both had set his teeth on edge. No one else seemed to mind, though; certainly not Eunice, who had sat in her chair, knitting, her foot tapping in time to the music. Samuel, more often than not, had fallen asleep on the sofa, the newspaper on his chest rising and falling with his snoring breaths. And as for Jeffery, he only smiled with a husband's pride and gently applauded each number.

Having tethered his horse to a branch of a tree, Colin came toward Bethany.

"Are you enjoying your stay at Glencoe?" he asked, suddenly realizing how much he had missed her. The urge to take her in his arms was so strong he could barely contain himself. Pausing before her, he regarded her expectantly, hoping to find a welcome in her amber eyes, a sign that would tell him that she was pleased to see him. All he saw was a pleasant but impartial expression on her lovely face.

"It's a beautiful place," Bethany replied noncommittally, then tilted her head to look up at him. "What are you doing here?"

His shoulders moved beneath his brown jacket. "I came to remind you that the *Nola Star* is sailing tomorrow." Although he spoke lightly, his eyes narrowed at her continued preoccupation. He wasn't even certain that she had heard what he said. "You will be aboard, won't you?"

"Ah . . . yes. Yes, I'll be there," she murmured, averting her face.

Colin peered closely, mouth compressed to a flat line. He sensed a conflict within her, and it disturbed him. "What is it? Are you weakening?" he demanded. His dark eyes glittered with a sudden surge of anger as he grabbed hold of her.

"I'm not weakening!" She pulled her arm away.

"It appears to me you are," he insisted, his voice taking on a brittle quality. "Have you forgotten how you came to me, groveling for help . . ."

Drawing a sharp breath, Bethany turned to stare at him, twin spots of angry color splashed across her cheeks. "I do not grovel, Colin!" she said in a sharp voice. "How dare you speak to me like that!"

"I'm sorry." The apology came quickly. His hand moved in a vague gesture, and his attitude immediately softened. "It's just that I don't want to see you fall under the spell of the Bayou Fox."

"I'm not under the spell of any man," she retorted in the same tone. "Not even you, Colin—though you'd like to think so."

Presenting her back to him, Bethany's gaze sought the calm surface of the lake. She stared at a cluster of cornflowers on the bank, their blossoms as blue as the water.

He stared at her a moment, then said, "I thought we had an understanding." Placing his hands on her shoulders, he caressed the soft roundness. This contact made his body tense with the sudden surge of desire that swept over him. Never in his life had he wanted to possess a woman as much as he did this one. When Colin spoke again, his voice was choked with emotion. "My God, Bethany, you must know I'm in love with you." In a quick movement, he spun her around, crushing her to him, no longer able to control himself.

Bethany was so surprised that for a moment she didn't react. She remained passive in his arms, feeling his mouth against hers. When he tried to part her lips with his tongue, she attempted to twist away, but he was holding her in a grip so tight she couldn't move. She felt the quickening throb of his heartbeat against her breast and the distinct outline of his erection as he pressed into her.

There was no answering response in her own body, and the only emotion Bethany could summon was anger. Feeling his hands cup her buttocks, she reached back and dug her nails into his wrist.

With a moan, Colin removed his lips from hers and buried them in the soft hollow of her throat.

"Colin!" she exclaimed through clenched teeth. His grip was so tight, her breasts were flattened against his chest, and she was finding it difficult to breathe.

Turning her head away from him, Bethany stiffened. At the sound of her sharply drawn breath Colin at last drew back, staring into her wide eyes with a puzzled look on his flushed face. Following her glance, he saw Edward standing a few feet away from them.

Edward's eyes were like the sea: bottomless, unfathomable. He ignored Colin as he stared at Bethany, his face tight with fury.

"Forgive the intrusion," he said coldly. "If I'd known you were otherwise occupied, I'd have asked Rissa to delay dinner."

Although he addressed Bethany, Colin gave him a nasty smile. "You certainly have a knack for putting in an appearance at the most awkward times, Hammond." He released Bethany and was about to say more. Instead, he took a step back as he viewed the black look on Edward's face. Colin then took a quick glance at Bethany, but he was uncertain as to what he was seeing.

Her face had paled, but her eyes were bright as she stared at Edward.

Giving Bethany a stony look, Edward turned on his heel and strode away without a backward glance, driven by an anger he could not conceal.

Bethany glared at Colin, her hands clenched at her sides. He had mounted his horse and sat there, a triumphant smile curving his lips as he watched Edward's receding figure.

"Damn you, Colin," she shouted and his gaze swung toward her. "If you ever do anything like this again, I'll take a horsewhip to you!"

Reaching down, Colin touched her cheek with his fingertips. The smile had vanished and his eyes were serious. "I love you, Bethany," he said softly. "I swear to you, I've never felt this way about a woman before "

Bethany stepped back to where he couldn't reach her. "Colin . . ." She sighed deeply and shook her head. "There can be nothing between us. I've told you that before."

His eyes grew hooded as he picked up the reins. "Time will tell, Bethany," he said quietly. "I'm not a man who gives up easily." Giving her a mock salute, he spurred the horse forward.

Pivoting sharply, Bethany walked away.

Entering the house a few minutes later, she went into the front parlor, halting abruptly at the sight of Edward. He was standing by the window, hands clasped behind him, the dark look still on his handsome face. As he came toward her, he spoke in a harsh voice that she had never heard him use before.

"Has Colin made love to you?" The anger he felt at

the assumption took Edward totally by surprise. Even the incident with Lydia hadn't provoked the murderous rage that now shook him.

Giving a small gasp, Bethany flushed and turned away. "I don't think that's any of your business. . . ."

"I take it you're not going to answer my question?" he muttered in a savage undertone.

Raising her chin, Bethany clenched her hands at her waist and looked him in the eye. "I see no need for you to know the intimate details of my life," she snapped, perversely glad to see the flash of pain that swept across his face.

Taking a step forward, Edward grabbed her upper arm, holding it painfully tight. "He did, didn't he?" His mouth twisted into a grim line, and dark color flooded into his face. "I was not the first, I know that!"

She wrenched away. "And was I your first woman?" she demanded, nostrils flaring in indignation. "Would you care to give me an accounting of how many women you've made love to?"

His eyes narrowed, and he headed for the door, where he turned to look at her. "No wonder you don't want to discuss your past," he growled. "Though I imagine it would make quite an interesting story."

Anger simmered, then exploded within her. How dare he look at her like that! As if she were no better than a prostitute!

"You want everything your own way, don't you!" she blurted out, dismayed to hear the shrillness in her voice. "People like you just take whatever they want and give no thought to whatever destruction they leave behind!"

A deep frown creased his brow, and he stood very still. "People like me? What the devil are you talking about?"

"I know you for what you are." Her chin jutted out. "A scoundrel of the worst sort!"

Edward was staring at her, his eyes no longer mocking. Their blue depths smoldered, and a muscle pulsed angrily in his jaw. "It's fortunate we're leaving tomorrow," he stated tersely. "I wouldn't want to offend you by extending the hospitality of this house to you for any greater length of time."

Bethany's eyes flashed, resentful of the forceful assurance she was seeing. She longed to accuse him of what she knew he had done. With effort, she bit back the words. She would stand no chance at all if he knew she even suspected him of cheating.

She quickened her steps and walked from the room, brushing past Edward without looking at him, more determined than ever to do what she had set out to do.

Running up the stairs, Bethany headed for her room, eyes blinded by tears she could not control and would not allow him to see. When she closed the door, she buried her face in her hands and wept.

That night, Edward stood in his darkened room, gazing out the window. The breeze had quickened, and the moon was hidden behind a veil of clouds.

He clenched his hands, intensely aware that Bethany was just down the hall, a few steps away. Despite his anger—and it was acute—his desire for her was suffocating.

Running an agitated hand through his golden hair, Edward tried to analyze his feelings. He thought he had been in love with Lydia. Yet this . . . emotion that now had such a grip on him was nothing at all like that. Angered and disgusted by Lydia's wanton behavior, he had turned from her without a backward glance. Even at the height of his infatuation for her, when she was out of sight she was literally out of his mind. Certainly he had never lost a night's sleep over her.

So, if that had been love, what the hell was this?

The next morning, while Henry loaded the luggage into the carriage, Edward went to his father to say good-bye. Cyrus viewed him with just as much disapproval as he always did on these occasions.

After listening to his father's usual comments, Edward passed a weary hand across his forehead. "I'm doing my best, you know that," he murmured.

"I know, I know." Edward didn't see the fierce pride in his father's eyes. "It's been hard on you. Nobody's going to deny that, least of all me. But we're horse people, damn it! Not gamblers." He pounded the quilt in an effort to emphasize that point.

"There's no easier way to make fast money," Edward retorted, sounding tired.

Cyrus noticed the change in his son's voice and suspected that Edward had spent a sleepless night. "And if you lose," he finally said, deciding not to comment on his observation, "what then?"

"I don't lose," Edward replied curtly. "Not substantially, anyway. When the cards turn cold, I leave."

Cyrus had no answer, so he changed his tactics. "And your mother? Have you ever thought of what grief you would have caused her?"

For the first time since he had come into the room, Edward smiled at his father. "Mother was a practical woman, Pa. Even you can't deny that. A man does what he has to do. She taught me that."

Before his father could offer any further protest, Edward gave a hasty farewell and quickly went outside. Bethany and Amy were already in the carriage. Without speaking, Edward took his seat and stared off into space.

Standing within the relative seclusion of the shed row, Matthew watched as the carriage bearing Edward, Bethany, and Amy sped down the drive.

He saw Amy turn and knew she was looking for him, but he stepped back so she could not see him.

Although he knew he should have, he hadn't been able to bring himself to say good-bye. His sense of loss was a lead weight, causing his broad shoulders to slump. It was foolish of him to think a beautiful girl like Amy could care for him, a nobody. Wasn't it? But he'd never know for sure unless he saw her again and told her how he felt. He wondered if he'd ever see her again. He *had* to see her again!

Turning, he glanced at the meadow where Sea Foam was placidly grazing. The stallion could easily overtake the carriage. But then what? He couldn't possibly declare himself in front of Edward and Bethany.

Slamming the palm of his hand on the hard surface of the wooden stall, Matthew swore softly; then his mouth firmed. When the *Nola Star* returned to Louisville, Matthew promised himself he'd be there.

The journey to Louisville was made in silence, painful and uncomfortable for everyone but Amy, who was lost in her own thoughts. Matthew hadn't said good-bye. Each roll of the carriage wheels echoed the words, imprinting them in her mind, searing them into her heart. Her eyes remained dry, however, for she knew that even tears wouldn't ease the aching loneliness she now felt.

Amy viewed her gloved hands folded in her lap. Matthew's attentions had been kind, she realized; nothing more. But she, foolish girl that she was, had lost her heart. Was this love? If so, it was not the pleasant sensation she had thought it would be.

She raised her head, eyes wide as a thought struck. What if there were someone else! Her breath caught in her throat. Why hadn't she thought of that before? She had automatically assumed that Matthew was unattached, but perhaps he had a sweetheart. A betrothed? Her mind shied away from that possibility.

Oh, Matthew, she thought, dismay paling her cheeks. *Please don't have anyone else. . . .*

It was late afternoon by the time Henry halted the carriage at the wharf.

Alighting, Edward assisted Bethany and Amy as they got out.

"Henry will see to it that your luggage is put on board," Edward said to Bethany, his face inscrutable.

Taking Amy's arm, he turned and walked away, heading for the gangway, leaving Bethany standing there to fend for herself. Her mouth gaped at this less than gallant gesture. Then, her jaw set, Bethany wended her way through the roustabouts, defiantly staring at the men as they grinned and leered at her.

Leaning on the railing of the texas deck, Colin had

watched the little scenario with a half smile on his attractive face. Trouble in paradise? Well, if so, that would suit his purposes just fine. From the look of Bethany's stormy countenance, it appeared that her unwilling attraction for the Bayou Fox was finally at an end.

That evening, as Bethany seated herself next to Colin, she wondered whether she would be able to concentrate. The noise of ice against glass, the scraping of chairs, an occasional cough, sounding loud over the voices of those gathered in the Grand Saloon—all punctuated the beginning of the evening's games.

Just after ten o'clock, Edward entered the room and sat at a table not far away. This was accomplished, Bethany noticed with some annoyance, without so much as a glance in her direction. A moment later, she heard him laugh heartily at a comment made by one of his companions, and the sound seemed to echo through her mind long after it had ceased.

"Bethany!"

She started at Colin's voice, saw his frown, and gave him a blank stare.

He motioned to the cards in front of her. "It's your deal!"

"Oh, yes," she murmured, trying to summon a smile. "Sorry. . . ."

For the next hour, Bethany played each hand as best she could, trying to keep her attention from wandering, but she was acutely aware that Edward was nearby. Although she glanced at him from time to time, he never once looked in her direction. She could not have been in the room for all the attention he bestowed upon her. Her anger rose and ebbed at this display of icy reserve. Bethany tried to will him to look at her so that she could turn away, but he never gave her the opportunity.

Then, suddenly, he did, and her resolve melted as though it had never existed. If her life depended on it, Bethany doubted she could even move. The gaze he leveled at her was contemplative, brooding, and devastating in its intensity. She paled and once again found herself caught by that blue flame that always seemed to hold her captive.

It was Edward who finally looked away.

Bleakly, Bethany forced her attention back to the cards in her hand, seeing only meaningless numbers and pictures on rectangular pieces of cardboard.

At last the tedious evening came to an end.

"It appears we've been outclassed, gentlemen," Colin said cheerfully to the other men at the table, and viewing the pile of money in front of her, Bethany wondered dully how she had managed to win when she had been playing so absentmindedly.

After complimenting her on how well she had played, Colin ambled over to the bar for his usual late-night drink. Turning, Bethany noticed that Edward had already left the room. Blinking her eyes against the hazy smoke, she got up and went out on deck. Only the beacon lights on the river alleviated the dark, for there was no moon.

She walked aimlessly, tightening her shawl against the night air. Even though it was chilly, it felt clean and fresh after the close confines of the Grand Saloon with its rank atmosphere of alcohol and smoke.

Seeing the glow of a lighted cigar tip, Bethany came

to an abrupt halt, then drew her breath as she saw Edward.

"Oh," she murmured, caught off guard. "I didn't know you were out here."

"Didn't you?" he drawled laconically.

"Of course I didn't!" she bristled, not wanting him to think she'd come looking for him. She waited a moment, but he neither spoke nor moved. He could have been a statue for all the animation he displayed. Bethany bit her lip and regarded the tips of her shoes. "I . . . never got a chance to thank you for . . . well, for showing me such a nice time." Again she waited, and again there was no response. "I did enjoy my visit to Glencoe, in spite of . . ." She broke off, feeling helpless.

Edward continued to observe her in silence for a moment longer. Bethany couldn't see his face clearly, but she easily heard the sardonic amusement that altered his voice when he finally did speak.

"Yes. It was . . . nice, wasn't it?" Edward's jaw worked, and he forcibly tore his gaze away from her, not daring to notice the dark cloud of her hair, the fullness of her breasts, the sweet mouth that tempted him beyond endurance.

Another awkward silence fell, then Edward said curtly, "You'd better go back inside. I'm sure Colin is waiting for you."

Her chin rose. "Colin has no say in what I do!" she retorted stiffly.

A short laugh adequately conveyed his disbelief, but he made no comment that would contradict her.

Without wanting to, Bethany found herself thinking of that night in her room. So clear and sharp were her memories it was as if she could still feel that strong hard body pressed against her own, still feel the texture of his tanned skin as she caressed those broad shoulders with the palms of her hands. . . .

"Edward . . . I . . ." A sudden longing prodded her, causing her words to emerge in a breathless whisper as it crested into a wave of desire that took her completely by surprise. It was so unexpected that she felt defenseless beneath its shattering impact.

Hearing the altered tone of her voice, Edward turned to look at her, his expression effectively hidden in the darkness. A great weakness came over Bethany. For one crazy moment she wanted to throw herself into his arms, to yield to the aching need that washed over her like a molten fire. Reason fled, and in its place only feeling remained.

Give it up! her mind cried, trying to seduce her from her goal. *It's over and done with. It doesn't matter anymore. What you're trying to do will not bring back your father.*

She narrowed her eyes, trying to pierce the dimness that separated them. Edward's nearness drew her like a magnet. Bethany couldn't help herself as she moved closer to him.

"You're not happy with one man, are you, Bethany?"

She went rigid with his words, feeling as though she had been plunged into an icy stream.

"Women like you never are," he added bitterly.

The cigar sailed over the railing in a shimmering orange arc to be consumed in the black water. Edward gave her one more of those unfathomable looks, then strode away.

Bethany compressed her lips to muffle a strangled sob, then swallowed against the tightness in her throat. *Damn you!* she thought, clenching her hands. But her anger turned inward at the realization that she had permitted her emotions to get the better of logic. She must have truly lost her senses! she thought, shocked by what she had almost done.

White-lipped, Bethany went back inside. So upset was she that she never even noticed Colin coming toward her.

"Bethany! I thought you'd gone up already," he said as they both headed up the stairs.

"I went outside for a breath of air," she replied tersely, striving for composure that, right now, seemed beyond her.

He raised an eye-brow. "It seems to have left you a bit ill-tempered," he commented with a laugh. Then he added, "I saw Edward storming upstairs a few minutes ago. He looked more than cantankerous and about took my head off when I spoke to him." Colin regarded her speculatively, suddenly wondering whether there was a connection between Edward's dark mood and Bethany's obvious agitation. But he had an idea she wouldn't tell him, so he didn't ask.

They had reached her door. Colin touched her arm and lowered his voice.

"Bethany, I think it's about time you let me set up a game between you and Edward..."

"I don't want to discuss that now!" Removing the key from her reticule, Bethany went to put it into the lock, but her hand was shaking so badly that she had to make several stabs at it before she could insert it properly.

Colin ran a hand through his hair and sighed. "If you have doubts that you can beat him, I told you there are ways to make certain—" He broke off at the sight of her face, not at all sure she wasn't about to strike him.

"Don't ever mention that to me again, Colin!"

"All right, all right," he said swiftly, in an attempt to pacify her.

Plunging his hands in his pockets, Colin stood there looking forlorn, and indeed felt it. Although she had made no further reference to it, he knew she still had not forgiven him for the passionate embrace he had forced upon her. But she would, he reasoned, trying to make himself believe that. When Bethany came to realize just how much he cared, she would have to forgive him.

Bethany was still staring at him with blazing eyes. "I mean what I say!"

"It's only your welfare I'm thinking of. . . ." Colin laced his voice with grievance and added a dollop of reproof, hoping to spark at least a hint of contrition in those amber eyes.

Although still tense, Bethany made a conscious effort to soften her attitude. She realized she was being unduly snappish with Colin, not so much because of what he had just now said to her, but because of what had happened with Edward a few minutes ago. Although she really did wish he would refrain from harping on that absurd notion of his. Viewing his hang-dog expression, she said, "Colin, it may be that you just don't know me very well. I could take no pride at all in winning like that. The victory would be meaningless."

"I understand," he murmured, sounding resigned. "But will you at least let me make arrangements for the game?" He took a step closer and appeared about to reach for her.

"We'll talk about it in the morning. Good night, Colin." Bethany pushed the door closed before he could speak again.

Crossing the room, she lit the gas lamp, dispelling shadows that danced on the wall. Then she headed for the porcelain ewer and hastily splashed cold water on her face. Her whole body was trembling with outrage, with embarrassment, . . . and with a yearning she tried very hard to ignore.

In an effort to calm the thudding beat of her heart, Bethany sat down on the edge of the bed, taking a deep breath as she did so. With the back of her hand, she brushed her cheeks, attributing their dampness to the remaining clinging drops of water.

Finding herself too restless to sit still, Bethany pushed herself up and went to the window. She stared outside, seeing only a pool of blackness . . . and her own reflection superimposed on the glass. To her amazement, she looked like a scared, hurt little girl. Where was the poised, self-assured young woman she knew herself to be?

Taking a step back, Bethany frowned at the image she saw, welcoming the hard knot of determination that formed within her. Edward Hammond had destroyed her father, but she'd be damned if she would allow him to do the same to her!

Chapter 20

Her paddle wheels frothing the muddy water, the _Nola Star_ moved away from the wharf at Baton Rouge and headed downriver. From here on they would be in the sugar region.

Occasionally the banks of the river opened onto small tributaries: murky swamps inhabited by alligators, reptiles, and deadly patches of quicksand.

The weather was growing warmer now, the sun pouring down with a suggestion of tropical intensity. But to the south, ominous gray clouds were gathering, giving sullen notice of the impending storm that would arrive before the day was over.

Bethany left her stateroom, intending to go out on deck, where she was to meet Colin. She had gone only a few steps when she found her way barred by a young and handsome Creole named Leon Clere. He was dressed flamboyantly in a suit of peach satin and carried a walking stick and soft, brown kid gloves.

White teeth flashed at her with his broad smile. "You are Miss Kincaid, are you not?" His dark eyes dropped to her breasts in an insinuating manner.

"I am," Bethany replied, frowning at him. She had seen the man in various places around the boat in the last few days. Each time her gaze happened to land on him, she found him staring intently at her. She tried to move around him, but he took a step to the side, again barring her way.

"I saw you in the Grand Saloon last night." He touched her cheek, caressing it with his fingertips, and appeared amused when she jerked her head back. "But then, such beauty as yours is not to be missed, whatever the setting."

Bethany's frown deepened. "Will you please let me pass!"

Leon didn't move. He knew Bethany was traveling with Colin Thatcher; he also knew she wasn't married. But then, a man didn't marry a woman like this; he made love to her. Leon thought he would very much like to have that opportunity.

"Would you do me the honor of joining me at my table for supper this evening?" he asked softly.

Supper indeed! Bethany thought, noting the lustful way he was leering at her.

"Certainly not! Now will you please get out of my way!"

He gave a low chuckle and leaned on his walking stick. "Am I to understand that you reserve your charms for only one man?" He raised a brow and stared at her in a suggestive manner.

Behind Bethany, a door opened and Edward stepped

into the corridor. It took him only a few steps to
position himself between Bethany and Leon Clere.

"Perhaps you didn't hear the lady ask you to move
out of her way!" he said in a sharp voice.

Clere's brows met over the bridge of his nose as he
stared up into Edward's face. He had played poker with
Edward two nights before and had lost heavily. The
sting of losing was well remembered by Leon, and he
gave Edward a look that clearly conveyed his scorn.

"On your way!" Edward said, his jaw tightening at
the other man's hesitation.

His face flushing with quick anger, Leon raised his
glove, and Edward's mouth quirked into a smile that
bore no trace of humor.

"I wouldn't if I were you," he said in a soft voice
laced with menace. "If you do, the choice of weapons
will be mine. And it will not be pistols or swords."
Taking a step closer to the Creole, Edward raised a
massive fist, pausing only inches from Leon's aristocratic nose. "It will be these. . . ."

Leon's nostrils grew pinched and white. Edward was
standing so close that Leon had to raise his head to look
him in the eye. "Like all Americans, you are a barbar-
ian!" he exclaimed heatedly. "I would not soil my
hands on the likes of you." Turning, he walked stiffly
toward the stairs.

Bethany was about to offer a tentative smile of
gratitude, but the look on Edward's angular face precluded her from doing so. If he was amused, she saw
no signs of it.

"I suggest you do not wander about the halls

unescorted," he said curtly. "It can lead to unpleasant situations."

With that, he turned and walked away. Leaving her standing there alone. And unescorted.

Bethany blinked against the hot sting of furious tears. Once she had thought Edward Hammond to be a scoundrel. Now she could think of several other names that would fit him very well, names that no lady would permit herself to utter.

Edward continued downstairs, heading for the Grand Saloon, where he sat down at an empty table and stared moodily out the window.

What the bloody hell was he doing here on this boat, knowing Bethany would be on it? He should have stayed home this trip. Just looking at her created a painful ache in his loins.

A steward appeared, but Edward waved him away.

And, like it or not, she was still traveling with Colin. Bethany hadn't answered his question, and it still tormented him. Was Colin her lover? Had he ever been? The thought made him see red.

Turning in his chair, Edward barked at the steward to bring him a drink after all. It was early in the day, but so what?

He could still see those incredible eyes regarding him only minutes ago. She had seemed surprised by his interference. Amused? Yes, he had seen the beginnings of a smile on those lovely lips.

Leon Clere was, after all, wealthy, attractive, and unmarried. Perhaps she had even been annoyed by his interference.

Of course she was. A woman like that could take care of herself. An innocent she was not!

He had half a mind to get off at the next landing. Yes, maybe he would do just that. Get on another boat, get as far away as he could from Bethany Kincaid.

The steward placed his drink in front of him and was treated to a black scowl that caused him to retreat hastily.

A while later, walking along the texas deck beside Colin, Bethany was aware of the heavy and distinct scent of magnolias. She concentrated on the pleasant aroma, not wanting to think about Edward and not wanting to listen to Colin's voice. She was still a bit annoyed with him; yet when she had viewed the incident dispassionately, the only thing she could accuse Colin of was stealing a kiss and professing his love for her. Hardly a crime in any sense of the word, though God knew she didn't want either from him.

Glancing at the shore, Bethany noted that the foliage was changing, the green now interspersed with the bright orange of palmettos. Here and there, she could see magnificent manor houses, fronted by emerald lawns that provided a smooth carpet for strutting peacocks spreading tails that were exotic fans of color.

"I thought you were a woman of principle, my dear Bethany," Colin was saying, more than a hint of petulance in his voice, prompted by her unresponsive manner. He tugged at his silk cravat as if it were suddenly too tight.

For the past four days now he had been trying to convince Bethany that it was time she put her plan into action, but she had been resisting him. Although she played cards every night, she refused to sit at the same table with Edward.

Colin turned to look at her, but Bethany's face was partially hidden beneath the lacy parasol she was carrying. He tried not to think about how lovely she looked. Her fine lawn dress was striped in brown and yellow, the darts on the bodice making her waist appear even slimmer than it was. A pert bustle swayed with each step she took.

Knowing Bethany as he did, Colin was certain she wasn't moving in that provocative way deliberately. Nevertheless, he kept glancing at it time and again, even though he tried to resist the temptation.

He frowned and directed his gaze elsewhere. "When you first approached me—and I would remind you that it was you who came to me—you were strong in your convictions. You knew what you wanted, and you sought my help in attaining it. Yet now, you continue to avoid the issue." He made an exasperated gesture. "Do you expect my patience to be unending?"

She didn't look at him, letting her gaze travel the riverbank to the lacy moss that hung from deeply foliated trees swaying beneath the prodding of a quickening breeze. The clouds had darkened to lavender, and a distant rumble of thunder disturbed the stillness of the afternoon.

"And what of your father," Colin persisted, undeterred by her silence. "Have you forgotten him so soon? Has the sight of a handsome face banished your memories of him?"

Bethany still made no response, and Colin touched her arm. His temper was up, and though he was aware he was sounding like a pompous lecturer, he couldn't help himself. "I've seen women fall all over themselves in an effort to gain Hammond's attention. Though for the life of me the charm of the man escapes me."

Turning, she gave him a level look. "Is that why you dislike him so? Or perhaps envy would be a better word!" Mentally, Bethany winced, sorry that she had spoken to him like that. A restless irritation prodded her, but Bethany was uncertain as to whether it was directed at Colin or herself.

Colin had shifted uneasily at her words. "I dislike Hammond because he is, as you well know, a cheat!" It gratified him to see her recoil. Then his voice softened. "I just didn't think you would be so gullible."

"It's not that," she murmured, biting her lip. Colin was right, she thought gloomily; she was vacillating. What was she doing here if she wasn't going to follow through? The dream came to mind, chilling in its vividness, appalling in its accusation. But the anger that had been her mainstay was gone, and she couldn't seem to bring it back. In its place was nothing; she felt hollow.

"Then what is it?" Colin's voice shimmered with irritation. "Have you forgotten the debt owed your father's memory?" Putting a hand on her elbow, he steered her over to the deck chairs.

"Of course I haven't forgotten," she said tersely as she sat down. She closed the parasol and moved farther back in the chair.

"Then perhaps you doubt your father's word?" he suggested softly.

She took a sharp breath, stung by the insinuation.

"No!" Oh, God, no, she thought, truly upset. "It's just . . . I don't know," she said at last, feeling helpless. "I cannot seem to reconcile the two: the man my father told me about, and the man I have come to know. . . ."

A soft growl came from his throat. "And just how well have you come to know him?"

She ignored that. "Why was the engagement broken between Edward and Lydia?" she asked, absently twirling the handle of the parasol. Edward had never said a word to her about Lydia, had never even mentioned her name.

Colin viewed her from the corners of his eyes. "I don't know," he lied smoothly, wishing she hadn't asked that question. "A . . . lover's spat, I guess."

He had hesitated a moment too long, and Bethany strongly suspected there was more to it than that. Suddenly she remembered Kane's words in reference to the enmity between Colin and Edward. Something to do with a woman, he'd said. Lydia? The thought came as a surprise to her, and Bethany viewed Colin curiously.

"Do you . . . do you think Edward is still in love with her?"

Colin hesitated. He really didn't know the answer, but for his own purposes, it would be best that Bethany think he did. He spoke with as much decisiveness as he could muster.

"Of course he's still in love with her. They were childhood sweethearts, you know. Grew up together and all that sort of thing. Lydia has a temper. She and Edward quarreled, and in the heat of the moment she flung his engagement ring at him." Colin was pleased with himself. It sounded just like something Lydia would do.

Bethany moistened her lips and kept her tone casual as she asked, "You mean she broke the engagement, not Edward?" Why had she thought it was the other way around?

"That's right," Colin replied in an offhand manner, as if the subject were of no interest to him.

"Then why did she come aboard the *Nola Star*?"

Colin gave a short laugh. "I suspect you know the answer to that without being told. Certainly it's not the first time a woman's changed her mind." He glanced sideways at her, noting her distress but adding ruthlessly, "Mark my words. Lydia has only to crook a finger and Edward will come running."

Bethany had no doubts that Colin spoke the truth, but why had Edward invited her to Glencoe? To make Lydia jealous? Possibly. Or . . . perhaps Edward had no other reason in mind than to seduce her, something he'd done quite admirably and without much effort on his part. The thought left a bitter taste in her mouth.

Colin leaned closer and spoke firmly. "You have a score to settle with Edward. Now, don't you think we should get on with it?"

And still, Bethany found herself drawing back, wanting to be certain, unable to put aside her uneasiness. Everything pointed to Edward's being guilty as charged. Why was she having such difficulty in accepting it?

Extending her hand, Bethany let it rest lightly on Colin's arm. "You were there that night, Colin." Her amber eyes entreated. "You must know the truth. Please tell me."

Colin hesitated a moment, his features hardening when he finally replied. "You're right, I was there. Edward won, and he won heavily." He smoothed his mustache with a fingertip. "I suspected at the time that he was using a holdout, but I wasn't about to risk getting shot in order to find out."

Tilting her head, Bethany regarded him with a puzzled look. "A . . . holdout? What is that?"

"A simple mechanical device that holds one or more cards," he explained. "It can be strapped on the arm, on the chest, even on a leg. It holds one, perhaps two cards that can be called forth at a crucial moment."

Bethany frowned. "Where would a person get the extra cards to do that? We begin each evening with a new deck, and I've seen the stewards collect and destroy them when we're through playing."

He laughed at her naiveté. "It's a simple matter to bribe a steward," he noted, "and even easier to pocket a few cards. While it's true the stewards collect the decks at the end of the night, I've yet to see one of them take the time to count the cards."

Bethany gave him a sharp glance. "And you think that's how he did it?"

"I do," Colin nodded, brushing an imaginary speck of dust from the sleeve of his dark green frock coat. "I know for a fact that the cards weren't marked," he went on. "On most boats you can buy marked decks from the bartenders, but not here. Mary is very strict about that. She has the cards made to her own specifications and stamped with the name of the *Nola Star*."

Bethany's smooth brow furrowed. "But what assurance do I have that Edward will not use this . . . this holdout on me?''

He turned and smiled. ''Because, my dear Bethany, I will be the dealer. Neither one of you will handle the cards except to play them.''

Bethany leaned back in her chair, a pensive look on her face. Colin said no more, but he was determined to act before another day went by.

Chapter 21

When Colin and Bethany entered the Grand Saloon that evening, Colin's eye quickly scanned the room. Edward was standing in front of the buffet table, drink in hand, conversing with a group of people that included Mary and Captain Baxter.

Taking Bethany's arm, Colin firmly led her in their direction.

Edward nodded coolly as they approached, striving for a detachment that he couldn't achieve when he saw how lovely Bethany looked. Her pale-lilac silk gown was in stark contrast with her black hair. Her skin gleamed like polished ivory, and he wouldn't allow himself to remember how soft it was. Edward had spent the last four days telling himself that Bethany was no different from any other beautiful woman. He hadn't quite come to believe it, but he was working on it.

"And how is the Bayou Fox this evening?" Colin inquired in a casual way. He studied the array of food on the buffet table with an air of intense interest, then helped himself to a piece of cheese.

Edward frowned at him. He disliked the silly nickname and knew that Colin was aware of his feeling.

Colin's face twisted into something resembling a smirk. He chewed the last of the cheese and swallowed it.

"You know," he said conversationally, with a look that embraced the whole group, "it appears to me that if a man is considered to be a champion, he ought to welcome a challenge to his title." He stared directly at Edward. "What do you think, Hammond?"

Edward's frown deepened. "Are you challenging me, Colin?" he asked dryly.

"Oh, no. I'm not good enough," Colin replied quickly, with a deprecating wave of his hand. "But I know someone who is . . ." He paused a moment, then asked: "What do you say, Hammond? Are you willing to sit at a table with someone whose skills are as good as your own? No limit?"

Leon Clere, who had changed into a more conservative outfit of oyster-gray broadcloth, lifted a pinch of snuff to his nose and quirked a brow in interest. He moved closer. "I for one would very much like to witness such a contest," he murmured, staring at Edward in a meaningful way.

Edward's own eyes held a hint of scorn as he viewed the aristocratic features of Leon Clere, who was making no effort to disguise his aversion for what he termed "Americans." Edward wondered how the Creole had survived his more than twenty years without prompting someone into making the attempt to wipe the arrogance from his olive-complexioned face.

Nearby, Mary's worried gaze took in first Edward, then Bethany. A game of poker was one thing; but no limit . . . ? She'd seen men lose everything, even commit suicide under such rules; there could, after all, be only one winner.

Edward sipped his drink, watching Colin cautiously, wondering what the man's scheme was. "What do you have in mind?"

"I suggest a game of poker with Miss Kincaid. No limit . . . and I will be glad to offer my services as dealer." A supercilious smile came to his lips at Edward's hesitation. "Of course, if you're afraid of being bested by a woman . . ." He paused dramatically with a knowing look at everyone.

A long moment of silence ensued; it was charged, as if all those present were sharing a moment's awareness of high drama. The crowd looked at Edward with avid anticipation, sensing his reluctance but knowing he could not refuse without detriment to himself. The gauntlet had been thrown; only a coward would refuse to pick it up.

At last Edward gave a slow nod in Bethany's direction. "If Miss Kincaid has no objection, it would be my pleasure to best her in a game of poker."

Although taken by surprise by Colin's actions, Bethany quickly recovered. She noted Edward's display of self assurance. She felt as though he were waving a red flag in her face.

"On the contrary, the pleasure will be mine," she said curtly, with a lift of her chin.

A table was chosen in the center of the room, so that the spectators could stand around and watch. The few games already in progress came to an abrupt halt as everyone congregated to witness the contest. Bets were being made on the outcome.

Mary drew Bethany aside and regarded her with anxious eyes. "Bethany, perhaps you should give this more thought. . . ."

The suggestion drew a rueful laugh from Bethany. "Even if I wanted to—and I do not—things have gone too far for me to back down now."

"There is still time—" Mary sighed deeply when she saw Bethany shake her head in a curt movement. "Have you any idea how rough a no—limit game can be?" she persisted. A note of urgency crept into her voice, and she put a hand on Bethany's shoulder as if to detain her. "You could lose everything!"

"Or win everything," Bethany countered quickly.

"Need I remind you that it was in just such a game that your father lost all he owned?"

When Bethany looked at Mary, her mouth was set with determination. "That's one thing you don't have to remind me of." Mary's hand was still on her shoulder, and Bethany took hold of it, giving it a gentle squeeze before she released it. "Don't worry about me. I know what I'm doing."

As she started to walk away, Mary said in a low voice, "And when it's over? Are you going to tell Edward who you really are?"

Bethany flashed a bright smile that didn't quite come off. "Win or lose," she promised. Going back to the table, she sat down.

Mary fetched an unopened deck of cards, which she put in front of Colin, and he broke the seal.

"Five card draw?" Colin asked, viewing Edward and Bethany, both of whom nodded their assent. After shuffling the cards, he began to deal.

The next hour passed swiftly. Mary opened the doors in an effort to expel some of the cigar smoke.

At the end of the second hour, Bethany had a slight edge, which increased during the third hour.

Both Bethany and Edward had purchased ten thousand dollars worth of chips. In the fourth hour of play, almost all of them were in front of her.

Leaning back in her chair at one point, Bethany inhaled deeply, trying to fight the mental fatigue that was asserting itself more and more with each passing minute. Glancing at her watch, she was astonished to see that they had been playing for more than five hours! Her back felt stiff, and her eyes were dry and gritty. Edward, she noted with annoyance, was showing no sign of strain. He looked as fresh and alert as when they had first sat down.

Not so the onlookers. Most of those who had crowded around the table at the beginning—including Mary—had long since retired. The remainder were either drunk or half asleep on their feet. The exception was Leon Clere, who was still watching with avid interest.

Outside, it had begun to rain. Thick, heavy drops produced a monotonous cadence that had a lulling effect.

Concentrate! Bethany told herself sternly, trying to shake off the numbing lethargy she was beginning to feel. *This is the reason you came here. Ignore those blue eyes that seem to be asking for so much more than you can give.*

She was less than successful. Visions of that love-filled night before the fire at Glencoe kept intruding, teasing her mind with what might have been.

Edward had opened. Studying her cards, Bethany kept two and drew three, noticing that Edward had a pat hand. He was completely relaxed and sat there staring at her. Bethany refused to look at him.

A slight aberration in the movement of Colin's hand caught her eye, but the motion was so swift that when Bethany focused on the movement of the cards he was dealing to her instead of his hand, she could see nothing out of the ordinary.

Upon seeing which cards she had been dealt, Bethany firmly resisted giving in to her elation. Glancing up, she was caught by Edward's direct gaze, and a tremor flashed through her with such force she almost dropped them. Damn him! And damn his arrogant confidence. She would not allow herself to be distracted; she had not come this far to let her goal elude her.

Calmly, Bethany pushed all her money to the center of the table, then fixed Edward with a level look.

There was a moment of absolute silence, as if everyone in the room held their breath.

"Would you accept my marker?" Edward asked quietly, knowing he could not possibly cover the bet.

Bethany opened her mouth, but Colin's voice preempted her reply.

"A marker!" He laughed loudly and with high amusement, then viewed the spectators with an incredulous look. "Come, Hammond. You can do better than that.

If your hand is good enough to bet, it's good enough to be backed up with something more substantial.''

Edward gave him a cold look. "I believe I addressed my question to the lady," he said in a voice that matched his expression.

"And I speak for the lady," Colin shot back, eyes gleaming. He leaned forward. "I understand you have a horse by the name of Dawn's Light. Suppose you put up the papers for her!" Leaning back again, he waved a hand in a careless gesture. "Unless, of course, you're willing to concede defeat right here and now." He viewed the spectators again. "What do you say? Should the Bayou Fox live up to his reputation—or admit that he has been bested by a woman?"

Jeers and taunts filled Edward's ears—Leon Clere's were especially loud and explicit—and he shifted his weight in his chair, feeling decidedly uncomfortable.

Sensing that Bethany was about to protest, Colin fixed her with a hard look. "It is my understanding that Dawn's Light was purchased with Mr. Hammond's winnings at the card table; it seems only fitting that he use her to back up his bet now—don't you agree?"

Bethany swallowed. Her palms felt damp against the cards as she avoided Edward's piercing gaze. This was what she had come here for, she told herself sternly. She had no right to show pity or weakness now.

Defiantly then, Bethany met the blue flame of his eyes, ignoring the thud of her heart as it pounded against her breast. She, at least, had played an honest game, unlike Edward, who had tricked her father.

Edward lit a cigar, appearing to be completely re-laxed. He didn't review his cards; he knew very well what he had. Four of the five cards were kings. The remaining card was an ace; obviously Bethany could not be holding four of those. She had drawn three cards, possibly against a pair she held. A straight, maybe a full house, he reasoned; neither of which would beat him. Even four of a kind couldn't beat him. Only a straight flush or a royal flush could do that, and the odds were too high to credit Bethany with having either of them.

"Very well," he said at last, putting the cigar in an ashtray. "Fetch the pen and paper."

There was a flurry of movement as a steward hurried to comply.

Bethany, too, leaned back in her chair to wait, feeling the distinct beginnings of a fierce headache.

Her mind, so weary, seemed to empty itself of conscious thought, a sensation not unlike the twilight calm one experiences in those few moments before falling asleep; that time when the answer to a problem, or a familiar name that has eluded one all day long, suddenly becomes clear and sharp.

The flooding realization was like being awakened with a pail of cold water on a winter's morning. Colin's constant playing with the silver dollar took on a new meaning for Bethany. Why was it necessary for a gambler, even a professional one, to have such dexterity when dealing? And that girl—the one Colin had with him on that night, the one who had so conveniently bumped into the table just as the cards were being dealt—was she a distraction?

And, finally, something she herself had just now witnessed but had not immediately recognized. She suspected that Edward would have immediately noticed what Colin had done—if he had been looking at him. But he had been staring at her!

The feeling of dismay that came over Bethany was so intense that it took her breath away.

My God, it hadn't been Edward who cheated; it had been Colin! Hattie had said that her father had no proof or he would have done something at the time. There had been only two other players in the game that night. Knowing he was cheated, her father would have automatically assumed it was the man who won!

She became aware that Edward was regarding her in a quizzical manner, waiting for her to make a move.

"I'll call," he said again, wondering at her sudden preoccupation.

Hesitating only a moment, Bethany nodded.

Edward laid his cards down, and Bethany viewed the four kings and the ace. Of course he would be confident with a hand like that, she thought; just as her father had been. Something must have gone wrong that night, but Bethany was too numb to be able to fit the pieces together at this point.

Raising her head, she stared at Edward for a long moment; then she put her cards on the table...facedown.

"You have won," she said quietly, ignoring Colin's sharp indrawn breath and the flush of quick anger that stained his cheeks. His reaction was final, conclusive evidence for her.

Pushing herself away from the table, Bethany got up and left the Grand Saloon, feeling the need for fresh air. The rain had stopped, but clouds still obscured the sky.

She took several deep breaths, trying to clear her

mind. Strange, she mused to herself. She had never thought past this moment. It was to have been her moment of triumph; it had turned out to be anything but.

And now?

Walking toward the railing, she put her hands on the smooth wood. It was cool and damp beneath her palms. Humid air enveloped her, feeling clammy on her bare arms.

How was she to tell Edward the truth about herself? she wondered. Would he even listen?

Hearing footsteps, Bethany turned to see Colin storming in her direction, his face livid.

Grabbing her arms, he shook her with a force that loosened the pins in her hair, spilling dark tresses about her shoulders.

"What have you done?" he said in a choked voice. "You've ruined everything!"

She pulled away from him. "It was not my intention to do it that way! You planted those cards!" Her voice rose to a shout. "Didn't you? Didn't you!" The urge to strike him was so strong she clenched her hands tightly, welcoming the pain of her nails digging into her palms.

"Of course I did. You don't really think you would have beat him on your own, do you?" His lip curled in a sneer.

"It wasn't Edward who cheated my father, was it?" Bethany was trembling so hard her voice emerged breathless. "It was you! And all this while, you knew! You lied to me from the very beginning." The extent of her naïveté left her incredulous.

Anger drained away, and Colin appeared defensive.

"Look, Bethany, I did not cheat your father. It was an accident..."

"How can a deliberate action be an accident?" she demanded.

Colin cringed from the scorn on her lovely face. Wetting his lips, he said, "George had no business being in that last hand. I felt certain he would drop out..."

His look begged for understanding, but Bethany stared at him, saying nothing, her eyes eloquently expressing her contempt.

"It was Hammond I was after," he went on, his voice taking on a pleading note, "not your father. The cards he got were meant for Edward—and it was Edward, who got the cards intended for me! Your father had no business being in that last hand," he repeated. "The fool picked the wrong time to try a bluff."

They both turned as Edward came out on deck, heading in their direction. He was smiling at Bethany.

"You played a good game," he said, pausing in front of her. "Although in truth I can't say I'm sorry you lost that last hand." He shrugged. "The luck of the draw."

"Luck!" Colin grabbed Bethany's arm again, his lips drawn back from his teeth as anger returned. "Luck had nothing to do with it." He pulled Bethany a step forward. "May I present to you Miss Bethany Forrester. She's George Forrester's daughter, and she's aboard the *Nola Star* for no other reason than to beat you at your own game. We were working as a team. That last hand belonged to Bethany. You were set up, Hammond! Set up!" he repeated harshly. "And if Bethany had had her mind where it belonged, she would have won.''

Edward turned to look at Bethany's white face. He had no need to ask if Colin spoke the truth. He saw all he needed to know in her stricken expression. Turning on his heel, he walked away.

Bethany made as if to follow, but Colin's grip was tight on her arm.

"Listen to me, Bethany," he implored. "You can't go after him. Stay with me. Marry me. We'd make an unbeatable team. . . ."

Turning to look at him, Bethany was seized by a terrible anger. She wrenched away. "I don't ever want to see you again, Colin!" she cried out. "You can forget about us being a team or anything else!"

Hoisting her skirts, Bethany ran after Edward, finding him at the stern of the boat staring moodily into the black water.

"Edward, please let me explain," she began. "My father thought you had cheated him. . . ."

"And you thought so, too?" He kept staring into the water.

"Yes . . . No! I don't know!"

When he looked at her, his eyes were as cold as the Arctic. "Are you in fact Bethany Forrester?"

"Yes, but—"

He turned from her. "I don't care to hear anything you have to say, Miss Forrester."

His lips twisted, and Bethany felt her heart wrench painfully. He was sneering at her, mocking her. It was more than she could bear. Through her blurred vision she never saw his anguish.

"Please let me explain," she entreated again.

He glanced at her with that same cold expression, and his voice was brutal in its frankness. "I'm not interested in your explanations. Do you consider yourself to be a better person than the one you thought I was?" he asked harshly. "You are as much the cheat as you thought me to be. Assuming a false identity, pretending to be someone—and something—other than you are!" His face was rigid as he stared at her pale face, unmoved by the welling tears in those lovely eyes.

"You don't understand—" she began with a strangled cry.

"I understand all I need to know," he interrupted. "I do not wish to hear any more of your lies." He moved so that he was facing her directly, hands clasped behind him. "In fact, madam, you *are* a lie."

He flung the words at her, each one striking her with the force of a hurled stone. She pressed her hand to her lips to contain the sob in her throat. Why hadn't she listened to her own heart? she thought frantically, unable to bear the look of contempt she was seeing. Why had she denied her own instincts!

The sob could not be held back. Turning, Bethany ran in the direction of her stateroom.

Closing the door, she leaned against it, feeling drained, wondering how she could continue to live the endless days that stretched before her, days without Edward, without love.

She closed her eyes, and immediately the image of his face sprang into being against the darkness of her lids. With an anguished moan, she quickly opened them again, unable to endure the memories that stalked her mind.

On legs that felt stiff, she walked across the room, nerveless fingers undoing buttons and ribbons, unaware of the tears that continued to dampen her cheeks.

Chapter 22 __

More shaken than he would admit, Edward's hands gripped the railing as he stared at the frothy line of water strung out behind the boat like a tattered lace ribbon. He had known that George had suffered a fatal attack, having been informed by the attorney on the day the debt had been settled from his estate. But he hadn't known that Forrester had a daughter. Certainly not one who would go to such lengths to ruin him under the misguided notion that he came by the money dishonestly.

Torment moved in his chest as the sickening realization sunk in: Bethany was not the woman he had thought her to be. Their whole relationship had been a sham from the start.

And that night they had made love . . . had she only pretended passion? Of course she had. She'd done nothing but pretend from the first day they had met.

Everything was so clear to him now: her evasiveness, the abrupt change of moods, her unwillingness to discuss her past. And as for her relationship with Colin . . . Edward made a sound of disgust. Obviously they were partners in more ways than one.

With a sigh, he headed back to the Grand Saloon. He felt badly in need of a drink. The hour was so late the room was empty except for a sleepy-looking steward who was clearing the leftover food from the buffet.

Passing by the felt-topped table, Edward looked down at the cards. They were in the same position as when he had left. He began to walk toward the bar. Then, on an impulse, he went back to the table and picked up Bethany's cards.

His eyes widened in disbelief. Six, seven, eight, nine and ten of spades! His hand shook as he put the cards down. He knew Bethany well enough by now to know that she could never have misread a straight flush. She had put down a winning hand, had let him win!

Bethany, he recalled, had drawn three cards. The odds against filling in a straight flush under those circumstances were astronomical. Most assuredly, Colin had contrived that last hand, and probably had been doing so all night. But Bethany couldn't have known about it, he realized, or she would have played out the hand as dealt. Somewhere along the line, she had discovered that Colin was manipulating the cards, and she had dropped out.

Turning from the table, Edward went to the bar for his drink. He ordered a bourbon from the steward, who looked unhappy with the interruption, then he sat down, his mind working in furious circles.

Mentally, he reviewed the game with George Forrester.

Had that last hand also been contrived by Colin? If so, why hadn't Colin won?

Unless . . .

Edward slammed his palm down on the table. Unless Colin had thought Forrester would drop out. Forrester either knew or suspected he had been cheated; naturally he would have assumed it had been done by the man who had won the hand. Obviously he had told Bethany of his suspicion. George had been a man of honor, and Bethany would have no reason to doubt her father's word.

Not bothering to finish his drink, Edward went to Bethany's stateroom, where he knocked softly on the door. At her murmured permission to enter, he opened it.

She had removed her clothes and was garbed in a confection of flowing silk that subtly outlined the sculptured perfection of her body. He caught his breath at the sight of her.

"Bethany . . ."

"Oh, Edward!" She came running into his arms. "Please let me explain . . ."

"No." He put a fingertip to her lips. "There've been too many words spoken already."

Bending his head, he kissed her tear-stained cheek, achingly aware that he had caused those tears to fall. Drawing her closer, he felt his body rising to meet the softness pressed against him. Picking her up, he carried her to the bed. Removing his clothes, he got in beside her. Then he kissed her again, a long and deep kiss that set her heart to pounding. All her desire for vengeance evaporated in the storm of passion that erupted within

Bethany, roiling her senses to a pitch she had never thought possible.

Without removing his lips from her own, Edward untied the satin ribbon at her throat. When he drew back, he buried his face in the dark cloud of her hair, murmuring her name.

Squirming out of her nightgown, Bethany flung it carelessly on the floor.

She leaned forward to kiss him, but he put his hands on her buttocks, raising her up until his mouth found her nipple. Warmth flamed through her as she rested her cheek on his hair, feeling the golden softness on her skin. Bethany felt her flesh tingle with excitement wherever he touched her.

Urging her back against the cool sheets, Edward moved himself on top of her, feeling her hand guide him into the warm treasure he had sought for so long. As he moved within her, growing waves of pleasure rippled throughout Bethany's body, each one stronger than its predecessor. Each burning thrust was met by her own aching need.

With his hands firmly around her waist, Edward rolled over on his back, allowing her the freedom to move at her own pace. Every fiber of her being sprang to life, and although her skin shone with the efforts of her exertion, Bethany couldn't contain herself. She moved wildly, feeling his hands grip her buttocks, urging her faster, deeper, until Bethany was aware of nothing but this rhythmic joining of flesh and spirit.

She moaned, shuddering with the hot liquid fire that filled her body with rapture. She collapsed against

Edward's chest, both of them trying to catch their breath.

Finally, she settled herself at his side, her arm flung across his chest. "Will you let me tell you now?" she whispered.

His arm tightened around her. "The only thing I want to hear from you is that you love me as much as I love you."

She raised her head to look at him. "More . . . much more," she answered, pulling him close to her again.

"That's not possible," he said softly and smiled when she began to argue the point.

Dust motes danced in the bright sunshine that infused the cabin as the morning sun tipped the trees. Her paddle wheels churning against the current, the *Nola Star* was moving away from the refueling station, heading for the middle of the river.

Bethany's lips parted as she released a sigh of contentment. Although her eyes were closed, she was aware of Edward's warm breath as he nuzzled her neck, prodding her to wakefulness.

With her eyes still closed she turned to him, putting her arms around him, feeling his hard body against the softness of her own.

"Are you awake?" he whispered against her cheek.

She smiled lazily. "If I'm not, I hope this dream goes on forever."

His hands were caressing the length of her beneath the covers, and her breath quickened with the aching need that his touch always seemed to provoke within her.

"Bethany. . . ." He kissed her eyelids. "Will you marry me?"

Her eyes flew open at last. "Oh, Edward . . ." She blinked against a sudden sting of happy tears.

With a fingertip, he gently brushed her dark lashes. "Is that a yes?" he asked, smiling at her quick nod. Then his eyes darkened as he drew her close to him in a fierce embrace. "My God, I love you." Her answering response was lost as his mouth slanted over her lips.

When he drew back, Bethany regarded him with a solemn look. "How could I have ever doubted you? Can you ever forgive me?"

She looked about to cry, and Edward spoke hastily. "There is no need to speak of forgiveness, my love. For either of us. In all honesty, I must confess that if I had been in your place, if it had been my father, I would have done as much, and more." He smiled and rubbed his cheek against hers. "In retrospect, you have my admiration. And," he added softly, "I have an idea that George would have been very proud of you."

That was all the assurance Bethany needed to hear. She pressed close to him, her nails digging into his muscular shoulders as she sought his lips.

His ardor met and melded with her own as their bodies united with a passion that brought them both to a height of ecstacy neither had ever experienced until now.

When they were spent, Bethany turned on her stomach and snuggled into her pillow in the grip of a dreamy lassitude that left her feeling as though she were floating on a cloud.

Edward, however, seemed charged with energy. When

he had washed and dressed, he stood by the bed looking down at her, seeing dark curls tumbled in appealing disarray. The sheet was wrapped around her ankles, and his eyes feasted on the splendid curves of her well-rounded form.

"Get up, lazybones," he said to her.

Bethany didn't stir. "I'm going to stay in this bed forever," she declared, her words muffled by the pillow.

Grinning, he gave her a playful slap on the delicious mound of her rump. "Well, I can't wait to tell the world our good news. I'm going down to breakfast. Come and join me as soon as you're dressed."

Another mumble greeted that last entreaty, and still grinning, Edward headed for the dining room.

Spying Mary and Amy, who were having their breakfast at a corner table, Edward hurried over to them. In a voice more breathless than he could have imagined, he told them that he and Bethany were to be married.

"And we want you both at Glencoe for the ceremony," he concluded. A steward put a cup of café au lait in front of him, and Edward took a quick swallow, hearing Mary accept with excited enthusiasm.

Neither Mary nor Edward noticed Amy's somber expression. The news of the impending marriage left her with a conflict of emotions. On one hand, she was happy. Edward was one of her favorite people, and Bethany was fast becoming part of that elite group. On the other hand, she'd been unable to shake the despondency that had enveloped her since her departure from Glencoe.

On two separate occasions she had started to write Matthew a letter. Both times she had crumpled it and thrown it away. She had no idea what to say to him. Her feelings were too intense to put on paper, and she had been unable to bring herself to write words that were light, chatty.

She found herself missing Matthew more than she thought possible. Obviously he didn't care for her. He hadn't even bothered to say good-bye when she left. Amy knew her mother had noticed a change in her. In fact, she was afraid to analyze her emotions too closely, afraid she would be faced with wanting something more than she had ever wanted anything in her life—and knowing there was no way for her to get it.

In her mind, Amy had gone over every minute of the time she had spent in Matthew's company, reliving it over and over again as though it were a treasured memory she could not bear to release.

Still unaware of anything amiss with her daughter, Mary placed a hand on Edward's arm. "I can't tell you how pleased I am. Bethany's a fine young woman, in spite of . . ." she broke off, appalled that she had almost broken Bethany's confidence.

"I know," Edward said, his mouth stretching in a broad smile. "I'm aware of Bethany's reasons for being here. But she knows now that it was Colin who cheated." In as few words as possible, Edward explained the situation to her.

Mary wiped her mouth with the linen napkin, then threw it on her plate in a gesture of angry exasperation. "That man! If he ever does anything like that again on my boat, I'll see to it that he cools his heels on the nearest sandbar!" She was furious. It was bad enough that Colin had pulled a stunt like that on the *Nola Star*.

But even more upsetting was the fact that she had been fooled by him.

"I don't think you have to worry, Mary," Edward said quietly, seeing her agitation. "Colin was after me, not George. Much as I dislike the man, cheating is not his normal style."

"It damn well better not be," Mary declared emphatically. "If he—"

Her words ended in a scream as the sound of an explosion rent the quiet morning.

"One of the boilers must have exploded!" Mary's shriek was lost in the turmoil that erupted.

The explosion had ripped a hole in the floor of the dining room. Splintered planking and debris sailed through the air. The boat lurched with a sickening impact that threw people every which way. Both Mary and Amy had been thrown to the floor. Edward was slammed with terrific force against the table, sending a spasm of pain through his rib cage.

Righting himself, he helped Mary and Amy to their feet. Then, in dismay, he saw the ring of fire. The hole looked like a blazing inferno.

"Get out on deck, both of you," he shouted over the din of terrified screams and shouts. "Go to the prow! The wind's sending the flames to the stern!"

Bethany! In spite of the heat, Edward was cold with terror. He fought his way through the hysterical crowd of passengers, all of whom were either running aimlessly or jumping overboard, and elbowed his way around crew members frantically trying to contain the fire.

Above the commotion, Edward could hear Captain

Baxter's frantic cries. "All hands on deck!" he was shouting, his voice sounding hoarse.

Taking the stairs two at a time, Edward flung open the door to Bethany's cabin. She was dressed and apparently had been on her way out when the explosion occurred. She was on the floor, half sitting, a hand to her forehead.

"Bethany!" He knelt beside her, and with hands that were shaking, put his arms around her. "Are you all right?"

She looked a bit dazed, but her voice was steady enough. "I think so. Just a bump on the head. What happened? Did we collide with another boat?"

"No," he said, helping her to her feet. "One of the boilers blew up. Come on. It'll be safer on deck. There's a fire. . . ."

Edward led her outside, and Bethany drew a sharp breath when she saw the gaping hole from which flames were shooting into the sky. Shards of stained glass and splintered wreckage were scattered on the deck, and they carefully stepped around the debris. Leading Bethany to where Amy and Mary were standing, Edward removed his jacket and helped the crew fight the fire.

In the pilothouse, John Forbes held onto the gigantic wheel with fierce determination. Will Bishop was frantically tugging on the ship's whistle in an effort to summon all craft, large or small, to the aid of the stricken *Nola Star*.

Peering ahead, the boy's face whitened. "Reef!" he shouted, pointing. "Reef!"

"I see it," Forbes growled, swinging the wheel hard to larboard. It seemed to take forever before the *Nola*

Star gallantly responded. There was a loud scraping noise as the boat caught the outermost tip of the reef, and Forbes held his breath, releasing it only when they cleared it and were once again in easy water.

On deck, Mary stood very still, well aware of the close call they had just had. She returned her attention to the crew. Pail after pail of river water was being flung onto the insatiable fire, which seemed to gobble it up like raw meat thrown to a wild beast. She knew that buckets of sand were situated at strategic points on all decks, but these had apparently all been used already.

Mary's brow creased in concern as she thought of the deck passengers, for that was where the furnaces and boilers were located. The full impact of the explosion would have hit there. She prayed that most had had the opportunity to go overboard.

She glanced over the side, seeing bobbing heads and flailing arms. Some people were swimming for shore; others were clinging to planks and debris, just trying to stay afloat.

Looking up at the clear sky, Mary mentally cursed the perfect day. Rain would have been a blessing; instead, the sun shone with a relentless benevolence that was galling under the circumstances.

Leaning as far as she could over the rail, Mary took note of the hull. Although listing, the *Nola Star* was holding her own. She did not appear to be in imminent danger of sinking. Mary touched Amy's arm.

"Amy, stay close to Bethany. I'm going up to the pilothouse."

"Mary, please be careful," Bethany urged, putting an arm around Amy.

"I'll be all right," Mary called over her shoulder. "If the old girl stayed afloat this long, I think we can make it to New Orleans if the bilge pumps are still working. Shouldn't be more than three miles downriver."

Suddenly, the flames flared again, sending a shower of sparks into the smoke-filled air.

Bethany stared in mounting horror as she lost sight of Edward in the cloud of black smoke that belched into a towering wall. She heard screams and felt as if her heart had ceased to beat.

"Oh, God, no!" Bethany made the effort to lunge forward, but Amy, with surprising strength, put both arms around Bethany's waist, pulling her back from the searing heat.

"Edward!" Panic caught in Bethany's throat and terror robbed her of breath. She couldn't lose him; not now, not after they had found each other.

The smoke finally cleared. Relief weakened her knees as Bethany caught sight of Edward. His face was black with soot, but he appeared unharmed. The fire was lower now, apparently under control at last.

She looked about her. People were sprawled on the deck, some moaning, some motionless. Aware that Amy still had her arms around her waist, Bethany turned to the girl.

"Amy, we must help!"

The girl studied her face for a moment, as if to assure herself that Bethany would do nothing foolish, then, with a quick nod, released her.

Kneeling at the side of a man, Bethany looked down into the face of Leon Clere. A nasty gash cut across the

Creole's forehead and down one cheek. He was unconscious, but breathing.

She motioned to Amy. "Get one of those pails of water..." Raising her skirt, Bethany began to tear strips of cloth from her petticoat.

For the next half hour, Bethany and Amy worked side by side, tending to as many people as they could. When she finally took note of her surroundings again, Bethany saw that the fire was finally out.

Ropes were being thrown to those who had jumped overboard. Grabbing one, Edward hurled it into the water and dragged Colin up on deck. Regarding the dripping figure, Edward's face lit up with amusement.

"Welcome aboard, Colin," he said dryly. "I thought only rats deserted a sinking ship."

"Very funny, Hammond." Colin growled. He turned, his shoes slushing with every step as he strode in the direction of his stateroom.

"Is Colin all right?" Bethany asked as she came to stand at Edward's side.

He nodded, putting an arm around her waist, hugging her tightly. "Aside from his dignity, which I fear has suffered a mortal blow...."

Bethany answered his grin with one of her own. "Couldn't happen to a more deserving person," she confided, eyes dancing.

Chapter 23

Amy opened her eyes, anticipating something that momentarily eluded her in that first instant of wakefulness.

Then she remembered: today she would see Matthew. Although her mother had stayed in New Orleans in order to make preparations for the repair of the _Nola Star_, Amy had accompanied Edward and Bethany back to Glencoe.

When they had arrived at Glencoe the night before, it had been close to midnight. Too late, Edward had said, to rouse anyone.

They had each gone to their own rooms as quietly as they could, so as not to disturb the Masons, whose rooms were on the third floor, nor Matthew, who occupied a small room to the rear of the house, next to the kitchen.

Despite the mishap on the boat and the long journey back to Glencoe, Amy had been certain that she would be unable to sleep. But she had done so, deeply and dreamlessly.

Now it was morning, the sun shining with a buttery warmth that beckoned her outdoors.

Leaping out of bed, Amy ran toward the window, peering in the direction of the stables, a bit disappointed that Matthew was nowhere in sight.

But everything else was just as she remembered it. With a soft smile, she hurriedly dressed and went downstairs.

How wonderful, she thought, to live in a house, to be able to walk out a front door and be greeted by the sight of greenery and grazing horses, to lie in the grass and stare up into a sky that seemed to embrace all eternity.

Amy ate her breakfast just as hurriedly as she had dressed; then she went outside, trying to maintain a sedate pace. She raised her chin, feeling the gentle breeze on her face. It carried the unmistakable scent of spring.

Matthew was in a fenced-in meadow, exercising one of the horses. Her step was hesitant as she approached him, not certain that he would be as happy to see her as she was to see him.

Reaching the railing, she stood very still, eyes fastened on the young man who had become as important to her as life itself. Her doubts came back in full force, and she bit her lower lip. What if Matthew didn't want her the way she wanted him? And _want_ she did, with all her heart.

When Matthew caught sight of the slender figure standing quietly on the other side of the fence, he abruptly halted the horse.

"Amy, . . ." he breathed. Dropping the reins, he

dismounted and ran toward her, scaling the wooden barrier with little effort.

When he paused before her, they both stared at each other for a long moment. Matthew had been certain that his remembered image of her beauty had been exaggerated—but it hadn't been. If anything, she was even lovelier.

Not trusting himself to speak, Matthew raised his arms. Without hesitating, Amy stepped into the protective circle as though she had come home. With a deep sigh of happiness, she rested her head on his chest, hearing the beating of his heart, feeling the warmth of his body against her own.

Bending his head, Matthew's mouth held hers in a soft and lingering kiss. Then, taking her hand, they began to stroll. Words suddenly seemed unimportant to them both.

Five miles away, Colin stepped out of a hired carriage, paid the driver, and surveyed The Willows with an appreciative eye. Set almost five hundred feet off the dirt road that fronted it, the house was an imposing three-story brick structure with a wide, columned front porch. Black wrought-iron gates opened onto the carriage drive that curved gracefully to the front entrance. Despite the name by which the farm was known, Colin saw no willows in evidence; the towering trees that lined the drive were ancient oaks.

If he ever did settle down, this was the sort of house he would like to have, he thought, walking up the broad front steps. There was an air of grandeur about it that appealed to him.

A black woman wearing a white apron over a dark brown dress let him in, led him into the library, and went to fetch Lydia.

The room was rectangular. The bow windows at one end were diamond-paned and draped with crimson velvet bordered with gold fringe. Two deep-cushioned sofas were positioned at right angles to the fireplace. The remainder of the walls were fitted with glass-fronted shelves housing leather volumes of assorted sizes and thicknesses.

A large oil portrait hung over the peach-veined mantel. At first, Colin thought that the woman portrayed in it was Lydia. But upon closer inspection, he decided it must be her mother, painted when the woman was in her twenties. The green eyes were identical to Lydia's, but they lacked fire. The mouth, too, was of the same shape, but the smile was hesitant, uncertain.

Going to one of the sofas, he sat down.

"Colin! This is a surprise," said Lydia. The short train of her pale green chiffon morning gown swayed across the carpet as she came into the room.

On his feet again, Colin gave her a weak smile. "I do hope you're not one of those people who insists upon cutting the head off the bearer of bad news."

She frowned at him. "What do you mean?" Before he could answer, she gave him a quizzical look. "And what are you doing here? I thought the *Nola Star* wasn't scheduled to arrive in Louisville until tomorrow."

Hesitating a moment, he said, "There was an accident. One of the boilers blew up—"

"Oh, my God!" Lydia put a hand to her face, feeling a weakness in her legs. "Edward?"

"He's all right," Colin assured her quickly as he sat down again. "There were only two casualties, both of them deck passengers. The *Nola Star* put in at New Orleans." He gestured. "Sit down, Lydia. The accident is not the reason I'm here."

Trying to control the sudden apprehension that engulfed her, Lydia seated herself on the opposite sofa. Nervously, she tugged at the short puffed sleeves of her gown, uneasy with the uncharacteristically solemn expression she was seeing on Colin's face.

There was, he knew, no way for him to soften the blow, so he said it bluntly. "Edward and Bethany are to be married."

Color drained from her cheeks with his words. "I don't believe it!"

He inclined his head and spoke quietly. "It's true." He waited for her to speak, but she seemed incapable of it at this moment.

A heavy silence was in the room. Outside a horse nickered, but it caused only a brief interruption of the stillness.

"No!" There was a rustle of chiffon as Lydia jumped to her feet, hands clasped tightly at her waist. "I don't believe you. Edward loves me! He's always loved me." Her voice shook with emotion.

Colin sighed deeply. "Lydia, . . ." he began, but she continued as if he had not spoken.

"He's angry because of that night I went to your room." Her expression turned eager, as if by convincing him she could convince herself. "Don't you see? If Edward didn't love me, he would never have become so furious, so jealous." Lydia nodded her head once to emphasize that point. "That's what he was—jealous! And a man doesn't feel jealousy without love. . . ." The words tumbled out of her mouth in a breathless tirade.

She was staring at him intently, but Colin said nothing. He hoped his face didn't express the pity he felt. Getting up, he went to a small table in a corner of the room. There, resting on a silver tray, was a decanter and several crystal glasses.

Picking up the decanter, he removed the top and sniffed at the contents. Brandy. He poured a couple of stiff drinks. Returning to her side, he handed her one of the glasses.

"Please sit down, Lydia."

She did as she was told, her motions resembling those of a puppet that had lost its strings. Colin gave her a worried look, hoping she wasn't about to lose control of herself. He wasn't much good around hysterical females.

"I can't believe it," she said again, her voice not much louder than a whisper. "He hardly knows that woman . . ." Her fingers curled around the glass in her hands, but she made no move to raise it to her lips.

Colin made a wry face and swallowed the last of his drink. "There's more truth to that than you know," he murmured, putting the glass on the low table in front of the sofa. "Bethany's name isn't Kincaid . . ." Leaning back, he told Lydia everything that had happened from the day Bethany first came to his hotel room.

"So you see, my dear," Colin concluded, "I very much fear our plans have gone awry."

Lydia gave him a stony look. She had regained her composure. The brandy had done its work: it restored color to her cheeks and calmed her agitation. "I have no intention of giving up so easily."

"I daresay there's little you can do about it at this point," he remarked glumly. He was surprised at the extent of his own feeling. When Mary had told him of the impending marriage—and in retrospect Colin realized that she had done so with a certain degree of malevolent satisfaction—he'd been so upset that he couldn't even reply. He could not, in all honesty, say that his feelings were as deep as Lydia's; but then, Lydia was not only in love with Edward, she was obsessed with him.

Lydia's eyes narrowed. "Are you in love with that woman?" she demanded. Leaning forward, she studied him closely. "Or is this just another one of your passing fancies?" She saw the quick pain in his eyes, but her own anguish was too great for any answering compassion. What was his stupid little infatuation compared to her own deep and abiding love?

"It's no passing fancy," Colin admitted in a low voice. He spread his hands. "But I can hardly ride to Glencoe on a white charger and carry her off now, can I?"

A slow smile drifted across Lydia's beautiful face. "Perhaps you don't need a white charger, Colin," she mused thoughtfully. Although she spoke calmly enough, anger tore at her insides. Bethany was the cause of it all. The lying, deceitful little bitch! She had no intention of allowing that woman to steal Edward from her.

Colin's brow furrowed. He recognized that determined look on her face and wondered what was on her mind. "You're not thinking of going to Glencoe, are you? I've an idea that Edward wouldn't welcome either one of us.''

"He might,'' she contradicted softly. She raised her chin and arched a brow as she looked at him. "You see, I have something he wants.''

Getting up, Lydia moved with a feline grace to the window, motioning for him to follow. Chiffon swirled like a soft-green cloud before falling to stillness around her ankles. Holding the drapery aside, she directed his attention to the golden stallion grazing placidly in the meadow.

"Pretty,'' Colin observed, wondering what she was getting at. He knew nothing about horses other than how to ride them, although even his untutored eye could see that this animal was better looking than most.

Lydia made a face. "Pretty? That, my dear Colin, is the understatement of the year.''

Colin shrugged. "I suppose there is something special about him,'' he conceded, taking a closer look at the unusual sheen of the coat.

"Oh, yes,'' she murmured softly, with a nod of her head. "There's something very special about Baron. He's the only stallion of his breed in the state of Kentucky, in the whole country, for all I know.''

Lydia had had no trouble at all in convincing her father to buy the stallion. Once he had seen Dawn's Light, he had been, as she'd known he would be, convinced of the horse's superiority and potential. Samuel had gone to Glencoe to view the Akhal-Teke; he had, of course, been denied admission to the house. Cyrus had refused to see him, a situation that didn't concern Lydia in the least. It was Edward with whom they would negotiate. She turned as Colin spoke.

"Where did you get him?"

"I wired a friend in London, Jeremiah Hadbury. I've been very busy while you've been sailing up and down the river. Baron arrived the day before yesterday."

"You mean you bought him sight unseen?" Colin seemed surprised.

Lydia nodded. "Exactly. But it wasn't much of a risk. Father's done business with Jeremiah on more than one occasion in the past." She let the drapery fall back into place. "Edward has a mare of the same breed. He's been looking for a stallion to service her." She slipped her arm through his. "Now, here's what I propose we do, Colin . . ."

Bethany came down the front steps and smiled at Henry as he assisted her into the landau. Several afternoons a week she drove into Lexington for fittings of her wedding gown. The small shop was owned by a woman named Michele Arnaud. Rissa had recommended her, pronouncing her the best dressmaker in town.

As she drove, Bethany was aware of a sense of well-being. She was certain that no one was ever as happy as she was right now. She treasured every night that she spent sheltered within Edward's strong arms. Their relationship, in her opinion, had become progressively idyllic. They whiled away hours whispering, exploring each other's minds, dreaming aloud, planning their future. And in the mornings, as they shared a leisurely breakfast, their eyes met and glowed with remembrance of the evening's lovemaking, and in anticipation of the night to come.

Stopping the landau in front of the small shop, Bethany hurried inside, never seeing Lydia Madison, who had just emerged from a dry-goods store across the street.

Lydia halted abruptly as she caught sight of Bethany. Crimson flared in her cheeks, fueled by the sudden surge of hot anger that coursed through her.

Confronting Bethany was not part of the plan Lydia had outlined to Colin, but her smoldering fury demanded some sort of immediate satisfaction.

Eyes glinting and mouth compressed, Lydia hoisted her skirt, crossed the street in a determined manner, and entered the shop.

At the tinkling of the bell on the door, Michele turned, her smile of greeting faltering at the sight of Lydia's face. Michele was a small, dainty woman of forty-one. Above large brown eyes, her brows were penciled in a way that gave her a look of perpetual surprise. She was a widow and supported her two young sons and herself by dint of her expertise with a needle.

"Mademoiselle Madison," she said, coming forward, "how nice to see you again. How can I help you?"

Lydia's green eyes scanned the room, sliding over bolts of material, laces, ribbons, before coming to rest on Michele again. "The woman who just came in here. Where is she?"

Michele blinked. "You mean Mademoiselle Forrester? She's in the dressing room . . . wait!" she exclaimed hastily, as Lydia headed to the rear. "You cannot go in there—she's undressing for her fitting."

"I can go anywhere I damn well please," Lydia retorted harshly, without breaking her stride.

In the back, she flung aside the curtain with a gloved hand, ignoring Bethany's startled gasp of surprise. She had already removed her dress and was clad only in a lace camisole. Lydia took in the well-rounded shoulders, the pure curve of perfect breasts, the long limbs, and uncontrollable anger tightened her throat, squeezing the breath from her lungs.

Seeing the cream satin wedding gown draped carefully over a chair, Lydia walked toward it. Picking it up, she flung it to the floor, then deliberately stepped on it.

Bethany drew a sharp breath at the look of murderous rage that contorted Lydia's beautiful face.

Michele appeared and gave a cry of alarm when she saw the gown on the floor beneath Lydia's feet.

"Oh, mademoiselle!" she cried out in a shocked voice. "I've spent hours on that dress. You'll soil it!"

Lydia's green eyes focused on Michele, who felt as if a shard of ice had pierced right through her.

Moving a step back, Lydia slowly bent over and picked up the dress. Michele put a trembling hand to her lips. Lydia was holding the dress as if she meant to rip it apart. Michele was vastly relieved when Lydia only threw it at her.

"Take it!" Her mouth twisted around the words. "Soiled or not, it will never be used."

Clutching the dress, Michele beat a hasty retreat.

Bethany had recovered, and now her own eyes blazed in anger. "Get out of here before I lose my temper."

"I have no intention of leaving until I say what I've come to say," Lydia countered. The bodice of her apple-green silk dress rose and fell with her deep breaths.

Bethany made a face and drew a deep breath of her own. "Then get on with it!" she said heatedly. "Edward expects me back within the hour. I don't think he'd be too pleased to learn of what happened here today."

"You think you know him . . ." Lydia pointed the tip of her parasol at Bethany's breasts, and Bethany resisted the impulse to back away. "You know nothing about him." She lowered the parasol, but her manner remained threatening. "I've known Edward all my life. He *is* my life!"

At the sight of Lydia's genuine anguish, Bethany's anger drained from her. "I did not take Edward from you," she said in a softer tone. "No one can predict when they will fall in love. . . ."

"Love?" Lydia's voice emerged as a shriek. A feral gleam lit her emerald eyes as she thrust her face closer to Bethany. "You little fool! It's me he really loves." Her voice took on a note of desperation. "Don't you understand? He's trying to punish me by pretending he's going to marry you."

Bethany was so astonished at Lydia's words that her mouth gaped, and she could think of no immediate reply. Sighing deeply, she looked away. "You can't believe that, Lydia."

"You dare appear injured," Lydia seethed, with a toss of her head. "I'm the one who has been betrayed. You are the usurper, not me. Oh," she exclaimed, one hand on her hip, "I knew of your little game from the start. As soon as you saw Edward, you wanted him. You used every trick you had at your disposal to whet his appetite. And," she added scathingly, "I'll wager a woman like you has a lot of them!"

"That's not true," Bethany said quietly. "Please, I don't want to quarrel with you. I'm sorry you feel this way—"

"Sorry!" Lydia screamed. "You steal the only thing of value in my life, the only thing that matters to me, and you offer me an apology?"

Studying Bethany's face, Lydia saw a compassion she couldn't endure. With stiff limbs she began to walk away, skirts aswirl with venomous fury, flashing a black look at Bethany as she did so.

"You can forget about your fitting," she said tersely. "The wedding will never take place!"

She stormed from the room. A moment later the front door slammed shut with a jarring impact that sent the little bell into a quivering lament.

Lydia had no sooner left than Michele came hurrying into the dressing room, the gown cradled in her arms. "Oh, mademoiselle, I'm so sorry—I don't know what to say. She has never done anything like that before. . . ."

"It's all right, Michele," Bethany said quietly. "This had nothing to do with you."

The woman viewed her uncertainly for a moment, then sighed in relief. Shaking the dress, she held it up and inspected it with a critical eye. "Just one small spot by the hem," she pronounced. "When I clean and press it, it will be good as new."

"I'm sure it will be," Bethany smiled, then allowed Michele to help her into the dress, submitting patiently to the final alterations that were needed.

Chapter 24__

Bethany allowed the horse to travel at its own pace on the way back from town, using the time to calm her unsettled nerves. She was both angry and upset. In truth she was troubled by Lydia's words.

"The wedding will never take place," she had said.

Why had the woman sounded so confident? Bethany wondered, then shook off her unease. It was foolish to give credence to Lydia's ravings.

By the time the landau turned into the drive, Bethany had resolved to put the incident from her mind. Seeing Edward waiting for her, she put a delighted smile on her face. Helping her out of the carriage, he gathered her close.

"I've missed you," he whispered. Burying his face in her neck, he nibbled on her earlobe, sending pleasurable darts of warmth throughout her.

"Edward, . . ." she protested laughingly, but he only pulled her closer.

"How did the fitting go?" he asked.

Bethany hesitated. Looking up into his so very dear face which reflected only tenderness and good humor, she didn't have the heart to tell him of her encounter with Lydia.

"It went fine," she said at last. "One more visit should do it."

Bethany was determined to banish thoughts of Lydia from her mind. What, after all, could the silly woman do? she reasoned, as they walked into the house, feeling the protective assurance of Edward's arm around her. Best to forget the whole incident, she decided. Her wedding was less than a month away. She wasn't about to allow that woman to mar her happiness.

Bethany was still in an optimistic frame of mind when she saw the carriage coming up the drive later that afternoon.

Her heart plummeted at the sight of Lydia and Colin. At first, she didn't notice the horse roped to the back of the carriage. When she did, her eyes widened at the sight of the beautiful stallion. One look told all she needed to know.

Seeing Edward coming from the stables and heading in the direction of his visitors, Bethany had an irrational surge of hope that he would send them away. But as she saw him inspecting the stallion with unconcealed admiration, she knew it wasn't to be.

Although chiding herself for being like the ostrich who kept its head in the sand, Bethany still decided to stay in her room until it was time for supper. She wasn't at all certain she could keep her temper in check around Lydia or Colin.

Around four o'clock, Amy came to her room with a request that Bethany assist her in arranging her hair in a more sophisticated coiffure, for she had overheard Edward invite Matthew to join them for the evening meal.

Bethany was grateful for the girl's company, for the distraction she provided.

During the next two hours, they tried first one style then another, finally deciding on a sweeping pompadour that accented the slender column of Amy's neck.

"You look lovely, Amy," Bethany said, patting the newly devised coiffure. She smiled, watching the girl inspect herself in the mirror. "This sudden desire for a new hairdo wouldn't have anything to do with a certain young gentleman with whom you've been spending so much time of late, would it?" she teased, her smile turning into a delighted laugh at the sight of Amy's deep blush. She kissed the soft cheek. "Well, I'll venture a guess that he's going to be pleasantly surprised when he sees you."

Bethany was still smiling when Amy returned to her room to dress. Then, although she knew it was inappropriate for the occasion, she donned a black satin gown with huge puffed sleeves, the folds of which revealed creamy white satin inserts. A string of pearls was the only jewelry she wore.

Feeling reassured by the reflection she saw in her mirror, Bethany set her jaw and went downstairs.

As soon as she caught sight of Lydia, she was glad she had taken such pains with her appearance. The other woman was clad in a silk gown the color of hyacinths. The back was cut almost to her waist, where a jeweled pin shaped like a sunburst gathered the material before it fell to the hem in soft folds. Bethany couldn't help but notice how the outfit accented the perfect hourglass figure it clothed. The discovery did nothing to raise her spirits.

They had assembled in the library, where Henry served them brandy cocktails with thin shavings of ice in narrow crystal glasses.

For Amy, there was a tall glass of iced lemonade. She, too, had dressed with the utmost care, wearing the same pearl-gray dress she had worn to the cocktail party.

As Bethany entered, Edward immediately came forward to escort her into the room. She glanced at Lydia, who was standing by the marble fireplace. Returning her look, Lydia's green eyes seemed to dare her to speak of what had taken place in Michele Arnaud's shop.

Bethany turned away. She gave Colin a short nod, quickly averting her face from the longing she saw in his eyes. She was more than annoyed by his presence. She had not, and would never, forgive him for what he had done.

"Good evening," she said, keeping her voice calm as she came farther into the room. If there was to be any unpleasantness, it would not originate with her, she told herself firmly, listening to Edward as he spoke of the stallion with undisguised enthusiasm.

"For the time being," he was saying, "I've had Matthew put Baron in the adjacent field."

"I'm glad you're pleased, Edward," Lydia put in, giving him a warm smile that did not escape Bethany's attention. Coming forward, she stood before him, looking up into his eyes as though they were alone. "And I hope it goes as planned," she purred, resting a hand on his arm. "My father is of the opinion that the friction between our families should come to an end. I needn't tell you that I feel the same way."

Edward nodded and took a sip of his drink. "It would be nice if we could be friends and neighbors again," he agreed pleasantly.

While Edward wasn't at all pleased to see Colin, he was relieved to see that Lydia had apparently accepted the fact that their relationship had come to an end and was conducting herself in a businesslike manner.

His words notwithstanding, however, Edward had decided to say nothing to his father about the stallion for the time being, not until he was certain that Dawn's Light would accept Baron. Mares were not unlike women in that respect. They would accept a mate—or they would reject him—in no uncertain terms. The choice was theirs to make.

Lydia had turned, and her eyes now swept Bethany in a contemptuous manner. "Are you familiar with the process of breeding horses, Miss Kincaid—?" She broke off with a light laugh, picking up her glass from the table. "Forgive me. I understand that your name is Forrester. Silly of me to have forgotten."

"Bethany will do just fine," came the murmured reply. She kept her tone casual, refusing to let herself be baited.

"I must say you had us fooled by your little charade. Perhaps you should have taken up acting instead of gambling." Lydia's eyes glittered coldly. "But you're right, of course. Since we are, in a sense, to be neighbors, it is only right that we should be on a first-name basis.''

''Bethany's last name is of no consequence,'' Edward interjected quickly, his arm going around her, ''because I plan to change it to Hammond.'' He gave them all a broad smile.

Lydia looked as if a fist had landed in her stomach, and she turned away for a moment to regain her composure. Even though she'd known of the coming marriage, hearing Edward confirm it was almost more than she could bear. When she faced Edward again, her smile trembled on her lips.

''Am I to offer congratulations then?'' she asked. The hurt in her eyes belied the lightness of her tone. But in spite of his announcement, Lydia could not face the thought of having lost Edward, would not face it. After all, they were not yet married. There was still time for him to change his mind.

Hearing Edward's murmured affirmation, Lydia turned away again. She went to place her glass on the table. It slipped from her trembling fingers, hit the base of the brass lamp, and shattered into tiny, glittering shards. She stared in dismay, as if viewing the pieces of her broken dreams. Her hand reached out.

A small ''oh . . .'' was all she could manage. Colin had gotten up and now gripped her arm, trying to infuse strength into her.

''No, . . . don't try to pick it up,'' he said. ''You'll cut yourself.''

She was disintegrating, the pain too great to be voiced in anything less than a scream. Lydia clamped her teeth together, refusing the howl of anguish that tore at her throat.

"Come over here and sit down," Colin said, giving her a worried look. The color had fled from her face, and her eyes were overbright.

Moving as though in a trance, Lydia heard Edward say, "Yes, don't bother with it. Henry will take care of it."

Sitting in a chair by the fireplace, Amy tilted her head as she watched the actions of the others in the room. She didn't especially like Lydia Madison. Not because the woman had ever slighted her in any way, for she hadn't. It was, Amy decided, because her smile seldom reached her eyes. Any graciousness Lydia displayed was affected, a studied mannerism that had little basis in sincerity. Yet now, Amy felt a stirring of compassion for the woman, realizing that she was still in love with Edward.

At that moment, Matthew entered the library, so handsome in his brown frock coat, his usually windtossed hair neatly combed, and all thoughts of Lydia fled from Amy's mind. As Matthew crossed the carpeted floor, she studied his reaction closely, reveling in the delighted admiration she saw reflected on his handsome face.

And as their eyes met, Amy had the distinct impression that for the first time Matthew was seeing her as a woman.

Tearing his gaze from the vision Amy presented, Matthew murmured a greeting to the others in the room. Everyone, except Lydia, responded. Matthew didn't even notice. Crossing the room, he sat down beside Amy, resisting the urge to take hold of her hand.

"You look so beautiful," he whispered to her.

Her rosy lips mouthed a silent thank-you, and Matthew's heart thumped at the sight of the warm and tender smile she gave him.

Henry appeared in the doorway to announce that supper was ready. As they all moved from the room, Colin caught Bethany's hand.

"Bethany, wait . . . just a minute. Please . . ."

"What do you want, Colin?" She looked toward the door, noting with some annoyance that Lydia had tucked her arm beneath Edward's, leaving him no alternative but to escort her into the dining room. She was leaning on him in a way that suggested she would fall to the floor if he removed his support.

"I . . ." Colin wet his lips, wishing she didn't look so beautiful. She quite took his breath away. "I just want to say how sorry I am. For everything."

Bethany gave him a look of pure loathing as she drew away, rubbing her hand as though she had come in contact with something distasteful. "The only thing you're sorry for, Colin, is the fact that your dishonest nature has finally come to light."

Beneath the trim mustache, his mouth hardened. "You don't give me credit for possessing any decency, do you?" His voice sounded bitter.

"I've not seen a measure of it." she retorted, walking from the room, not seeing the glint of anger that sparked to life in his dark eyes. Until this very moment, Colin had been undecided as to whether he would go along with Lydia's plan; but as he watched Bethany walk gracefully from the room, he knew he would do it.

Supper was an awkward affair, with Colin and Edward addressing each other in stiff, overly polite tones. But there was nothing anyone could do to dispel the underlying tension.

Edward managed to keep the conversation on a general level, and Bethany did what she could to help; but it wasn't easy with Lydia's green eyes boring into her. The woman was sitting rigidly in her chair, as though she were in danger of shattering like the wineglass she had accidently broken. Her smile was a red slash fixed in place. Hatred blazed like green fire each time Lydia's eyes met Bethany's.

But Bethany noticed something else besides that ugly emotion on Lydia's face: determination. It left her with an uneasiness she couldn't explain.

The only two people unaffected by the swirling undercurrents were Amy and Matthew, both of whom seemed oblivious to everyone else but themselves.

Bethany gave a great sigh of relief when the tedious evening at last came to an end. She fervently hoped that Lydia would conclude her business in the morning, and that both she and Colin would leave Glencoe as soon as possible. It had been decided that they would put the stallion in the same meadow with Dawn's Light first thing in the morning. If all went well, they would leave the horses together for a few weeks and let nature take its course. If not, Lydia would take the stallion back with her to The Willows.

Closing the door to her bedroom, Bethany undressed and donned her nightgown. Seating herself at the dressing table, she began to brush her hair, pausing when the door opened and Edward came in.

Dropping the brush, she ran toward him.

"I thought you weren't coming," she whispered. Her arms went around his neck, and she pressed her cheek against his. She had never thought it possible to love another human being as much as she loved this man.

"Nothing could have kept me away." Edward held her close. "I wanted to make certain that everyone was settled for the night." Drawing back, he grinned at her. "It wouldn't do for my future wife to be exposed in a compromising situation."

She giggled softly. "Even if it's you who's doing the compromising?"

"Even so."

He shucked his robe, which was all he was wearing. Bethany swept off her nightclothes and crawled into bed beside him.

"Shall I extinguish the lamp?" she asked, in the same hushed whisper.

"Don't you dare," he said, reaching for her. "You're too lovely to be hidden in the dark."

As his mouth sought hers, the banked fire of their passion for each other began to glow, flaring into a blaze that grew higher with each touch, each kiss, until they both felt consumed by the raging inferno that engulfed them.

It was well after one when Edward gave Bethany a final, lingering kiss and left her bed. He certainly didn't want to go, but he thought it prudent in view of the fact that Colin and Lydia were in rooms nearby, not to mention Amy.

For himself, Edward didn't give a damn what people

thought. But for Bethany, he cared a great deal and decided it was best that the intimacy of their relationship be kept at a discreet level.

In his bedroom, Edward removed his dressing robe and threw it on a chair. Then, standing there naked, he stretched, feeling a deep sense of well-being in the warm afterglow of shared passion.

It annoyed him that Lydia and Colin were in the house. He probably shouldn't have gone to Bethany's room tonight; even as he thought that, Edward knew that nothing could have kept him away.

Drawing back the covers on his bed, he plumped the pillow, reflecting that soon he and Bethany would be spending every night in it. He couldn't wait for the time when he could put an end to this foolish sneaking in and out of rooms. It really galled him to have to do it.

Hearing the door open, Edward didn't turn around, thinking it was Henry. The Negro often came in just before Edward retired to see if there was anything he wanted.

When he did turn, Edward's mouth gaped. Lydia was standing there, garbed in a negligee so transparent that it revealed more than it covered.

In what seemed to him to be one motion, she closed the door with a slight push of her hand and dropped her robe to the floor. Edward was so startled by her actions that he made no immediate move.

She didn't speak as she came toward him. When she pressed herself against him, Edward took a step back, but he was so close to the bed, the calf of his leg hit the side and together they fell onto it.

Chapter 25

As soon as Edward left, Bethany got up, put on her nightgown, and was completing the interrupted brushing of her hair when the door opened. She stared at Colin, too surprised to react to his abrupt entrance; and when he came forward and took her arm, she automatically got to her feet.

"How dare you come into my room like this?" She twisted away from him and stared angrily. "If you don't leave this instant, I'll call Edward."

Colin seemed unruffled by her words. "I don't believe he would welcome an interruption at this time," he mused.

She blinked. "What are you talking about?"

An unpleasant smile distorted the lips beneath the thin mustache. "I think it's time you learn the true nature of the man you think you love." He grabbed her wrist again, this time with a force that precluded her escape.

"Let go of me, Colin!" Outrage blazed in her eyes. "What do you think you're doing?"

"Giving you an education, my dear. One you're sorely in need of."

Somewhat roughly, he propelled her along the hall, pausing before Edward's door, which he opened with his free hand. Only then did he release her.

Bethany put her hands to her lips, but couldn't repress a gasp at the sight that greeted her eyes.

They were on the bed, naked. Lydia's arms and legs were wrapped around Edward's body. So tightly were they entwined, it was difficult to see where one left off and the other began.

Bethany registered it all, but what she really saw was the ecstatic, triumphant expression on the face of Lydia.

Turning, Bethany ran back to her room, her night-gown billowing behind her in her haste. She heard Edward call her name, but she put her hands over her ears, refusing to listen.

Just before Colin had opened the door, Edward had been attempting to disengage himself from Lydia's avid, heated embrace. He'd never seen her so wild. With a strength he wouldn't have believed possible, she'd clung to him as though her life depended on it. He hadn't wanted to hurt her, and so he had not used the extent of his own strength against her. But he could just imagine what Bethany thought at the sight of them struggling on the bed.

And it had been planned; Edward realized that now.

He became aware that Lydia, still on top of him, was staring at him with passion-filled eyes. Far from aroused, he felt the fury coil tight in his stomach, threatening his self-control. His hands on her wrists, Edward pulled Lydia's arms from around his neck and pushed her away with a force that sent her tumbling to the floor. He glared at her, his rage so great he feared he would do her bodily harm.

Blind anger propelled Edward as he then lunged at Colin. The force of the impact knocked the man to the floor, where they both rolled about, fists flailing at each other.

Taking a step back, Lydia pressed her knuckles to her mouth, horrified at the sight of Edward's uncontrollable rage. He had his hands around Colin's throat and gave every indication of choking the life out of him.

Colin finally managed to scramble to his feet, breathing heavily. Unlike Edward, his was a sedentary life, and the exertion took its toll rapidly. Raising his hands, he spread them in front of his face.

"Calm down!" he shouted, truly alarmed at the expression on Edward's face and knowing he was no match against the taller and more muscular man. He had the unsettling idea that Edward could break him into little pieces if he wanted to.

And from the look on Edward's face, Colin thought that that was just what Edward had in mind. He put a hand to his throat, tried to swallow, but couldn't.

Edward paused. He was breathing as heavily as Colin, but it wasn't with exertion. Rage drummed along his nerves and pounded in his ears. He clenched his fists and took a threatening step forward.

"For God's sake, Hammond!" Colin gave Lydia a pleading look. "Do something before he kills me!"

Lydia had been just as shocked as Colin. She had

never seen Edward react with such violence. Even on that night when she had gone to Colin's room, Edward had not acted like this. A lot of shouting and one punch to Colin's jaw had composed the sum total of the dispute.

On legs that felt wooden, she moved forward and placed herself between the two men, not entirely convinced that Edward wouldn't strike her. She was still naked, but neither man so much as glanced at the tempting array of her charms.

"Edward, . . ." she said in a quiet voice that nonetheless wavered with apprehension, "this has gone far enough. . . ." She had expected him to be angry, but Lydia had been certain she could turn that anger into passion once Bethany and Colin left the room. She saw now that it wasn't to be.

Edward's eyes narrowed dangerously as he looked at her. "For once you've spoken the truth, Lydia," he gritted. "I want you both out of this house. Now!"

The fight drained out of Lydia, and she suddenly felt exhausted. She had lost Edward: totally, irrevocably. There was a chasm between them now, one so big it could never be bridged. The display of violence toward Colin could not have affected her more deeply had it been directed at her; and somehow, Lydia suspected that Edward wished it could have been.

"Now!" Edward repeated in a voice that would brook no contradiction. His hands were still balled into fists as he strained for control.

Reasoning it would be better not to argue, Lydia hastily grabbed her negligee and donned it. Colin was out the door before she was, vowing to put as much distance between himself and Edward Hammond as was possible from now on.

"And take your damn horse with you!" Edward shouted after them.

Picking up his robe, he shrugged his arms into it and went to the window, making certain of their departure. With a regret he couldn't deny, Edward watched the magnificent stallion being led away. Even washed by pale moonlight, the horse looked as if he had been cast from gold. Edward was glad now that he hadn't said anything to his father. Fortunately, Cyrus had been taking a nap when Lydia and Colin arrived with the horse.

Stepping into the hall a minute later, Edward glanced at Amy's door, wondering if the commotion had awakened the girl. He hoped not.

As quietly as he could, he walked toward Bethany's room. Putting a hand on the knob, he discovered the door was locked. Several times he knocked softly, calling her name, but only silence answered him. He put an ear to the wood paneling in an effort to hear whether Bethany was crying, but he heard nothing.

And, in truth, Bethany was not weeping. She was packing her clothes, vowing to be gone from this house—and Edward—at first light.

Edward frowned at the door. He was of a mind to break it down, but glancing toward Amy's room again, he thought better of it.

With a sigh, he went downstairs to the library, where he poured himself a generous glass of bourbon. Downing it in one swallow, he viewed the bottle; then, after a moment's reflection, he picked it up and left the room.

Tomorrow, he thought, making his way upstairs, feeling weary to the bone. Tomorrow he would explain everything, make Bethany understand that what had happened had not been his fault.

Chapter 26

It was seven-thirty in the morning when Bethany crept down the stairs. Edward's door was closed. She stared at it, wondering whether Lydia was still in his bed, then decided she didn't care. The two of them, she thought angrily, deserved each other.

Emerging into the cool, slightly overcast day, Bethany paused a moment, then headed for the stables. She carried only a small valise, planning to send for the rest of her things when she was settled—wherever that might be. For now, she planned to take the train to Harrodsburg and stay with Hattie.

If Matthew had any questions as to why Bethany was going into town at such an early hour, he didn't express them. At her instruction, he readied the landau, and in a short while they were on their way.

The drive into Lexington took just over an hour, but to Bethany it seemed endless. She didn't want to think and sat there staring at the passing landscape without really seeing it.

When they finally arrived at the station, Matthew carried her valise inside, put it down on the tiled floor, and politely asked if he could be of any further service.

Ignoring the young man's somewhat inquisitive look, Bethany declined, thanked him, and sent him on his way.

Moving toward the wooden cubicles, Bethany purchased her ticket, unhappy to learn that the only train scheduled for Harrodsburg was due to depart at noon. It was now five minutes after nine. Resignedly, she went across the street to a small restaurant and had something to eat. Returning to the depot, she bought a magazine and settled down on one of the hard benches to wait.

Lydia had been right, Bethany thought with growing bitterness. The wedding would never take place. No doubt Lydia had also been right when she said Edward still loved her and was only trying to punish her by threatening to marry someone else.

She clenched her hands in her lap, furious. The mental picture of Edward and Lydia—their naked bodies gleaming in the glow of the bedside lamp—was still fresh in her mind. And Edward still warm from her bed!

Colin's words came rushing back at her as well. "Mark my words," he had said, "all Lydia has to do is crook her finger, and Edward will come running." Well, Lydia had done more than crook her little finger, but the end result had been the same.

Bethany felt her nails digging into her palms but didn't care. How could she have been such a fool! Moisture welled in her eyes, but she sternly blinked it away. Tears solved nothing; she ought to know that by now.

After what seemed an endless amount of time to her, the train finally arrived. Grabbing the magazine and her valise, Bethany quickly boarded.

Settling herself as comfortably as she could, she glanced out the window, impatient for the train to move, absently watching as people bid each other good-bye, some happily, some sadly.

"Oh!" she cried, eyes widening as she caught sight of Edward stalking up and down the platform, peering into the windows. Putting a hand to her lips, Bethany stiffened, her back ramrod straight, every muscle frozen in her body. She turned her head away, pulling the brim of her hat lower in an effort to cover her face.

When she dared to look a minute later, she released her breath, seeing no sign of him.

To be on the safe side, she got up and moved from the window to a vacant aisle seat a couple of rows ahead. Hearing the conductor's call for all passengers to board, Bethany exhaled a sigh of relief and opened her magazine.

She had no sooner turned the first page when a hand flashed out and caught her wrist in a none too gentle manner. Too startled to react, she felt herself being hauled to her feet. She managed to keep hold of her reticule, but the magazine fell to the floor.

Looking up at Edward, Bethany gave a gasp that emerged as a cry of alarm. His blue eyes blazed fiercely, and his jaw was set to the point of causing damage to his teeth. Overall, his face had the look of an impending thunderstorm as he picked up her valise. He gave every indication of being on the verge of exploding, as indeed he had when Matthew told him that he had taken Bethany to the train station and that she had been carrying a suitcase.

Still clutching her wrist, he turned, ignoring her loud protests as he all but dragged her out to the platform. One man, nattily dressed in a tweed jacket and beaverskin hat, stood up and glared at Edward in indignation at this assault upon womanhood. But whatever words he had been about to utter died in his throat when Edward's burning gaze swept over him.

They no sooner stepped off the train when it began to move.

"You brute!" Bethany gasped, almost losing her footing. "Take your hands off me!"

Her voice had risen to a shout, but Edward didn't bother to answer, much less shorten his long strides. His head ached in deference to the half bottle of bourbon he'd consumed the night before, and he was in no mood for niceties.

"I will not go anywhere with you..." Bethany exclaimed, trying to pull away.

"There's been enough foolishness," he muttered tersely, before she got any further. His grip tightened on her hand. "We are getting married. And we're not waiting weeks or days—not even one more hour!"

His step long and purposeful, Edward headed up the street for the nearest minister's house, which he knew was two blocks away. Passersby stopped in their tracks to view the young man and woman, but Edward ignored them, his face appearing hewn from granite as he moved relentlessly forward.

With one hand on her hat to keep it in place, the other in Edward's firm grip, Bethany had to quicken her steps until she was literally running beside him. Even if she wanted to protest, she had no breath left with which to do it.

Striding up the flagstone walkway that led to the small brick parish house next to the church, Edward paused at the front entrance. He put down the valise, and banged on the door with his fist, without once looking at Bethany.

Inside, the Reverend Elijah Stone was sipping his afternoon tea. He was a tall man in his late sixties, with large bones that seemed even more so, due to the fact that he was so thin. Putting down his cup, he reached across his desk for a sheaf of papers and leaned back in his chair to read the sermon he planned to deliver on Sunday. He'd not gotten very far when his housekeeper opened the door to his office.

The woman was about to announce the young couple, but they brushed right past her before she could speak. Quite overcome with this inconsideration, she stood in the doorway with a quivering hand against her lips.

The reverend scowled, put his sermon back on the desk, and listened as Edward, in clipped tones, informed him that he wanted to get married—right now, this minute. Elijah Stone recognized Edward Hammond, although his attendance at church left something to be desired, but he had never seen the young woman before.

Raising bushy brows, the reverend calmly studied his visitors. The groom appeared about to erupt like Vesuvius, and the bride was so breathless she appeared about to swoon at any moment.

Taking note of Edward's dark countenance, the reverend had the distinct impression that if he refused to marry them, the couple would head directly to the justice of the peace. While Elijah Stone could not argue the legality of such a move, such ceremonies appalled him. Everyone knew that for a union to be blessed, it must be accomplished in the sight of God.

Well, he thought as he summoned his wife and his housekeeper to act as witnesses, from the look of them it was best he proceed with all due haste.

Even so, it would have to be done properly. He picked up his Bible, cleared his throat, then regarded the young couple with a stern eye. With great dignity, he proceeded with the ceremony in measured tones, refusing to be hurried by Edward's impatient attitude.

Finally he paused and let his gaze rest on the lovely woman standing in front of him. "Do you, Bethany Forrester, take this man to be your lawful wedded husband, to have and to hold from this day forward, in sickness and in health, till death do you part?"

Bethany glanced up at Edward. He was still holding her hand so tightly that her fingers were growing numb. The blue flame of his eyes seemed to burn right through her.

"I do," she replied in a small voice, and her heart echoed her vow with each beat it made.

Edward finally released her hand, and Bethany resisted the urge to rub it. From his vest pocket, he brought forth a gold band and slipped it on her finger. His kiss was no more than perfunctory, a mere brushing of lips.

When the ceremony was concluded, Mrs. Stone bustled forward to offer congratulations, insisting that the newlyweds stay for dinner. In contrast to her husband's thinness, Bessie Stone was short and plump, with warm brown eyes and a ready smile that she now displayed as she looked at Bethany.

Bethany hesitated, then looked at Edward, affronted at the sight of his still scowling countenance. *He certainly doesn't look overjoyed at being married,* Bethany thought with some annoyance. *And I'm the one who was dragged here!*

"Yes, yes," the reverend interjected quickly before Bethany could reply. "By all means, you must stay for dinner. Mother makes the best sweet-potato pie you've ever tasted."

Bessie Stone's smile widened at her husband's compliment. Taking Bethany's arm, she began to lead her from the office.

"We wouldn't want to be any bother," Bethany murmured, glancing back at Edward, suspecting he wasn't especially thrilled at the prospect of staying for dinner.

"No bother at all," Mrs. Stone assured quickly, patting her hand. "It's already made. Come along, my dear. The dining room is right across the hall."

By the time Edward and Bethany finally returned to Glencoe some hours later, twilight had thrown a lilac veil across the land.

They had spoken only a few words during the trip. Edward seemed aloof; Bethany was still angry. All through dinner the reverend's good wife had so graciously prepared, Edward sat with the same scowl on his face, answering in monosyllables whenever he was asked a direct question—the only time he had bothered to speak at all—leaving her to gloss things over as best she could.

Bethany's ears still tingled with embarrassment, recalling the sympathetic looks cast in her direction by Mrs. Stone, who murmured a few comforting words about the rights and privileges of husbands, and how it was the duty of wives to remain complacent and good-natured, even when they were out of sorts. Bethany wasn't at all certain she believed in that philosophy, but she had felt it would be ill-mannered to argue the point.

Fine wedding, Bethany was thinking morosely as she got out of the carriage. A shotgun wedding had more dignity than the one she just went through.

In the foyer, chin high, Bethany gave her husband a short, cool look and, hoisting her skirts, went directly upstairs to her room, closing the door with a slam that resounded through the house.

Who does he think he is? she fumed, unbuttoning her pelisse with hands that were shaking with anger. Running after her like the devil on horseback, dragging her through the streets, and then having the nerve to be angry with her! She was the one who had the right to be angry. And he hadn't even tried to explain what he was doing in bed with that woman!

Throwing her pelisse on a chair, unmindful that it fell to the floor with her careless aim, Bethany gritted her teeth. *Oh, he was a complete wretch!* she thought angrily. Why hadn't she been stronger and stood her ground?

Damn, she thought, sniffing. She was married, but she certainly didn't feel like it.

And her wedding gown! Bethany blinked against tears of frustration. She had wanted Edward to see her in it. She had wanted to see the look in his eyes when she walked down the aisle garbed in the beautiful cream satin creation.

He'd ruined it all!

Downstairs, Edward gave Rissa a few instructions, took the time to inform his father that he and Bethany had been married, then went upstairs.

Opening Bethany's door he stood there, staring at his wife. She had already undressed and drew a sharp breath at his abrupt entrance. He wasn't smiling. Bethany viewed him in some apprehension. Surely he didn't mean to force her? That was one thing she would not allow, husband or no.

"I believe you are in the wrong room, madam," Edward said to her in a quiet voice that set her nerves to jangling.

Without waiting for a response, Edward crossed the carpeted floor in a few long strides, took hold of her arm and firmly propelled her toward the door, ignoring her sputtering protests.

In his room, Edward released her, then closed the door, seeing with satisfaction that Rissa had filled the cast iron tub with warm water as he had told her to do.

Turning to Bethany, he calmly began to undo the ribbons and ties of her nightdress.

"What do you think you're doing!" Bethany snapped, her words muffled as he raised the gown over her head. In a reflex motion, she folded her arms across her bare bosom, growing more furious with each passing moment. If he thought she was going to fall into bed with him before he did some serious explaining, he had another thought coming. Married only a few hours and already he was acting like her lord and master.

Without answering, Edward picked her up in his arms and deposited her in the warm, perfumed bath.

Bethany sat there, rigid, arms still across her breasts, glaring at him. Stepping behind her, Edward put his hands on her shoulders. His thumbs working firmly in a circular, kneading motion, he began at her neck, working his way slowly down her spine, taking the better part of five minutes to conclude the journey.

With a sigh, Bethany closed her eyes, feeling her body relax, unable to resist the combination of warm water and the insistent pressure of his hands as he massaged her tense muscles.

Then her eyes flew open as she felt his hands on her leg. Raising it out of the water, he massaged her thigh, his movements unhurried and deliberate, working his way down to the calf of her leg. When he reached her foot, he bent forward and brushed his lips across her toes.

The contact sent a stab of fire up her leg, and she drew a shuddering breath. In some fascination, Bethany watched as her other leg was treated in the same way. Far from being relaxed now, a small quiver deep inside her was making its presence known.

Reaching over, Edward now lifted her out of the water. For a moment, he let his gaze travel her body with pleasure, noting how her white skin glistened with moisture and glowed in the soft light of the single lamp.

Then he briskly toweled her from head to toe. In spite of herself, Bethany's whole body was beginning to tingle in a most pleasurable way.

Taking a moment to undress, Edward then whisked the towel away and clasped her tightly against him. Tilting her chin, he gazed into her amber eyes.

"I love you, Mrs. Hammond," he said in a soft voice that was in itself an embrace.

As her anger melted away, Bethany swallowed deeply and once and for all gratefully gave in to the emotion she had for so long denied.

"And I love you," she replied breathlessly. "So very much."

His mouth slanted across hers and she parted her lips. His tongue found the satin of her inner cheek and slowly began to caress it. His hands slid down her back. Cupping her firm buttocks, Edward pulled her against his hardness, while his tongue continued its pursuit of the tantalizing nectar of her mouth.

The small quiver within Bethany had increased to the point where she was trembling, grateful she was being supported by his strong hands, certain she would be unable to stand without it.

As if sensing her growing weakness, Edward picked her up and carried her to the bed, where he kissed every inch of her with such intensity that she cried out for him to release her from the frenzied wave of delicious torment he had built up within her.

But, unhurriedly, he led her into uncharted planes of passion, building the tension, and together they explored every plateau with abandonment, delighting in each new discovery that raised them both to the pinnacle of pleasure. Here, time had no meaning, and only sensation prevailed, a symphony of rhythm that was rapture's own music.

It was a long time before Bethany's breath finally slowed. They dozed then, still entwined in love's embrace.

When Bethany awoke some thirty minutes later, she saw that Edward had gotten up, donned a robe, and was sitting at the small table by the window, helping himself to some of the food Rissa had put there.

Quickly, she put on her peignoir and joined him. Going to the table, she looked down and smiled.

"Cold chicken and champagne?"

"Rissa's an incorrigible romantic," Edward said with a quiet laugh.

Realizing that she was indeed hungry, Bethany sat down and helped herself to a wing while Edward filled the wineglasses. He handed one to her and raised his own.

"To us," he said softly.

She drank, then gave him a kiss. "This is the way I want us to celebrate all our anniversaries," she told him, a contented sigh following her words.

He raised a brow in mock surprise. "All fifty of them?"

"All fifty," she declared firmly, again attacking the chicken.

"Bethany . . ." He bent toward her.

"Umm?"

"You haven't asked me about last night. . . ."

"I know." She licked her fingertips, amused by his perplexed expression.

Edward moved uncomfortably and cleared his throat. "I think I'd better explain."

She got up, went to him, and sat down on his lap, snuggling close to him. "Wasn't it you who said there'd been too many words spoken?" She raised her head to look at him. "Besides, I think I know. It was staged . . . that's why Colin came to get me. I should have realized it from the beginning. It's just that I was so . . ."

"Jealous?" he suggested, sounding hopeful with the possibility. Her robe was parted, and he slipped his hand inside, cupping the softness of her breast.

She gave him a playful poke in the ribs. "And you? You were impossible when you thought that Colin and I . . ." Biting her lip, she looked at him through lowered lashes. "We didn't, you know. Never. It wasn't Colin . . ."

Edward kissed her before she could go on. "I don't want to know," he said quietly. "I don't care. Everything that happened before today is of no importance."

Turning slightly, Bethany put her lips on his neck. "Perhaps . . . but I warn you, Edward Hammond," she murmured, nibbling at his earlobe. "If I ever find another woman in your bed, I'll cut your heart out. . . ." His hand dropped lower, and she moaned in pleasure as his fingers caressed her womanly depths, sending a firey ecstacy singing along her veins.

"You've already got my heart," he said huskily. Picking her up, he carried her back to bed.

The next morning, Bethany awoke feeling the warmth of Edward's arms around her. They were both still naked, but at some time during the night Edward had pulled the quilt over them.

She stirred, moving closer to him and looked up to see him gazing at her.

"How long have you been awake?" she asked, kissing his neck.

"Not long," he murmured. "Just long enough to notice that even in the morning you're beautiful." He hugged her tighter. "Fine bones. That's the true test of beauty, you know."

"I know nothing of the sort," she replied, raising herself up on an elbow and giving him a mock frown. "And would you mind telling me how you know?"

He pursed his lips. "Did I forget to mention that I'm an expert? Horses and women—not necessarily in that order."

"Well, from now on, it'll be only horses you'll be judging!"

His hands caressed her satiny back. "Agreed," he said, kissing her nose.

Shifting her weight, Bethany held her hand up, admiring the ring that Edward had slipped on her finger when they had been married.

"Do you like it?" he whispered, watching her.

"Oh, yes!" She looked at him curiously. "But when did you have time to buy it?"

He smiled. "I didn't. It belonged to my mother."

She drew a sharp breath. "Does your father know?"

"He knows," Edward replied. "In fact, he was the one who suggested it." He frowned slightly. "If you prefer, I will get you one of your own."

"Not on your life," she said quickly and emphatically.

Then her smile softened. "It's the only one I'll ever want, or wear." She smiled down at him, then her brows knitted into a real frown. "Edward—what are we going to do about all the wedding preparations?"

"We'll have a wedding," he said blithely, working the silky tresses of her hair through his fingers.

Her eyes widened. "For whom?"

"For us," he answered quickly. "There's no law saying we can't get married twice. Besides," he grinned wickedly, "that will give us two wedding nights to celebrate."

"Will it be like our first one?" she whispered, easing herself on top of him, feeling his answer in the quick hardening beneath her before he spoke.

"I will personally see to it," he promised. His voice deepened as he folded her close to him. "But right now, it's the first day of our marriage." The blue flame of his eyes sought hers. "And I think we should begin by having our first bath together."

Turning her head, Bethany regarded the tub doubtfully. "It doesn't look big enough for us both."

"I know," he agreed cheerfully, smothering her ready laughter with his warm mouth.

He got out of bed, shrugged into his robe, and went to tell Rissa to replenish the bath water.

A while later, having accomplished that, Rissa turned to look at Bethany, who had remained in bed, covers pulled up to her chin, unable to quell the blush that tinted her cheeks.

"And what would you be wantin' for breakfast, Missus Hammond?" she asked, her brown face wreathed in a wide smile.

Bethany thought a moment. "Steak, eggs, and biscuits." She looked at Edward.

"Sounds fine to me," he agreed with a nod of his head as he ushered Rissa from the room. "We'll be down shortly," he said to her as she left, turning to look at Bethany. "Then again, we might not make it till dinner," he speculated, closing the door.

Chapter 27

Even though the morning sun seemed disinclined to put in an appearance on this day, Amy awoke with her usual enthusiasm and jumped out of bed, filled with the delicious sense of anticipation that had marked her stay here at Glencoe.

Arriving downstairs a while later, she was a bit surprised to see that neither Bethany nor Edward were present for breakfast; but the situation didn't bother her in the least.

When she concluded her solitary meal, she went outside. Adam came loping toward her, tail wagging a welcome. Bending, she ruffled his thick fur and planted a light kiss on a soft ear. Then she continued on to the stables, the dog trotting happily at her heels.

The day was heavily overcast. Thick, pewter clouds ambled across the sky, giving the landscape a peculiar greenish-gray color.

Matthew was nowhere in sight, and Robert informed

her that he had taken one of the mares to the farrier in Lexington to be reshod.

With the help of the young stable boy, Amy managed to saddle Sea Foam, then she took him for a run around the track.

Amy set an easy canter, enjoying the cool misty air on her face, feeling more alive than she had ever felt in her life. She hated the thought of having to go back on the boat, of having to return to that confining existence.

Resolutely, she made the effort to put those thoughts from her mind, refusing to spoil the pleasure of enjoying what days remained of her visit to Glencoe—and her time with Matthew.

A flurry of movement caught her eye as she came around the back turn. Amy turned in the saddle, drawing a sharp breath at the sight of Adam. The dog was racing at full speed, zigzagging, in pursuit of a terrified rabbit. Too late she saw that they were on a collision course with Sea Foam. Onto the track they came in a blur of fur and flying feet, almost colliding with the horse.

Frantically, Amy jerked the reins and her mount reared, almost unseating her. In that split second, a flash of lightning glowed with eye-searing brightness, followed almost immediately by a deafening crack of thunder that seemed to rend the skies in two.

Emitting a shrill neigh of fright, Sea Foam panicked. With his four feet on the ground again, he took off at a flat gallop. Amy tugged on the reins to no avail.

Her eyes grew round when she saw that the horse was no longer following the curve of the track. He was heading straight for the rail!

Leaning forward, Amy closed her eyes and pressed her knees tight against the horse as she prayed for a safe jump. Beneath her, she felt the animal surge upward, as if he had suddenly sprouted wings and was heading for the sky.

In a smooth and graceful motion, Sea Foam cleared the railing, and when Amy dared open her eyes again they were speeding across the meadow.

Amy inhaled deeply, and instead of trying to halt the panicked animal, she gave him free rein, deciding to let him run. His hoofs seemed barely to touch the carpet of bluegrass as he sped onward. The feeling was exhilarating, and Amy felt as one with the great stallion.

Over the rhythmic drumming of Sea Foam's hoofs, Amy gradually became aware of another sound: her name being called with frantic urgency. She sent a swift glance over her shoulder, seeing Matthew coming in her direction astride a bay mare. But Sea Foam was still unresponsive, giving Amy no recourse but to ride him until he grew tired.

Above his checkered shirt, Matthew's face was white, and his heart pounded in a painful way that made him gasp for air. He'd seen virtually everything that had happened, having just turned into the drive when he saw Sea Foam sail over the railing.

Though past his prime, Sea Foam was able to outrun the mare, but after a few long and harrowing minutes his age began to tell, his pace began to slow. The younger horse started to gain on him until at last they were running neck to neck.

In that instant before Matthew grabbed the reins, Amy turned her head toward him, a breathless smile on her lovely face. Mildly astonished, he saw no sign of fear, only an excitement that pinked her cheeks and left her gray eyes shining with exuberance. His heart swelled with pride at her courage.

Sea Foam finally allowed himself to be halted. Amy slipped from his back and into Matthew's arms. She rested her head on his chest, trying to catch her breath.

"If you must race," he said shakily, "I wish you'd do it on the track."

Her hair grazing his chin was as soft as the wings of a butterfly. Bending his head, Matthew found her lips. Holding her slender body tight against him, he kissed her deeply and urgently.

An as yet unawakened passion began to stir within Amy. For the first time in her life, she wanted a man to make love to her. And not just any man. She wanted this man, wanted him to hold her, to touch her, to teach her how to become a woman.

Matthew dared hold her no longer. His face flushed a deep crimson at the thought of her becoming aware of the extent of his intoxication with her nearness. Releasing her, he looked down at her, his brow still creased in concern from the mishap that could have so easily turned into tragedy.

The sudden, sensual thoughts that invaded Amy's mind caused her own cheeks to flame in embarrassment, and she moved a step away, fearing he would see the desire in her eyes. She had never felt this way before and found herself trembling with a need she had no idea how to satisfy. Rather than alleviating this strange feeling, when Matthew held her in his arms it seemed only to increase the tingling sensation that afflicted her from head to toe.

After a long moment, Matthew walked toward Sea Foam. Reaching out, he patted the animal on the neck, feeling the dampness of sweat beneath his palm. He handed Amy the reins and picked up those of his own horse.

"We'd better walk them back," he said, putting an arm around her tiny waist and renewing those disturbing sensations that left Amy with a sweet ache in the pit of her stomach.

When they reached the stables a while later, Amy helped Matthew as he carefully rubbed down both Sea Foam and the mare. She was now feeling contrite, afraid she might have caused harm to Sea Foam. If so, she would never forgive herself. When they were through, Robert led the horses back to their respective stalls.

Looking at Amy's anxious face, Matthew smiled and said, "They'll be all right. Don't worry about them." He took her hand, marveling at how small and soft it felt beneath his calloused palms. Emotion rose up in him, taking his breath away. "Your mother is coming for the wedding, isn't she?" he asked in a low voice.

Amy gave a slow nod, knowing what he meant.

Matthew wet his lips. His mouth suddenly felt dry and parched. "And she's going to take you with her when she leaves . . ."

Amy bit her lip and turned away, feeling the pressure of his hand move to her arm.

"Amy, . . ." Matthew's voice cracked. "Oh, Amy, I can't let you go. You must know how I feel . . ."

She was in his arms, almost weightless. Her face

tilted up toward his, displayed such a loving trust that Matthew's knees went weak at the sight of it. Bending forward, he placed his lips on hers and felt them part like a budding flower beneath his own. He wanted to make love to her right here, wanted it so badly his senses swam in a whirlpool of desire that aroused him beyond endurance.

At last he drew away. "I love you, Amy," he whispered, touching the silkiness of her pale hair.

Although Matthew spoke the words tenderly, they seemed an inadequate definition of the emotion he was feeling. Each beat of his heart echoed her name. Her tremulous smile touched him deeply, and his own eyes stung with threatening tears as he saw hers mist.

Amy moved closer, feeling the warmth of him envelop her, wishing with all her heart that she could tell him how much she loved him.

Unable to resist her nearness, Matthew again gathered her in his arms, and his hand, with a will of its own, gently cupped her breast. He felt the tremor that shook her slim body, but she did not draw away from him. Adoration flooded Matthew's heart, and he knew he would never know peace until he made her his own.

"I want to love you," he whispered, "to cherish you for the rest of our lives." He looked deeply into the gray depths of her eyes. "I don't have much to offer you . . ."

He paused as Amy put a fingertip to his lips. *But you have everything to offer me,* she thought, wondering how she could let him know how her heart cried out for him.

Matthew kissed the softness of her fingertip and caught her hand in his own. "Marry me, Amy..."

Her eyes brimmed with happy tears, and she could manage no more than a quick nod before his lips were again upon hers.

A few drops of rain began to fall, cloaking them in a silvery mist that went unnoticed as they clung to each other.

Chapter 28

Moving briskly around her spotless kitchen, Rissa hummed a little gospel tune to herself.

The kitchen faced east to catch the early sun, and on this Tuesday morning nature was obliging, flooding the room with warm gold that highlighted the oilcloth on the floor and pinpointed the porcelain fittings on the cabinets. Showy red curtains fluttered by the open windows, prodded by a fresh spring breeze.

Rissa was proud of her kitchen and proud of the fact that Edward always consulted her each time he purchased anything for it. The coal stove was new and of the latest design. Rissa herself had made the curtains and selected the cheery, floral-patterned oilcloth that never went a day without a vigorous scrubbing.

Despite her absentminded humming, Rissa was a bit disturbed. Edward had informed her that he was hiring extra help for the wedding, insisting that she could not do everything by herself.

While Rissa welcomed assistance in making beds and serving food, she wasn't too happy about having strangers in her kitchen; she envisioned plates being broken and pots being scratched by careless hands.

At the sound of the door opening, Rissa looked up and smiled as Bethany and Henry entered the kitchen at the same time.

Bethany had come downstairs a short while ago and had seen Henry in the hall. The Negro had just come out of Cyrus's bedroom, holding yet another tray of untouched food.

Placing the tray on the table, Henry gave his wife a look that was almost apologetic, as if he had somehow been at fault. Rissa's smile had turned into a frown that deeply creased her otherwise smooth brow.

"He has an appetite like a bird, that one," she complained heartily to Bethany as Henry hastily made an exit. She viewed the griddle cakes and rasher of bacon with a disgruntled eye, then scraped it into the dog's dish, which she placed outside the rear door. "Sometimes, when Mistah Edward eats with him in his bedroom, he don't do so bad," she continued, coming back to the table. "But alone . . . ," she shook her head sadly, "he just picks at his food."

"But why doesn't he come into the dining room to eat his meals?" Bethany asked. She found the idea upsetting that Cyrus spent day after day in his room. Even more disturbing was the fact that he ate so sparingly.

Rissa shrugged. "Can't stand to be carried by Henry. Says it makes him feel like a helpless baby. An' he just won't use his crutches or that fancy chair Mistah

Edward bought him." Picking up the plates and utensils from the tray, she deposited them in the sink. "Many's the time Mistah Edward tried to talk him into comin' out of his room," she went on, putting the tray into a cabinet. "But Mistah Cyrus pays him no mind. Stubborn as a mule, he is."

Bethany frowned in thought, absently biting her lower lip. "Rissa, would you mind terribly if I made Mr. Hammond's breakfast tomorrow morning?"

The black woman regarded her doubtfully for a moment, then shrugged again. "Don't matter none to me, Missus Hammond."

Bethany touched her arm. "Thank you, Rissa. If you have a spare apron, I'll make some batter now; it can rise overnight."

The next morning, Bethany got up early, even before Edward was awake. Carefully, she moved his arm, flung across her waist, and squirmed out of bed as quietly as she could. Looking down at his sleeping form, her heart swelled with love. She brushed her lips across his forehead, then dressed and went downstairs.

As early as she was, Rissa was about her chores, explaining that her sons, Paul and Robert, rose at four; Matthew got up an hour later.

Rissa poured coffee for them both, then sat down at the kitchen table and watched Bethany with interest.

Using muffin tins, Bethany filled them halfway with the batter she had made the night before which was now light and spongy. She placed the rings on a hot griddle, then turned her attention to making Hollandaise.

"You gonna put that there sauce on the eggs, missus?'' Rissa asked skeptically. *Mistah Cyrus sure won't like that,* she thought to herself.

''Yes,'' Bethany answered, adding a generous sprinkle of cayenne to the mixture. ''It's really quite good,'' she added, seeing Rissa's expression. ''I had it for the first time about a year ago, in Paris.''

''Paris?'' Rissa murmured, her attention diverted. ''I've never been further than Louisville. Henry and me go there almost every May to watch the Derby, specially if Mistah Edward has a horse entered in the race.''

Turning from the stove, Bethany looked at her with quick interest. ''Has he ever won?''

Rissa shook her head. ''No. Had a filly entered last year.'' She chortled. ''I told Mistah Edward that no filly ever won that race. Only colts. But he wouldn't listen to me.'' Her plump shoulders moved in a way that clearly conveyed how wrong Edward had been to disregard her expert advice. ''Went ahead an' entered that there Moon Song, and that little gal didn't even show. Come in fifth, she did.'' Picking up her cup, she took a deep swallow, smacking her lips appreciatively.

Bethany laughed. ''Well, surely one day a filly will win.'' She paused and pursed her lips. ''I'll bet Dawn's Light could win.''

Slowly, Rissa shook her head again. ''Too old. Only three-year-olds can run in the Derby,'' she explained. ''But I think you're right, missus. That little horse got the best speed I ever seen.''

Bethany leaned over the stove, the steamy heat flushing her cheeks with warm color. The eggs were poached just right. Assembling the meal, she put it on a tray. Getting up, Rissa poured coffee into the silver pot and placed it alongside the plate, adding an extra cup at Bethany's direction.

"Mistah Cyrus takes his coffee black," she advised, viewing the strange steaming meal with fresh doubt. She sincerely hoped Bethany wouldn't be too offended when it came back untouched.

Balancing the tray in the crook of her left arm, Bethany left the kitchen and proceeded down the hall to Cyrus's room, tapping lightly on the door. Receiving permission to enter—which Cyrus extended in a decidedly gruff tone of voice—Bethany opened the door, ignoring the look of surprise on her father-in-law's face.

"Good morning," she said brightly.

Pulling the covers up high on his chest, Cyrus scowled at her. "Where's Henry?"

"I suspect he's about his chores," she answered, placing the rectangular tray, which was fitted with short legs on each corner, on his lap. "I thought I would join you for breakfast this morning. I hope you don't mind."

"What's that?" he grumbled, viewing the food before him with a suspicious eye, wondering what was under that carpet of yellow sauce. He wasn't at all certain he wanted to find out.

"A dish I had in Paris last year."

His frown was tinged with disgust. "Rissa knows I like plain food. Never did like fancy stuff."

"Rissa didn't make it," Bethany said calmly. "I did." She poured two cups of coffee, taking one of them for herself.

Cyrus looked at his plate again, then up at her. She was smiling in what he took to be an encouraging way. With a sigh of resignation, he picked up his knife and fork and cut into the eggs. He was certain he wasn't going to like it, but he didn't want to offend his daughter-in-law after she had gone to the trouble of making it.

Bethany sipped her coffee and looked out the window as Cyrus proceeded to clean his plate. Then she returned to the bed. Removing the tray from his lap, she placed it on the table.

"Would you like more coffee?" she asked.

Cyrus shook his head, blotting his mouth with the napkin and suppressing a contented belch. "No, no. I've had enough, thank you."

Taking a deep breath, Bethany gave him a level look before she spoke. "You know that Edward and I will be having a formal wedding ceremony here in the house in a few weeks, don't you?"

He nodded and plumped his pillow. "I know."

"It would mean so much to Edward, and to me, as well, if you would attend the wedding. I know Edward has told you how hurried our first ceremony was." She gave a short laugh. "Legal though it might be, we both want our friends and family to witness it."

Raising his head, Cyrus gave her a startled glance. "Can't see how I can do that, unless you want to bring the preacher in here . . ."

She ignored the hopeful look in his eyes. "The wedding will take place in the drawing room," Bethany said firmly. "You can use the wheelchair," she suggested. "Henry will help you. . . ."

Eyes wide, he glared at her, affronted by the suggestion. "I won't use that contraption! I'm no—" He bit down on the word "cripple." Strangely, he had never considered himself to be one.

Stepping closer, Bethany rested a warm hand on the thin arm. "Please make an exception this one time," she said softly. "You must begin to look to the future..."

"The future is yours," Cyrus said sadly, averting his face. "I have nothing but the past."

"You're wrong," she cried out, upset with this display of defeatism. "Edward needs you. He would welcome the wisdom and experience you can offer."

Cyrus blinked, considering that. "Do you really think so?"

"Oh, yes." She bent toward him and spoke earnestly. "I would so very much like it if you would give me away..." Seeing him hesitate, waver with indecision, she added, "It is the only wedding gift I shall ask of you...."

Cyrus observed the beautiful face, the amber eyes welling with tears of entreaty—and the frozen tundra, which for so long had been his heart, melted. He could easily see why his son was in love with this woman. Edward had told him that his gambling days were over. Cyrus was certain that Bethany had influenced this decision, and he would be eternally grateful to her for that.

And, he thought, sitting up a little straighter, maybe it was about time he got out of this damn bed and saw to the business of living again. A man could moon about just so long.

"Well..." He glanced over at the hated wheelchair. "Since you put it that way, I don't see as how I can refuse."

Bending forward, Bethany kissed his cheek. "You've made me very happy."

Cyrus blinked away the annoying moisture in his eyes. "And that son of mine better make you happy, too," he declared gruffly. "Or else he'll answer to me."

Bethany laughed. "I'll tell him that . . . Papa." She rested a hand lightly on his arm. "May I call you that?"

Looking down at her gold band, Cyrus thought of his wife for the first time in many years. Remembering was always painful for him. He had never been able to get over his grief at losing his darling Annabella. And the fact that she had died without him being able to comfort her during the last hours was a never-ending source of anguish to him.

Seeing the direction of his gaze, Bethany said, "Thank you. It really is quite lovely. I feel honored to be wearing it."

"It belongs on a pretty woman," he murmured, then looked up, staring at her for a long moment. "I'd be honored to give you away." On an impulse, he reached for the slim hand, feeling the coolness of smooth flesh beneath his own weathered palm. It was like touching youth, touching life. "It will be good to have life and laughter in this house again," he said, clearing his throat. "It's been empty too long, filled with memories that leave a bitter taste in a man's mouth."

She pressed his hand and gave him another light kiss. Then she picked up the tray and headed for the door.

"Oh, um . . . you might tell Rissa how to make that," he waved at his empty plate. "Wasn't too bad."

"I'll do that," Bethany said with a smile as she closed the door.

The wedding was scheduled to take place on the third Saturday in April. The first guest to arrive, fully a week ahead of time, was Mary.

When she learned that Bethany and Edward were already married, she gave them a dismayed look.

"Why couldn't you have waited until I was here?" she grumbled.

Bethany laughed and hugged her. "I didn't say there wouldn't be a wedding," she said, explaining the situation.

It was ten-thirty in the evening. Amy had already gone to bed, and Mary insisted that she be left undisturbed.

"I'll see her in the morning," she said, settling herself in a chair in the library.

Rissa bustled in with a tray of sandwiches and a pot of coffee. Helping herself to one of the little sandwiches, Mary asked, "How is Amy? I hope she's not been too much trouble. I can't tell you, Edward, how much I appreciate you allowing her to stay here."

"Amy's fine," Edward said quickly, pouring himself a cup of coffee. "And I assure you, she's been no trouble at all. You know you're both welcome here, for as long as you want to stay." He sat down, leaning back in his chair. "As a matter of fact, she's hardly ever in the house. She's learned to ride and has taken to it as if she had been born in the saddle."

Mary's brows rose. "Ride? You mean on a horse?" At the sound of Edward and Bethany's laughter, she raised a hand. "Forgive me, Edward. But I really can't imagine anyone wanting to ride one of those beasts."

"You haven't ever ridden?" Bethany asked in some surprise.

"No," Mary replied, giving her an amused look. "And I have no intention of ever doing so." Having finished her sandwich, she wiped her mouth with the linen napkin and settled back in her chair.

"How are the repairs coming along?" Edward asked, lighting a cigar.

Mary's shoulders moved. "Not too well." Her mood shifted and she spoke in a somber tone. "You know, at first, I blamed myself," she said quietly, with a deep sigh. "I should never have sent the old girl out onto the river with a patched boiler."

Expelling a sigh, Bethany got to her feet. "You must be exhausted, Mary. Come, I'll show you to your room."

Chapter 29

The next morning, from her bedroom window on the second floor, Mary regarded the scene that greeted her eye. Used to the muddy waters of the river, it was a pleasant change to view the sea of bluegrass that stretched as far as the eye could see. Opening the French doors, she went out onto the verandah and stood there, breathing deeply of the fresh morning air.

Looking down, she smiled as she saw Amy running with a light step in the direction of the stables. The weeks here have done her good, Mary thought to herself. She looked healthy and happy, and there was a glow about her that made her appear positively radiant, noticeable even at this distance.

Mary was about to turn away when she saw a young man emerge from the stables. Amy came to a halt before him and stood with her face tilted upward. To Mary's utter astonishment, he bent forward and kissed Amy on the lips. Mary opened her mouth to scream at the young scoundrel, but before she could get the words out, she saw Amy's arms go about his neck. Standing on tiptoe, she was returning the kiss with obvious enthusiasm.

Suddenly feeling as though she were intruding, Mary retreated into the bedroom, her heart a whirlpool of troubled emotion.

Too soon! her maternal inclinations cried out. And yet, why? She herself had been married at eighteen, a full year younger than Amy. But that was different. Wasn't it?

During breakfast, Mary studied her daughter's face and actions with great care and decided to have a talk with Edward.

Despite her resolve, it was late afternoon before an opportunity presented itself. Bethany had gone up to her room to change for supper, and Amy was taking a bath. No wonder, Mary thought disgruntledly. A person would need a dozen baths after spending all day around those horses.

"Yes," Edward said carefully in answer to her cautious question. "I had noticed that Amy and Matthew seemed attracted to each other." He regarded the older woman's concerned face. "Matthew is a fine young man," he went on quietly. "I can vouch for that." When Mary's expression didn't change, he added: "Look, if it upsets you, I'll speak to him, tell him to keep his distance."

"Oh, no. No. Don't do that." Mary made a helpless gesture. "The last thing I'd do is interfere with Amy's happiness. God knows she's had little enough. I've known that sooner or later she'd meet someone; in fact

I've prayed for it to happen. I won't always be around to care for her.'' She gave a rueful laugh that ended in a small sob. "And let's face it, I can't give her a decent life. I'll always be what I am...."

Edward put his arms around Mary's waist and hugged her. ". . . And that's one hell of a fine woman," he said softly. He patted her arm, watching as she dabbed her eyes with a lace handkerchief. "Just a minute."

Edward left the room, and when he returned a few minutes later, he carried a bottle of blackberry brandy in one hand and two glasses in the other.

"Here." He filled one of the snifters and handed it to Mary. "My mother used to swear by this stuff," he said, filling the other glass. "Claimed it cured everything from tummy aches to migraines." He put the bottle on a nearby table and nodded approvingly as Mary sipped her drink.

She grinned at him. "Your mother was a wise woman, Edward." Then she frowned. "Do you..." She wet her lips. "Do you think it's serious?"

Edward took a swallow of the fruited brandy before he answered. "I can't answer that, Mary. But I wouldn't worry about it. They're both young. Most likely it's no more than an infatuation."

Despite his words, Edward decided to have a talk with Matthew. The one thing he didn't want was for Amy to be hurt. As it turned out, Edward didn't have to say anything. He had no sooner approached Matthew than the young man told him that he and Amy wanted to get married.

"Well," Edward said, "I can't in all honesty say that

this comes as a surprise." He inclined his head at Matthew. "But I'm not the one you should be telling...."

Shifting his weight, Matthew took a deep breath. "I...thought perhaps that you could talk to Amy's mother—"

"Oh, no," Edward cut him off with a laugh and raised a hand when Matthew seemed about to persist. "You'll have to talk to Mary yourself."

"I've never met the woman!" Matthew protested, sounding dismayed.

Edward grinned at him. "Well, if she's to be your mother-in-law, don't you think we should take care of that as soon as possible?" He put a hand on Matthew's shoulder. "Tell you what I'll do. I'll let her know that you're going to join us this evening for supper and that you have something important to discuss with her afterward." He tried not to laugh at the sight of Matthew's stricken expression. The young man looked as if he had been condemned to a fate worse than death.

Supper that night seemed endless to Matthew, and he had the disconcerting feeling that Mary's dark eyes were boring into him. *She doesn't like me*, he thought in anguish. Only the sight of Amy's serene face gave him the courage to remain seated in his chair and not give in to his urge to bolt from the room in panic.

When the meal finally ended, they all went into the library, where Henry served them an after-dinner drink.

Mary accepted the sherry gratefully, feeling the need of fortification. Matthew took his glass from the tray but put it on a nearby table, fearing in his nervous state that he would drop it. He sat on the sofa, leaning forward slightly, almost on the edge of his seat, elbows on his knees, hands clasped between them. As if he sensed his posture was unfitting, he straightened, then placed his hands on his knees, palms down.

He gave Amy a pained look, and she smiled at him in what she hoped was an encouraging way. She was aware that her mother knew very well what Matthew was leading up to. Mary and Edward had had a long talk before supper, and Amy knew everything that had been said; she had been in the room and had made her feelings quite plain to them both.

Matthew looked at Mary. "Mrs. Dennison..." He paused and cleared his throat. He threw an imploring look at Edward but saw only mild interest on the older man's handsome face. No help there, he thought morosely; he was going to have to do this all by himself. "Mrs. Dennison," he began again in a stronger voice. "I am not a rich man...."

Mary raised her glass to her lips and looked at him over the rim. "Who among us is?" she noted dryly.

Matthew frowned. "Even so," he pressed onward. "I have a respectable job and have managed to save a few dollars."

"Commendable," Mary murmured noncommittally, refusing to make it easy. She couldn't help but feel rankled with this young man who had appeared out of the blue to steal her daughter.

Matthew nodded, feeling he had scored a point. His eyes again sought Amy's, and he took strength from their calm gray depths. "Amy and I... we...," he faltered at the sight of Mary's stern, forbidding countenance, wondering how such an imposing woman could have a daughter as sweet and fragile as Amy.

Getting to his feet, Matthew walked over to the fireplace, feeling an advantage in having to look down at her, forcing her to look up at him.

"Your daughter and I have discovered that we have a great deal in common and have come to enjoy each other's company very much." His mouth felt dry. Matthew cast a longing look at the glass of sherry on the table, but his feet felt rooted to the floor.

Seated in her chair, Amy sighed, both amused by and exasperated with her mother's attitude. She knew Mary well enough to know that she was deliberately making Matthew feel uncomfortable; she knew, too, that if Mary was going to refuse, she would have already done so. She tried to catch her mother's eye, but Mary wouldn't look in her direction. Matthew was looking so miserable that Amy could take no more of it.

In a graceful movement, she suddenly stood up. Moving to Matthew's side, she slipped her hand in his, her lips curved sweetly.

Clutching the small hand tightly, Matthew looked directly at Mary, all fears and uncertainty gone.

"I want to marry Amy," he stated quietly, with a firmness that Mary approved of but would not acknowledge out loud.

Mary finally looked at her daughter, but Amy was gazing up at Matthew with a rapt expression. She had no need to ask what thoughts were chasing through her daughter's mind; they were written clearly on her face for all to see, but Mary felt she must.

"Are you certain this is what you want?" she asked quietly. Seeing the emphatic nod, she turned to Matthew. "Then you have my blessing," she said with a catch in her voice and prayed with all her heart that she was doing the right thing.

Had Matthew been anyone else, worked anywhere else, been vouched for by anyone other than Edward Hammond, Mary seriously doubted she would have consented without asking the young couple to wait and reconsider.

She sighed deeply, remembering how quickly she had fallen in love with Lucian Dennison. One look had been all that was necessary for her to know her heart's desire. Nor, despite all the heartache in between, had she ever regretted it. It had never happened to her again, and probably never would.

Mary regarded her daughter's glowing face as she continued to gaze up at Matthew. She had done the right thing, Mary decided. Happy was the woman who recognized love at first glance, for the heart was seldom wrong.

Abruptly, Mary got to her feet. "Wait here," she said to Amy and Matthew. "I'll be right back."

As Mary left, Bethany took Edward's hand and drew him to the far side of the room.

"Edward," she said, her voice a trifle breathless with excitement. "We are already married...."

He chuckled. "I know that, my darling. And happy about it I am, too."

She shook her head slightly. "No, you don't understand what I'm getting at. It would be such a waste— all the preparations, the guests, the food, the decorations— just to renew the vows we have already taken."

He frowned at her. "Are you saying you want to call it off?"

"No, no." She glanced across the room and nodded at Amy and Matthew who were still gazing into each other's eyes as though the world had ceased to exist for everyone but themselves. "I'm saying I think there ought to be a real wedding, one with a bride and groom—not a husband and wife." Bethany looked at Edward and saw his broad grin as he caught her meaning.

They both turned as Mary came back into the room. Walking toward Matthew, she handed him an envelope.

His puzzlement evident, Matthew removed the bank draft, then drew his breath sharply as he saw it was made out for five thousand dollars. He thrust it at Mary as if it burned his hand.

"I can't take that!" He was so shocked his voice cracked.

"This money is not mine," Mary stated calmly, refusing to touch the paper that fluttered in Matthew's hand. "It is my daughter's dowry. Amy will not go to her husband penniless!" She raised her head, sounding affronted at the mere thought of such an occurrence.

Matthew looked at his prospective mother-in-law for a long moment, then nodded, putting the envelope in his pocket. Amy thrust her arms around his waist and rested her head on his chest.

Quickly, Mary reached out and firmly drew Amy to a distance. "There will be none of that until after the wedding!" she declared emphatically, frowning at Matthew with such ferocity his blush burned his ears.

"And speaking of weddings," Bethany said, coming to stand at Mary's side, "let me tell you what we have planned for Amy and Matthew. . . ."

Edward smiled as he watched the two women leave the room, their voices rising in excitement as they discussed the wedding preparations.

The invitations had already been sent out, and Bethany could do nothing at this date to advise the guests that the name of the bride and groom had been changed. But the very next day, Bethany, accompanied by Mary, took Amy to Michele Arnaud's shop, cajoling the bewildered woman into altering the cream satin gown yet one more time, so that it would fit Amy's smaller frame.

Chapter 30

Coming out onto the front porch, Edward squinted in the bright sunshine, hoping the perfect weather would hold through tomorrow. Although the wedding itself would take place in the house, the reception was to be held outdoors.

Hattie McDowell had arrived the night before, and Edward had just left Bethany, Hattie, Amy, and Mary lingering over their morning coffee, engaged in an animated conversation that dealt almost exclusively with the coming festivities.

A sigh built up in him, and Edward sternly repressed it. This wedding had been his own idea, he reminded himself; even if it had turned out to be for someone else. But he fervently wished it were over, so that he and Bethany could be alone again.

How selfish I am, he chided himself, with a rueful shake of his head. _I don't want to share her with anyone!_

341

Standing there, Edward turned his head and regarded the stone cottage with a thoughtful expression. It was still an eyesore, a chore he had been putting off long enough.

Seeing Matthew in the shed row, Edward walked down the steps and headed in that direction.

"Matt, have you given any thought as to where you and Amy will live?" Edward asked, watching Matthew apply the chamois to the saddle he was cleaning.

"Well, sometime next week, I was going to look for a small place in town." Matthew paused in his task. "For now, I thought we'd stay in my room—if you have no objection," he added.

Edward frowned. "That room is hardly big enough for you," he observed. "Would you consider living in the cottage by the lake? It would be a damn sight more convenient than making the trip into town every day."

Matthew's face lit up at the suggestion. "Amy would like that," he exclaimed enthusiastically, his first thoughts, as usual, for her.

"Then it's settled. You can't move in until it's made suitable, of course. In the meantime, I think it best that you both stay in the main house. I'll tell Rissa to prepare one of the guest bedrooms for your use." Edward paused and clapped the young man on the shoulder. "You're a lucky man, Matthew. Amy is very special indeed."

That night, when Edward closed the bedroom door, he heaved a sigh of relief.

"I haven't been alone with you all day," he complained, crawling into bed beside Bethany. The lamp was lit, but he didn't extinguish it, wanting to fill his eyes with the sight of her. She lay on her stomach, arms around her pillow, her smiling face turned toward him. Her unclothed body glistened from her recent bath. She smelled of soap and roses.

Edward looked at her for a long moment. "I adore you," he whispered, moving closer. His hand swept down her body from the nape of her neck to the hollow of the small of her back, paused a moment on the delicious swell of her buttocks, then continued down long, well-shaped limbs. "Gad, you're a beautiful filly," he murmured admiringly, loving the satiny feel of her.

Raising herself up on an elbow, Bethany stared at him. "Edward . . ." She put a hint of playful exasperation in her voice. "You've got a look in your eye like you're getting ready to breed me!"

He grinned in a leering manner, his eye on her rounded breasts. "That's not a bad idea," he said, reaching for her.

Bethany snuggled against him, her hands working through his golden hair. "Perhaps you've already done so," she murmured in a barely audible voice, feeling her heartbeat quicken as his tongue played with her nipple.

Intent on kissing every available inch of her body, it took the better part of a minute for her words to sink in. Then Edward's head shot up. He stared at her with a stunned expression. Bethany broke into a delighted laugh at the sight of his gaping mouth.

Edward put his hands on her shoulders, and she felt them trembling against her bare flesh. "Bethany, . . . do you mean we're to have a child?" His voice broke on a note of incredulity, and her laughter bubbled forth again.

"That usually happens when you mate a virile stallion with a beautiful filly. Hadn't you noticed? Surely I don't have to tell you that" she teased, running her fingertips through the soft hair on his chest.

"Are you sure?" he asked, still staring at her, wondering why the thought had never occurred to him.

Bethany gave him a soft smile. "I'm fairly certain," she replied, moving her hand to his cheek. "Are you pleased?"

"Oh, my darling." He took her in his arms. For the moment he couldn't speak and had to make two attempts before the words could pass the choked feeling in his throat. "Ecstatic would be more like it. Oh, Bethany, . . . you could give me no greater gift than a child of our love." He held her a moment longer, gathering his whirling thoughts, then drew away, scanning her face with anxious eyes. "You must stay in bed. I'll send for the doctor immediately." Throwing the blankets aside, he got to his feet.

"Whatever for?" Bethany protested with a laugh as he began to tuck the covers around her. "Edward, the baby won't be here for almost eight months! I have no intention of staying in bed for that length of time." She made a face as she looked at him, wondering if he had heard what she said.

Kneeling at the side of the bed, he put a hand on her stomach, still flat and smooth. "My son . . . ," he murmured with a note of reverence.

She cocked a brow. "Son?" A small grin teased her lips. "What if it's a girl?"

Edward looked startled at the possibility, then a bit uneasy. "I've never raised a girl. . . ."

She giggled at that. "And have you raised a boy?"

"No. But I was one," he said quickly and in all seriousness. "There's nothing difficult about raising boys." He waved a hand. "They just grow up all by themselves."

She gave him a doubtful look. "Well . . . I'll do my best."

"Oh, Bethany . . ." Edward bent forward, kissing her gently, as though she had suddenly turned into a delicate piece of china that might shatter beneath his touch. He was feeling so damn proud of himself. Lucky he wasn't wearing a shirt. He'd pop the buttons right off it.

She returned his kiss, then rubbed her cheek against his. "Edward, . . . let's not tell anyone about it until after the wedding. Tomorrow belongs to Amy."

"All right," he agreed softly. "It will be our secret. But I have an idea that eveyone will know about it just by looking at my face," he added with a laugh.

"And now," Bethany said, putting her arms around his neck, "I do believe there is the matter of some unfinished business between us." She kicked off the covers and drew him close to her.

"My love," he said uncertainly. Mentally, he cursed himself for his lack of control, for he felt himself becoming aroused to the point where he was shaking with his need. "Perhaps we shouldn't; I'd never forgive myself if I caused harm to you or the child—"

She nuzzled his neck, taking little nips on his ear-lobe. "The only way you could harm me or your child is to withhold yourself from us," she interrupted in a voice that was becoming breathless with her longing to feel his fullness within her.

The day of the wedding dawned clear, the sun shining brightly from a cloudless sky.

At The Willows, Eunice Madison clasped a string of pearls around her neck and checked her reflection one final time in the mirror. The red hair that she had bequeathed to both Lydia and her son Jeffrey had long since turned a becoming shade of gray. Even the added pounds that now plumped her once–slender body didn't hide the fact that she had been a handsome woman in her youth. Satisfied with her appearance, Eunice left her room.

Crossing the hall, she tapped softly on Lydia's door, then opened it, even though silence had greeted her knock.

Except for meals, Lydia had spent the past week in her room. Eunice had no idea what had taken place at Glencoe. Another quarrel, she assumed. Lydia really should try to control that temper of hers. The only good thing that had happened, in Eunice's opinion, was the departure of Colin Thatcher. Eunice didn't like the man. Aside from the fact that he gambled for a living, he had cold, shifty eyes. Certainly he wasn't to be considered a suitable match for her daughter. Eunice had breathed a sigh of relief when she saw that Lydia's interest in the man had been only superficial.

Standing just inside the doorway, Eunice glanced around the room. Lydia was seated in a chair by the window and didn't turn as her mother came further into the room. Although it was close to noon, she was still wearing her nightgown. A satin robe was draped carelessly over her shoulders, the emtpy sleeves trailing over the arms of the chair. Her hair fell loosely, its slightly tousled appearance attesting to the fact that it had not yet been combed this day.

"How are you feeling?" Eunice's voice was low, solicitous.

"Fine." And that was a lie, Lydia thought to herself. Oh, God, would she ever get over him? How long did a broken heart take to mend? A week, a month, a lifetime?

"Lydia, my dear," Eunice said softly. "It's almost time to leave. The wedding is scheduled for two o'clock."

"I'm not going."

Eunice frowned. "I wish you would reconsider. Your father thinks that this would be the perfect time for us to heal the breach between our families."

"I have no intention of going," Lydia said tersely. "I thought I made that plain. I will not watch Edward marry that trollop!"

Looking distressed, Eunice came closer. "Dear . . ." She paused, wringing her hands. "The wedding . . ." She sighed deeply. "Edward is not the one who's being married."

Turning in her chair, Lydia gave her mother a sharp look. "What are you talking about?" she demanded. Her hands gripped the armrests as if she were about to leap from her chair. "I saw the invitation . . ."

"Yes, I know," Eunice said slowly, fingering the pearls at her throat. "Really, I don't know the details. Micky Ivers met Matt Fletcher in town yesterday."

Lydia nodded impatiently. Micky Ivers was their senior groom.

"Well, it appears that the wedding to be held at Glencoe is for Matthew and a girl named Amy Dennison."

Lydia got to her feet, her heart racing wildly. "You mean Edward isn't getting married?"

Eunice bit her lip. "Lydia . . . Edward is already married. He and Bethany—is that her name?—were married by Reverend Stone some weeks ago." She made a vague gesture. "It was all done on the spur of the moment. I have no idea why . . ."

Lydia's face was the color of chalk.

"My dear, I really think you should go," Eunice said with a forcefulness that was unusual for her. "Everyone knows that you and Edward were engaged not too long ago. Your absence would make it appear as though you had been the one who was jilted."

Lydia's laughter was infused with a note of hysteria, and Eunice viewed her with alarm.

"But I *have* been jilted, Mother," she said with false brightness. "Did I neglect to tell you that?"

Eunice wet her lips and looked annoyed. "It is unnecessary for anyone to know that . . .," she began firmly, then turned as she heard Margaret's voice from the doorway.

"There you are!" she said to Eunice. "Jeffrey said to tell you that the carriage is ready." She looked at Lydia and blinked in assumed surprise. "Lydia! You're not even dressed . . ."

Eunice came hastily forward, placing a hand on Margaret's shoulder. "Lydia isn't feeling well. I'm quite certain she has a fever. It would be better if she stayed home."

"Oh, how sad," Margaret said, sounding anything but. A bright smile flashed across her thin face as she regarded her sister-in-law. "Everyone will be there. I've heard that half the town's been invited. But don't you worry, Lydia. I'll tell you all about it when I get back."

But for once Margaret's jibes had no effect on Lydia, who had collapsed in her chair again. She stared out the window and tried to banish the memories that tormented her with their sweetness.

Chapter 31 _

The ceremony was scheduled for two o'clock, but by noon guests were already arriving at Glencoe.

Dressed in a silk gown of tawny gold, Bethany circulated among the guests, trying to remember everyone's name once she had greeted them. She'd had no idea that Edward knew so many people.

Bethany had been afraid that when Cyrus learned of the new arrangements, he would refuse to attend the wedding. To her delighted surprise, however, she saw Henry solemnly and with great dignity pushing the wheelchair with its fancy wicker back into the drawing room . . . and in it was Cyrus. He was dressed in a tan frock coat that was unbuttoned, revealing a yellow satin vest. His dark brown cravat was adorned with a diamond pin. Rushing over to him, Bethany kissed him soundly and gave him a quick hug.

"Thank you for coming," she whispered.

"Nothing could have kept me away," Cyrus replied

cheerfully, nodding to neighbors he hadn't seen in years. He didn't tell Bethany of those long minutes filled with indecision while he had been dressing. But in the end, Cyrus reminded himself that he had given his word. Hammond men never reneged on their word.

Well before the appointed hour, the house was filled with people. Buggies and carriages lined the drive and spilled onto the road.

Standing on the front porch, more in an effort to get out of the way than to greet arriving guests, Matthew's eyes lit up when he saw his brother alight from a hired cab. Although his whole family had been invited, Alexander was the only one scheduled to attend.

"Alexander!" Matthew came forward to shake his brother's hand. "I'm so glad you could make it. I can't tell you how good it is to see you again." He viewed his older brother with a wide grin. It had been more than five years, but Alexander hadn't changed much. He was of a height with Matthew, but his hair was a darker brown, falling into thick sideburns at his lean jaw.

"I'm sorry I was the only one able to come. Roberta is expecting again. The doctor thought the trip too much for her. And Mother, as I wrote you, has been ailing."

"How is she?" Matthew asked quickly. Alexander had written some weeks ago that their mother had taken a fall down the stairs.

Alexander sighed. "As well as can be expected. Her hip is healing slowly. But after the fall she took, we were all glad she didn't suffer an even worse injury. Roberta is staying with her until I get back. Now, what about you?" He laughed. "Never thought the woman existed who could capture you!"

Matthew flushed, looking altogether pleased with himself. "It was the other way around, I assure you." He paused, compressed his lips, then flashed another grin. "You know, I feel I owe you an apology, Alexander."

The other man registered surprise. "Whatever for?"

"When you first saw Roberta and announced your intention of marrying her before you'd even been properly introduced, I ... well ..."

Alexander broke into a hearty laugh. "You couldn't believe it until the lightning bolt struck you, is that it?"

Somewhat ruefully, Matthew nodded his head. "I guess that about sums it up."

Alexander draped his arm about Matthew's shoulders as they headed into the house. "You've gotten your just rewards, little brother. And I for one couldn't be more pleased. I cannot wait to meet the bride."

Entering the foyer, Matthew cornered Edward and introduced him to his brother. After exchanging a few pleasantries and assuring Alexander that he was welcome to stay as long as he liked, Edward returned to the drawing room, viewing the milling crowd of people that was growing with every passing minute.

It was some fifteen minutes later when Edward glanced toward the door and saw the Madisons standing uncertainly on the threshold. Samuel Madison was fifty-three, two years older than Cyrus, but unlike that man, Samuel gave the impression of being considerably younger than his age. His brown hair was thick and wavy, his body lean and wiry.

Edward had faced a momentary dilemma regarding

the Madisons. Knowing how his father felt about them, he hesitated to send them an invitation. Yet he himself had always maintained a cordial relationship with them.

And then, of course, there was the matter of Lydia....

In the end, Edward had sent the invitation, addressing it to Samuel Madison and family. Lydia, he reasoned, could make up her own mind as to whether she would attend the wedding or not.

Now, a quick look told him that Lydia was not with them. Edward wasn't aware of the sigh of relief he expelled as he hurried forth to greet them.

Cyrus, too, had noted the arrival of the Madisons, but when Samuel offered a tentative nod in his direction, Cyrus quickly looked away, his expression leaving no doubt about his displeasure.

More carriages were coming up the drive, and Edward viewed the swelling crowd in amazement. He hadn't realized they'd sent out so many invitations.

Joan Princeton arrived with her husband, as did Emily Simmons, who had come with her parents. Both young women were startled to learn that they would be attending the marriage of two people they didn't know. Bethany spent the better part of twenty minutes explaining the situation to them until Edward took her arm and drew her aside.

"Reverend Stone is here," he said to her. "I think we're ready to begin. Is Amy dressed?"

She nodded. "Mary is upstairs with her. I'll go and tell them—"

"No you don't!" Edward said firmly, blocking her passage. "I don't want you running up and down the stairs. I'll go."

"All right," she said softly, with a knowing smile. She watched him ascend the stairs, then urged all the guests to be seated.

Chairs had been placed on either side of the room, creating a makeshift aisle between them, which Mary and Bethany had decorated with white satin ribbons. With the exception of the grand piano, the rest of the furniture had been removed from the room.

The Reverend Stone, Bible in hand and looking particularly severe and gaunt in black broadcloth, stood patiently waiting for everyone to be seated. Bessie Stone, tightly corseted beneath her mauve satin dress, an expectant look on her kindly face, sat erect at the piano, hands poised over the keys. At a nod from her husband, the first chords of the wedding march drifted through the house.

A moment later, Amy appeared, her hand on Edward's arm, the three-foot train of her gown rustling softly as it flowed across the carpet. A low murmur wafted from the crowd, sounding like a sigh of appreciation.

Bethany felt a tiny twinge of regret that vanished almost as soon as it made itself known, turning into a small smile on her lips. Married and pregnant, she would be foolish even to consider wearing a wedding gown.

Michele Arnaud, who was among the guests, had done her work well. The cream satin gown molded Amy's slim body like a loving caress. Tiny seed pearls had been sewn into a floral pattern across the bodice and were repeated at the hem. A crescent-shaped cap covered her silvery blond hair, from which a white veil fell to cover her face, floating in back nearly to the floor. The long sleeves came to a point on the back of her hands, one of which was holding a bouquet of white roses.

Matthew's face as he watched the approach of his bride held an expression of reverence that brought tears to Mary's eyes.

But there were no tears in Amy's eyes as she came slowly down the aisle. Though her eyes were shining, it was not with tears, but love.

Reverend Stone cleared his throat as Amy and Edward paused before him. "Who gives this woman away?"

"I do," Edward responded quietly, placing Amy's hand in Matthew's waiting one.

Sitting in the first row, Mary at her side, Bethany dabbed at her eyes with her lace handkerchief. She and Edward exchanged a long glance during the simple ceremony, and she knew that he, like she, was silently renewing their vows. She held his gaze until the ceremony was concluded, mentally offering him a kiss.

Because the day was fine, tables had been set up on the front lawn. Trees were adorned in pale green leaves, and daffodils and lilies of the valley bobbed lazily in the soft spring breeze. The monotonous hum of bees informed everyone that these insects were diligently going about their duties.

The servants that Edward had hired for the occasion scurried about, making certain that everyone had a glass of champagne with which to toast the newlyweds as they cut into the huge four-tiered wedding cake that Rissa had labored over for two days. Edward then gave a brief speech of congratulation, after which everyone milled around heavily laden tables that offered an abundance of food.

Helping himself to a piece of cold salmon, Edward smiled as he saw Bethany coming toward him.

"Everything has worked out so wonderfully," she declared happily, giving his arm a squeeze. "I'm so glad you agreed to all this."

Inclining his head, he asked, "You're not sorry that we didn't have a second ceremony?"

A small smile played at the corners of her lips. "The more I think about it, the more I'm convinced I would not have had our wedding any other way."

He looked at her for a long moment. "You know," he said musingly, touching the softness of a curl, "I wonder which of us would have won that game of poker if Colin hadn't interfered."

"Don't you know?" she teased. Reaching out, she adjusted his perfectly situated cravat. "That can be easily resolved, my love. Some long, cold winter night— when we have nothing better to do—let's find out. . . ."

He grinned and caught her hand, giving it a quick kiss. "It's a date, lovely lady." Hearing his name called just then, Edward turned.

Eunice Madison bustled toward him, resplendent in red-and-yellow–striped taffeta and carrying a lace-frilled parasol. At her side, Margaret quickened her steps to keep up with her mother-in-law, casting a backward glance at her husband, Jeffrey, who was talking to some friends. She was also garbed in a striped dress, the effect of which served to emphasize her thin, flat-chested body.

"The ceremony was lovely," Eunice exclaimed, pausing before Edward and Bethany. "Thank you for inviting us."

"It's nice to have you here," Edward said sincerely with a nod of his head that included Margaret, who made no response. She was staring at Bethany.

Eunice licked her lips. "Ah...I'm sorry Lydia couldn't make it. She's...she's not feeling well."

"I understand," Edward said quickly to cover the awkward moment. "Have you met my wife?"

The woman's lips stretched to a thin smile as she observed Bethany. "I've not had the pleasure..." Eunice was almost as distressed as Lydia was with the way things had turned out, for she was fond of Edward and thought that the match would have been a good one for her daughter. But Eunice was not one to hold a grudge, and she, in fact, wished Edward well.

While Edward presented Bethany, Margaret took note of everything. Beneath her sweeping, wide-brimmed hat, her eyes were openly curious. A secret smile worked its way across her narrow lips. She had always been jealous of Lydia's fiery beauty and caustic wit. Still staring at Bethany, Margaret mentally prepared herself for the enjoyment of telling Lydia in detail of the day's events: how attentive Edward was to his wife, how his eyes softened each time he looked at her, and how beautiful Bethany looked in the fashionable tawny-gold gown that so closely matched her eyes.

Samuel Madison, feeling a trifle uncomfortable in the formal attire his wife had insisted he wear, stood on the front porch, drink in hand, and surreptitiously regarded Cyrus Hammond. Henry had wheeled his chair outside and placed it beneath the spreading branches of a huge oak tree. Hammond was holding a glass of champagne but had taken no more than a sip from it.

Samuel hesitated, set his mouth firmly, then walked toward him, ignoring the scowl that etched Cyrus's brow as he noted the approach. He was, Samuel noticed with a nudge of surprise, wearing shoes.

"You're looking well, Cyrus," he said, coming to stand before him.

"What the hell are you doing on Glencoe land, Sam Madison?"

"I was invited."

"Not by me," Cyrus declared in his usual blunt way. He hadn't known the Madisons would be here, and the discovery didn't please him at all.

Samuel ignored that. "You know, Cyrus, I'm thinking it might be time for us to lay aside our differences and be the friends and neighbors we once were." He kept his tone neutral, having decided he would not allow himself to be goaded into anger.

Cyrus's eyes narrowed dangerously. "I'll not embarrass my son and his wife by causing a disturbance on this day." His voice was low, his expression hard and unyielding. "But I'll ask you kindly to partake of any refreshments offered . . . then leave my house!"

"It's been fifteen years, Cyrus," Samuel said mildly, refusing offense.

Cyrus looked away. "Fifteen or fifty; makes no difference to me," he retorted, not feeling obligated to offer Samuel Madison the usual courtesies one would accord a guest.

Samuel regarded him for a long moment. "I wasn't the only one in the state to stand with the Federals," he pointed out in the same quiet voice. "Besides, we're united under one flag now, Cyrus—the stars and stripes."

The elder Hammond's head moved quickly as he turned to glare at the man before him. "That flag will never fly here," he muttered harshly. "Not while I'm alive."

"You always have been obstinate, Cyrus," Samuel said with a small smile, as if it were intended as a compliment.

"Know my own mind, if that's what you mean," Cyrus murmured with a disdainful sniff.

Samuel fell silent, sipping his drink. His gaze fell on Henry, who was standing at a discreet distance but close enough to respond should Cyrus need assistance. Although Samuel was certain the man could hear what was being said, the black face was expressionless, eyes fixed on a distant point somewhere behind where Samuel was standing.

Then Samuel let his eye travel across the sea of bluegrass to Dawn's Light.

"That horse," he murmured after a moment. "The Akhal-Teke . . ."

Cyrus frowned. "What about her?"

"One hell of a fine-looking animal."

"On that we agree," Cyrus said quickly. Inclining his head, he regarded his polished shoes. Henry had carefully stuffed the tips with soft cloths. Cyrus had thought they would be uncomfortable, but they weren't.

Staring down at his empty glass, Samuel pursed his lips. "Too bad you can't find a suitable stallion to service her," he said casually. "It would be a shame to put her to any other kind of breed."

"We'll get one." Cyrus waved a hand, dismissing the comment.

Samuel glanced sideways at his erstwhile friend. "I happen to know where you can get one right now, today," he remarked quietly.

Raising his head, Cyrus viewed him suspiciously.

Turning, Samuel beckoned to Jeffrey, who was standing with his wife, chatting with Edward and Bethany. When the young man approached, Samuel murmured something in his ear, too low for Cyrus to hear.

Puzzled, Cyrus watched as Jeffrey got into the Madison carriage and drove down the drive.

During his son's absence, Samuel managed to keep up a conversation, dealing in generalities, interspersed with anecdotes of horses and races, to which Cyrus responded or not as the mood took him. Although his curiosity was piqued, Cyrus wasn't about to give Samuel the satisfaction of hearing his questions.

Standing a few yards away, Edward turned to look at his father and Samuel. He could not, of course, hear their words, but he took heart from the fact that the two men had been in each other's company for several minutes now, without any noticeable incident occurring. That in itself was a milestone.

Cyrus shifted his weight in the chair, a bit surprised by his own reactions. The anger should be there, deep inside him, where it always was. Yet he seemed unable to summon it forth.

Maybe, he thought, it was the occasion. He eyed the crowd of people as they ate, walked about the grounds, or clustered in small groups, talking. He couldn't remember the last time Glencoe had hosted a social function. There were quite a few children scampering about, for everyone who had been invited had brought their families with them. The sound of their piping voices and occasional high-pitched laughter was pleasant to his ear.

With a small start, Cyrus realized he was enjoying himself! He couldn't remember the last time that had happened either. Samuel was now relating the fact that he planned to enter a horse in the Derby this year, and Cyrus found himself listening intently.

As the two men conversed, the wedding reception continued, the low hum of shared gossip and laughter going unnoticed by them.

Bethany walked to where Hattie was seated, sipping her champagne and nibbling on cold chicken. She sat down beside the older woman, happy to see that she was apparently enjoying herself.

"Are you comfortable, Hattie? Is there anything I can get for you?"

"Everything is just fine." She took a sip from her glass and put it back on the table. "Oh, Bethany, I still can't believe it. You married . . ." She shook her head and gave a small laugh. ". . . And to Edward Hammond!"

"Yes, at times I'm hard pressed to believe it," Bethany confessed with an answering laugh of her own. "But . . . oh, Hattie, I love him so much!"

"As long as you're happy, nothing else matters," Hattie declared firmly.

"And you?" Bethany grew serious. "Are you happy living with your sister?"

"Now don't you worry about that," Hattie responded quickly, wiping her lips with a linen napkin. "My sister and I get along just fine. It's a bit crowded, I suppose. Connie has five children, as I told you. But her oldest is getting married soon."

Bethany took hold of her hand and smiled into the thin, angular face. "Hattie," she said softly, "would you consider coming here to live?"

Startled, Hattie's hazel eyes grew round. "Oh, I couldn't impose."

"Impose! Good heavens, you'd be doing me a favor!" Bethany gave Hattie an affectionate hug. "I need you, Hattie. I really do..."

Hattie looked at her, and her smile was a bit wistful as she shook her head. "No, Bethany. You have your own life to lead now. We're not that far apart that we can't visit each other." She squeezed Bethany's hand. "And we will!"

Bethany's eyes clouded. "Hattie, ... are you sure?"

The older woman nodded. "I'm sure, Bethany."

Aware that a sudden hush had fallen over the group of guests, Bethany fell silent. Everyone had paused to watch the carriage coming up the drive, their eyes riveted on the golden stallion tied to the rear.

Edward glanced at his father and smiled at the animated expression he was witnessing. Wisely, he resisted the impulse to join his father and Samuel Madison; the two men were better left alone.

"My God," Cyrus breathed, looking from the stallion to Dawn's Light. The stallion was larger and broader, standing just over fifteen hands high. Except for that and the obvious anatomical differences, the two horses were identical.

Cyrus narrowed his eyes and studied the proud and

calm bearing of the stallion. The animal seemed unperturbed by the attention he was now receiving as everyone crowded around him for a closer look.

Twisting his upper body in the chair, Cyrus looked up at Samuel. "What's your price?" he demanded, trying not to show his excitement.

"Well, I wasn't exactly thinking in terms of money," Samuel replied slowly, twirling the stem of his wineglass. "I thought we might work out a trade."

Cyrus frowned and spoke cautiously. "What did you have in mind?"

"I've a mare named Sheba. Pretty as a picture. She was sired by Medallion. You remember . . . he won the Derby two years back. I thought maybe you'd lend me Sea Foam for a few weeks. I'd like to mate him with Sheba."

"Sea Foam!" Cyrus was indignant. "You know what I get for a stud fee for that horse?"

"I speculate it's about as much as I plan to charge for Baron," came the unruffled reply.

Cyrus moved in his chair and a low growl rumbled in his throat.

" 'Course, you don't have to make up your mind right now," Samuel went on, inclining his head. "On the other hand, if you agree, I could just leave Baron here and take Sea Foam back with me."

Cyrus again viewed the magnificent stallion. In the late afternoon sun, the animal appeared to have stepped from an illustrated book of Greek mythology. The well-shaped head was high, and the long neck flowed into perfectly formed withers. Like Dawn's Light, both the mane and tail were short, honey-gold in color, and of an incredibly silky texture. He leaned back. "You talk to Edward about this?"

Samuel looked surprised at the question. "No," he said truthfully. "I figured you'd be the one who'd make the decision."

"Damn right!" Cyrus agreed, then lowered his head in a thoughtful manner. "I might consider it," he said at last, rubbing his chin. "But I don't want Sea Foam tied up too long."

"Appreciate that," Samuel allowed. "Shall we say three weeks?" At Cyrus's slow nod, Samuel turned to the hovering Henry. "Bring us two bourbons. Mr. Hammond and I want to close a deal."

Cyrus glared at Henry with an air of importance. "Yes, yes. And be quick about it." He regarded his half-full glass of champagne and with a sound of disgust dumped it on the ground. "Never could abide the stuff," he confided to Samuel Madison.

Chapter 32

It was growing dark, but none of the guests gave any indication of departure. Lanterns had been lit, and overhead a finely-etched crescent moon looked down on the ongoing revelry.

Matthew stood behind Amy's chair and fidgeted, shifting his weight from one foot to the other and back again. He was uncomfortable in this sort of setting, preferring the company of horses to most people.

Right now, the only thing he really wanted was to be alone with his wife. He sensed that Amy, too, was growing restless, glancing up at him time and again with a shy smile that caused his heart to thump.

Alexander ambled by and put his glass down on the table. He smiled at Amy, making no attempt to conceal his admiration and approval. "Matt told me you were the prettiest girl he'd ever seen. I'd like to add that I think so, too." He grinned at Matthew. "Am I allowed to kiss the bride?"

Matthew laughed, more pleased with the compliment than was Amy, who had flushed in pleasure in response to the words of her new brother-in-law. "If it's on the cheek," he replied, watching as Alexander quickly did so.

The young man then took Amy's hands in his own. "I want you to promise me that you'll have Matt take you to New York for a visit. And soon! The whole family wants to meet you." Seeing her nod, Alexander squeezed her hands, then released them, facing his brother again. "I'm leaving very early in the morning, Matt. If I don't catch the train that leaves at five, I'll have to wait until evening. I promised Roberta I'd be back as soon as possible."

"I understand," Matthew said, trying not to look disappointed. "Although I do wish we had more time to spend together."

"So do I," Alexander responded with a nod. "Edward was kind enough to offer me accommodations, but I think it would be best if I return to Lexington tonight and stay at a hotel there."

Matthew's nod was reluctant. He hadn't known how much he'd missed his older brother until he'd seen him. "I'll get someone to drive you—"

"No need," Alexander interrupted quickly. "It's all been taken care of." He held out a hand and Matthew gripped it tightly. "Good-bye, Matt. I can't tell you how good it is to see you again." He put his free hand on Matthew's shoulder. "I meant what I said . . . about you and Amy coming to visit." As Alexander's boyish grin appeared now, Amy was able to see the strong resemblance between the two men. "You've got a passel of nephews you haven't even seen yet,'' Alexander added, referring to his three boys with obvious pride.

"We'll be there." Matthew said the words, but he knew it would be a long time before they'd be able to make the trip.

With Alexander's departure, Amy heard Matthew's deep sigh and quickly reached for his hand. As he viewed her lovely face everything fled from his mind except his desire to be alone with her.

Finally, at nine o'clock, Matthew took a careful look around him. Most of the guests were tipsy, in high spirits; the men clustered in groups indulging in their endless discussion of horses, the women still gossiping, the children looking sleepy but unwilling to miss a moment of the party atmosphere.

Bending forward, Matthew put a hand on Amy's shoulder. "I think if we leave now," he whispered in her ear, "no one will even know we're gone."

Amy immediately got up and followed him into the house and up the stairs. Closing the door, Matthew issued a long sigh of relief. He looked at her and his smile was a tender expression of love.

Shyly she lowered her lashes but did not feel in the least bit nervous. Amy knew she would never be uncomfortable around Matthew. Indeed, she longed for him to take her in his arms. She'd thought of nothing else all day.

"Do you want me to wait outside while you undress?" he asked softly.

Her lashes still fanning her cheeks, Amy shook her

head. A blush flowed up her throat to blossom like a budding pink rose in her cheeks.

Matthew came closer. "Let me help you with the buttons..."

Obediently, Amy turned, for the dress buttoned down the back. Matthew's hands trembled slightly as he worked them loose. Reaching out, he lifted the shining curls from her neck and kissed the warm softness beneath them, causing a shudder that set Amy's whole body to trembling. As the gown and shift fell to the floor, Matthew caught his breath.

"You know," he said wonderingly, his voice unsteady, "even an angel couldn't be as beautiful as you...." He watched as the corners of her lips tilted upward. Expressive to begin with, Amy's face really came alive when she smiled.

In a moment, his own clothes lay beside hers.

Putting his arms around her, Matthew drew her close, his lips buried in the shimmering paleness of her hair. For a long time they stood, flesh against flesh, the warmth of their bodies intermingling. His hands moved on her back, sliding across smooth skin. Reaching up, he removed the pins from her hair. Matthew's eyes drank in the sight of her from the shining mass of silvery blond hair that flowed halfway down her back, to her small and tapered feet.

"So beautiful," he murmured. Catching a silky strand of hair, he brought it to his lips.

No, my darling, Amy thought to herself. *It is you who are beautiful*; but she was pleased that he found her worthy of his admiration.

Overcome by her nearness, his need making itself

felt in no uncertain terms, Matthew picked Amy up in his arms.

On the bed, he began to kiss her, holding himself in check until he was certain she was ready. His mouth explored the satin skin, lingering over her small and perfect breasts, gratified when the rose-tinted nipples hardened beneath his questing tongue.

Amy's hands grew more insistent as she clutched him. She felt no shyness, no reservation, but gave in willingly to the turbulence that claimed her. It felt so right, so perfect that she never even thought to question her eager responses.

Easing himself on top of her, Matthew put his lips to her ear. "You'll have to help me, Amy," he whispered, putting her hand on his hardened member.

Raising her knees, Amy entwined her legs around his hips, instinctively guiding him into her.

He probed gently, moving slowly, feeling her heartbeat quicken beneath his chest, becoming as one with his own.

Amy was enveloped in pure sensation. She recoiled slightly with the sudden, searing bite of pain, but it was momentary. She shuddered and arched upward in response to his quickening pace. His stroking thrusts evoked deep womanly instincts, and her body began to move as if it had a will of its own.

Suddenly, Amy caught her breath, feeling deep within her an explosion of such intense pleasure that for the moment it was almost unbearable. Liquid fire ran through the veins of her newly awakened young body.

"Oh, Matthew!" she cried out, unaware that she did so. "I love you . . . I love you so much . . ." Her arms went around his neck and with her legs still holding him fast inside her, she clung to him.

At first, Matthew was so caught up in his own flooding release that he didn't realize what had happened. For a long moment he lay cradled in her fierce embrace. Then he gently disengaged her arms from about his neck. Raising himself up on his elbows, he looked down at her face. Her eyes were closed, lips parted slightly, her skin shining with the exertion of lovemaking.

"Amy?" he murmured in a barely audible voice, so as not to startle her.

She opened her eyes and smiled at him, a slow and contented smile of love.

"Amy, . . . tell me again," he said quietly, watching her intently. "Please, my darling, tell me again. . . ."

For an instant her stare was uncomprehending. Then her eyes widened. She had said it, she thought wonderingly. She had spoken the words aloud, the words that had filled her mind in these past weeks every time she looked at this man.

"Matthew, . . ." she said tentatively. Then her voice emerged half laughing, half sobbing. "Matthew—I love you!"

She could say no more because his lips were upon hers again.

Finally, he drew away. Propping the pillows together, he sat up and drew Amy into his arms, her head on his chest.

"Talk to me, Amy," he urged softly. "I want to know every thought you've ever had. . . ."

She gave a small laugh. "Most of them are of no consequence—"

"To me, they are," he interrupted with a kiss. "And they always will be." Her voice was like warm honey; Matthew thought he'd never heard anything as sweet in his whole life.

Her words were hesitant at first; then they came in a rush, interspersed with soft laughter and interrupted occasionally by Matthew's kisses, until at last, both of them feeling the strain of excitement and exhaustion of the day, they fell asleep, still clinging to each other.

The next morning Mary sat at the dining table, staring dejectedly into her coffee cup. She had come down early for breakfast, but Edward, Bethany, and Hattie had already begun to eat. The four of them were now on their second cup of coffee.

"I don't know—maybe I ought to sell the old girl and settle down somewhere," Mary was saying. She had just informed them that the *Nola Star* was still not serviceable, and the cost of the repairs had consumed fully a year's profit.

Edward laughed at her statement. "You know you'd never be happy away from the river. I've often thought you had the Mississippi flowing in your veins."

"Well, I suppose that's true. All the same . . ." Mary broke off as she saw Amy and Matthew paused on the threshold that led to the dining room.

Viewing them, Mary smiled. From the glow on Amy's face, she had no need to question whether her daughter was happy. It was evident that she had been treated gently and had in no way been mishandled. Mary felt a great relief.

"Mama . . ."

Mary heard the single word and her eyes flew open in astonishment. At first she thought she had imagined it. But then that single word came again, and Mary's heart swelled within her breast. Her hand went to the ruffle at her throat to contain the cry of joy she feared would erupt in a most unladylike manner.

Then, to hell with propriety! She jumped up so abruptly, her chair toppled backward. But before she could take a step, Amy flung herself forward into her mother's arms.

"It's all right, Mama," Amy said, brushing the tears from her mother's cheeks. "It's all right. I can speak again. And...oh, Mama, I have so much to tell you...."

Mary hugged the slender form, tears blurring her vision as she looked across the room at Matthew, who was grinning from ear to ear.

Into the crescendo of babbling voices that now erupted around her, Amy laughed with pure delight, a silver sound of happiness that Matthew likened to a clear fresh mountain stream.

Later that same day, Amy and Mary walked along the shore of the lake. It seemed to both of them that they had been talking non-stop for hours; and so they had.

Amy slipped her arm through Mary's as they paused in front of the cottage. "I can't wait to move in," she said, viewing the small house as if it were a mansion.

"Well, I hope Matthew fixes the roof before you do," Mary said with a laugh.

"He will. He and Edward are going to start work on it next week." She removed her arm and took a step away, for the moment not looking at Mary. "Mama, . . .

about the money. Matthew has serious reservations about accepting it, and so do I."

Mary shook her head. "The money's yours, Amy." She touched her daughter's cheek. She still couldn't get over the sound of Amy's voice. A startling metamorphosis had occurred, it seemed to Mary, overnight. In a sense, Amy seemed to be another person. A mature woman who suddenly knew exactly what she wanted.

A small frown creased the smooth brow. "Right now, you need that money, Mama," she said firmly. "You know you do. The cost of the repairs must be exorbitant."

"If they are, that's no concern of yours," Mary said quickly. Her voice grew softer. "I've had that money put aside for your use for years. I've never touched it. No matter how bad things got, I've never used a cent of it." She straightened. "Nor am I about to begin using it now."

The adamant look on her mother's face told Amy that further protest would be futile. But that was not what precluded her from further effort. It was the pride she saw in her mother's face, in her bearing. Suddenly Amy realized how important it was to Mary.

She smiled and said simply, "Thank you, Mama. We'll use a part of it to furnish the cottage."

When Bethany awoke on one early May morning, her hand automatically reached out for Edward but found only the softness of his pillow. Sitting up, she looked at the clock and frowned. She had overslept again. While she was experiencing no discomfort with nausea, her pregnancy was causing her to sleep more than she had ever done in her life.

Entering the dining room a while later, she smiled at Amy and Cyrus.

"Good morning, Amy," she said. "Papa..." She gave Cyrus a quick kiss.

"Morning, Bethany." He laid aside the paper he had been reading and smiled at her as she settled herself.

"I'm sorry I'm late," she said, leaning back as Henry placed a bowl of oatmeal before her. "It seems as though all I want to do is sleep."

Cyrus reached out and patted her arm. "Don't you fret about it, Bethany. You need your rest...." His eyes glowed as he spoke. The excitement he was feeling at the prospect of becoming a grandfather took him by surprise. Cyrus decided he'd never been as happy as he was right now. For the first time in more years than he could count, he was looking toward the future, anxious for its arrival.

Bethany took a spoonful of the porridge before she asked, "Where's Edward?"

"At the cottage," Amy responded. "He and Matt got an early start. We hope to move in by the weekend." She gave a soft laugh. "I can't wait."

"I don't blame you," Bethany said, smiling at her enthusiasm. "I know you'll be very happy there." She looked at Cyrus. "Have you seen it yet?"

He shook his head. "Not yet. But Henry's going to take me down there this afternoon." He took a sip of his coffee, then regarded Bethany. "Steve Willard stopped by last night. You met him at the wedding, I think."

"Yes, I remember him. He owns a stable in Louisville...."

"That's the one. He's made an offer for Red Cloud. He wants to buy her." Noticing Amy's suddenly dismayed look, Cyrus laughed. "Amy, that's what we do here. Breed horses to sell."

"Oh, I know," she said, sounding even more distressed than she looked. "But I've become attached to her."

Cyrus wagged a finger at her. "Mustn't make pets of them."

Amy sighed but made no comment. She knew she was doing exactly that, but couldn't help herself. "What about Dawn's Light?" she asked tentatively.

"That's different," Cyrus said quickly. "Only her offspring will be sold."

Amy appeared comforted by that. She scraped the last of the eggs from her plate, then got up. "I have some things I want to do this morning. Bethany, try to stop by later today. I hung the curtains yesterday, and they look beautiful."

"I will, dear," Bethany replied, watching Amy leave the room.

Outside, Amy took a deep breath of the clean air, then ran in the direction of the cottage.

The sound of hammering and sawing filled the spring air, occasionally interrupted by Matthew's happy whistle.

The guests had long since gone. Hattie had stayed for three days following the wedding, promising Bethany she would return for a visit after her niece's wedding. Mary had stayed for two weeks, returning to New Orleans when she received word from Captain Baxter that the *Nola Star* was finally ready to resume her trek upriver.

For the past month, Matthew and Edward had been working on the cottage. Another room had been added and yet one more planned in the near future. It had been whitewashed, the roof repaired, and a brand new coal-burning stove installed in the kitchen. Amy and Bethany had spent the time sewing curtains and stocking the shelves of the small pantry. As a wedding present to the young couple, Edward had installed one of the huge four-poster beds from one of the guest bedrooms in the main house.

Amy poked her head inside and saw that Matthew and Edward were at work putting up shelves in the kitchen. Not wanting to disturb them, she stepped outside again. Last week she had started a small vegetable garden. Now she was ready to plant flowers.

Picking up the trowel, she plunged it into the soft black earth, scooping out a hole big enough to support the rose plant that waited for its new home. From inside the cottage, she heard Matthew whistling, and she smiled at the sound of it. In the month that they had been married, she and Matthew had become closer than she thought it possible for two human beings to be.

Amy worked steadily throughout the morning, determined that her garden would be a showpiece.

The idea of having her very own house, complete with front and rear gardens, was an exciting prospect, one that drew her mentally into the days and years to come. Fruit trees. She mustn't forget fruit trees, she thought happily.

It was close to noon when Matthew came outside, smiling as he saw Amy on her hands and knees.

"I had no idea you had a green thumb," he teased, squatting down beside her.

She laughed, pushing an errant tendril of hair from her cheek and leaving a streak of dirt in its wake. "Only time will tell."

With his thumb, Matthew brushed the spot of earth from her face. "Umm, now if only you can cook. . . ."

"I can," she said with an answering laugh. Bending forward, she kissed him with a display of enthusiasm that sent them both sprawling to the grass.

Emerging from the cottage just then, Edward opened his mouth to ask Matthew a question, then closed it again. The exact position of the shelves could wait until tomorrow, he decided, averting his eyes from the young couple.

Noting the time, Edward began to head back to the house for dinner. The sun was bright, fanning the land with shafts of gold and orange.

Suddenly he paused, his brows knitting together as he caught sight of Lydia Madison. She was astride a white gelding, staring intently at Dawn's Light. A stiff-brimmed hat covered her flaming hair. Garbed in her Spanish riding habit, she had swung her right leg over the pommel, and it appeared at first glance that she was sitting side-saddle.

She didn't turn as Edward approached, but he knew she was aware of his presence.

She nodded once in the direction of the golden horse. Baron had been returned to The Willows, for Dawn's Light now carried the seed of the great stallion.

"That's one thing I don't regret," she said in a low voice, still not looking at him.

"Nor I," Edward responded, wondering why she was here. He hadn't seen her since that night she came to his room.

"But it is, perhaps, the only thing. . . ." Lydia turned her head slightly, and now looked directly at him. She wished with all her heart that she could hate him. And knew she never could.

Edward took a deep breath and stared at the ground. "I . . . don't know what to say, Lydia. . . ."

A small smile tilted her mouth, but never reached the emerald eyes. "This is not an apology," she said quickly, her chin rising slightly with her words.

Edward couldn't prevent a rueful smile. "No, . . . I didn't think it was." He shifted his weight uncomfortably, wanting her to go, but not wanting to put his feelings into words.

"I'm going away for awhile," she told him. "Jeremiah Hadbury and his wife have invited me for a visit. They have a lovely town house in London." She arched a brow and tilted her head to one side. "Who knows—I might meet a gentleman of the nobility." She stared at him for a long moment, then held out a hand. "Goodbye Edward," she said softly.

He touched her hand briefly and nodded. "I wish you the best, Lydia."

She swung her right leg down and into the stirrup again. Nudging her mount to an unhurried walk, she _____ the drive. Edward watched her receding _____ didn't turn around.

_____ hts didn't follow her. Slowly, he began to

walk toward the house. Looking up, he saw Bethany emerge onto the front porch, her smile radiant as she waved to him.

Breaking into a run, Edward headed toward his wife, suddenly wanting very much to hold her in his arms.